Praise for *A Desolation Called Peace*

"Martine spins a dizzying, exhilarating story of diplomacy, conspiracy, and first contact. . . . This complex, stunning space opera promises to reshape the genre."
—*Publishers Weekly* (starred review)

"It left me breathless with awe, this book that so effortlessly balances being a high-octane, science-fiction action thriller while also simultaneously being a thoughtful, complicated examination of identity, language, personhood, and truth. Arkady Martine has done it again, and made it bigger, bolder, and more beautiful than ever. Don't hesitate. Read this book."
—*Tor.com*

"A worthy follow-up that demands and rewards the reader's attention."
—*Nerds of a Feather, Flock Together*

Praise for *A Memory Called Empire*

"Perfectly balances action and intrigue with matters of empire and identity . . . All-around brilliant space opera. I absolutely love it."
—Ann Leckie

"Super fun and ultrafascinating."
—Charlie Jane Anders, author of *All the Birds in the Sky*

"The best SF novel I've read in the last five years."
—Yoon Ha Lee, author of the Machineries of Empire trilogy

T0004198

ALSO BY ARKADY MARTINE

A Memory Called Empire

A DESOLATION CALLED PEACE

ARKADY MARTINE

TOR

A TOM DOHERTY ASSOCIATES BOOK

NEW YORK

This book is for all the exiles:
the displaced, the refugee, the stateless;
the abandoned and the abandoner;
those made desolate and those cast free.

(And for Stanislav Petrov, who knew when to question orders.)

A DESOLATION CALLED PEACE

Copyright © 2021 by AnnaLinden Weller

All rights reserved.

A Tor Book
Published by Tom Doherty Associates
120 Broadway
New York, NY 10271

www.tor-forge.com

Tor® is a registered trademark of Macmillan Publishing Group, LLC.

The Library of Congress has cataloged the hardcover edition as follows:

Names: Martine, Arkady, author.
Title: A desolation called peace / Arkady Martine.
Description: First edition. | New York : Tor, 2021. | "A Tom Doherty Associates book."
Identifiers: LCCN 2021001147 (print) | LCCN 2021001148 (ebook) | ISBN 9781250186461 (hardcover) | ISBN 9781250186478 (trade paperback) | ISBN 9781250186485 (ebook)
Subjects: GSAFD: Science fiction.
Classification: LCC PS3613.A786325 D47 2021 (print) | LCC PS3613.A786325 (ebook) | DDC 813/.6—dc23
LC record available at https://lccn.loc.gov/2021001147
LC ebook record available at https://lccn.loc.gov/2021001148

ISBN 978-1-250-18647-8 (trade paperback)

Our books may be purchased in bulk for promotional, educational, or business use. Please contact your local bookseller or the Macmillan Corporate and Premium Sales Department at 1-800-221-7945, extension 5442, or by email at MacmillanSpecialMarkets@macmillan.com.

First Tor Paperback Edition: 2022

Printed in the United States of America

0 9 8 7 6 5

First, reality was suspended. All breaches to Inca protocol occurred at once: the rules governing personal contact (visual, oral, and corporal), drinking, and eating were broken. When Ciquinchara first met the conquerors he was allowed to do what no Indian could, and now the tables were turned. Since there was no signifying context to frame their interactions, the actors exposed themselves to limitless risk. Atahualpa could have been slaughtered, or Soto and Hernando poisoned. . . .

—Gonzolo Lamana, in "Beyond Exoticization and
   Likeness: Alterity and the Production of Sense in a
   Colonial Encounter," *Comparative Studies in Society
   and History* 47, no. 1 (2005): 4–39

To ravage, to slaughter, to usurp under false titles—this they name empire; and where they make a desert, they call it peace.

—Tacitus (quoting Calgacus), *Agricola* 30

PRELUDE

TO think—not language. To not think language. To think, *we,* and not have a tongue-sound or cry for its crystalline depths. To have discarded tongue-sounds where they are unsuitable. To think as a person and not as a wantful voice, not as a blank-eyed hungering beast, not as a child thinks, with only its own self and the cries of its mouth for company. To look outward from the two-ring or three-ring of one of our starflyers, and see every pinpoint light, every fusion-heart star. To see the pattern these stars make in our eyes reflecting the pattern of our eyes in the dark on the old planet. How our eyeshine glowed in the dirt-home, the blood-home! How we closed them and were invisible, dark-scavengers, secret-hunters! How our starflyers glow in the void-home, the light-home of us! How we slip sideways, like a closing eye, and are invisible! To think as a person, with the singing fractal swarm of *we,* and see these places that we have not yet scavenged, not yet torn open, claws as delicate as surgeon-scalpels, for their secrets!

Oh, the other hunger, the hunger of *we* that is nothing to do with the body. The hunger of *we* to reach out.

This body or that body: flesh full of the genes for strength and savagery, flesh full of the genes for patience and pattern-spotting. This body a curious body, an observer body, trained well for celestial navigation and surveying, its claws laced through with the filaments of metal that allow it to sing not only to *we* but to any starflyer it touches. This body a body that almost did not become *we,* almost became meat instead, but is *we,* and sings *we,* and is a body for making other bodies meat, for making also other bodies with itself: this body full of kits and clever with its hands on the triggers of a starflyer's energy cannons.

These bodies, singing in the *we,* singing together of the flesh of bodies who are not *we* but have built starflyers and energy cannon. Bodies who are meat and cannot sing! Bodies who think *language,* who cry with their mouths and leak water from their eyes, who are clawless but vicious in their own hunger to reach out. Who have touched so much of the void-home already, and dwell in it, and have come so very close to the jumpgates be-hind which are all of our blood-homes, new and old.

These bodies sing: the clever meat dies like every other meat, like *we* do, but it does not remember what its dead meat knew. So we have brought down our sibling-bodies onto one of their planets, not a blood-home but a dirt-home, full of resources to scavenge, and we have rendered them up for usage, the meat and the resources both.

To sing—hunger satisfied. To sing—understanding. Except:

Another body provides counterpoint, a dissonant chord. This body a curious body, an observer body, a stubborn and patrolling body who has slipped sideways in and out of vision in the same sector of void for lo these many cycles and remains a curious body even so. This body sings in the *we,* sings of a few clever meat bodies that *do* remember what their dead meat knew. But not all of them. Not all the *same* knowing. Not like the singing of the *we.*

To think of a *we* that fragments! That does not flock, that re-members but could not hold the shape of a murmuration. We sing disturbance and we sing the hunger of reaching-out, to think of fragmentation! We sing, too: *What does this clever meat have that we do not? What singing is their singing, that we cannot hear?*

And we send our starflyers whirling, whirling close. Close enough to taste.

CHAPTER
ONE

. . . INTERDICT SUSPENDED—for a duration of four months, extensible by Council order, the interdict regarding Teixcalaanli military transport through Stationer space is suspended; all ships bearing Teixcalaanli military callsign are permitted to pass through the Anhamemat Gate—this suspension does not authorize Teixcalaanli ships, military or otherwise, to dock at Lsel Station without prior visas, approvals, and customs clearances—SUSPENSION AUTHORIZED BY THE COUNCILOR FOR THE MINERS (DARJ TARATS)—message repeats . . .

> —priority message deployed on diplomatic, commercial,
> and universal frequencies in the Bardzravand Sector,
> 52nd day, 1st year, in the 1st indiction of the Emperor
> of All Teixcalaan Nineteen Adze

* * *

Your Brilliance, you have left me with all the world, and yet I am bereft; I'd take your star-cursed possessing ghost, Six Direction, if only he would teach me how not to sleep.

> —the private notes of Her Brilliance the Emperor
> Nineteen Adze, undated, locked, and encrypted

NINE Hibiscus watched the cartograph cycle through its last week of recorded developments for a third time, and then switched it off. Without its pinpoint stargleams and Fleet-movement arcs inscribed in light, the strategy table on the bridge of *Weight for the Wheel* was a flat black expanse, dull-matte, as impatient as its captain for new information.

There was none forthcoming. Nine Hibiscus didn't need to watch the cartograph again to remember how the displayed planet-points had winked first distress-red and then out-of-communication black, vanishing like they were being swallowed by a tide. No matter how thickly laid the lines of incoming Teixcalaanli ships were shown on that cartograph, none of them had advanced into the flood of blank silence. *Beyond this point,* Nine Hibiscus thought, not without a shimmering anticipation, *we are quite afraid to see.*

Her own *Weight for the Wheel* was the second-closest vessel to the communicationless swath. She'd sent only one ship farther out than she'd take her own people. That was the hybrid scout-gunner called *Knifepoint's Ninth Blooming,* a near-invisible sliver of a ship that slipped free of her flagship's open-mawed hangar and into the silent black. Sending it might have been Nine Hibiscus's first mistake as Her Brilliance the Emperor Nineteen Adze's newest *yaotlek*—commander of Fleet commanders, with multiple Teixcalaanli legions under her control. An Emperor made new *yaotlekim* when that Emperor wanted to make a war: the one begot the other. Nine Hibiscus had heard *that* old saying the first time when she'd been a cadet, and thought it herself approximately once a week, absent confirmation of absolute observed truth.

Nineteen Adze, new-crowned, had very badly wanted to make a war.

Now, at the very forefront of that war, Nine Hibiscus hoped sending *Knifepoint* hadn't been a mistake after all. It'd be useful to avoid unforced errors, considering *how* new a *yaotlek* she was. (It'd be *useful* to avoid errors at all, but Nine Hibiscus had been an officer of the Six Outreaching Palms—the Teixcalaanli imperial military, hands outstretched in every direction—long enough to know that errors, in war, were inevitable.) So far

Knifepoint was running as quiet as the dead planets up ahead, and the cartograph hadn't updated in four hours.

So that gambit could be going any way at all.

She leaned her elbows on the strategy table. There'd be elbowprints later: the soft pillowing flesh of her arms leaving its oils on the matte surface, and she'd have to get out a screen-cleaner cloth to wipe them away. But Nine Hibiscus liked to *touch* her ship, know it even when it was just waiting for orders. Feel, even this far from its engine core, the humming of the great machine for which she served as a brain. Or at least a ganglion cluster, a central point. A Fleet captain was a filter for all the information that came to the bridge, after all—and a *yaotlek* was *more so,* a *yaotlek* had farther reach, more hands to stretch out in every possible direction. More *ships.*

Nine Hibiscus was going to need every one of them she had got. The Emperor Herself might have wanted a war to cut the teeth of her rulership on, but the war that she'd sent Nine Hibiscus out to win was already ugly: ugly and mysterious. A poison tide lapping at the edges of Teixcalaan. It had begun with rumors, stories of aliens that struck, destroyed, vanished without warning or demands, leaving shattered ship pieces in the void if they left anything at all. But there were always horror stories of spooks in the black. Every Fleet soldier grew up on them, passed them down to new cadets. And these particular rumors had all crept inward from the Empire's neighbors, from Verashk-Talay and Lsel Station, nowhere central, nowhere important—not until the old Emperor, eternally-sun-caught Six Direction, died . . . and in his dying declared that all the rumors were true.

After that the war was inevitable. It would have happened anyway, even *before* five Teixcalaanli colony outposts on the other side of the jumpgate in Parzrawantlak Sector went as silent and dull as stones, just where those horror-stories would have crawled out from, if they were going to crawl out of the black spaces between the stars at all. It merely might have happened *slower*.

Her Brilliance Nineteen Adze had been Emperor for two months, and Nine Hibiscus had been *yaotlek* for this war for almost half that time.

Around her the bridge was both too busy and too quiet. Every station was occupied by its appropriate officer. Navigation, propulsion, weaponry, comms: all arrayed around her and her strategy table like a solid, scaled-up version of the holographic workspace she could call into being with her cloudhook, the glass-and-metal overlay on her right eye that linked her—even here on the edge of the Teixcalaanli imperium—to the great data-and-story networks that held the Empire together. Every one of the bridge's stations was occupied, and every occupant was trying to look as if they had something to do besides wait and wonder if the force they had been sent to defeat would catch them unawares and do—whatever it was that these aliens were doing that snuffed out planetary communication systems like flames in vacuum. All of her bridge officers were nervous, and all of them were tired of being patient. They were the Fleet, the Six Outreaching Palms of Teixcalaan: *conquest* was their style, not massed waiting on the edge of the inevitable, paused in worrisome silence at the very forefront of six legions' worth of ships. Nearest to the danger, and yet still unmoving.

At least when Her Brilliance Nineteen Adze had made her *yaotlek* to prosecute this war, Nine Hibiscus thought, she'd let her keep her own ship as flagship. Each of these officers was a Teixcalaanlitzlim she'd worked with, served with, commanded—each of them she'd led to victory at the uprising at Kauraan System less than three months ago. They were *hers*. They'd trust her a little longer. Just a little longer, until *Knifepoint* came back with some actionable information and she could let them loose a bit. Taste a little blood, a little dust and fire blooming from the death of an alien ship. A fleet could last a long time, fed on those sips of sugar-water violence, as long as they believed their *yaotlek* knew what she was doing.

Or that'd always been how Nine Hibiscus had felt, when she used to serve under Fleet Captain Nine Propulsion before Nine Propulsion had gone off to pilot a desk planetside in the City. She'd risen all the way to Minister of War under the last, dead, lamented Emperor, and Nine Hibiscus—who spelled her name with the same number glyph Nine Propulsion used, and hadn't yet regretted that late-teenage star-eyed choice of how to style herself in written form—had thought she'd probably be Minister under the new one. Had *expected* that.

But instead, Nine Propulsion had taken retirement almost immediately upon Nineteen Adze's ascension. She'd left the City entirely, gone home to her birth system—no chance yet for one of her old subordinates to drop by and ask her what for, and why now, and all the usual gossip. Instead, Nine Hibiscus, bereft of the comfort of mentorship (she'd been lucky to have had it so long, if she was being honest with herself) had woken up one shift with an urgent infofiche stick message from the Emperor Herself—a *commission*.

If this war is winnable, I want you to win it. The Emperor's dark cheekbones like knives, like the edges of the flares of the sun-spear throne she sat on.

And now, calling her back to herself in this present moment, a low voice to Nine Hibiscus's direct left: one that wouldn't startle her at that distance. (The only one who could sneak up that close, regardless.) "Nothing yet, then, sir?"

Twenty Cicada, her *ikantlos*-prime, highest-ranking of all the officers who served directly under the Fleet Captain and not in another administrative division. He was her adjutant and second-in-command, which was *one* of the ways that rank could be used—she couldn't imagine having anyone else in the position save for him. He had his arms folded neatly across the cadaverous thinness of his chest, one eyebrow an expressive arch. As always, his uniform was impeccable, perfect-Teixcalaanli, the very image of a soldier in a propaganda holofilm: if you ignored the shaved head and how he looked like he hadn't eaten in a month. The curling edges of green-and-white-inked tattoos just visible at his wrists and throat, when the uniform shifted as he moved or breathed.

"Nothing," said Nine Hibiscus, loud enough for the rest of the bridge to hear. "Absolute quiet. *Knifepoint*'s running silenced, and at their usual speed they're not going to be back for another shift and a half, unless they're running from something nasty. And there isn't much *Knifepoint* would run from."

Twenty Cicada knew all that. It wasn't for him. It was for how Eighteen Chisel in Navigation's shoulders dropped an inch; how Two Foam, on comm, actually *sent* the message she'd been hesitating on for the past five minutes, reporting continued clear skies to the rest of their multilegion Fleet.

"Excellent," said Twenty Cicada. "Then you won't mind if I borrow you for a moment, *yaotlek*?"

"Tell me that we are not still having problems with the escaped pets in the air ducts on Deck Five, and I will not mind being borrowed," Nine Hibiscus said, widening her eyes in fond near-mockery. The pets—small furred things that vibrated pleasantly and ate vermin, a peculiar variant on *cat* that was endemic to Kauraan—had come aboard during their last planetfall there, when she'd still been Fleet Captain Nine Hibiscus of the Tenth Legion, not *yaotlek* yet. The pets had not been a problem—or something Nine Hibiscus had even *known* about—until they had decided to reproduce themselves, and moved into a Deck Five air duct to do it. Twenty Cicada had complained vociferously about how they were disturbing the homeostasis of *Weight for the Wheel*'s environment.

"It is not the pets," Twenty Cicada said. "That I promise. Conference room?"

If he wanted privacy to discuss whatever it was, it couldn't be good. "Perfect," Nine Hibiscus said, pushing herself upright. She was twice as wide as Twenty Cicada, but he moved around her as if he had solidity enough to match. "Two Foam, your bridge."

"My bridge, *Yaotlek,*" Two Foam called, and that was as it should be, so Nine Hibiscus went to see what was wrong with her ship—her Fleet—*now.*

Weight for the Wheel had two conference rooms right off the bridge—a large one, for strategy meetings, and a small one, for fixing problems. Nine Hibiscus had repurposed the latter from an auxiliary weapon-control station when she'd first been made captain. A ship needed a space to have private *official* conversations, she'd thought then, and she'd been largely right; the small conference room was the best place to solve personnel issues, recorded on the ship's cameras, visible and invisible all at once. She took Twenty Cicada inside, cuing the door to open with a micromovement of one eye that directed her cloudhook to talk to the ship's algorithmic AI.

Twenty Cicada wasn't given to preambles; Nine Hibiscus had always known him to be *efficient,* brisk and clean and mercilessly direct. He preceded her through the door—and to her surprise, did not turn to give his report. Instead he headed directly for the room's narrow viewport and put a hand up against the plastisteel separating his body and the vacuum. Nine Hibiscus felt a flicker of warmth at the familiarity of the gesture, warmth mixed with uncomfortable dread: like her, Twenty Cicada touched the ship, but he touched it like he was longing for space to come in and take his hand. He'd done that for as long as Nine Hibiscus had known him, and the two of them had met on their very first deployment.

Which was long enough ago by now that Nine Hibiscus didn't particularly feel like counting the years.

"Swarm," she said—the nickname he'd gotten back on that deployment, the one she had mostly given up calling him for the sake of officer hierarchy—"spit it out. What's going on?"

"Sir," he said, still staring out at the black, gentle corrective for the cameras, even if the recordings of this room would never be seen by anyone but her: who outranked a *yaotlek*? But he was so *correctly* a Fleet officer, a Teixcalaanlitzlim's Teixcalaanlitzlim, seamless in the role of *ikantlos*-prime and adjutant, a man who could have walked out of *The Expansion History* or *Opening Frontier Poems,* except that the system his people had come from hadn't even been absorbed into Teixcalaan when either of those works had been written. (Except that he still kept up some of that system's peculiar cultural-religious practices— but hesitance wasn't one of *those,* either. At least not one she knew about.)

"Yes, *ikantlos*? Report."

Finally he turned, widened his eyes in wry and resigned amusement, and said, "In about two hours, sir, you're going to get an official communiqué, addressed to you *specifically* as *yaotlek* in charge of this combined Fleet, from Fleet Captain Sixteen Moonrise on the *Parabolic Compression* of the Twenty-Fourth Legion, demanding to know what the delay in action is. It will be countersigned by Fleet Captain Forty Oxide of the Seventeenth and Fleet Captain Two Canal of the Sixth. We have a problem."

"The Seventeenth *and* the Sixth?" Nine Hibiscus asked. "They hate each other. That rivalry is two hundred years old. How did Sixteen Moonrise get them both to sign?"

They absolutely had a problem. Her combined Fleet was six legions strong: her own Tenth and five more, each with its own Fleet Captain newly subordinate to her authority. The traditional *yaotlek*'s six, both tactically effective and symbolically sound—if a somewhat limited amount of manpower to win a war with. Enough, though, to *start* a war, which Nine Hibiscus understood her purpose here to be. To start, and then to win with whatever resources she would need to call up from the core of Teixcalaan, if such resources were necessary.

But if *three* of her initial *yaotlek*'s six were already willing to sign an opening salvo against her authority as *yaotlek* . . . She didn't need to say it; both she and Twenty Cicada knew what a letter like this one meant. It was a test, a press to check for weak spots: a light barrage to find the best point to concentrate a wedge attack. It was bad enough that she'd been given both the Sixth and the Seventeenth Legions as part of her Fleet, but she'd expected any ensuing conflict to be *between them,* something to carefully manage by doling out the best assignments equally. Not this surprising show of political unity through displeasure.

"From what information I've received from my associates on their ships," said Twenty Cicada, "Sixteen Moonrise appealed on the one side to Forty Oxide's long experience compared to yours, and on the other to Two Canal's vehement wish that *she* had been made *yaotlek* instead of you, and neither of them knew the other one had agreed until right before they agreed to send the message."

There were reasons that Twenty Cicada was nicknamed Swarm, and it wasn't just his peculiar name: a name with a living creature in it instead of a proper object or color or plant. Swarm was Swarm because he was everywhere at once: he knew *someone* on every ship in the Fleet, and those someones tended to keep him well-informed. Nine Hibiscus clicked her teeth together, considering. "Politics," she said. "All right. We've had politics before."

Nine Hibiscus had had politics come after her more than once. Anyone who made Fleet Captain did. Anyone who made Fleet Captain and meant to keep the position and win victories for her legion—well, that sort of Teixcalaanlitzlim made enemies. Jealous ones.

(Every time there'd been politics before, though, Nine Hibiscus had also had Nine Propulsion in the Ministry as a threat of last resort. The new Minister of War, Three Azimuth, was no one's friend in particular—or at least she wasn't Nine Hibiscus's friend.)

"Two Canal and Forty Oxide aren't the point anyhow," said Twenty Cicada. "Sixteen Moonrise is. She's the instigator—*she's* the one you're going to have to defuse."

"Perhaps she'd like the point position when we do make our approach."

Twenty Cicada said, dry as processed ship's air, "So direct, sir."

She couldn't help grinning: teeth-bared like a barbarian, a savage expression. It felt good on her face. Felt like getting ready to act, instead of waiting and waiting and waiting. "They *are* insinuating I'm overhesitant."

"I can have that order composed. The Twenty-Fourth will be cast shouting into whatever void is eating our planets by shift-change, if you like." One of the problems with Twenty Cicada was that he offered her exactly what she wanted, for precisely long enough for her to remember that it was a bad idea. It was the kind of problem that ended up being one of a thousand reasons Nine Hibiscus had never thought of replacing him with a soldier who came from a more assimilated world.

"No," she said. "Let's do one better. The glory of dying first for the Empire is too good for Sixteen Moonrise, don't you think? Invite her to dinner instead. Treat her like a favored colleague, a prospective co-commander. A new *yaotlek* like me needs allies, doesn't she?"

Twenty Cicada's expression had become unreadable, like he was adjusting some value in a vast calculation of a complex system. Nine Hibiscus figured that if he was going to object, he would go ahead and object, and went on, assuming he wouldn't.

"Fourth shift—that'll give her the travel time to get over to *Wheel*. Her and her adjutant. We'll have a *strategy discussion*, the four of us."

"As soon as the letter officially arrives, sir, I'll send that invitation back—and alert the galley that we're expecting guests." Twenty Cicada paused. "I don't like this. For the record. It's too early for anyone to be pushing you like this. I didn't expect it."

"I don't like it either," Nine Hibiscus said. "But since when has that made a difference? We persevere, Swarm. We *win*."

"We do tend to." A flicker, again, of that dry amusement. "But the wheel goes around—"

Nine Hibiscus said, "That's why we're the *weight*," like she was one of her soldiers in the mess, ship-phrase slogan, and smiled. *Game on,* she thought. *Sixteen Moonrise, whatever it is you want from me—come play.*

Over the comm, then, Two Foam's disembodied voice: "*Yaotlek,* I have visual on *Knifepoint.* Three hours early. Coming in fast. Coming in—*hot.*"

"Bleeding *stars,*" Nine Hibiscus spat, a quick, instinctive curse, just for her and Twenty Cicada to hear, and then signaled her cloudhook to patch her into the comm frequency. "On my way. Don't fire on anything until we know we have to."

———

Lsel Station was a sort of city, if one thought of cities as animate machines, organisms made of interlocking parts and people, too close-packed to be any *other* form of life. Thirty thousand Stationers on Lsel, all in motion, spinning in the dark in their gravitational well, safe inside the thin envelope of metal which was Station-skin. And like any other city, Lsel Station was—if you knew where to go, and where to avoid—a decent place to take a long enough walk to exhaust yourself out of overthinking.

<A fascinating theory, that one,> said Yskandr, <which you are in the process of disproving at this very moment.>

Mahit Dzmare, by certain technicalities still the Ambassador to Teixcalaan from Lsel, even after two months spent returning from her post and one month more since she'd returned to Lsel in quasi-disgrace, had perfected the art of *thinking* the sensation of rolling her eyes. *I haven't walked far enough yet,* she said to her imago—to *both* her imagos, the old Yskandr and the fragmentary remains of the young one. *Give me time.*

<You've got twenty minutes before Councilor Amnardbat is expecting you,> Yskandr said—he was mostly the young Yskandr today, arch and amused, experience-hungry, all bravado and new-won fluency in Teixcalaanli manners and politics. The Yskandr-version she'd mostly lost to the sabotage of

the imago-machine which had brought him to her in the first place, nestled at the base of her skull, full up with live memory and the experience she'd needed to be a *good* Ambassador from Lsel, on the glittering City-planet heart of Teixcalaan. Sabotage executed—possibly, she remained unsure—by the very Councilor she was due to have dinner with in twenty minutes.

There was another life, Mahit thought, where she and Yskandr would have been in the City still, and integrated already into a single continuous self.

<There never was,> Yskandr told her, and that was the *other* Yskandr: twenty years older, a man who remembered his own death well enough that Mahit still sometimes woke up in the night choking on psychosomatic anaphylaxis, <any other world but the one we got.>

Mahit was too many people, since she'd overlaid her damaged imago with the imago of the same man twenty years further on down the line. She'd had a while to think about it. She was *almost* used to how it felt, the fault lines between the three of them grinding together like planetary tectonics. Her boots made soft familiar noise on the metal floor of the Station corridors. She was out near the edge of this deck—she could just barely see the curvature of the floor, here, stretching up. Walking endless loops around the Station had started as a refamiliarization tactic and turned into a habit. Yskandr didn't know the geography of the Station any longer—in the City he'd been either fifteen years or three dead months out of date, but here at home he was just a long-exiled stranger. In fifteen years the interior, nonstructural walls moved around, the decks were repurposed, little shops opened and shut. Someone in Heritage had changed all the fonts on the navigational signs, a shift Mahit hardly recalled—she'd been *eight*—but she found herself staring at them, a perfectly innocuous MEDICAL SECTOR: LEFTWARD sign suddenly compulsively fascinating.

We're both exiles, she'd thought, right then, and had hated herself for thinking it. She'd been gone a few months. She had no right to the name. She was home.

She wasn't, and she knew it. (There was no such place any longer.) But the walking was a semblance, and she *did* remember where some things were, the shape and rhythm of the Station, alive and full of people—and she and Yskandr both had the same joy in discovering new places. On that, the aptitudes had gotten them entirely dead to rights.

This deck—which contained Heritage offices, if a person kept walking through the residential section Mahit was traversing, everyone's individual pods hanging in warm bone-colored rows, interspersed with common areas—wasn't one she knew well at all. It was full of kids, older ones, three-quarters of the way to their imago-aptitude tests, sitting easily on top of bulkheads and clustered in chattering groups around shop kiosks. Most of them ignored Mahit entirely, which was comforting. One month back on the Station, and half the time she ran into old friends, her crèchesibs or classmates, and all of them wanted her to *tell them about Teixcalaan.* And what could she say? *I love it; it almost ate me and all of you together; I can't tell you a single thing?*

<Propaganda's fascinating when it's inside your own mind,> Yskandr murmured. <It endlessly surprises me, how good the City is at engendering compulsive silence.>

You died there rather than coming back to share your plans with our Station, and you'd like to lecture me on silence? Mahit snapped, and felt her smallest fingers go to fizzing sparkles: neurological afterimages of sabotage. That side effect hadn't stopped. It was more obvious when she stumbled into one of the places she and Yskandr *hadn't* managed to integrate yet, at all. But her sense of his presence withdrew to a banked and observant simmer. She'd ended up next to one of the kiosks while she was too busy talking to her imago to notice where she was going. (Probably she should mind those slips more than she did. The slips where she wasn't quite *her,* in her body.) Ended up next to a kiosk, and in a line for what it was selling.

Which seemed to be—handbound literature. The kiosk was labeled ADVENTURE/BLEAK PUBLISHING. Its display was full of graphic stories, drawn not on ever-changeable infofiche but on *paper*, made from flattened rag pulp. Mahit reached out and touched the cover of the nearest. It was rough under her fingertips.

"Hey," said the kiosk manager. "You like that one? *The Perilous Frontier!*"

"The what?" Mahit asked her, suddenly feeling as adrift as she had the first time anyone had asked her a question in Teixcalaanli. Context failure: *What frontier? Aren't they all perilous?*

"We've got all five volumes, if you're into first-contact stuff; *I* love it, the artist on volume three draws Captain Cameron's imago like Chadra Mav's, only visible in reflective surfaces, and the *linework*—"

The manager couldn't be more than seventeen, Mahit thought. Short tight-curled hair over a bright-toothed grin, eight hooped earrings up the side of one ear. That was new fashion. When Mahit was that age, everyone had been into *long* earrings. *I'm old,* she thought, with a peculiar delight.

<Ancient,> Yskandr agreed, dust-dry and amused. He was years older.

I'm old, and I have no idea what kids on Lsel like to read. Even when I was a kid on Lsel, I didn't know, really. It hadn't seemed important, before her aptitudes—why bother, when there was so much Teixcalaanli literature to drown herself in? To learn to speak in poetry for?

"I haven't read them yet," Mahit told the manager. "Can I have the first one?"

"Sure," she replied—ducked down underneath the counter and produced one. Mahit handed over her credit chip, and the manager swiped it. "They're drawn right here on this deck," she said. "If you like it, come back on second-shift two days from now and you can meet the artist, we're having a signing."

"Thanks. If I have time—"

<You have ten minutes before Councilor Amnardbat wants to feed you dinner.>

"Yeah." The manager grinned, as if to say, *Adults, seriously, what can you do.* "If you have time."

Mahit waved, went on. Walked a little faster. *The Perilous Frontier!* fit in her inside jacket pocket like it was a political pamphlet. Exactly the same size. That was interesting, in and of itself. Even if it turned out to be a horribly dull story, *that* was interesting.

The Heritage offices were a neatly labeled warren, seven or so doors on either side of the deck corridor, which had narrowed from the wide residential space to something more like a road. Behind those doors, all the extra space would be full of the offices of people assigned to jobs in Heritage: analysts, mostly. Analysts of historical precedent, of the health of art production and education, of the number of imago-matches in one sector of the population or another. Analysts and propaganda writers.

How Teixcalaan had changed her, and how *quickly*. The last time Mahit had come to the Heritage offices, for her final confirmation interview before she received both her imago and her assignment as ambassador, she'd have never thought about Heritage as being in the business of propaganda. But what else were they doing, when they adjusted educational materials for one age group or another, trying to have the aptitudes in five years spit out more pilots or more medical personnel? Changing how children *wanted* to be.

She was hesitating, poised outside the middlemost door with its neatly signed (*in the new font, and when will I get to stop noticing the fucking new font, Yskandr, it isn't actually a new font, it's only a new font for you*) nameplate reading AKNEL AMNARDBAT, COUNCILOR FOR HERITAGE. Hesitating because she hadn't seen Councilor Amnardbat since that last confirmation interview, and hesitating because she still couldn't understand why the woman she'd met then would have wanted to sabotage Mahit's imago-machine. Ruin her before she could even attempt to do right by the imago-line she was part of. If Amnardbat had even been responsible—Mahit only had the word of a *different* Councilor, Dekakel Onchu, Councilor for the Pilots, on that. And Mahit had that word because she'd received letters, while embedded in the Teixcalaanli court, which Onchu had meant for Yskandr.

She missed, with an ugly and sudden abrupt spike of feeling, Three Seagrass, her former cultural liaison, the woman who was supposed to make incongruous experiences make more sense to the poor barbarian in her charge. Three Seagrass would have just opened the door.

Mahit lifted her hand, and knocked. Called out her own name—"Mahit Dzmare!"—a Lsel-style appointment-keeping: no cloudhooks here, to open doors with micromovements of an eye. Just herself, announcing herself.

<You aren't alone,> Yskandr said, a murmur in her mind, ghost thought: almost her own thought.

No, I'm not. And Amnardbat doesn't know there are two of you— three of us—which is its own problem—

The door opened, so Mahit stopped thinking about danger-ous lies she had told. Not thinking about them made them eas-ier to hide. She'd learned that somewhere in the Empire, too.

Councilor Amnardbat was still slim and middle-aged, her hair worn in a spacer's cut of silvering ringlets, narrow and long grey eyes in a wide-cheekboned face that always looked like she'd been exposed to too much solar radiation—*chapped,* but in a rugged sort of way. She smiled when Mahit came in, and that smile was welcoming and warm. If she'd been working with her staff before Mahit's arrival, they weren't immediately visible. Heritage was a small operation, anyway. Councilor Amnardbat had a secretary, who wrote her correspondence—he'd been the one to send Mahit this invitation through the intra-Station electronic mail—but Mahit saw no one in the office at all. Just chairs, and a desk with infopaper piled all over it, and a screen on the wall showing some camera's view of what was outside Lsel just now. A slow rotation of stars.

"Welcome home," said Councilor Amnardbat.

<One month she's been waiting to tell you that?>

It's a gambit, Mahit thought. She felt Yskandr subside into a watchful, attentive hum. More awake than he'd been in a long time. She felt that way, too. More awake, more present. Having a dangerous conversation with a powerful person in their office. Just like she was supposed to do, on Teixcalaan.

"I'm glad to be here," said Mahit. "What can I do for you, Councilor?"

"I did promise to have a meal with you," Amnardbat said, still smiling, and Mahit felt an echo of Yskandr's flinch, his remembered fear: the Minister of Science in Teixcalaan, offering him food as a pretext to poison. She shoved it back. Not *her* endocrine trauma response. (She wished that she trusted Lsel's integration therapists with the secret of what she'd done when she'd overlaid two imago-Yskandrs. *Mahit* didn't have memory-linked trauma responses—probably—but Mahit and Yskandr were blurred, blurring more all the time, and she didn't know what to do with *his*.)

"It isn't that I don't appreciate *that*," Mahit said, "but I am sure you're busy enough to not *just* want to share some food with a returned Ambassador."

Councilor Amnardbat's expression didn't change. She radiated pleasant, brusque good cheer, laced with an almost-parental concern. "Come sit down, Ambassador Dzmare. We'll talk. I have spiced fish cakes and flatbread—I figured you'd missed Lsel food."

Mahit *had*, but she'd fixed that the first week back, gone to one of her old haunts and eaten hydroponic-raised flaky white fish stew until she'd ached from it and, feeling entirely ill, fled the place before any of her friends could show up accidentally and welcome her back with their questions. Something about Councilor Amnardbat's emotional timeline was skewed. Perhaps skewed on purpose. (And what purpose would it serve? Checking for some Teixcalaanli-derived corruption of taste? And what if Mahit had been one of those Stationers who hated fish cakes, it was a *preference*—)

"It's very kind of you to have it brought," she said, sitting down at the conference table across from the Councilor's desk and tamping back (*again*) on her imago's frisson of adrenaline signaling. The danger here wasn't going to come from the food. In fact, it smelled good enough to make Mahit's mouth water: the flaky fish spiced with red peppers, the carbon-scent of slightly charred flatbread, made from real wheat and precious thereby. Amnardbat sat across from her, and for a good two minutes they were just Stationers together: rolling flatbread around fish, devouring the first one and making another to be eaten more slowly.

The Councilor swallowed the last bite of the first flatbread she'd rolled. "Let's get the awkward question out of the way, Mahit," she said. Mahit attempted to not let her eyebrows climb up to her hairline and mostly succeeded. "Why did you return so soon? I'm asking this in my capacity as the Councilor for Heritage—I want to know if we didn't give you something you *needed*, out in the Empire. I know the process of integration was foreshortened . . ."

<Also you sabotaged me,> Yskandr said, and Mahit was worriedly glad that he was inaudible unless she let him be audible. Or slipped.

Possibly she sabotaged us, she reminded him. *If we believe Onchu. Who we also haven't spoken with—*

She'd been too afraid to. Too afraid of Onchu being right, *or* Onchu being wrong, and too exhausted by the sudden and irrevocable strangeness of what had been home to get around that being-afraid.

"No," she said, out loud. "There wasn't anything I needed that Lsel didn't try to give me. Of course I'd have liked more time with Yskandr before we went out, but what happened to me wasn't the shortest integration period in our history, I'm sure."

"Then why?" asked Amnardbat, and took another bite of fish. Question over, time to eat, time to listen.

Mahit sighed. Shrugged, rueful and aiming for self-deprecation, some echo of how uncomfortable she imagined Heritage would like a Stationer to be with things Teixcalaanli. "I was involved in a riot and a succession crisis, Councilor. It was violent and difficult—personally, professionally—and after I secured promises from the new Emperor as to our continued independence, I wanted to *rest*. Just for a while."

"So you came home."

"So I came home." *While I still wanted to.*

"You've been here for a month. And yet you haven't had yourself uploaded into a new imago-machine for your successor, Ambassador. Even though you know quite well that our last recording is extremely out of date, and we don't have one of *you* at all."

Fuck. So that's *what she wants. To know if the sabotage worked—*

<So you do believe she sabotaged us.>

. . . At the moment I do.

"It didn't occur to me," said Mahit. "It hasn't even been a year—forgive me, this *is* my first year having an imago at all. I thought there was a schedule? With appointment reminders?"

Refuge in bureaucratic ignorance. Which would also act as a shield—however temporary, however flimsy—against Amnardbat finding out that she had *two* imagos. Uploading would make short shrift of that little deception. And Mahit had no idea what policy there was on Lsel about doing something like what she'd done. Or if there even *was* any policy. She expected there wasn't. It was so clearly a bad idea. It had certainly given her enough squirming, revulsive qualms, before she'd done it.

<Do you regret—>

No. I needed you. I still need—us.

"Oh, of course there's a schedule," Amnardbat said. "But we in Heritage—well, I specifically, but I do speak for everyone here—have a policy of encouraging people who experience significant events or accomplishments to update their imago records more often than the automated calendar suggests."

Politely, Mahit took another bite of her flatbread wrap. Chewed and swallowed past the psychosomatic tightening of her throat. "Councilor," she said, "of course I can make an appointment with the machinists, now that I know about your policies. Is that really all? It's a kindness, to have this much fish cooked for us, and real flatbread, just to ask for an administrative favor that you could have written to me about."

Let her deal with the suggestion that she was being profligate with food resources. Heritage Councilors had been removed for lesser corruptions, generations ago. That imago-line wasn't given to new Heritage Councilors any longer. Mothballed, preserved somewhere in the banks of recorded memories, deemed unsuitable: anyone who would serve their own needs before the long-remembered needs of the Station shouldn't be influencing the one Councilor devoted to preserving the continuity of that Station.

<You are *annoyingly* clever.>

Some very nice Teixcalaanlitzlim and my imago have conspired to teach me to weaponize references.

But Amnardbat was saying, "It's not a favor," and as she said it, Mahit realized that she'd underestimated the Councilor, was underestimating the *reasons* for her behavior, expecting that she could be manipulated like a Teixcalaanlitzlim could be, with allusion and narrative. "It's an order, Ambassador. We need a copy of your memory. To make sure that whatever it was that made Yskandr Aghavn stay away so long from the uploading process hasn't spread to you, too."

Fascinating, really, how she felt so cold. So cold, her fingers gone to ice-electric prickling, no sensation around how she held the remains of her flatbread. So cold, and yet: hummingly focused. Afraid. *Alive.* "Spread?" she asked.

<Aren't we poisoned?> Yskandr whispered, and Mahit ignored him.

"It is a terrible thing, to lose a citizen to Teixcalaan," Amnardbat said. "To worry that there is something in the Empire that steals our best. The machinists and I will be expecting you this week, Mahit."

When she smiled again, Mahit thought she understood what made the Teixcalaanlitzlim so nervous about bared teeth.

———

Knifepoint was in visual range when Nine Hibiscus made it back to the bridge, briefly out of breath from the speed of that short transit. She took deep inhalations like she was an orator, settled her lungs, tried to keep any adrenaline response limited. It was her bridge now, her bridge and her command. All her officers rotated toward her as if they were flowers and she was a welcome sunrise. For a moment everything felt *correct*. And then she noticed how quickly *Knifepoint* was approaching the rest of the Fleet, growing in size even as she watched through the viewports. They had to be burning the engines at absolute maximum to be coming in this hot. *Knifepoint* was a scout—it *could* hit that speed, but not maintain it for very long; it was too small and would run out of fuel—and if its pilot had decided to run as fast as possible, then they were absolutely being *chased*.

"Do we know what's following them?" she asked, and Two Foam shook her head in swift negation from the comms chair.

"Everything's blank," she said. "Just *Knifepoint* and dead void behind them—but they'll be in hailing range in two minutes—"

"Get them on the holograph as soon as you can. And scramble the Shards. If there's something after them, we're not going to let it get far."

"Scrambling, *yaotlek*," said Two Foam, her eyes flickering in rapid motion behind her cloudhook. All around them the high

clear whine of the alarm rose through *Weight for the Wheel*. A
Fleet's first line of defense, and most mobile: a swarm of single-
pilot small craft, all weaponry and navigation, short-range and
absolutely deadly. Nine Hibiscus had been a Shard pilot herself,
on that long-ago first deployment, and she still felt the scramble alarm like a delicious vibration in the marrow of her bones:
go, go, go. Go now, and if you die, you die star-brilliant.

With the alarm singing through her, Nine Hibiscus said, "And
let's charge up the top two energy-cannon banks, shall we?"
She settled again into her captain's chair. Five Thistle, the duty
weapons officer, gave her a bright, wide-eyed grin.

"Sir," he said.

They all wanted this so *much*. Her, too. The fire and the blood
of it, something to *do*. A proper battle, blue and white energy
weapons arcing through the black, shattering and scorching.

Just as the first Shards spilled, sparkling, into the viewport's
visual range, the thing that *Knifepoint* was running away from
appeared.

It didn't *come into view*. It *appeared*, as if it had been there all
along, hidden in some kind of visual cloak. The black nothingness of space—this sector had so *few* stars—rippled, squirmed
like a nudibranch touched by a finger, an enormous and organic recoiling, and *there it was*, the first ship-of-their-enemy
any Teixcalaanli eyes had seen. (Any Teixcalaanli eyes which
had lived to describe it, at least.) Three grey hoops, rotating at
speed around a central ball. It was hard to look at, and Nine Hibiscus didn't know why—some of that recoiling, squirming visual distortion clung to it, made the grey metal of its hull seem
oil-slick and unfocused.

It had been not-there, and now it was there. Right up on
Knifepoint's tail, just as fast, and *closing*—

"This is the *yaotlek* Nine Hibiscus," she said, wide-broadcast.
"Cut that thing out of its vector and surround it. Hold fire unless you are fired upon."

Like they were extensions of her will, of her exhaled breath, the Shards flew outward on a fast approach toward the foreign object that had dared come so *very* near. It took them a moment to orient themselves around the alien ship; it wasn't a shape they knew, and it moved in unexpected ways, a slippery roll like a greased ball bearing. But the Shards were smart, and they were interlinked—each ship providing positional and visual bio-feedback not only to its own pilot through their cloudhook, but to all of the pilots in the swarm—and they learned quickly. *Knifepoint* shot out between the glittering sparkle of them like a shuttle breaking atmosphere and was caught safely by the out-reaching net of *Weight for the Wheel*'s hangar bay.

Two Foam had gotten *Knifepoint*'s captain on holo: he looked harried, wild-eyed and breathing rapidly, his hands visibly white at the knuckles as he gripped the controls of his ship.

"Well done," Nine Hibiscus said to him, "not a scratch on you—give us a minute to deal with this thing you brought us, and I'll bring you right up to debrief—"

"*Yaotlek*," he interrupted, "they're *invisible until they want to be*, that might not be the only one, and they have *firepower*—"

"Stand down, *Knifepoint*," Nine Hibiscus said. "It's our problem now, and we have firepower too." They did. The energy cannons, and the smaller, more vicious, more ugly power of nuclear core-bombs. If necessary.

"I intercepted a communication," he said, as if he hadn't heard her at all.

"Excellent. Put it in your report."

"It's not *language, yaotlek*—"

"Two Foam, deal with this? We are a *little* busy just now." The alien ship did have firepower—what looked like a fairly standard but very *precise* suite of energy cannons, arrayed on the outmost of those three spinning loops. Soundless bursts of light blinded her through the viewport, and when she blinked the afterimages away, there were three fewer Shards. She winced.

"All right, containment is no longer the protocol—Five Thistle, tell the Shards to clear a path for cannonry."

At their best, Nine Hibiscus's officers didn't need to confirm they'd heard her—they *acted*. Five Thistle's hands gestured inside the holographic workspace of the weapons station, moving ships and vector lines in the embedded starfield, a miniature version of her own cartograph table—and the Shards moved in response, forming a new pattern, clearing a space for *Weight for the Wheel*'s main cannon banks to aim and to fire.

Electric blue. The light that Nine Hibiscus had always imagined a person saw if they accidentally stepped inside an industrial irradiator, in the brief moment they'd have to see anything at all. Deathlight, with its hum like a scramble-alarm, as familiar as breathing or ceasing to breathe.

(For a fraction of a second, she wondered if she oughtn't try to *capture* the thing first—shut it down with targeted electromagnetic pulses while it was still far away enough that EMP wouldn't fry her own ships, pull it on board—but *Knifepoint* had said they had an intercepted communication, and this thing had killed three of her own soldiers already. Four—another Shard winked out in a silent shatter of flame, a candle going up and going out in rapid succession.)

Full cannon power lit the alien ship like a beacon, shook it, peeled some of that slick and squirming visuality away from it— the parts of the outer ring which had been blown off looked like metal, like space debris, entirely standard. But full cannon power didn't destroy it. It spun faster—it *whirred*—Nine Hibiscus imagined she could hear it spinning, though she knew that was impossible—and just before the second cannon barrage struck its inner ball, smashing it open into nothingness and destruction entire, it emitted from the second of its damaged rings some dark viscous substance that fell through null-grav in strange *ropes*.

Spit, Nine Hibiscus thought, repulsed.

Five Thistle was already calling *get away from it* on all channels, and the great reactor-fueled engines of *Weight for the Wheel* flared into life, pulled them backward, away from how the ropes tangled like a liquid net where the alien ship had been. What fluid moved like that? As if it was—seeking, mobile, far too cohesive. The *surface tension* on it—not so much that it clung together in a ball, but enough that it spun itself out in thinning, reaching strings—

One of the Shards, a glittering wedge tumbling easily onto a new vector, vernier thrusters firing, intersected with one of those spit-strings. Nine Hibiscus watched it happen. Watched all the gleam of the little fighter vanish, slicked over with alien ship-saliva, a fractal net of it that stuck and clung even when the Shard pulled free of the string. Saw, disbelieving *while* seeing, that net begin to bubble its way *through* the Shard's hull, corrosive, eating its metal and plastisteel like some kind of hyperoxidizing fungus.

The Shard's pilot *screamed*.

Screamed on the open channel Five Thistle had used, screamed and then shouted, "Kill me, kill me now, it's going to eat the ship, it's in here with me, don't let it touch anyone else," a controlled and desperate spasm of bravery.

Nine Hibiscus hesitated. She had done many things she'd regretted, as a pilot and a captain and as Fleet Captain of the Tenth Teixcalaanli Legion—uncountable things, she was a soldier, it was the nature of being what she was to commit small atrocities, like it was the nature of stars to emit radiation that burned and poisoned as much as it gave warmth and life. But she'd never ordered her ship to fire on her own people. Never once yet.

On that same channel, a chorus of anguish: *all* the Shard pilots, linked together by biofeedback, all of them feeling the death of their sibling ship, devoured alive. Sobbing. The sound of snatched breath, hyperventilation. A low moaning scream, that *echoed,* was picked up by other voices—

"Do it," Nine Hibiscus said. "Shoot her. As she asked."

Deathlight-fire, precise and merciful. A burst of blue, and one Teixcalaanlitzlim rendered to ashes.

Silence on all the comms. Nine Hibiscus heard nothing but the hideous pounding of her own heartbeat.

"Well," said Twenty Cicada, finally—sounding as shaken as anyone, but *briskly* shaken—"that's approximately eight new things about these people we didn't know ten minutes ago."

CHAPTER
TWO

[. . .] and of course your reputation precedes you, like an earth-quake precedes a city-drowning wave; the tremors of your arrival are already setting the Ministry to vibration as if we were all made of tlini-strings and you were the bow. Of course we regret the absence of former Minister Nine Propulsion—her guidance was a warm silk glove that has been taken off the Palms now that she has retired (and so abruptly!)—but I, for one, look forward to having meetings with a person who was the first successful Governor of Nakhar System. We have work to do. I remain, in anticipation [. . .]

> —letter from Third Undersecretary Eleven Laurel of the
> Ministry of War to the incoming Minister of War,
> Three Azimuth, dated to the 21st day, 1st year, in
> the 1st indiction of the Emperor of All Teixcalaan
> Nineteen Adze

* * *

Letters to the dead are poor practice; I'd do myself a service if I merely kept a journal like half the Emperors who have slept in this bed before me. But since when have you known me to do service to myself? And at least you *are* dead—or it is simplest to think of you so now—I have all the stars in my hands, Yskandr, and it is terribly easy to let them slip through a finger-width gap. Especially when some of them are going dark, eaten up by your successor's so-convenient alien threat. You slept here more often than I did—more often than I do, if we count sleeping and not nights. How often did you wish for the convenience of narrative

to bow to your whims? More or less often than our Emperor,
awake beside you?

  —the private notes of Her Brilliance the Emperor
  Nineteen Adze, undated, locked, and encrypted

KNIFEPOINT'S captain, Thirty Wax-Seal, clutched his cup
of coffee like it was the only thing keeping his hands from
shaking. He was a nasty shade of grey all through: Nine Hibiscus thought of oatmeal congealed in the bottom of a pan,
that leftover scrim of mealy grey-white that needed to be
scraped off.

"It's not language," he said, for the second time; that had been
his opening statement to her, when she'd gotten him retrieved
safely from his ship and had him brought to her smaller conference room to be debriefed. "I had Fourteen Spike with me,
she speaks five languages—that's why I took her, in case we got
to overhear something—and it was nothing like a language to
her. It's not got—parsable phonemes, she said. That was before
the enemy ship came out of nowhere and started chasing us. She
didn't get much farther than *we can't make noises like that*."

I am not equipped to run a first-contact scenario, Nine Hibiscus
thought, *especially when the things being contacted spit ship-dissolving
fluids at my people and don't make understandable noises.* She was
a *soldier.* A strategically minded one, with the vast punch of
Teixcalaanli power behind her, but a soldier nonetheless. First
contact was for diplomats and people who got into epic poems.

"If it's not language," she said, sipping at her coffee—Thirty
Wax-Seal drank a bit of his, mirroring, and she was glad of it—
"how did you know it was communication at all?"

"Because it didn't start until we showed up. And it was responsive, *yaotlek*—I mean, when I took *Knifepoint* in closer, the
transmission shifted, it sounded different, and when I backed
us away, it changed again, and when I tried to slide around the
far side of that dwarf sun and get eyes on what happened to our

colony on Peloa-2, it *shrieked* at us and then that ring-ship was *right there—*"

The edge of hysteria in Thirty Wax-Seal's voice was unsettling. It wasn't like him; he wouldn't be a scout-gunner captain if he was prone to the horrors. The ring-ship had been awful, and its spit had been *worse,* but still. It wouldn't do.

"You got back, Captain," Nine Hibiscus said, even, reassuring. "You came home to us and you brought us an intercepted communiqué and we know approximately eight new things about these people than we did before today." She was using Twenty Cicada's language, but this captain didn't know that. Didn't know how rattled *she* was, and never would, if she was careful. "You did very well. You can stand down awaiting further orders, unless there's anything else I should know."

"No, sir. The recording is with Chief Communications Officer Two Foam, if you want to listen to it. But there's nothing else specific. We didn't get close enough to Peloa-2 for actionable intelligence."

Nine Hibiscus wanted to listen to the recording very badly, and the idea made her skin crawl at the same time. But she had another hour and three-quarters before Sixteen Moonrise was scheduled to come aboard and discuss strategy—*discuss strategy,* such thin cover for a meeting meant to provide Nine Hibiscus with some leverage against Sixteen Moonrise's extremely untimely episode of Fleet intrigue—and she would like all the information she could get. Whether it was language or not.

———

Beneath the imperial palace there was a network of passages, secret and small. There was a poem for them, a good one with a walking rhythm to it. It went, *as many roots in the ground as blooms into the sky / daylight servants of the empire gather palace flowers / justice, science, information, war / but the roots that feed us are invisible and strong.* Eight Antidote liked two parts of that poem best: how his feet hit the tunnel tilework floor right along with the pulse of *roots* in the *ground* and *blooms* in the *sky*—and also how he wasn't a daylight servant at all. Daylight servants got palace flowers. Alone in the tunnels, Eight Antidote, sole heir to Teixcalaan entire (just recently *sole* heir, which meant something, probably, something about how he needed to think about himself), didn't need flowers. He was down in the dirt, where silent things grew strong.

He'd been in the tunnels tens of times, even before the Emperor—not the current Emperor, but his ancestor-the-Emperor, it was important also to clarify these things in his mind—had whisked him into them during the insurrection right before he died. He'd been in the tunnels enough to be beginning to know them, their secret ways, their listening-posts and open spy-eyes. His ancestor-the-Emperor had shown him, and had let him . . . go into them.

It was one of the only things Six Direction had *let* him do, like it was a prize, a passcode between the two of them, an indulgence. Eight Antidote wondered a lot about why. He'd wondered that even before his ancestor had killed himself in a sun temple for the glory of Teixcalaan.

Here the tunnel narrowed, dipped left—it smelled of petrichor, rain and the underneath parts of flowers. Eight Antidote trailed his fingers against the wall where it was damp with condensation, and imagined a small Six Direction, just his own eleven-years-old size, walking around under the palace, exactly like this. He wouldn't have needed to duck through the narrow parts either, not when he was eleven. If there were physical differences between Eight Antidote and his ancestor, he didn't know about them yet. Ninety percent was a lot of clone to be, physically. Also he'd seen holos.

But Six Direction hadn't grown up in the palace, had he. All those holos came from some planet with *grass* on it, a kid with his own face a hundred years ago, green-grey plants up to his narrow chest. Six Direction'd never been down here at all, until later.

After the narrow part there were some stairs, a long climb in the dim. He knew the way now, even lightless; in the past few weeks he'd come up these stairs seven times. Today was eight. He was too old to believe in numerical luck anymore, but *eights* felt right even so: eight times for luck particular to him. (Particular to him and to everyone else who shared the glyph he used for the number-sign in his name, so also lucky for the Minister of the Judiciary, who was technically his legal parent since she'd adopted him, and also tens of thousands of other kids, and this was why he didn't believe in numerical luck anymore, not since he'd thought about it properly.) There was a door in the ceiling, at the end of these stairs. Eight Antidote knocked on it, and it opened up for him, and then he was in the basement of the Ministry of War.

Eleven Laurel was waiting for him there. He was tall, and the carved planes of his face were very dark, with deep wrinkles around the eyes and the mouth. He was wearing a Ministry of War uniform, which wasn't the same thing as a legionary uniform, but *almost* was: not a suit like every other ministry, but breeches and a gunmetal-grey jacket that came down to the middle of his thighs and buttoned double-breasted with small flat gold buttons. He never seemed to mind sitting in the Ministry basement dust, waiting for Eight Antidote to show up. He just stood, brushed the dust off his pants unceremoniously, and said, "And how are you this afternoon, Cure?"

There were a couple of things Eight Antidote had learned from his ancestor-the-Emperor, and a couple more from Nineteen Adze, who was Emperor now and had promised to take care of him even if it killed her. The biggest one was probably *don't trust anyone who makes you feel good without knowing why they want you to feel that way.*

But Eleven Laurel, who in addition to waiting for him in basements once a week, and teaching him how to run a cartograph strategy table and shoot an energy-pulse pistol, was the Undersecretary of the Third Palm, one of six undersecretaries who only answered to the Minister of War—Eleven Laurel called him *Cure*, not *Your Excellency* or *Imperial Associate Eight Antidote* or anything else, and Eight Antidote really truly loved it. At least, he thought, he *knew* he loved it. Which had to help. He loved it, Eleven Laurel definitely wanted him to, and this might be a bad thing. But right now, right now it wasn't. Right now he widened his eyes in a grin, and scrambled out of the hole in the floor, and said, "I solved it, you know. Last week's exercise. The one about Kauraan System."

"Did you," Eleven Laurel said. "All right. Show me what you think the Fleet Captain at Kauraan did to win that battle, and what it tells you about her. We can go to the cartograph straight off."

It bothered Eight Antidote, a faint kind of upset like a hum off in one corner of his mind, that Eleven Laurel, a man who had served in twenty campaigns and seen more blood- and star-drenched planets than he could easily imagine, spent an afternoon once a week entertaining an eleven-year-old kid who had snuck in through the basement. There were extenuating circumstances, of course: the obvious one being that Eight Antidote was likely to be Emperor of all Teixcalaan at some point, much *more* likely to be so than before Six Direction had sacrificed himself and named a *sole* successor in the process. The Third Undersecretary to the Minister of War, who might see himself Minister in that hypothetical future, would have a lot of reasons to amuse that kid.

Also it wasn't like where they were was a secret. On the way to the cartograph room—one of a whole lot of them, the Ministry of War was a tactician's garden, Nineteen Adze had said that to him and it stuck in his head—Eight Antidote and Eleven Laurel passed in full view of at least ten soldiers, four administrative staff, one floor cleaner, and five City-eye cameras that Eight Antidote could spot. (That probably meant there were five more he hadn't spotted on this route.) He wasn't *escaping*. He wasn't doing anything *secret*, and neither was Eleven Laurel.

Nineteen Adze—Her Brilliance, the Emperor—had said *the Ministry of War is a tactician's garden* right after Eight Antidote had come back from his first trip through the tunnels. She'd come into his rooms, alone, and showed him the holograph-recording the City had made of him, moving through the Ministry like a bright bird in a net of eyes. He'd asked her if she'd prefer he not go, and she had said that line about tacticians and gardens and told him to do precisely what he liked, and left again.

Sometimes Eight Antidote wondered if anyone would ever trust him enough to not show him that they were watching him all the time.

The cartograph room made him happy anyway, happy enough to shove the whole mess of *why* away for a little while: Eleven Laurel called up Kauraan System with a few sweeps of his hands, last week's exercise displayed in slow-rotating lights hung in the middle of the air. Every ship in the Fleet had one of these tables, for solving problems before they happened. The problem here: *How did the Fleet Captain at Kauraan use only one ship to quell an uprising before it could spread past the southern tip of one continent?* And the constraints: *Less than five thousand Kauraani casualties, less than two hundred Teixcalaanli ones; she didn't call for help; she had no unusual weaponry not in the standard manifest for a ship of that size; she was outnumbered forty-to-one; and the Kauraani rebels had seized the spaceport and were using Teixcalaanli ships against her. Solve it.*

Eight Antidote loved the constraints best of all. Delimiters. *This happened, so it must be possible. Solve it.*

"Go on," said Eleven Laurel. "Show me what Fleet Captain Nine Hibiscus of the Tenth did here."

Eight Antidote came up to the table. He called it to his attention with small movements of his eye behind his cloudhook, and carefully allowed the simulation to run forward without making any changes to what was, now, functionally *his* Fleet: he stood in for Nine Hibiscus. And like he was almost, almost sure

she had done, he didn't send any of her Shards down toward
Kauraan, not even when the Kauraani rebels came floating up
off the planet in their stolen Teixcalaanli ships. He paused it
right as the stolen fleet entered firing range—between all of
them, they could have destroyed Nine Hibiscus's *Weight for the
Wheel,* even though it was an *Eternal*-class flagship.

"There's only one solution I can find," he said, not looking at
Eleven Laurel—imagining, instead, that he was a War Minister
or a Fleet Captain himself, talking to his people, his troops.
"Nobody fired at all."

"How would that have happened?" asked Eleven Laurel,
which wasn't *no, you're wrong.* Eight Antidote didn't smile,
but he felt very bright, very focused—like flying would
feel, like being a Shard pilot, tumbling on a vector of his own
choosing.

"On Kauraan," he went on, "the rebellion was small. Just one
faction of one ethnic group. But they were smart enough to
know that we keep a garrison on that southern continent. A lot
of ships. Enough to kill an *Eternal* if they had to. The rebels were
very smart when they captured the port first instead of going
after the provincial governor's offices. But there really weren't
a whole lot of them, I think. Not enough to not—take allies
where they could get them."

"Not implausible thinking." Eleven Laurel was paying out
the rope, Eight Antidote thought, giving him just enough space
to get in trouble, but he wasn't *going* to get in trouble, because he
was right.

"So the Fleet Captain, Nine Hibiscus. She's got this
reputation—her soldiers would do anything for her. And it's not
just the every-captain's-soldiers-love-them thing, it's not *just* poetry. I looked up her prior campaigns, and her people will do
a lot of, um. Dumb shit, in my opinion, Undersecretary. If she
asked them to."

Eleven Laurel made a noise that might have been laughter a
few decades back. "You did look her up. I'd say *dumb shit* is a fair

description, yes. Go on. What sort of dumb shit did she get her soldiers to do at Kauraan?"

"If she'd sent some of them down to infiltrate the rebels," said Eight Antidote, "and she trusted that they'd succeeded—then I think she let the rebels take the stolen ships up into space, *this close* to her ship, and asked her own people to trust that they wouldn't fire while the coup went down and the rebels got killed on the same ships they'd stolen. Nobody fired at all. They didn't *need* to. She'd already won."

The cartograph went blank. Eight Antidote blinked, afterimages of *Weight for the Wheel* and Kauraan's sun bright across the inside of his eyelids.

"That's very close to right," said Eleven Laurel. "Well done."

"What did I miss?" Eight Antidote asked, because he couldn't help it. *Very close* wasn't good enough. Not when he'd come up with *they never fired* in the middle of the night like a sunburst explosion of *I know it, I see it.* Woken up with it on his tongue like a bursting fruit.

"Infiltration is part of Fleet counterinsurgency protocols, yes," Eleven Laurel said. "But who should be in charge of it? Who makes that call, Cure, to send our people to lie for us?"

"Not a Fleet Captain?"

"The Minister of War, or the Undersecretary of the Third Palm."

"You?" The Third Palm—for the East direction, for—he struggled, reached for it. Palace-East was where Nineteen Adze had lived before she was Emperor, where ambassadors stayed, where the Information Ministry was. But the Information Ministry was *civilians*.

Eleven Laurel was waiting for him.

Eight Antidote hated that; it made him feel like he was being indulged. He said, "You. Third Palm, because the Third Palm is what's left of the *military* part of Information."

"Quite. Me, and the rump end of the separation of our spies from our soldiers. The Third of Six Outreaching Palms:

intelligence, counterintelligence, and Fleet internal affairs. Now, Cure—did our Nine Hibiscus receive this authorization from me, or from Minister Three Azimuth—ah, no, it was still Minister Nine Propulsion then, but even so?"

". . . No," Eight Antidote said. "She didn't have authorization to give that order. And her people did it anyway."

"You're going to make a hell of a tactician when you're the rest of the way grown," Eleven Laurel said, and Eight Antidote felt warm all through. He ducked his head, not wanting to blush. "That's right. She didn't get permission, she just *decided,* and none of her people asked a single question about it."

The blankness of the cartograph table felt abruptly heavy, threatening. "Where is she now?" Eight Antidote asked. "What happened to her after Kauraan?"

"Oh, we made her *yaotlek*," Eleven Laurel said, as if this was something that happened every day, "and sent her out to die bravely for Teixcalaan and Her Brilliance the Emperor as quickly as possible."

———

It took a particularly vicious sort of self-recrimination for Mahit to wish herself alone inside her own mind: alone like she'd been as a child, imagoless and longing, instead of replete with memories that were only beginning to belong to her, and were doubled and distorted and full of Teixcalaan anyhow. A particularly vicious sort of self-recrimination that also involved lying on the bed in her egg-shaped residence pod and staring at the comforting off-white curve of the ceiling as blankly as possible while not thinking about how completely fucked she was. Having whole hours to contemplate her degree of fuckedness was a luxury. Back in the City she'd never had time to sit with the dawning horror of revelation: she'd kept moving. She'd had to. The ceiling was very nice and very Lsel, and no one could look at her in here; she'd set all her tell-lights on the outside of the pod to *privacy, emergency only.*

<You're going to have to come out of the pod eventually,> said Yskandr, and Mahit felt nothing so much as that she was being reprimanded by a parent or a crèche-carer: *You'll have to go to bed eventually, Mahit.*

"I could wait a week," she said, quite out loud. No one could hear her in here; no one could *notice* how she wasn't one integrated person but a suspect, secret, virulent merge of three. "And then steal a shuttle and try to make the Anhamemat Gate before the Councilor noticed I missed my appointment and *yes* this is a stupid idea and *no* I won't do it and if I was going to betray Lsel's interests for *your sake*, Yskandr, I would have done it back in the Empire."

<How about for yours? What do you think Amnardbat is going to do to us when she finds out what we are?>

That depends, Mahit thought at him. *Did she sabotage us the first time, and if so, why did she? You knew her, Yskandr, you have more*—time, *more years than I do.*

<In her office you were sure she'd done the sabotage.>

In her office I was scared. There was a waiting sort of silence, an abeyance that wasn't acknowledgment as much as it was frustration, and Mahit was so tired of not thinking half of her own thoughts. *Are you happy now, Yskandr? I was frightened, and you were spilling trauma reaction all over my endocrine system, of course I was sure Amnardbat had sabotaged us right then. And now I'm alone and I can think, and I can't just work with I was scared, I have to*—

<Mahit,> Yskandr said, very gentle in her mind. <We were scared together. It's all right. Breathe.>

She took a breath; it came short, and she realized she'd been breathing in little fast useless inhalations for at least a minute and hadn't really *noticed* when she'd started. She took another, and it was still so *hard*, to breathe like her lungs weren't going to seize up, like she wasn't trapped—she *was* trapped, even in the safety of her private pod, she was absolutely trapped, the Councilor for Heritage wanted to *carve her open* and she still—months later, and she *still didn't understand why Amnardbat would have tried to sabotage her, or how, or* anything, and—

She breathed, deep, a circular breath through the nostrils and the mouth; it wasn't her choice, but she knew (or Yskandr knew) the pattern of it, the calming way of breathing. He took over their body entirely so rarely. Only when he needed to. The last time—the last *real* time—he'd run them through a riot unscathed, with all of the City in conflagration around them.

<There,> Yskandr said, and then, <Really, oxygen is helpful for clarity of thought,> a snatch of that bright rag of a man, the remains of her first imago, the sabotaged-Yskandr who never remembered his own dying, who only remembered decades of anticipated life in Teixcalaan to come, and a vast ambition, and a cleverness Mahit wanted to own, to inhabit, to allow into herself.

Thank you.

Warmth—all the little hairs on her arms and legs standing up and lying down again in a shivery wave, like her own neurology was touching her gently. This, too, was in none of the imago-training, none of the expectations for what would happen after a person received a live memory and a line of experience to be part of. Nothing in Mahit's education had told her about the strange kindnesses of living in a body with a—friend.

<Sentimentality is *not* helpful for clarity of thought,> said Yskandr.

An intensely *annoying* friend.

Electric laughter, and that vicious spike of ulnar-nerve pain; it wasn't always a shimmer now. Sometimes it just hurt.

<So. We're scared and we're trapped and since you're not planning on abandoning station like the hero of some graphic story like the one you bought—what *are* we going to do, Mahit?>

She sat up. Pressed her spine against the comforting inward curve of her pod. *What we should have done when we first got back, Yskandr. I think we should tell Dekakel Onchu that her messages for you didn't go unread entirely.*

Again she felt alive—*awake* in a way she hadn't seemed to be ever since she'd come back to Lsel. Awake was close to frightened, and exhilarating. There were remarkable similarities between how her aptitudes and Yskandr's had spelled for *risk-seeking;* she'd always assumed that had been a necessary precondition for the sort of xenophilia that made a person fall in love with a culture that was slowly eating her own, but perhaps it was something simpler, something gut-deep: *I can't leave anything well enough alone.*

<Ah, so you've decided to be political after all,> said Yskandr, so close in tone to her own thoughts that there was hardly any space between imago and inheritor, an intimation of future blur—one of her own memories being echoed, Twelve Azalea in her ambassadorial apartment back in the City, before anything had begun to go truly wrong, before she'd gotten him killed. Saying to her, *So you've decided to be political after all.*

Petal, she thought, with fond grief—not what she'd called him, that had been Three Seagrass's pet name for a man named for a pink extravagance of a flower. *Yes, I guess I have.*

———

It wasn't language. *Knifepoint*'s captain had been right about that much. The recording they'd made from the intercepted enemy-ship transmissions could have just been bad static feedback, cosmic radiation interference jacked up into a sharp crackle, at least to Nine Hibiscus's inexperienced ears. A sharp, ugly noise with the intimation of a headache inside it, that ended in a scream that had *taste*—a foul, oilslick, tongue-coating taste that made her nauseated. Synesthesia wasn't in Nine Hibiscus's usual suite of neurological oddities, and sound that made humans crosswire to taste was at *best* unpleasant and at worst actively harmful.

Nevertheless she listened to it twice, confirming for herself that *Knifepoint* had been right about the pauses in the crackling: even if this wasn't language, it was responsive to what *Knifepoint* had done. So it was communication. Of one sort or another. She made Twenty Cicada join her for the third time through. When the noise skittered higher and louder, he winced and put his hand over his mouth, swallowing a gag. He'd always been more sensitive than Nine Hibiscus was to local environments. She wished, abrupt and useless, that she hadn't made him hear this.

"—I can't," he said, once he'd gotten control of himself again, "imagine that their mouths are very pleasantly shaped, if they talk like that."

Nine Hibiscus shrugged, one shoulder up and down again. "They could be using a distorter. Or this is machine communication, one ship to another—"

"Or they could be machines communicating."

She wondered if Twenty Cicada would find that comforting: machines that accidentally talked in a way that disturbed human homeostasis, rather than something organic that could hurt other organic things by speaking. If she wasn't so short on time—shorter now, with Sixteen Moonrise due in an hour for a strategic defusing of politics over dinner—she'd ask him about it. "I doubt it," she said instead. "The spit that ate the Shard—See? I'm already calling it *spit*. Too organic. They're not machines."

Twenty Cicada said, "You don't *know* that," and she nodded.

"I don't *know* anything. We need a linguist. Who have we got on board for translation?"

Twenty Cicada leaned back in his chair, laced his hands behind the smooth dome of his head, and dipped his eyelids shut, consulting with the internal lexicon of personnel he seemed to always have easy memory of. "*Cuecuelihui* Fourteen Spike— that's who was on *Knifepoint*—but she *is* a translator, not a linguist. Outer Rim languages. One of your spy-types, she was on the ground team at Kauraan. Clever but better with humans than whatever this is, I think."

"Not her," Nine Hibiscus said. "I need someone without any

preconceptions, who hasn't heard the transmission before." Fourteen Spike *was* one of her "spy-types"—not *spies,* she didn't have spies unless Swarm himself counted. Third Palmers—*political officers,* in common parlance, the Ministry of War's intelligence branch—weren't the sort of people that a Fleet Captain kept around on purpose. Fourteen Spike was just one of her soldiers who she'd picked out for quiet charisma, language skills, the ability to become indispensable to anyone they were near. Usually someone of *cuecuelihui* rank, not command-track but the highest level of nonofficer specialist soldier. Someone flexible enough for independent work, strong enough to keep their loyalties regardless, like a metal that didn't go brittle when bent. Sometimes people like that could talk to barbarians so well that the barbarians forgot they were Teixcalaanlitzlim until it was too late for the barbarians. Fourteen Spike was for barbarians. Not aliens. Not something that not only wasn't *civilized* but wasn't even *human.* "Who else?"

"I could pull up the rest of the Kauraan team—"

"I don't want someone who can make *people* trust them, Swarm, I want someone who can talk to aliens without mouths."

Twenty Cicada covered his mouth again, but this time it was to hide a snicker. "Not you then either, my *yaotlek.* Only *people* trust you."

Her people trusted her, yes—the Tenth Legion trusted her, would die for her like she'd die for them: that was a captain's bargain. The rest of this Fleet? Not *yet.* Not with Sixteen Moonrise and her letter of political discontent already working its way through the other legions. Nine Hibiscus couldn't pull translators from some other legion's contingent, she was almost sure. Not without knowing Sixteen Moonrise's business, and how far it might have spread. She hated working on fractured ground, without the comfort of the Minister of War to contact as a last resort—but perhaps she'd grown too used to having that comfort.

Perhaps it was time to learn what sort of *yaotlek* she'd like to be remembered as, in her own right.

"This," she said at last, sitting down next to Twenty Cicada like they were both still palest-leaf-green cadets, shoulder to shoulder, "is a job for the Information Ministry."

CHAPTER
THREE

Top panel, two-thirds of the page: Captain Cameron and the rescued Heritage archivist Esharakir Lrut huddle in the shadow of the ruined caravanserai. It is snowing hard. Esharakir is feeding the papers and codex-books she has been guarding for twenty years into the fire, one by one. The flames look like words, curling up the panel: Teixcalaanli poetry, Heritage documents, maybe even a passage from the Lsel Record of Origin, a super-recognizable one—but altered slightly. A secret version that Heritage has kept from the rest of us, being destroyed so they can live through the storm.

Lower panel, one-third of the page: Captain Cameron's hand, snatching at the burning Record of Origin words, and Esharakir's face. She's serene.

CAMERON: You don't have to—Esharakir, what's the point if we can't keep what you've found—stop—

ESHARAKIR LRUT: This is dross, Captain. It's precious, but it's not a memory. Did you think you were coming here for *documents*? What sort of Stationer guards *documents* when she could preserve an imago-line that would be lost without her? I'm everything you need.

—graphic-story script for *THE PERILOUS FRONTIER!*
vol. 1, distributed from local small printer
ADVENTURE/BLEAK on Tier Nine, Lsel Station

* * *

[. . .] meals, supplement to hydroponics (meat substitute, taurine substitute)—twelve shipping containers; meals, supplement to hydroponics (preserved fruit)—one shipping container; missiles (projectile, hand weapon)—three shipping containers; missiles (projectile, ground cannon)—four cannons [. . .]

—appropriations for Fleet supply, Western Arc sector

(page nine of twenty-two)

THE request came in during the early hours of the morning, and so it was the Third Undersecretary to the Minister of Information, who had slept, or not slept (not slept, yet again) in her office, who got to it first. Three Seagrass saw it flash through on the internal Information Ministry network, a bright grey-gold-red cycling pulse in the upper-left quadrant of her cloudhook display: a *priority nineteen* message in War Ministry colors, the sort of thing that wouldn't even show up on a regular *asekreta*'s feed. Three months ago Three Seagrass never would have seen it.

(Three months ago, even if she'd somehow reached this exalted position in the Ministry, complete with her own tiny office with a tiny window only one floor down from the Minister herself, Three Seagrass would have been *asleep* in her *house,* and missed the message entirely. There: she'd justified clinical-grade insomnia as a *meritorious action,* one which would enable her to deal with a problem before anyone else awoke; that was half her work done for the day, surely.)

The request cycled again, blinking. No one was picking it up. Priority nineteen messages cycled four times and then dumped themselves into the First Undersecretary's private cloudhook, on the basis that an emergency message from someone command-level in another Ministry would at least get answered fast if otherwise it was clogging up Information's second-in-command's workflow. If it cycled one more time, Three Seagrass could safely forget about it until whatever it was settled on the Ministry like a fog of pollen, irritating everyone's mucous membranes—

Even your allusions are becoming terrible. Fog of pollen? *Like that is going to be the base of a decent poem—*

Two and a half months ago, Three Seagrass had written a decent poem, a lament for her dearest friend, stupidly and uselessly dead, and after that, well. Fog of fucking pollen, and this exquisite prison of an office.

She flicked her eyes up, micromovement to the left, and claimed that request message for her own.

Twenty minutes later, just as the dawn began to flood through her window to pool in extravagant, vision-obscuring beams across her cloudhook display, Three Seagrass put the finishing touches on the second-stupidest idea of her career in the Information Ministry. She did it accompanied by the determined cheerful voice of Fourth Undersecretary Seven Monograph humming the newest top-ten hit arrangement of "Reclamation Song #5" (the same song for *three fucking weeks now* and at least Seven Monograph had an exquisite command of prosody and imitation, even if he also had a tendency to get songs stuck in his head and share them with the office . . . but no one could sing two harmony lines at once without artificial help, and some people shouldn't try), wafting its way down the hall, as it did every morning. The Third Undersecretary—well, *any* Undersecretary of the six of them, really—had discretionary authority over assigning Ministry personnel on priority nineteen requests, and *oh*, had this ever been a request and a half. The *yaotlek* Nine Hibiscus, out on the edges of Teixcalaanli space, wanted a first-contact specialist with diplomatic chops, and wanted one *yesterday*. To talk to those same incomprehensible aliens that Mahit Dzmare had used to defuse a civil war while Three Seagrass watched, caught up in the strange gravity of her very own barbarian ambassador.

Her cloudhook pulsed pale gold: message incoming.

Patrician First-Class Three Seagrass, asekreta, *Third Undersecretary to Information Minister Four Aloe, you have been reassigned. Your new temporary designation is Envoy-at-Large, seconded to the Tenth Legion on the* Eternal-*class ship* Weight for the Wheel, *commanding officer* yaotlek *Nine Hibiscus. Please report to the central spaceport for expedited travel by sunset on 187.1.1–19A (TODAY). Your pay grade: remains the same; your clearances: remain the same; span of assignment: three months, with unlimited extensions. Assigning officer: Three Seagrass, Third Undersecretary to Information Minister Four Aloe. For questions regarding this assignment, please contact your assigning officer. To accept this assignment, reply to this message—*

Last chance, Three Seagrass thought to herself, last chance to have second thoughts. Last chance to not set yourself up for an *intensely* boring disciplinary meeting when you get back.

And blinked a *reply affirmative* before she could stop herself, feeling shimmering, feeling like she was already weightless and off-planet and terrified, feeling *real.* She thought of Eleven Lathe, her poetic model, her hero, writing *Dispatches from the Numinous Frontier* out alone amongst *his* aliens, the Ebrekti. Could she do worse? Certainly, but perhaps not *much* worse— and then, gleeful and bitter, she thought, *Fuck you, watch me try,* in Twelve Azalea's eternally silenced voice. That had been the first-stupidest idea of Three Seagrass's career: believing, wholeheartedly and entire, that the Ministry she and Twelve Azalea had served would protect them both from senselessness, even in the face of imminent civil war. Oh, how *very* stupid a decision that belief had engendered. And she hadn't been the one to die for it.

Not her, and not Mahit Dzmare. Mahit, who had kissed Three Seagrass once, in the middle of going more native than Three Seagrass had ever seen a barbarian go, and before she'd run away from the whole concept of Teixcalaan. She missed her, Three Seagrass decided. Maybe she should fix that, while she was exploding her nascent political career for the sake of the Empire.

The last time Mahit had gotten herself involved with court politics—and wouldn't the Lsel Council absolutely hate being

compared to the Teixcalaanli imperial court, that pit of internecine intrigue and backstabbing, villain of every faintly anti-
imperial holoproj drama—she hadn't been *consciously* aware of
the clock. This time—walking soundless on soft-soled shoes
through the decks of the Station, wending a deliberately ran-
dom path toward the central ship-hangar—she could almost
hear the seconds counting down. She had at *absolute most* six
days before Councilor Amnardbat wanted her in the neurological suite, six days before (in the best case) everyone on Lsel
knew that she had not one, but *two* imago-versions of Yskandr
Aghavn in her mind.

<What's the worst case?>

We die on the table. Carved open, a Heritage neurosurgeon's
scalpel slipping just enough to accidentally (surely accidentally)
sever her spinal cord. The surgical scar from where Five Portico had inserted the dead-Yskandr's imago-machine into Mahit's
skull ached. She'd grown her hair out to cover it; the tight curls
were longer than they'd been in years.

<I can think of worse than *that*,> Yskandr said, with too
much brittle cheer.

Don't.

The clock had existed in the City too. She'd started it running the instant she'd begun to investigate her predecessor's
death—or Yskandr had started it a long time previously, when
he'd promised a dying, brilliant Emperor an imago-machine and
eternal life. Like priming the detonator on an explosive. But
Mahit hadn't noticed the acceleration of time, the reduction
of options, until she'd been on Teixcalaan for *days*. At least this
time she could see the flat blank wall of the deadline coming
for her. She wouldn't be *surprised*.

<Councilor Onchu doesn't keep an office,> Yskandr mur-
mured to her as the Station's hangar opened up in front of
them, a busy cavern studded with ships, <or she didn't when
I knew her. She likes being with her people. There won't be a
central location you can walk up to—>

I don't want a meeting, *Yskandr, I want a conversation. We're going to a bar.*

Mahit still felt his laughter as an electric shimmer down her nerves, like she always had; it was only that now it shaded into the neuropathic ulnar pain when it reached her smallest fingers. She'd gotten used to it, somewhat. As much as she could manage to get used to it. As long as it didn't spread, or turn to numbness, she'd be fine. It wasn't an obvious tell. So very *few* people knew what had happened to her and Yskandr in Teixcalaan, and all of them were either—well, either her-and-Yskandr, or the entire person they sometimes managed to be, or back *in* Teixcalaan.

The bar she'd chosen wasn't one she'd been to before. She hadn't made a habit of hanging around pilots' bars as a young person or a student; her aptitudes in spatial mathematics had ruled out pilot-imagos as feasible matches early on, and she'd never quite stopped feeling like they'd all *know* she wasn't quite good enough to join them. Now that emotion felt like a vestige of another Mahit entirely, a child-Mahit with a child's fears and desires. The Mahit she was now wanted a drink, and she wanted a drink with Dekakel Onchu, the sort of Councilor who liked to socialize with her people. And this was Onchu's drinking establishment of choice—there were publicity holos of her coming out of it on more than one of Lsel's internal newsfeeds.

Finding her wasn't difficult. The publicity holos hadn't lied. She was at the bar: a dulled chrome expanse well scratched by glasses, graffiti, the remains of the original inlaid design, diamond hatching around curved fan-shapes. Mahit thought, *What sort of flower is that?* Thought it in Teixcalaanli, and had Yskandr chide her with a memory; how popular this particular pattern had been in pilot-deck décor back when he'd been a teenager taking his own aptitudes right here on Lsel. Mahit paused just to the left of the doorway, let the door swing closed behind her and leave her in shadows when an actual set of pilots walked in after. Onchu wasn't dressed like a Councilor; she was dressed like a spacer, scalp shaved to stubble, bright paint on her mouth and on the rim of her glass, deep lines around her eyes like solar rays. She wasn't in conversation. She was drinking companionably with the man to her right, a peaceful mutual silence, and there was an open stool on her other side.

<How do you want to play this?>

I think, Mahit said inside her mind, in the strange-echoing place where she was sometimes herself and sometimes a herself who was also Yskandr Aghavn, *that I want you to say hello.*

He didn't *take* her body, like he had in Teixcalaan or to calm her out of useless panic in her residence pod—Yskandr *slipped forward,* helped her muscles remember a walk they'd never used, a center of gravity they did not have. A smile wider than Mahit's own, and a way of leaning on one elbow when she'd arrived at the bar and sat down beside Councilor Onchu.

"Councilor," Yskandr said—Mahit said, the space between them hardly a space, thought and action fractionally separated—"it's been a long time. Sixteen years now?"

Onchu blinked. Blinked again, a slow narrowing and release of eyelids, an entirely evaluatory expression. "There are several people you might have been, with that sort of introduction," she said, "but only one who would be quite as audaciously rude as to make it. Hello, Mahit Dzmare."

Mahit smiled Yskandr's smile. "Hello, Councilor Onchu. I hope you don't mind if I have a drink."

"It's a pilots' bar, but we don't check your imago at the door for membership," said Onchu. "What's your poison?"

<*Ahachotiya.*>

We are not drinking fermented fruit, ever again, and also we are on Lsel, and also I wanted you to say hello, not to play Teixcalaanlitzlim for effect—

<Order a drink. She's watching us.>

"Vodka," Mahit said. "Chilled, straight up."

Onchu gestured to the bartender, a familiar hand flip, and he fetched down a chilled shot glass and a bottle of vodka so cold it poured thick and viscous. "As poisons go, I might like you," she said.

"Only as poisons go?"

Onchu grinned, white teeth bright against the dark red stain on her lips. "The rest, I'll see. It's funny, Dzmare, I thought you might show up a lot earlier than now. Or else not at all."

Mahit shrugged, the motion still more Yskandr's than her own. "Didn't mean to keep you waiting, Councilor."

"I wasn't waiting."

Talking to Dekakel Onchu was like trying to fix a target on a fast-rotating ship; she *looked* like she was right there, but she kept showing new faces, shifting too fast. Mahit thought (flood of memory, as sharp as scent, as the taste of Teixcalaanli tea, the light in Nineteen Adze's old offices), *Be a mirror,* and went on. "You sent me—well, not *me.* You sent several messages to the Lsel Ambassador. I regret to note that they reached the *current* one, not the former one."

The expression that crossed Onchu's face—a thinning of the mouth, one side of the lips curling up in a swift, barely visible smile, chagrin or pleasure, too fast to tell—made Mahit think of how she herself had felt, every time the world (the Empire—it was proving impossible to lose the valence of the Teixcalaanli fusion of the two words, even thinking in Stationer language)— shifted around her, reframed itself. Some new piece of information with its load of clarifying horror, slotting into place. Her upsurge of sympathy wasn't going to be useful here, she knew, but it was real nonetheless.

Onchu drank some of her beer, a swallow neither too large nor too small, a perfectly normal movement (and oh, fuck, how had one meeting with Heritage dropped Mahit right back into the kind of vigilant observation which had kept her alive in the City and which she had been trying so diligently to unlearn enough to imagine she had really come home), and nodded. "Interesting," she said. "From your behavior up until now, I would never have expected those went anywhere but a dead-letter office."

"I read them," Mahit told her. "I—at the time when I read them, I was very glad to have some external confirmation of what I myself was noticing."

"Drink your vodka," Onchu told her. "We're going to take a walk."

<Oh, she's interested in you,> Yskandr murmured.

Good, Mahit told him, and then—because he heard everything she thought anyway, because she was never alone again, *Let's see if interested means "would like me safely dead," as usual.*

The warm prickles of imago-laughter made the vodka shot burn sharper as she took it. "Where to, Councilor?"

"Think I'll show you around," said Onchu. "I'm due to inspect the hangar this shift. Come along. It'll be an education."

Mahit had been in Lsel Station's hangar before, but always as a passenger leaving the Station or on the yearly evacuation-safety-training days required for every Station resident. Walking into that cavernous space—cacophonous with talking, the thump and whine of maintenance machinery, the huge hum of cooling fans—next to the Councilor for the Pilots herself was a rather different experience. No one told Dekakel Onchu where to go: she walked amongst her people as if she had never quite wanted to be possessed of an office and a legislative responsibility. Mahit followed at her shoulder, feeling acutely ungrubby and uncalloused. There were so many *parts* of a spacecraft, and all of them were *everywhere,* being worked on by Stationers who understood them as intimately as Mahit understood the cadence of Teixcalaanli poetry.

"So," said Onchu, just loud enough for Mahit to hear over the roar of the fans, "you read my letters, and you thought what?"

"That you must have had real reasons for sending a warning like that," Mahit said. "An unauthorized communiqué, that—if it had ever reached Ambassador Aghavn—would have meant that our Station's official ambassador was a danger to him."

"I knew what I had done," said Onchu. "You don't need to prove that you're competent enough to figure that out." They were walking in a slow zigzag, tracking back and forth across the hangar floor. Half of Lsel Station's short-range transports were docked in here, being loaded or unloaded—the usual minerals and refined molybdenum, more unusual (to Mahit's eyes, at least, and she knew she was less informed than she'd like to be on Lsel's standard set of exports) pallets of compressed kelp, dried fish, rice . . . and most of those pallets were stamped with Teixcalaanli import papers. It looked very like Lsel was feeding the Teixcalaanli warships passing through Bardzravand Sector, the ones which were on the way to the war that had begun almost as soon as Mahit had come back to the Station.

<The war that we started,> Yskandr murmured.

The war that Councilor Tarats started, to preserve us, Mahit thought at him—and then stopped thinking, because Dekakel Onchu was watching her, watching every shift of her body language. Watching for Yskandr, or not-Yskandr. (For evidence of sabotage.) And even as she watched Mahit, she was moving amongst her people, stopping every so often to comment on a piece of work being done, or merely say hello to the pilot or maintenance engineer in question.

Some emperors are emperors of very narrow spaces, just enough to fill entirely with themselves, Mahit thought. When they were passing by a particularly noisy hull repair job, she asked as directly as she could, "What made you suspect Heritage?"

Onchu snorted. "Because it wasn't Tarats, and the others on the Council had neither access nor motive. Who else but the person who has control over all of our memories, whose responsibility is keeping us *safe* and *cohesive?*"

"Culturally safe," Mahit said.

"Amnardbat is a patriot," said Dekakel Onchu, who had flown ships in combat for the sake of Lsel Station, who Mahit thought would have given her life for her fellow pilots, and thus for the Station as a whole. She waited to see if the Councilor had anything more to add. In the silence between them the sound of metal banging on metal filled the whole world.

"And so am I, it turns out," Onchu went on, with an infinitesimal shrug of one shoulder. "Heritage should not be making such unilateral decisions about diplomacy. We're a council of six, and *Miners* breaks the ties, not Heritage."

"What did Councilor Amnardbat do to me?" Mahit asked, and let herself be as miserably upset about the question as she wanted. Which was a great deal.

"Ah," said Onchu, "then she *did* succeed," and Mahit had to stop herself from breaking into snickering, helpless and horrified—Onchu hadn't even been *sure,* she'd *guessed* at the sabotage, and thought it was worth warning the dead Yskandr about regardless.

"Someone did," she managed, just on the edge of that hysteria. "Quite effectively, really. I thought it was my fault—neurological failure, there *are* cases where an imago doesn't take—"

"You're not alone," Onchu said. "You don't move like Mahit Dzmare when I first met her."

No. No, she didn't. She'd shown that off very pointedly in the bar, and was probably showing it still—she herself didn't exactly *know* how she moved. If she ever moved like the person she'd been when she had been alone. "Some of the damage turned out to be reversible," she said, which wasn't *not* true. It just wasn't very much of what was true.

"In less complex circumstances, I'd be sending you over to medical to have that very thoroughly investigated, for the purposes of possibly reproducing the reclamation of function," Onchu said. "I hate losing imago-lines to neuro damage, and pilots—well. Lots of ways to get hit on the head. It'd be good to have a way of reestablishing a line that *did* manage to come back from an incident—I lose enough people as it is, lately."

"In less complex circumstances," Mahit replied, so dry that her tongue felt withered in her mouth, "there wouldn't be anything to investigate, would there."

Onchu laughed, soundless under the whine of a metal-cutter saw; laughed, and waved a half salute to the man operating it, who grinned back at her, signed *all good,* and went back to his work. "We suffer under complexity, Dzmare. So tell me. What made you finally decide to get off your ass and come down to the hangar?"

In six days I'm fucked sideways seemed too much like a confession. Like an appeal for sanctuary. She'd tried that on Teixcalaan, and look where it had gotten her: home, except never home again.

<Look where it got Nineteen Adze. Her Brilliance.>

Mahit ignored him. Yskandr—she, too, but mostly Yskandr—had a *history* of sleeping with emperors. Sleeping next to emperors, or proto-emperors, anyway, while they went their sleepless rounds of work. A thoroughly distracting history. And even if Onchu was worried about losing too many pilot-lines, too many deaths out in the black where Tarats's alien threat hunkered; Mahit couldn't trust Pilots to keep her safe through the revelation of her doubled imago any more than she could trust Heritage.

No one can know.

<You begin to see why I never came back.>

Not now, Yskandr.

"Heritage got off *its* ass," she said to Onchu. "Thought I should do the same. Now, how about you tell me what you thought you were trying to accomplish by warning Aghavn about me?"

Onchu pressed her lips together, dark red line like a cut beading blood. "Patriotism," she said, again. "Ask your imago—if that's still something you can do, if you've got more than muscle memory—about Darj Tarats and his *philosophy of empire,* and then, if you have more questions . . . I drink in that bar every seventh shift. Come on by."

Darj Tarats? Mahit asked, internal query . . .
. . . and what she got back was <Shit.>

———

A formal meal on *Weight for the Wheel* was a precise affair, a protocol dance, a prescribed sequence of events from the entrance
of the commanding officer to the final libation poured out for
the Emperor, a few drops of alcohol substituting for blood in
this latter fallen age—not that Nine Hibiscus was the sort of
Fleet Captain who would rather bleed into a bowl for propriety
rather than give up her last swallow of peat liquor. This was a
very *small* formal meal: four settings around a table in a conference room hastily made grand with Tenth Legion banners
and the black-and-gold starburst-cloisonné plates that matched
their banner colors. Nine Hibiscus herself wore exactly what
she'd been wearing while listening to the hideous alien noises,
which was her regular uniform with its new rank stars at the
collar: not just her Fleet Captain's four, but the spear-arc collar
tabs of a *yaotlek,* like the top of the imperial throne cut off and
turned sideways.

Guests were seated first, and thus Nine Hibiscus and Twenty
Cicada came into the room to find Sixteen Moonrise and her adjutant, the *ikantlos*-prime Twelve Fusion, already seated poised
over their empty plates, waiting like scavenger birds. She'd
never met Sixteen Moonrise in person before, only over holo—
the Twenty-Fourth Legion and her own Tenth had never been
posted in the same sector of space before this particular campaign. Sixteen Moonrise was tall, and her skin and hair were
the same suite of colors, like she'd been stamped from a die: the
color of the moon if the moon was a coin. Pale face, long and
straight pale hair, electrum-sheeny, left—for this official, cere-
monious meeting—loose of the queue she usually kept it
in. She was younger than Nine Hibiscus by a half indiction,
according to her official record. Those three and a half years

meant they'd never known each other as cadets. She looked serene and hungry at once.

"The *yaotlek* Nine Hibiscus, Fleet Captain of the Tenth Teixcalaanli Legion," murmured the soldier acting as steward, and both Sixteen Moonrise and her second bowed over their fingertips, deep inclinations.

"Welcome aboard the *Weight for the Wheel*," Nine Hibiscus said.

"We are welcome indeed," Sixteen Moonrise replied, the rote and required response, "your hospitality is as boundless as the stars, *yaotlek,* and as light-giving."

Nine Hibiscus sat. The table was small enough that all four of them were practically brushing elbows, save for Twenty Cicada, who was too skinny to brush elbows with anyone. The soldier at the door gestured fractionally, and another one of her people came in with real bread—every ship had *some* flour and yeast, for the particular rituals of hospitality that required their products—and the palest distilled wheat spirit, so alcoholic just inhaling it felt like being drunk: starshine, the Emperor's drink. Every ship had that, too. (Some more than others. Nine Hibiscus kept *Weight for the Wheel* well stocked.)

When she'd planned this meal—a *strategy dinner,* a transparent I-know-you-know-I-know ruse for Sixteen Moonrise to chew on along with her bread—Nine Hibiscus had meant to start with that letter demanding an explanation for the long delay in engagement with the enemy. Start with that, with her knowing about it before it had even officially arrived; cut Sixteen Moonrise's little political maneuver down at the knees and leave it to bleed out. But since then she'd been listening to aliens. Since then she'd seen their spit eat up one of her own.

"Fleet Captain," she began. Sixteen Moonrise inclined her head a fraction. "About an hour ago, while you were in transit, we engaged the enemy forces for the first time."

There was an expression there, but not much of an interpretable one. Twelve Fusion was more obvious: he put his glass of

starshine down on the table with a sharp click. "And you're having us for *dinner*?" he asked. "Why aren't you on the bridge?"

"Because you're my guests, and my Fleet Captains—
particularly the *eager* ones—are my best tools in the campaign
that is about to begin in earnest," Nine Hibiscus snapped.
There, that was the *I-know-what-you-did* portion of the meeting
gestured at. If she moved fast enough, she wouldn't need to ex-
pand into a full dressing-down. Sixteen Moonrise *was* a Fleet
Captain, and Nine Hibiscus was going to need the full complement of the Twenty-Fourth Legion—she could have used a triple six of legions, not just a *yaotlek*'s standard complement of
one six, if she was being brutally honest with herself about the
situation at hand. Unknown numbers of aliens, a force strong
enough to silence whole planets, and here she was with only
one six of legions—but she'd been outnumbered before. She'd
been outnumbered on Kauraan, and Kauraan had won her this
posting, for whatever good it would do her. "And besides," she
finished, ripping a chunk of bread off her roll with her teeth, "the
enemy that dared engage us has been neutralized entirely.
We aren't in an active combat situation, Twelve Fusion. Do you
think I'd have let you risk yourself and your Fleet Captain coming aboard during one?"

"No," Sixteen Moonrise answered, cutting off her subordinate
with a sharp gesture of one hand. "You haven't *half* enough legions to waste one on a stunt strategy dinner, *yaotlek*. Nor are
you stupid—"

That was rich, coming from a woman who was legally her
subordinate.

"*Stupid* is not the invective usually shouted at me, no," she
said, and tore off another mouthful of bread. It was sour, and
delicious, and the crust was sharp enough to cut her soft palate. Eating it showed her teeth, and she caught Twenty Cicada's
faintly reproachful expression. But propriety wasn't at *all* what
she wanted to convey just now. No, she wanted a sense of rapid
motion, of hunger. "A holo of the combat is already on your

shuttle for you to peruse on your way back, Fleet Captain," she continued. "And the Twenty-Fourth will come and join us at the point position in case more of these spitting, ship-dissolving *things* attack us. We'll be ready, with your able assistance. Twenty Cicada, play the audio."

She had warned him she was going to do this. She wasn't *cruel*. (And she'd noticed he hadn't eaten a single thing save for his obligatory sip of starshine, and hoped she'd keep her own bread down in her belly where it belonged.)

"You picked up a transmission?" Sixteen Moonrise began, and then the air was made of the hideous *noise* of the aliens again, and Nine Hibiscus at least had the pleasure of seeing the other woman go even paler than her standard color, and snap her jaw shut against an upsurge of bile.

After it was over, Nine Hibiscus said, "I've sent for a translator from the Information Ministry."

"You don't need a translator, you need a winnowing barrage," Twelve Fusion said. "Whatever made that shouldn't *exist*."

"Ah, I expect they think the same of you and me," Twenty Cicada said, as viciously dry as evaporating starshine liquor. "Perhaps we should try to talk to them and find out if there's anything *else* they'd like from us instead. Unless you enjoy watching Shard pilots dissolve from the ship inward. *Ikantlos-prime.*"

Nine Hibiscus could not *ask* for a better second than the one she had. She knew he knew she knew it, too, even if he wasn't looking at her.

Sixteen Moonrise placed her hands flat on the table. Nine Hibiscus wondered if they were shaking, or if she was trying to claim space—touching *Nine Hibiscus*'s ship, getting her palms on it. "*Yaotlek*," she said, with the highest level of formality. "Leaving aside the opinion of the entirety of the Twenty-Fourth, which I represent here, that talking to something that talks like that is a waste of all of our time, why the fucking *Information Ministry*?"

"What, do you want to talk to it instead?"

"I'd like to shoot at it. Without the interference of a bunch of manipulative spooks."

Nothing in Sixteen Moonrise's records as Fleet Captain of the Twenty-Fourth had suggested to Nine Hibiscus that she was more bloodthirsty than a standard Teixcalaanli soldier; Nine Hibiscus could imagine saying something similar. *I'd like to shoot at it.* She would, in fact, like to shoot at anything that came near her right now, including Sixteen Moonrise her own self. And *no* one in the Six Outreaching Palms was terribly fond of Information; Information were civilians. The eyes of the bureaucracy, of the City, out beyond the jumpgates where the actual City couldn't see. Eyes, quite often, on Fleet ships, reporting in secret to whoever their master was—either the Minister of Information, spidered away safe planetside (if you believed Fleet rumor), or all Teixcalaan expressed through the person of the Emperor (if you believed the propaganda Information put out). Nine Hibiscus usually neglected to believe the propaganda. Information were—oh, it would work to use Sixteen Moonrise's term, in her own mind, just for the moment—manipulative spooks.

But she had no one in her legion who could handle learning to talk to aliens that made human planets vanish into silence. And Sixteen Moonrise wasn't a trustable ally, not with her transparent power play of a challenge via concerned letter. Not with her immediate distrust of Information—that sounded like Third Palmer talk, *Fleet* intelligence, with their habitual distrust of anyone else's spywork. The Third Palm had never been one of Nine Hibiscus's favorite divisions to deal with. They were obstructionist, insistent on using only their own methods, their own people, anytime a Fleet engagement drifted out of strict combat and logistics and into overt psychological manipulation. Usually, Nine Hibiscus gave the orders she would have given anyway, and neglected to ask permission of the nearest political officer.

Sixteen Moonrise was a Fleet Captain, of course, not a political officer, but—she'd have to check the woman's early service record. Perhaps she had been, once. Either way, Nine Hibiscus didn't have the luxury of agreeing with her. Not now. Perhaps not at all.

"Information," said Nine Hibiscus, "talks to aliens as a habit. All of that bullshit with *Dispatches From the Numinous Frontier*, xenophile poetry and philosophy? These things can't fuck with Information's head, Information comes prefucked. It'll save us time, having them do the diplomacy and extract as much intelligence as possible, while we do the maneuvering. I want you to bring the *Parabolic Compression* up to meet *Weight for the Wheel*, with your full complement of Shards, and your stealth cruiser—what's it called, Twenty Cicada? The fast one."

"*Porcelain Fragment Scorched*," Twenty Cicada said, as smooth as an AI on cloudhook. "It's a very nice ship, Fleet Captain, you should be proud of the acquisition—where did you get it? From the Sixth Legion in trade . . . ?"

Sixteen Moonrise said, "You'd know, *Swarm*, wouldn't you," and fuck but she was going to push every inch of the way. Nine Hibiscus knocked back her glass of starshine, leaving only the Emperor's share, the last sip.

"He would," she said. "We're going to take back Peloa-2, even if there are more spitting ships waiting out there in the dark. You're going to, with *Porcelain Fragment Scorched*. Ask for whatever expertise you need from the Tenth, though I'm sure you're well staffed. This sector is Teixcalaanli. Let's remind ourselves of that while we wait for Information's input."

"This is a sop," Sixteen Moonrise said, her voice flat. "I am not a fool, *yaotlek*."

"On the contrary, Fleet Captain. You're just smart enough to know what I'm doing and that it will make you look like you've won when you come back to your co-conspirators in the Seventeenth and the Sixth Legions. Here's the action you requested. And here's my plan for a larger-scale engagement. You get both. Shall we go to work?"

Sixteen Moonrise made her wait, drawing out the tension between them for a long and ugly moment, and then she flipped over her starshine glass. The last mouthful spilled onto the table and glistened like the spit of their enemy.

"The Twenty-Fourth will execute this mission as you command, *yaotlek*," she said. "It is our honor to serve the Empire. Your hospitality has been impeccable—you remind me ever so much of Minister Nine Propulsion."

Ex-Minister Nine Propulsion, her former patron. That was the core of this, somehow. Nine Hibiscus couldn't quite see what Sixteen Moonrise wanted. Not yet, not with how she was still half-hearing the alien noise and watching the best alcohol in the Empire evaporate, formal gesture of détente-ended. Not yet, but it was surely Ministry politics, out here at the edge of the world; the long reach of the Palms mattered for politics as much as for firepower. Which was a sort of pity. She smiled instead of saying anything, her eyes wide, and tipped out her own glass. Thought, rote pattern, *May His Brilliance see a thousand stars,* and then corrected, internally. *Her Brilliance.*

"Fourth shift," she said to Twenty Cicada and the retreating backs of her guests. Eighteen hours away. "Recrew *Knifepoint* and ready *Dreaming Citadel* as support for the Fleet Captain's advance into the Peloa System."

———

It was kind of brilliant, really, how fast the people in Inmost Province Spaceport got out of Three Seagrass's way now that she was dressed as a special envoy. Teixcalaanlitzlim loved a uniform, a well-turned suit in shining colors—and Information cream and flame had never spun her wrong before when she'd needed to make an impression—but an envoy's suit, with its faint echo of a Fleet uniform done all up in that same flame-colored fabric? People *deferred*. She was tiny, and her rib cage was never going to be broad enough to write home about—no wide orator's lungs for her, no *substance* to her, at least physically—no matter how many poems she declaimed at court. And yet *absolutely no one had gotten in her way,* even though Inmost Province was as swarmingly crowded as ever. Merchants and freight pallets and soldiers and a thousand thousand Teixcalaanli citizens scattering like seeds to the stars. It was *heady.* She felt just exactly like she had when she'd been a trainee and skived off from class: a gorgeous and unfolding sense that she was getting away with something.

And it was all entirely, completely, and thoroughly legal. She'd signed off on it herself.

Admittedly, having done so, she'd left an *out of office* message on repeat outside her office door in cheerful doggerel glyphs, gone home to her flat to pack underwear and hair products and receive delivery of five identical envoy-at-large uniforms, and pointedly ignored any communiqués by cloudhook or infofiche stick that might have arrived with contradictory orders. Also she'd not done the dishes before she left for the spaceport and points unknown, but that wasn't *unusual.* She hadn't done the dishes all week.

A disturbing flicker of thought: neglecting the dishes all week was standard-overworked-Information-agent, neglecting the dishes before a three-month trip to a war zone was the sort of tell that a good interrogator would notice. Three Seagrass could imagine the conversation perfectly: *You weren't really planning on coming back,* asekreta, *were you?* asked the imaginary interrogator, and imaginary future-Three-Seagrass would have to shrug and say, *I wasn't thinking about that, I was preparing to serve Teixcalaan,* and then it'd be up to the two of them to figure out if she was lying.

None of this was her current problem, and all of it was unpleasant to consider. Three Seagrass strode through a group of off-planet tourists disembarking from a passenger cruiser and scattered them like leaves; wove her way past an enormous crate of brightly scented, spiky-skinned fruit being offloaded onto pallets; and walked straight up to the ship she knew would get her to the first stop on her route fastest of any ship currently at port in Inmost Province. It wasn't a military vessel. The *Flower Weave* was a medical resupply skiff, made for darting out-City loaded with equipment that had an extremely limited shelf life. Potent botanicals straight out of the Science Ministry's laboratory, offgassing to uselessness if they sat around too long, for example. Or—like this particular ship on this particular run— organs for transplant. Hearts. Nice fresh ones on ice, loaded up with antigens that were apparently—according to her quick and dirty research—quite common in the City but in very rare supply on a small planet right next to the first jumpgate that Three Seagrass wanted to move through.

She blinked directions to her cloudhook, microshifts of her eye, and cued a *government official is here to annoy you* message to the *Flower Weave*'s captain. It didn't take him long to show up, the doors of his hangar bay folding back like a membranous fan. He looked harried. *Excellent.*

"Captain Eighteen Gravity," Three Seagrass said, "My name is Special Envoy Three Seagrass, and I need you to take me along with your cargo when you break orbit."

He blinked. "Envoy," he said, and bowed over his fingertips, which gave him enough time to collect himself; she could watch him do it. "I'm a medical supply ship," he went on, as he straightened up. "I can't detour. My cargo is time-sensitive. I know the regulations say I'm supposed to take envoys anywhere they want to go, but—"

"You're headed to Calatl System. I am *also* headed to Calatl System, Captain. And you're leaving fastest of any ship in this whole spaceport." Sometimes it was very difficult for Three Seagrass not to smile like a barbarian: bared teeth and gleeful. She'd probably learned that from Mahit. The impulse remained repressible, however, so she repressed it.

"Oh," said Captain Eighteen Gravity. "If you don't mind the

cramped quarters in the hold, that's fine, then. We don't really have a passenger cabin, it's just me and my first officer and the *ixplanatl* tech."

"I am very small," Three Seagrass said, delightedly. "I squish. Put me in between the boxes of hearts, I'll do just fine."

There was a moment where the captain seemed to be attempting to marshal an appropriate response, and then he visibly gave up. "We break orbit in an hour and forty-seven—forty-six, sorry—minutes," he said. "If you're squished in with the hearts in an hour and thirty, you can go wherever we go. Envoy."

"Excellent," Three Seagrass told him. "Your service to Teixcalaan and Her Brilliance Nineteen Adze does you credit! See you soon."

An hour and thirty was enough time to grab dinner from one of the multitude of spaceport bars, and Three Seagrass figured she'd need it, if she didn't want to contemplate carpaccio of medically significant human heart at an inopportune moment. *Teixcalaan devours,* she thought, and then—*no, that wasn't how Mahit said it at all.* She could ask her, maybe, when she got to Lsel Station.

It was *on the way* to the war. It was in fact *right next to* the war, in a way that her barbarian must have known would happen when she gave the coordinates of their enemy as sinecure for her Station's freedom and thought the danger worthwhile. So Lsel was, in fact, a reasonable stop to make—especially if Three Seagrass was meant to *learn to talk to aliens,* which she was. She could use an alien who was good at talking to humans. Barbarians were the next best thing to aliens. Mahit was the best of the barbarians Three Seagrass had ever met, and also she missed her.

In the bar she ordered thick noodles in soup with chili oil and shreds of smoked beef, on the basis that it would be a long time before she could have proper in-City food again. She amused herself by drawing her route on one of her cloudhook's graphics vector programs: to that nearby jumpgate on the *Flower Weave,* and then to three more jumpgates by whoever was fastest at each stop, doing a complex end run around the two months of sublight travel that getting to Lsel *usually* took. She would come out the wrong gate, when she got there, and have to convince whoever was piloting her ride to take her to the Station. The wrong gate—which Mahit had called the *far gate*—would be much closer to Lsel than the usual gated approach to Stationer space, from territories properly controlled by Teixcalaan. The far gate was outside the Empire, and she'd have to switch to non-Teixcalaanli vessels to access it at all, especially from the non-Teixcalaanli side. That side of the Amhamemat Gate was in territory nominally controlled by the Verashk-Talay Confederation, who had an absurd habit of electing their leaders by popular vote. Or at least Three Seagrass thought it was. Verashk-Talay space wasn't mapped very well, and the Anhamemat Gate also led to places where incomprehensible aliens were making trouble for the Fleet's newest *yaotlek,* trouble bad enough to call Information for help rather than stick with the Third Palm's military-intelligence services . . .

"Good evening, Three Seagrass," said someone behind her, and she dropped her fork with a clatter and turned around.

"You might consider reducing the intensity of your startle reflexes, with where you're going," said Five Agate, once Nineteen Adze's prize student and chief aide, and now one of her *ezuazuacatlim,* the Emperor's sworn band of loyal servants. She hadn't changed her style of dressing with her elevation in status. She was still in white, like all of Nineteen Adze's people had been, in imitation of their mistress's former signature style.

"Your Excellency," Three Seagrass said, in the highest level of formality she could muster with noodles in her mouth.

"Chew your food," Five Agate told her, and Three Seagrass suspected that she used exactly the same tone when addressing her small son, Two Cartograph; absently parental. Three Seagrass had met the kid once, during the insurrection three months ago. He was very healthy and clever for someone who had been born from a uterus, on purpose. She chewed her food. Swallowed.

"What can I do for you, Your Excellency?"

"Her Brilliance has a question for you."

Her first reaction was an entirely terrifying spike of *But if I go to Palace-Earth, I'll miss my ride,* an absurd thought: her Emperor wanted to talk to her and she was concerned with her own somewhat-unauthorized exit from all the responsibilities that same Emperor had been gracious enough to grant her? There was something wrong with her for even experiencing the emotion. Best to pretend she hadn't.

"Of course," she said, and waved for the nearest waiter. "Let me settle the bill and then—"

"No need," Five Agate said. "I can ask it, and you can finish your meal."

"Please."

"The Emperor would like to know your opinion of Eleven Laurel."

Three Seagrass blinked, and tried to summon up her mental inventory of people named Eleven Laurel who the Emperor would want to know her opinion of—rejected out of hand the *asekreta* trainee serving as an office assistant on the eighth floor of the Ministry, and also the poet-orator who had died when Three Seagrass was thirteen and convulsed the capital in an ecstasy of internal rhyme for months—and was left with the Third Undersecretary to the Minister of War. Who she technically shared rank with, though that also seemed hilarious; Eleven Laurel was a war hero, and she was . . . herself. So far.

"Of the Third Palm?" she asked, just to make sure. (Of course the Third Palm; the passed-over military spymaster. The one the *yaotlek* Nine Hibiscus was for some reason avoiding, preferring to go through Information for her diplomats.)

"If Nineteen Adze wanted your *literary* opinions, she'd send a better messenger than me," Five Agate said, dust-dry. "I hate that poet. Yes, the Undersecretary. Do you know him?"

". . . I've met him," Three Seagrass said. "We haven't ever spoken personally. Do you—or Her Brilliance—want my *professional* opinion of him? The Information Ministry's opinion? Because if you do, I really can't have this conversation in a spaceport bar."

Five Agate shook her head, a dismissal—not a professional query, then. "Would you swear on the sacrifice of your blood that you're telling the truth, *Envoy*? You've never spoken to Eleven Laurel personally."

A professional query would have been less disturbing. This was a darker thing: that an *ezuazuacat* would ask her for her blood in a sacrifice bowl as a promise that she didn't have some prior relationship with the Third Undersecretary of War made Three Seagrass feel as if she'd fallen, vertiginous, back three months in time. Back to when all of Teixcalaan was convulsed in succession-crisis and almost-civil-war, death and blood, and she'd watched the old Emperor die on *full broadcast*, poured out in a sun temple like a spilled glass of water, red everywhere. The noodles she'd eaten felt leaden in her stomach.

"I would swear," she said. "Here, or wherever you and Her Brilliance would like. I don't know him, I've never spoken to him personally." She held out her hand, palm up. No scars there, not yet. She'd never sworn an oath large enough to scar. Even the one she'd sworn two months ago, with Mahit and Nineteen Adze, had healed to invisibility. The body didn't care about the size of the promise, only the size of the cut.

"No need," said Five Agate. "Your promise is enough. Do be careful out there on the front lines, Three Seagrass. Her Brilliance thinks well of you, and it's frustrating for the rest of us when she loses someone she likes."

"How frightening," Three Seagrass said, before she could stop herself. "I'm honored?"

"Go catch your ship," said Five Agate. "The *Flower Weave*, yes? You've got twenty minutes. I'd run for it. Don't worry about the check. It's on the government."

They must have been watching her the whole time, ever since she'd answered the *yaotlek*'s request. The City's camera-eyes, Nineteen Adze's favorite tools. They always had been, and now that she was Emperor, she'd have *every* access—the algorithms and the machinery, the Sunlit Three Seagrass had passed coming into the spaceport, who shared a kind of access to the algorithms that Three Seagrass never wanted to think about too closely. Every eye of them the same—and every eye opening to the Emperor Herself. It almost felt benevolent. Almost. If Three Seagrass worked at feeling like she was being protected, not *seen*.

And had the Emperor wondered, seeing her impulsive decision, if she'd somehow—been suborned by Eleven Laurel? What a complex idea. She'd have to think about it on the trip. She'd have time. Not much, but maybe enough. The Ministry of War was one of the barely-patched-up parts of government—still reeling from the former Minister Nine Propulsion's ever-so-convenient early retirement. Three Seagrass had immediately understood that move as being a way for Nine Propulsion to get out of the City with her reputation intact, before she could be dismissed by a new Emperor who knew she'd supported an insurrectionist general when push came to shove—

—and most of the War Undersecretaries had turned over with her, replaced by the new Minister's people . . . except for Eleven Laurel. Perhaps it was as simple as that.

Nothing was as simple as *that*.

"Thank you," she said to Five Agate. "For the warning. And covering the bill."

Then she ran for it before anyone else could stop her.

CHAPTER
FOUR

Teixcalaan, once we were in the First Emperor's hands and flying out into the black, learning jumpgates as we went, carrying
with us our seeds of civilization like sacrifice-blood welling from
the palms of those first planet-breakers—once the Empire was
the Empire, extending throughout the universe from jumpgate to jumpgate? Our Emperors were soldiers, and still are, but
an empire that holds a galaxy-net of stars in its teeth learns also
to speak our poetry in a thousand languages. A soldier-emperor
might be a soldier on the field of negotiation, and numbered
thus amongst our greatest *yaotlekim*. For in the latter centuries,
those that draw close to this present time, Teixcalaan rules as
much through words as through deeds. So it was with the Emperor Twelve Solar-Flare, whose life began in the City, second
crèche-child of her ancestor, the Emperor One Lapis's beloved
advisor Twelve Sunrise . . .

> —*The Secret History of the Emperors*, 18th edition, abridged
> for crèche-school use

* * *

[. . .] having considered the latest status report on the state of the
Station's evacuation procedures, including the level of community training on rapid lifeboat deployment, supply lines, and the
capacity of the mining outposts to shelter refugees, I suggest that
we consider what I would previously have dismissed as fearmon-
gering: if we are displaced permanently, how would we rebuild
a Station of this size before we ran out of resources to support
thirty thousand in diaspora? And where would we build, if we

are fleeing a conflict? The following memo begins to outline our deficiencies . . .

—internal research memorandum addressed to the Councilor for Hydroponics, composed by Life Support Analyst III Ajakts Kerakel and team, 67.1.1-19A (Teixcalaanli reckoning)

ALL *right,* Mahit said to her imago, a direct query like gritting her teeth inside her mind, *what don't I know about Darj Tarats that I need to know?*

She'd retreated to her residence pod from the hangar bay. It was quiet in here, curved and soothing-smooth, and in the intimate privacy of whatever internal landscape an imago and successor shared—she thought of it as a room sometimes, a room with unexpected mirrors—she discovered without much regret that this conversation was easier to have in Teixcalaanli.

Not that it was *easy* to have. Yskandr was chimerical, slippery; an imago wasn't really a separate person, but sometimes, *sometimes* Mahit felt like she was sharing herself with a possessing, secretive alien. Right now even the direct question didn't do her much good: there was no answering Yskandr-voice, no sense of partnership, just a flicker of visual memory (*hands on a table, grey-brown, the veins prominent right up to the knuckle, and the reflection of stars through a Station window*) which dissolved if she tried to look at it closely. Imago-memory wasn't always accessible; it was associational at best, not like her own living memories. She couldn't reach back into what Yskandr remembered and pull up Darj Tarats like a holofilm. The only transfers which worked like that were *skill* transfers. Language, decorum. How she could do partial differential equations now, because Yskandr had known how. Partial differential equations, and matrix algebra, and ciphers based in both.

But if he didn't *want* to help her—and oh, every time he went silent she was afraid, so desperately afraid of being alone and broken again, it was a horrible worm at the core of her, *how* afraid she was that it had never been sabotage at all, that she was merely broken, merely somehow corrosive to her imago, never suitable, not a rightful inheritor for *any* memory—

<Oh, stop it,> Yskandr said, and Mahit exhaled all of the breath in her chest, folding over herself.

You could stop scaring me, also.

<Unlikely, given the circumstances, our history, and the continued unorthodox nature of our link in the imago-chain. Not to mention Darj Tarats.>

Mahit was not going to let him bait her into enjoying herself, taking pleasure in the wry and vicious cast of his humor (*What did you do, Yskandr? Oh, sedition, probably*, fragment-memory, her first hour on Teixcalaanli soil, when she'd only had the edges of how wrong being the Lsel Ambassador could go), not when she really, really needed him to stop fucking around and give her what information he had.

Get on with it, Yskandr. Darj Tarats, Councilor for the Miners, he who rescued us and this Station by sending me coordinates of ship-destroying aliens to feed to Teixcalaan in exchange for our freedom. Your patron, according to absolutely everyone, including you. Spill. Or at least let me see.

<You know it doesn't—we don't—work like that.>

I know. Let me see.

And the mirrored room that was her mind unfolded like a flower, floating in some jeweled pool in Palace-East, blue petals like drowning.

Not a cohesive string of memory—not the being-Yskandr she'd experienced in flashes, under sedation and a laser-knife, when she'd had her damaged imago-machine replaced with one carrying an older version of the same imago. Not *narrative* at all, but a way of seeing. A way of knowing a man for a long time. What a distant, antagonistic friendship was like, conducted over interplanetary distances. They'd written letters, Yskandr Aghavn and Darj Tarats had—back and forth for twenty years, in the same cipher Tarats had used to send her the coordinates of the alien incursion. A long time to talk into the dark at someone you didn't like—

<I liked him. Sometimes.>

Yskandr had liked him at the moment of receiving a new letter, liked him in the anticipation of being challenged and surprised and having to figure out how to push back, keep what he himself intended in Teixcalaan unobserved. Liked, too, the brazenness of Darj Tarats's own planning, the equality-in-revolutionary-thought he'd found in that long, slow epistolary. Liked being just useful enough to his patron back on Lsel to be part of *his* dream of a future for Teixcalaan as well as Yskandr's own—

Mahit still wasn't getting to the heart of it. The elision, the *blank*. The drowning-blue unfolding that felt like terror and incomprehensibility and was probably just Yskandr not wanting to show her what Darj Tarats's imagined future *was*, like he hadn't wanted to show her how he'd loved the Emperor Six Direction with his mind and his body and eventually his loyalty to Lsel. All of that, all of him, given over. She *leaned*—a kind of internal pressure, like trying to remember the cadence of a poem, the stroke order of a glyph she'd only seen once, the *specific* word in Teixcalaanli for *ibis,* that long-legged bird that dipped its narrow feet through the pools of Palace-East, disturbing the lotuses, that same blue—

The spike of feeling down her ulnar nerves wasn't numbness or electric fire but actual pain. *Idiopathic,* she thought, biting back a hurt little noise, *idiopathic and psychosomatic, and it's probably just going to get worse, every time something goes wrong with us. Yskandr—*

Her hands felt like lumps that burned, fingerless, as if pain had rendered them invisible, insensible.

Blue, in a glass. Alcohol with a faint blue tint—<Gin,> Yskandr supplied, distant, <the blue is from a peaflower in the distillate, Nineteen Adze introduced me to it.>—and earliest-morning light, near-dawn glowing through the glass, the color falling onto one of Tarats's ciphered letters. Yskandr in his (their) apartment in the City. The sensation of being struck without being struck physically, an emotional blow, the world (the Empire) suddenly destabilized, and Yskandr had dropped the glass, spilled blue everywhere, blue and sharp glass shards and the smell of juniper rising in a sickening perfume.

You know I pushed for you to be Ambassador because I knew you'd make Teixcalaan need you, trust you, love you and through you, us, Tarats had written, *but perhaps you never managed to alight on why I would want such a hideous thing as imperial desire focused on our Station or on its representative. But what better way to draw a monstrous thing to its death than to use its functions against itself? Teixcalaan wants; its trust is rooted in wanting; it is in this way you and I will destroy it.*

The words were too clear to be organic memory—they were grooved in, words that Yskandr had repeated and reread, thought about so often that they'd become part of his internal narrative. Whether they were Tarats's actual words almost didn't matter. They were the story that Yskandr had told himself, remembered being true; they were scent-linked, color-linked, and they were her memory now too, as much true for her as they were for her imago, live memory carried over on sense and image.

Very carefully, like tonguing a wound, Mahit let herself wonder which part of those words had been what made Yskandr recoil away from them and drop his glass of gin. *To draw a monstrous thing to its death* was what had hooked in her like a barb in her lip, a phrase that might tear.

<That,> Yskandr said, a flicker of thought, so close to her own that it was more like confirmation than anything foreign or disparate. <That, and *its trust is rooted in wanting*—I knew what I was doing, with Six Direction, but to hear it so bluntly put . . .>

To hear that there was nothing of how you loved one another that was clean.

<A man pretends,> Yskandr murmured. <A *barbarian* pretends that civilization might grow in the small hours of the night, between two people.>

Mahit imagined it, civilization—humanity—blooming like tiny flowers, caught between mouths in the dark, lips that kissed and talked and built. It was a gorgeous phrase, in Teixcalaanli. *You might have been a poet, if you hadn't died—*

<No. You might have, had I not been the Ambassador before you.>

That stung. She smeared tears out of her eyes (and when had she started crying?) with the back of one numb, painful hand. It felt like using a mitten. It also hurt less than it had before, which was some bare comfort. She tried to breathe slowly, an even flow of oxygen.

Did you know? she asked, after a long while. *Did you at least suspect, that the Councilor for the Miners was using you as bait to draw Teixcalaan into the war the Empire is fighting now? You, and the whole Station right along with you?*

Mahit didn't get a straight answer; she got the emotional equivalent of a flinch, a squirming sense of avoidance, of needing to think of something else. Got that, and took it for *yes,* and also for *and I wished I hadn't understood.* The silence in her pod felt hollow, oppressively bleak. She had helped to start that war, out of desperation and need: doing exactly what Tarats had always wanted Yskandr to do, what he'd always refused. Squirming guilt rose up in her stomach. No wonder Yskandr hadn't wanted to share this with her. No wonder her hands hurt so badly.

Resigned, from a very long distance away: <He wanted—wants, I assume—for us to be free. Us Stationers. That was always the center of him. Trying to come up with some way we would end up free, as if Twelve Solar-Flare had never found us at all.>

Mahit tried to imagine it herself: Lsel Station, if the Teixcalaanli Emperor Twelve Solar-Flare had never found a jumpgate that spilled her out into this sector of space. If there had never been a historical epic written about that discovery by Pseudo-Thirteen River, if Mahit had never learned that epic in language classes and quoted it to imperial subjects to prove her erudition. She failed entirely. She wouldn't *exist*. There would be no constellation of endocrine response and continuity of memory that bore a single bit of resemblance to Mahit Dzmare. The feat of imagination that Tarats was attempting was—there was no other word for it but heroic.

Like something out of a Teixcalaanli epic poem. *That* heroic.

Mahit laughed, a raw sound that ended in a bubbling, weepy cough, choking on her own ridiculous fluids. She couldn't do it at all. She *thought* in Teixcalaanli, in imperial-style metaphor and overdetermination. She'd had this whole conversation in their *language*.

Deliberately, she thought in Stationer, *We're not free.*

And in the same language, Yskandr agreed: <There's no such fucking thing.>

————

Inside Palace-Earth there were three kinds of ways to be seen. There was the normal way, where Eight Antidote was in a place with other people and they looked at him with their eyes or their cloudhooks. He was good at avoiding the normal way, if he wanted to. It helped that he'd never lived anywhere else, and most of Her Brilliance Nineteen Adze's staff had come over from Palace-East and were still getting lost in corridors even two months later. It also helped that he was small, and had a tunic and trousers in soft grey that eyes slid off of, in addition to all the bright gold and red and grey things that stuffed his wardrobe otherwise. He managed not being *seen* all the time.

But there were two other ways, and he hadn't figured out how to disappear from them yet at all. There were the City-eyes, its cameras and locational tracking and the collective link of the Sunlit to crosscheck any errors, how the Emperor always

knew exactly where he'd gone. Eight Antidote had checked his
clothes for a tracking bug once, and found absolutely nothing,
and felt pretty stupid afterward: locational tracking was algorithmic. He'd learned that from one of his tutors, one of the
ones Minister Eight Loop sent him from the Judiciary, like an
economist was the kind of present a kid would want. The City
mapped him based on capturing his image and the location
of his cloudhook, and predicted where he'd been when he'd
dropped out of view for a minute, and it was *really* accurate. He'd
done the math, for that same tutor. Most of it. Some of it was
too hard still, kinds of equations he'd never seen.

The third way was the trickiest. The third way was being
seen because of asking questions. Having someone—some
adult, usually—see inside his head. And the person who was
most dangerous to ask questions of (well, most likely to use
those questions to figure out what Eight Antidote was thinking
without him ever saying anything out loud) was the Emperor
Nineteen Adze. It figured that she was definitely the person
he *needed* to ask about the Kauraan campaign. Everybody else
wouldn't tell him the truth, or would tell him something that
sounded true and was slanted away from it, like a tree growing out of the side of a building where it didn't belong. A tree
that looked like you could put your weight on its branches and
swing, but if you tried, the whole wall would come down along
with you and the tree instead.

He'd never get any better at hiding his thoughts when he
talked without practicing. This was definitely true and also
not very comforting at *all*. True things weren't, mostly. Still, it
helped to think about: even if the Emperor knew why he was
asking her questions, he'd learn what gave him away, and next
time he'd do better. He needed to learn. He was already eleven,
and some of the cadets in the Ministry of War were only fourteen and had real responsibilities; that was just three years
away, and he wasn't a cadet, he was the heir to the Empire. He
might not have three years to get ready.

The Emperor was in the Great Hall, as usual for midafternoon: she took public meetings and petitions, like Six Direction had before her, and sometimes she gave pronouncements, and once or twice a week Eight Antidote came to sit by the sun-spear throne and listen, on the Emperor's request. *Watch,* she'd said. *Watch who comes to ask for help, and who doesn't.* Today wasn't one of his scheduled days. Today he slipped into the Great Hall, quiet in his grey clothes and his soft shoes, the only thing that didn't gleam, that wasn't patterned. The Emperor was wearing gold and white, layers of suiting, the points of her lapels echoing the points of the throne, and she was talking to some *ixplanatlim* wearing poppy-red, the color of doctors and medical scientists. The verse in the children's song about the kinds of Palace employees went *red for blood and for the ease of pain* and had a tune that Eight Antidote wished was either less memorable or less cheerful. He wondered what the Emperor wanted to talk to medical people about, or what they had to say to her.

She was young. Not like his ancestor-the-Emperor, who had been dying, and talked to medical *ixplanatlim* all the time. She shouldn't need them. Not for a long time yet.

He crept closer. The City-eyes had spotted him, of course, but he wasn't trying to fool them right now; he just wanted to be quiet. He kept his back to the wall and shifted sideways between the fan-arch ribs of the roof where they met the ground. Sank down on his heels and sat cross-legged there, in a shadow. Grey like a shadow, a darker spot on the tiled floor, not really here— just here to *listen.*

"—find out," Nineteen Adze was saying. "I don't want your *supposition* that this woman died in a shop fire in Belltown Two because she was carrying an incendiary device and it went off prematurely. I want your *certainty,* and I want to know who she was. If it was her device, or if she was carrying it for someone else, or if it wasn't an incendiary at all but some poor unfortunate in the wrong place at the wrong time."

The *ixplanatlim* didn't look happy—they glanced at each

other, like they were all trying to get out of being the person who had to say something to the Emperor she didn't want to hear. Finally, one of them—a woman, her ash-brown hair in a triple queue down her spine, dull against the bright red of her uniform—took a step forward. "We wouldn't have come without completing the investigation," she said, "if the dead woman hadn't had one of those anti-imperial posters pasted over what was left of her face, the ones that were all over the City before the recent—um. Difficulties. Your Brilliance."

Eight Antidote could tell when Nineteen Adze was paying attention because she wanted to, instead of because she had to. She made all the air go out of a room, even a room as big as this one. Her fingers tapped on one of the arms of the throne, one-two-three-four-five, and then stilled again. "A defaced battle flag poster?" she asked.

The *ixplanatl* dragged her eyes off the Emperor's hand and back to her face. She nodded. "Plastered to her face with the same glue they'd use to stick it to a wall."

"Postmortem."

"Yes, Your Brilliance. Someone else stuck it to her corpse. Before any investigation personnel arrived."

"And there's no visual record of this mysterious corpse defacer."

"The fire took out the nearest City-eye, and—"

Nineteen Adze waved a hand, cutting her off. "Go to the Judiciary with this. The corpse, too—any further autopsy should be run out of their facilities," she said. "You'll have an appointment with the Minister of the Judiciary by the time you walk over there. Tell Eight Loop what you just told me. And Teixcalaan *does* appreciate your concern, and your expertise."

When people left the vicinity of the sun-spear throne, it was like watching starships try to break orbit—an *effort*. Eight Antidote had never felt that, that pull. It was probably because he belonged here, and they didn't.

"You can come out of the shadows now, Eight Antidote," said the Emperor, and Eight Antidote sighed.

It would be so nice if Nineteen Adze were less good at noticing. But that would make her a less good Emperor, too, according to every poem he knew: Emperors saw the whole of Teixcalaan, all at once, so why wouldn't they see one eleven-year-old kid in a corner? He got up and came over to the throne, thinking, *When I'm Emperor, will I see too?* and then deciding not to worry about that right this minute. It wasn't the question he wanted to ask.

Neither was "Did someone get murdered?" but that was what came out of his mouth first off.

"Unfortunately people get murdered all the time," said the Emperor, which was condescending—Eight Antidote *knew that;* he wasn't a baby.

"Most murders don't have three medical examiners talking to the Emperor about them," he said.

"True," that Emperor told him, her eyes wide-smiling, and Eight Antidote didn't trust her, really, didn't *know* her, really, but his ancestor-the-Emperor had loved her enough to make sure she ended up on the sun-spear throne, and that was something to remember when her smiling at him made him feel seen in the way that he *wanted* to be seen. "Come sit, little spy, since you've been listening already." She patted the wide arm of the throne.

Little spy wasn't half as nice as *Cure,* but it was more honest. Eight Antidote perched on the throne arm, like a palace-hummer alighting, comfortable—it was more than wide enough for him—but poised to leave at any moment. When he was sitting there, he looked at Her Brilliance and waited, keeping his face as expressionless as he could manage.

". . . You look so much like him, it's almost reassuring that you spend half your time hiding in shadows," said the Emperor, and Eight Antidote felt a rush of satisfaction at having made her react to him. He knew he looked like Six Direction. Knew that he'd only look *more* like his dead ancestor the older he got, and if he tilted his head just a little to the right, and lifted his chin and his eyebrows—

—Nineteen Adze pulled back from him a good inch before she caught herself doing it. *Interesting.*

"My ancestor-the-Emperor would have had a difficult time not being seen," he said. "*You* do, too. It is a very large throne."

"It is a very large empire, little spy," said Nineteen Adze, and sank back into that throne. Eight Antidote wondered if it was comfortable if your legs were long enough; it certainly wasn't comfortable when your legs were eleven-year-old size, like his. He'd tried it out. But Nineteen Adze looked so very much like she belonged in it: the corona of spearpoints like a crown behind her, metal-grey and gold. Like Six Direction had looked. Like a pilot embedded in a ship . . .

"I wanted to ask you something," he said, and knew that he was going to give away what Eleven Laurel in the Ministry of War was teaching him, if he asked his question. It wouldn't be his secret training anymore, it would be—oh, like everything else. Just part of being him, being him inside the palace. Inside his life.

From the depths of the throne, Nineteen Adze said, "I'll try to answer."

"Why wouldn't you be able to?"

"Ask," said the Emperor. "Find out."

Eight Antidote sighed, shoving air through his nose, curving in on himself until his elbows were on his knees, his chin in his hands, still perched on the throne arm. "Why did you pick Fleet Captain Nine Hibiscus to be *yaotlek*, Your Brilliance?"

"What a fascinating question. Are you thinking of spending time in the Fleet?"

He might have been. He hadn't thought about it *out loud*, inside his head, where it could turn into a real desire, something he could ask for and not get. But—maybe. He'd be good at it.

He could solve the cartograph puzzles Eleven Laurel set him, even the hard ones.

"I'm too young," he said.

"In all likelihood that will change," said Nineteen Adze, which *she* seemed to think was funny and Eight Antidote wasn't very sure about. "What interests you about Nine Hibiscus, then?"

He could lie.

But then he wouldn't get the answer to his question.

"Undersecretary Eleven Laurel says you sent her out to die for Teixcalaan. As fast as possible."

Nineteen Adze made a noise, a click of her tongue against her teeth, considering. "Honestly," she said, "I'd prefer she didn't die very fast at all, if she has to die for us."

That wasn't really an answer. He tried again.

"Is it because of Kauraan? That you picked her?" Another secret given away. Eleven Laurel probably wouldn't like him anymore, wouldn't tell him anything important if he was just going to go tattle to the Emperor Herself.

The Emperor was leaning up out of the throne and putting her hand on Eight Antidote's shoulder, a warm weight. There were calluses on it. He knew the stories about her, how she'd been a soldier, how she'd met his ancestor-the-Emperor on a *ground campaign*, where they fought with shocksticks and projectiles. On a planet, in the dirt.

"Yes," she said. "But not because I thought she was too dangerous to keep alive, little spy. Because I thought she might just be dangerous enough to *stay* alive."

———

By the time Three Seagrass reached her sixth commandeered passenger berth (six different ships taking her through six different jumpgates, and none of them very nice to ride in), she'd packed up her special-envoy suits in favor of an expensive, difficult-to-wear jumpsuit-overall in some black wool crepe that made her look like she had a great deal of money and a vastly different cultural background than the one she'd actually got. It exposed most of her sternum when she wasn't wearing its matching jacket, and its matching jacket had *eight zippers*. She'd bought it at her fifth stopover, on Esker-1, a planet on the Western Arc she'd never been to before: full of rich import-export families, the sort that Thirty Larkspur, lately demoted to Special Advisor on Trade from the heights of attempted insurrection, had come from. Esker-1 produced trade, and also choral singing, which Three Seagrass found inexplicably overwhelming to listen to. The choral singing, not the trade. Trade was easy. It let her buy terrible wealthy-importer-family-scion jumpsuits and catch a ship off-planet that was headed someplace a member of the Information Ministry in good standing oughtn't be, unless she was on assignment.

Esker-1 was in a system situated squarely between three jumpgates: two full of traffic, in and out of Teixcalaanli space, and one that dumped you out near a backwater planetary system that was contested territory when some emperor bothered to contest it, but was otherwise content to be loosely attached to the Verashk-Talay Confederation . . . and was four days sublight travel from the back end of the Anhamemat Gate, or what Three Seagrass was almost entirely sure was the back end of the Anhamemat Gate. It was that backwater where Three Seagrass had gotten to, and she felt, vertiginously, like she really had exited the properly ordered and expected universe.

That might be the number of jumpgates she'd been through in three days. She'd never crossed this many in this short a time, and she kept thinking about those debunked tabloid newsfeed articles from half an indiction back—the ones that said too much jumpgate travel would scramble your genetics and possibly give you cancers.

It also might be that while she'd been off-City—had even done her mandatory stint on a distant border post, like any good *asekreta* cadet who wanted *all* the best marks on her work history before graduation—Three Seagrass had never once yet been outside of Teixcalaan entirely. Outside the world. In the places that were—*otherwise.* Where the stars rose and set by different rules, and no one bowed over their pressed fingertips to say hello, and too many people smiled like Mahit had: all teeth.

The ridiculous jumpsuit helped. It let her pretend she was the sort of person who would *like* being here, in a dingy resource-poor spaceport full of barbarians, looking for the right ride off this shithole. Not deeper into Verashk-Talay space—thank fuck, she was terrible at their languages, she'd taken the mandatory six-month class as a cadet and forgotten everything about it as soon as she'd passed the exam. She'd been on the political specialist track, not the negotiator-with-not-currently-hostile-enough-to-bother-with governments track. Her current and regretful capacity to communicate in either Verashk or Talay was limited to asking for the location of a washroom and ordering *one large beer, please,* the sort of phrase that bored cadets yelled at each other gleefully in hallways.

Right now she had ordered one large beer, please, and was trying to convince a cargo-barge engineer to shove her in along with whatever she was shipping to Stationer space. Whatever it was had to be somewhat circumspect, since this barge was headed through that back-end jumpgate she was pretty sure would spit her out right next to Lsel Station. The same jump-gate the aliens had come through, according to Mahit's intelligence. Three Seagrass wondered if this engineer was worried about alien attacks, or being caught in a war zone. Probably not—but fear of aliens could certainly be why Three Seagrass had only been able to find this *one* ship headed where she needed to go.

"I don't care what it is you have in the crates," she said in Teixcalaanli. "I want on your ship, that's all."

The engineer was stony-faced. Not politely neutral like a Teixcalaanlitzlim, but aggressively *flat.* "The shipping manifest is for cargo only," she said, shaping the syllables with deliberate care. "Cargo *only.* Not persons from Esker-1."

I'm not from Esker-1, Three Seagrass thought, with a tiny internal cascade of despair. *I'm from the Ministry of Information.* None of this would help her. It would make things worse. If this engineer didn't want a wealthy trader from the Western Arc on her barge, she *definitely* wouldn't want an Information Ministry agent.

"Where I am from is not important," she tried. "It is where I am going that matters."

"There are other barges. Go buy them beers."

There were other barges. None of them were trying this route, the skip into Stationer territory through the back end. It had taken her hours to track down this one.

"Your barge is fastest and most direct." Three Seagrass tried a Stationer smile, with teeth. It didn't do much; the engineer remained unmoved. "Really, I have no idea what is in your crates, and I don't *want* to know. I want you to take me through the Anhamemat Gate."

"And what then?" asked the engineer.

"And then you drop me with your cargo, on Lsel Station."

"And you will tell the customs agents what? I think no. I think this is a bad idea, for you, and also for us."

Three Seagrass knew how to do this conversation as an Information agent; she knew how to do this conversation back on Esker-1, where she'd just been City Teixcalaanli and thus mysterious and *interesting.* The first one was the exercise of social power, and the second one was *grift*: being too compelling to ignore, and too slippery to hang on to. Neither was going to work here. (She'd always liked aliens. But there was a difference between *liking* and knowing how to talk to—and this was why she needed Mahit—)

She had one option left, though less of it than she'd had before she'd acquired the ridiculous jumpsuit.

She blinked, micromovements of one eye behind her cloudhook, and projected a shimmering, twisting hologram of a very large number onto the table between her and the engineer. "I think this is a less bad idea than you do," she said, "and all I need is the address of your barge's financial institution to show you how . . . Perhaps you have some debts, some refurbishing costs, that you would like not to worry about?"

The engineer's face moved for the first time. She wrinkled her nose. Three Seagrass wasn't sure if that was distaste or interest. The silence went endlessly on. Three Seagrass suspected the engineer was talking over a private subvocal line to her captain, checking whether the amount was enough. It had better be; after this Three Seagrass was broke, and writing to the Ministry for more discretionary funds was very unlikely to produce them. Certainly not in time for it to matter. Maybe she'd be stuck on this nowhere planet forever. She'd have to improve her Verashk. Or possibly her Talay. Immersion would help—

"We won't be responsible for you on the Station," the engineer said at last. "And you pay *before* you board. You pay right now."

———

Darj Tarats had beaten her to the best seat at the bar. Seeing him—aged and cadaverous to Yskandr's eyes, familiarly skeletal to her own memory, the burnt-clean shell of a man who'd spent the decades of his early working life in an asteroid mine, and *then* had become a politician, who had been a philosopher of ruining-empire and quiet revolution all that time—made Mahit's stomach flip over, a quick nauseating spike, and then settle into shimmering alert. Alive to the possibility of disaster.

She was beginning to think this was the most comfortable state for her to function in, and wasn't that just delightful.

She sounded like Yskandr to her own self, sometimes. More lately.

Darj Tarats was sitting next to Dekakel Onchu, and they were both on their second-at-least glasses of vodka. Mahit was, clearly, late.

Late, and surprised: she'd expected to find only Onchu here, at the same pilots' bar as their first meeting; the Councilor's suggestion, when she'd sent an electronic note saying that she had, indeed, asked her imago about Darj Tarats. Darj Tarats, who wanted the war now being raged all around, but not *in*, Stationer space, and was content to use Lsel as bait to draw Teixcalaan out. Darj Tarats, who Yskandr trusted more than she did, even though she'd done what he'd wanted and Yskandr never had. Mahit resolved to ignore all of the signals her endocrine system would send her for the duration of this conversation, knowing even as she made the decision that it was both impractical and likely physically impossible to accomplish.

"Councilors," she said, and took the seat on the other side of Onchu. "There are twice as many of you as I expected."

"Dekakel has predictable drinking habits, Dzmare," said Darj Tarats. "This is the bar to find her in, if a man wanted to catch up with his friend in a less formal setting than the Council chambers. As I see you have noticed."

It was an obvious power play—so obvious that Mahit was briefly annoyed she didn't rate a better one. Use Dekakel Onchu's first name, intimate the longstanding friendship between the two of them, and then call Mahit by her surname without the title she still owned by rights. There was no Ambassador to Teixcalaan save her. She *was* the imago-line.

<So much for ignoring your endocrine reactions.>

Shut up, would you? she told Yskandr, and waved the bartender over.

"What the Councilors are having," she said, and then turned to Tarats and *smiled,* taking a certain vicious joy in how baring her teeth would always feel like a threat now, how smiling this brightly even on Lsel *was* a kind of threat. "Councilor Onchu was kind enough to introduce me to the best vodka on-Station, yes," she told him. "It's a pleasure to drink with you as well, Councilor."

He was unreadable. It was going to drive her crazy (no, that was Yskandr, Yskandr's twenty years of pent-up frustration and competition with this man). He didn't return the smile. "You came back home from the Empire," he said. They were talking right *through* Onchu, and she was letting them, sitting a little back on her bar stool. "That's unusual for your imago-line."

<I stayed on Teixcalaan so that *you wouldn't know*—>

That you were committing treason, yes, shut up, I need to talk and if I say what you're thinking, we're both fucked, all right?

Prickles up and down her spine, chiding. But Yskandr backed off, retreated—for a moment Mahit felt dizzyingly alone. Dizzyingly *herself,* which was a very naked thing to be.

"Haven't you heard?" she said, still smiling. "I was sabotaged. Who knows what I'll do? Heritage certainly doesn't."

Dekakel Onchu laughed, and shoved her lowball glass, half finished, the ice floating and clinking and turning the vodka cloudy white, over to Mahit. "Have the rest," she said. "Tarats owes me another—he bet you'd go all Yskandr Aghavn at us, superior and elusive. I told you, Darj, this one is *direct* when forced. And I was *right* about the sabotage."

Mahit took it. Drank it. All of it, including the ice chips, fast enough that the alcohol burned and she had to work not to cough. When it was empty, she put it down on the counter, upside down, with a sharp click, loud enough to make her feel brave—floating. *Flying.* "Councilor," she said, when she had her breath back. "Your compatriot for the Pilots told me to consult with my imago about you before I came back to her. So I have. Here I am. Heritage probably would prefer I wasn't. Or at least she'd like to see inside my skull a bit. How about you?"

The bartender approached with Mahit's drink, and she waved it over to Onchu instead. Playing musical drinks; playing *who has power here.* She didn't, she knew that; she was having this drink at all because she was in the sort of trouble with Heritage she didn't know how to get out of, but—

<Oh, but we play anyway,> Yskandr murmured, and she agreed. Onchu accepted the glass without the slightest bit of comment.

Tarats extended a grey-brown hand, tilted it side to side. "On balance," he said, "I'd also like to see inside your skull. If I could see my own reports on your imago-integration, as opposed to Heritage's, of course. Interesting, that you came back. Interesting, that you retain enough of your imago-line despite putative sabotage to *consult* with it. Interesting, that you spent the time since you returned doing absolutely nothing instead of informing someone about all of these intriguing facts."

Mahit wasn't going to flinch. She wasn't. She hadn't been doing *nothing*. She'd been trying to recover her balance, her sense of herself, the shape of a life—any life—that could encompass both Lsel Station and Teixcalaan, two Yskandrs and one of her and whoever they were going to be. Admittedly she'd done a lot of that thinking while walking aimless loops around the Station, but she hadn't come up with any better way of processing. Physical motion helped. That was right out of basic psychotherapeutic technique that every kid on Lsel knew.

She *didn't* flinch. She said, "It'll be Heritage who gets to see."

An offer. *If you do nothing, either of you, Aknel Amnardbat will take me apart and I will be useless to you.*

<More like a plea.>

I've had luck with sanctuary before—

<This is not the City. Tarats is not Nineteen Adze.> The flash of memory, tangled: gin-blue, Nineteen Adze's dark hands on her (his) cheeks, the texture of her lips, the taste of juniper. The scent of juniper, when Yskandr had learned that Tarats was willing to use Lsel as bait to lure Teixcalaan into war with some force larger than itself.

Onchu said, contemplatively, "For a while, I considered whether Heritage can legally commit imago-line sabotage at all. Considering that it's their purview to manage our collective memories in the first place."

Tarats nodded to her. "Your conclusions, Dekakel? Doubtless you have them." He was ignoring Mahit, entirely. Gambit refused. She didn't know *why*, either.

"*Heritage* can't," said Dekakel Onchu. "But an individual working for Heritage—even the Councilor for Heritage—absolutely can. Darj, someone should cut that woman's imago-line loose into hard vacuum."

On this, Mahit thoroughly agreed. Maybe Pilots would help her even if Miners wouldn't—she just needed *some way* to be too useful to be sent into the careful surgical maw of Heritage's analysts, who would know instantly that she'd had entirely un-scheduled adjustments to her imago-machine. If they didn't simply kill her outright, and cover up Amnardbat's sabotage thereby.

"I don't disagree," Tarats said. "I knew her predecessor, and he would have done nothing of the kind; and that imago-line of Heritage councilmembers is six generations long. Some-thing has slipped. This . . . business . . . with Dzmare is more of the same."

"Personally," Mahit said, as dry and unconcerned as she could manage, which wasn't very, "I'd prefer not to be Heritage's busi-ness at all."

"You should have gone back to the Empire, then," said Tar-ats, looking at her directly. *Finally,* looking at her directly.

"You spent such time trying to convince Yskandr to come home," she replied. "Here I am."

Here I am, you used to want this.

Upsettingly, Yskandr murmured, <He wanted *me* to come home. To control.> Mahit's stomach felt like she'd drunk more vodka than she'd even been served: a slow and crawling nau-sea. It would be nice to have had the alcohol if she was going to feel the effects.

"Your imago knows me," Tarats said, as if he could hear Ys-kandr as well as she could. "You say the sabotage you experienced was insufficient enough that you still have some continuity, even if it is out of date—I have what I wanted from him, thanks to your good work. If you'd stayed in the Empire, or if you'd come to me when you returned and been willing to go out again, perhaps I could have found a further use for you, too."

She needed to hear him say it. Out loud, in this bar full of pilots, where he could be overheard. "What did you want from Yskandr?"

Darj Tarats's eyes were the coldest brown Mahit could imagine; brown like dust, like rust in vacuum. "Teixcalaan's gone to war," he said. "Right over us; ships come through our gates all the time, and not a one stops here with legionary soldiers to annex this Station."

"It won't last," Onchu muttered. "That *not stopping*."

"It will," said Tarats. "They've larger problems than us. It's quite refreshing."

Mahit thought, vicious and distant and cold, that Tarats was too satisfied with himself—too satisfied with what he'd helped *her* do, back in the City. He'd created this war between the Empire and some greater, worse thing beyond the Far Gate as a political pressure point, a fulcrum to turn a succession crisis on and simultaneously divert a war of conquest away from the Station. He'd done it all to benefit his desire to lure the Empire into a destructive conflict. He'd *succeeded,* and that was too pleasant a thought for him to let the possibility that Onchu was right—that no power, whether Teixcalaanli or alien, could leave resource-rich mining stations alone forever—ruin his sense of accomplishment.

"How will you know if they change their minds?" she asked, out of pure, apolitical—if anything could be said to lack politics that came out of her mouth now, what the Empire had done to her tongue was more than language—spite.

"I assume I'll have about thirty minutes' warning to scramble our pilots," said Dekakel Onchu, "when the farther mining outposts start getting shot up."

"Before Dzmare came back to us, we might have had a clearer view, even from the City," Tarats said.

That was the crux of it. Why he wasn't helping her, why he didn't care if Amnardbat killed her or took her apart: he no longer had his window on the Emperor. Yskandr Aghavn was dead, and Mahit Dzmare returned home in what he considered to be a state of failure, sabotaged or not; what was the *point* of showing her some special treatment? Of offering a rescue?

"I am still Ambassador to Teixcalaan," she said. She was. She hadn't resigned. She'd taken—*leave,* really, an extended vacation. She'd tried to come home.

<No such thing.>

I know, I know, but I wanted—

Tarats shrugged, an infinitesimal, tired motion of his shoulders. "So you are, though I doubt that will last past Heritage's examination."

"And then you'll have no eyes at all, no one who has met and knows the new Emperor—"

She sounded desperate even to herself. But Tarats was looking at her, quite directly, as if she was a piece of molybdenum ore, something to hold up to the light and watch for reflective facets in. She held still. Made herself be quiet.

"You're not wrong," he said, finally. "You're quite like Yskandr, too. Maybe *enough* like Yskandr." Another pause. Mahit found that she was holding her breath. "You do this, Mahit Dzmare: you go to your scheduled meeting with Amnardbat and her surgeons. But it won't be her surgeons there. It'll be mine."

She didn't breathe out. "Yours, and they'll do what?"

"Strip you of your imago-machine," said Darj Tarats, "and check it for sabotage, in truth; and if it is whole enough, put it into the brainstem of a *new* Ambassador to Teixcalaan. One I— and Dekakel, here, perhaps—have chosen. Some young person right out of the aptitudes. Clearly you are damaged, Dzmare, and you were Heritage's choice to begin with. Best we start over."

For a strange objective moment, it sounded like a good idea to Mahit. Go in to this scheduled checkup as if she had nothing to hide; let Tarats take her imago-machine, all of the memories of two Yskandrs and one Mahit, out of her. Relieve her of the responsibility, entirely, of being either Lsel's representative in Teixcalaan or finding a way to love Teixcalaan while being a Stationer, and not suffocate of it. Be free.

There's no such fucking thing. Her own voice, this time, not Yskandr's. The same tonality. The reassurance of blur.

She asked, "And what happens to me? In this hypothetical scenario."

"This year's aptitudes are coming up," Tarats said. "Retake them. For a new imago-line, or for anything else you like. You came back to the Station: be a Stationer. And all you have done and learned and remembered will be enshrined forever in the imago-line of ambassadors."

It was the sort of offer that got made to people who ended up with incompatible imagos—whose gender identity was stronger than they had thought it was and found a cross-gender memory match unbearable, or who were too close to the web of relationships their predecessor had maintained and couldn't figure out how to navigate them without emotional damage, or whose imago-line was so weighty and long that they weren't able to integrate fast enough and shattered under the strain. One of Mahit's agemates had been one of those. A hydroponics engineer, given an imago thirteen generations of memory long. The highest aptitude scores on systems thinking and biology on the Station, and she'd just collapsed under the weight. Two weeks, and she was stripped out of the line, and allowed to retake the aptitudes a year later.

Mahit didn't know where she'd ended up.

It was a *bad* offer.

She couldn't imagine what she'd be without Yskandr. She didn't know how integrated they were—or weren't—or how deep the damage of sabotage went; she didn't know if there'd be anything *left* of her if this imago-machine was carved out of her skull like Five Portico had carved out the other one. Not to mention the poor, stupid kid who would get the hybrid of *three,* a double dose of Yskandr and whatever there was of Mahit herself—and the first of their line, the negotiator Tsagkel Ambak, who mostly existed as a *feeling.*

<I'd drown in us,> some Yskandr said. Both of them, maybe,

the young and the old. A kind of fear of what they were, all of them, together; a protectiveness of that same thing.

And besides, she didn't trust Darj Tarats to actually do it. She'd walk into the Heritage medical facility and lie down on the table, and it would be Amnardbat's people after all, and what then?

Both Tarats and Onchu were looking at her. She wondered what shape her expression was. Her face felt numb and wooden.

"I don't know what to say," she said, because she didn't.

"I could offer you a position on a mining station instead," said Tarats, "but it'd be a waste, unless you're a sight better at operational and financial analysis than the usual diplomatic types."

"Amnardbat would call me back," Mahit said, because that was true, and because she didn't want to live as Tarats's *creature*, preserved by his sufferance, in charge of an asteroid mine, out of the way. But what choice did she have?

"She would," Tarats agreed, and said nothing more.

They were all bad offers, and if Mahit turned them down, she had nothing at all. She waved for the bartender. If she ordered another vodka, maybe she'd have a chance to think—come up with some angle, something she knew that only *she* knew, that wouldn't be preserved down an imago-line—

<Offer him me,> Yskandr told her. <The fifteen years of me that I denied him. Tell him that there are two of us, two Yskandrs, and that I will talk.>

Mahit opened her mouth.

All the proximity alarms on the pilots' deck of the Station went off at once.

INTERLUDE

TO consider the uses of meat.

Sustenance: meat that explodes on the tongues of us, the taste of heme and the texture of bundled muscle fiber, taurine tang and rich putrescene. A body requires meat, because a body is meat, and we, singing, take joy not only in the building of starflyers and cities, the investigation of natural processes and song-variants, but also the simple pleasure of taking in nutrients, energy, *flavor*.

Reuse: some bodies in a litter are not suitable for being persons, and all bodies eventually senesce and cease. But nothing made is lost, in the singing *we*: all bodies that are not persons or have ceased to be persons are reclaimed, used again, broken down into components, consumed as appropriate.

Skill: all bodies are meat, and each body's meat and genetics and experience create *skill*. To consider the uses of meat in this way is to invite the consideration of grief. All bodies senesce, or are damaged beyond repair, and are no longer a voice harmonizing; to know loss of voices is to know grief, to know lack, to cease from singing and to lament.

To consider the uses of *this* meat, however, is methodologically complex. There are two bodies of this type of meat, carved neatly out of their starflyers like a claw scoops shellfish from the clasp of abalone. The two bodies did not come to the *we* at the same time, though they came from the same sort of starflyer: the starflyers that originate from the void-home the meat has built on the other side of the nearest jumpgate to a far-from-center dirt-home of *we*.

They are not persons.

They think language.

But they react *as if* they were persons. A single pattern, re-peated: but only in how they fly their starflyers, their under-standing of vector and thrust. In all other ways they are not persons, they do not hear the singing of *we*, they are sustenance and skill alone. Save for that pattern. Save for *piloting*.

After a time, they are no longer skill, but only sustenance. We, singing, wonder if the taste of them will import their sin-gular pattern into the harmony of us: it is a puzzlement that the taste of them is merely taste.

————

Aknel Amnardbat spends more time alone than she knows she ought to. She's the Councilor for Heritage, after all—she has six voices of other Councilors for Heritage echoing down her imago-line for company, to begin with, and besides that chain of memory, she is *Heritage*, culture and community and everything that makes Lsel Station itself, and she remembers being a person who went to every ridiculous local art event she could find on the Station intranet. Bad holofilm documentaries and new kinds of music, kids yelling poetry in bars, song-and-dance ensembles, zero-g dance, that one year she'd been ob-sessed with an imagoless restaurateur who had come up with a new way of using fungi and capsaicin and aldehydes to cre-ate meals that were an impossible sense-explosion—before she was Councilor, she had known the Station like she knew her own body.

It's more difficult now. She's *Heritage*. When she arrives at an event, it's either a statement of official approval or a mes-sage that the event might be *sanctioned*. She doesn't know when that started happening. When she stopped being trusted, even when she was at something that didn't even have a *hint* of Teix-calaanli cultural infiltration—something she'd never have even considered censoring—

It doesn't matter. She's Heritage, and she isn't alone—she has all of Lsel Station with her, all its history and its people to watch over. She comes to the station's secret heart, the imago-machine repository, whenever she feels too much like her office has built a glass cage between her and her home. All the memories of the Station's imago-lines, in her safekeeping here, where she stands now.

An echo, imago-memory flare, emotion quickly repressed: *Except those you mar.*

Aknel Amnardbat doesn't make mistakes often. When she does, she admits them to herself and holds herself accountable.

What she'd done to Mahit Dzmare hadn't been a mistake. Cutting the imago-line of Empire-besotted ambassadors out of the heart of Lsel was *right;* no one should have been heir to Yskandr Aghavn's memories at all. Dzmare was acceptable collateral. She was a perfect match on aptitudes for him—she would have been another one just *like* him, even without his live memory to infect her. Getting them both off-Station had been the best possible idea.

Adjusting—weakening—the imago-machine Dzmare carried in her brainstem was almost as good. Either have the new Ambassador short out somewhere no one could help her—or free her of Yskandr Aghavn entirely, and see what she'd make of *herself* out there.

(*Sabotage,* one of the voices of her imago-line murmured, and she ignored it.)

Except Dzmare *came back,* imago apparently intact, and now Teixcalaan was closer than it had ever been, sucking up Lsel resources into the bellies of its warships as they passed through Bardzravand Sector on the way to their war.

Aknel Amnardbat doesn't make mistakes that she refuses to acknowledge. She acknowledges this one: her mistake here was imagining that Aghavn and Dzmare were already so different from their fellow Stationers that Lsel would never be a place they'd want to come home to. She'd been wrong: the two of them weren't *so* far gone as to want to get away and stay away.

It makes Dzmare *more* dangerous than she could ever have been off playing Ambassador. Returned, her whole imago-line is capable of spreading its empire-infected, already-colonized ideas to *other* imago-lines, and live Stationers carrying them. It makes them a vector, a more subtle one than an approaching warship, but just as true and just as poisonous to Lsel. It is the minds of a people that have to stay free. Bodies die, or suffer, or are imprisoned. *Memory* lasts. And what would Lsel Station be, with its memory suborned to the seduction of Teixcalaanli culture? They're losing enough lines already—mostly pilots, recently, vanished out by the Far Gate, to whatever enemy Teixcalaan is fighting (or, Amnardbat thinks, viciously and sharp, to Teixcalaan itself, under pretense). They can't afford to lose more to *corruption*.

If Dzmare misses her appointment with the imago-machine technicians, Amnardbat thinks, she will have her arrested. Even Darj Tarats can't argue with the legality of arresting someone for disobedience to a direct order from a Councilor. The law is embedded in all of Lsel's codes, woven into the meat of what Stationer culture is. The Council can give emergency commands, which must be obeyed.

And once Dzmare is arrested, Amnardbat will have her imago-machine under her hands one more time. Once the Lsel Council were captains and commanders, and their words meant death, or life amongst the black between the stars.

Perhaps they should be again.

CHAPTER
FIVE

The set of practices derogatorily referred to as the "homeostat-cult" originate in a single planetary system, comprising two inhabited planets (Neltoc and Pozon) and one inhabited satellite (Sepryi), collectively referred to as the Neltoc System. Neltoctlim refer to their heritage religious practice as "homeostatic meditation" or, colloquially, "balancing," and consider it a cultural artifact (with attendant registration and protections—see entry 32915-A in the Information Ministry's Approved Cultural Artifacts Registry). However, Neltoc System has been within Teixcalaan for eight generations, and Teixcalaanlitzlim whose planetary origins are located there are certainly not all adherents of the homeostatic meditation practice. An active practitioner can be identified by their green-ink tattoos, which take the form of fractals, mold-growth patterns, and lightning-strike figures, amongst other forms inspired by natural patterings . . .

—excerpt, *Intertwined with Our Starlight: A Handbook of Syncretic Religious Forms within Teixcalaan,* by the historian Eighteen Smoke

* * *

PRIORITY MESSAGE—ALL PILOTS—Travel in the direction of the Far Gate is highly discouraged during the period of Teixcalaanli military activity and while the usual interdict on military transport is suspended. Avoid contact with Teixcalaanli vessels. Avoid allowing visual confirmation of numbers, size, and armaments of Lsel ships. This order stands unless specifically rescinded by the Councilor for the Pilots regarding a particular

vessel, journey, or communication—assume caution is the better part of valor—authorized by the COUNCILOR FOR THE
PILOTS (DEKAKEL ONCHU) . . . message repeats . . .

>—priority message deployed on pilot-only frequencies in
>the vicinity of Lsel Station, and on the Pilots' Intranet,
>54.1.1–19A (Teixcalaanli reckoning)

THE last time Nine Hibiscus had flown a Shard was several
model generations back. Her cloudhook spent a truly absurd
amount of time updating its programming before it would
even let her hook in to the collective vision that the Shard pilots
shared, and she was completely innocent of the new biofeedback
system that let them react like one large organism. That technology had come over from the imperial police into the Fleet,
Science Ministry to Ministry of War, around ten years ago.
Minister Nine Propulsion—*former* Minister Nine Propulsion,
Nine Hibiscus reminded herself—had been a great proponent
of it. She'd seen what it did for the Sunlit down in the Jewel of
the World—*an instant reactivity, hypercommunication,* she'd said
once to Nine Hibiscus and some other officers over a long night
of drinks—and had it reworked for the Shards. Gotten the Science Ministry to do it—Minister Ten Pearl, of the epithet "he
who writes patterns into the world," the algorithm master himself, had adjusted the code on Nine Propulsion's behalf. Now
the new system was hardwired into how the Shard interfaces
interacted with the pilots' cloudhooks, and into a set of external electrodes and magnetic sensors that were woven into
their vacuum suits, providing an artificial sense of collective
proprioception as well as vision. Proprioception, vision, and
(the rumors went) shared pain and shared instinctive reflexes
about danger. Casualty rates had dropped nine percent since
the new system came online, and that made the Fifth Palm—
armaments and research—very happy. But even if Nine Hibiscus had been inside a Shard and wearing a Shard vacuum suit,

she wouldn't have known what to do with the new proprioception aside from inconveniently vomit, which was apparently the most common training side effect—so it was likely for the best that she'd stick to Shard-sight, which her cloudhook could provide for her by itself, no Shard required. She sat in her captain's chair on the bridge of *Weight for the Wheel,* tipped 90 percent horizontal, cloudhook arrayed over both eyes. There was no way she was going to let Sixteen Moonrise attack Peloa-2 without keeping her under extremely direct observation.

Her people could call her out of Shard-sight with a touch, and she'd be back in command. But for now, since her flagship was doing nothing but sitting here receiving recognizance, she'd left Twenty Cicada in official control while her perceptions were elsewhere.

She rode along, an invisible presence, down with the Shard pilots seconded to the small-fighter support craft *Dreaming Citadel,* following Sixteen Moonrise's *Porcelain Fragment Scorched* into the silence that had eaten up Peloa-2. Absently, she wondered if the comms breakdown would affect Shard-sight, and figured with some anticipation that it would be a useful thing to find out.

Porcelain Fragment Scorched was a beautiful ship. Through the ever-shifting viewpoints of Shard-eyes, it cut through space like an obsidian blade, darkly reflective: a stealth cruiser, *Pyroclast*-class. If it wasn't the pride of Sixteen Moonrise's Twenty-Fourth Legion, it ought to be. As it came around the far side of the Peloa System's dwarf sun—where *Knifepoint* had been when they'd been intercepted by the three-ringed alien ship—it looked like a slightly darker piece of starfield. Almost invisible. *Dreaming Citadel* floated in its wake, letting Sixteen Moonrise (of course she'd taken the command herself; Nine Hibiscus would have done exactly the same) lead. No one had seen Peloa-2 since the communication blackout. Nine Hibiscus wasn't sure what she expected. Anything from a blackened, burnt-out shell to a bright-lit, healthy colony with some kind of blockade up around it—

It was neither. Peloa-2 looked like Peloa-2 was supposed to, from holoimages: a small planet, three continents, large silicate desert in the middle of the biggest one. The Teixcalaanli colony at the southern edge of that desert, the shape of refineries and cloudhook-glass production facilities just visible, like a glyph etched into the landscape. All that pure silica sand, white-glitter surrounding the colony, a setting for a rough industrial jewel. Day, down on the part of the planet where there was settlement, so it was impossible to tell if the colony had power or not. The usual collection of satellites was still in orbit—but half of those satellites were dark, and the planet itself was—there was *no movement,* no rise and descent of small craft. And no visible aliens.

Over the Shard-chatter feed she heard Sixteen Moonrise, smooth and unfazed, say, "Come in slow to orbit. It's a graveyard."

Nine Hibiscus had no biofeedback to shiver with, but she shivered anyway, imagined it collective—all the Shards feeling that crawling, silent peculiarity. *It's a graveyard.* Sixteen Moonrise wasn't wrong. As they slipped in close, *Dreaming Citadel* passed the darkened satellites. They were debris and nothing more, ragged, chewed open; parts of them torn away. Nine Hibiscus tried to see a pattern in the devouring—the aliens could want metal, could want reactor cores, oxygen, any manner of thing—and couldn't. The satellites merely looked ripped. Eviscerated. *Whatever is useful in them is what they wanted to take,* she found herself thinking. *The animating force. Whatever made them objects with a purpose and not discarded trash. That's what they took.*

She was aware that she was anthropomorphizing the threat, giving meaning and reason to what might very well be reasonless destruction. These aliens weren't people. They weren't even barbarians.

Sixteen Moonrise again, on comms, steady command: "Maintain orbit and stay in touch. I'm sending down a ground party—six Shards from *Dreaming Citadel,* ten from *Porcelain.* Peel off."

A risk. One that Nine Hibiscus might not have taken—if the

satellites were a graveyard (and no wonder all of Peloa-2 had gone dark to communication, they had nothing left to communicate *with*), what sort of mass destruction would exist on the planet below? But she had told Sixteen Moonrise to retake this colony. Had *challenged* her to do it. And merely surrounding it with Teixcalaanli ships was insufficient. If there were Teixcalaanli citizens down there, they deserved to be reclaimed. They deserved defending. To be brought back into the world. Nine Hibiscus shifted her focus to ride with the Shard pilots headed down through the burn of atmosphere, letting the remainder fade to background, peripheral vision on her cloudhook, flickers in the dark.

They hailed the colony's spaceport on the way in—the usual way, asking for a landing vector and an appropriate berth between the skynets. Shards came down on their own power—not like seed-skiffs or cargo, which had to be *caught*. It should have been routine. (Nothing about this planet was routine.)

Peloa-2 didn't answer the hail. They didn't answer the second hail, either, or the broadcast on all channels which instructed the port to be cleared, War Ministry override—Nine Hibiscus would have skipped that one, wide broadcast felt too risky. Even graveyards could be haunted by the things that made graves. The Shards landed where they could, made their descent through the orange-purple glow of plasma and the pressure and shaking of deceleration g-forces, and came to rest neatly enough. All these pilots had made far more complex landings, in far worse conditions than radio silence and no vector bearings, only visual confirmation on a safe spot to sink down.

The spaceport was dark, too. Silent. No Teixcalaanlitzlim and no aliens came to meet the sixteen ships. Full daylight—the readout on one of the Shards' instrumentation panels told its pilot that it was nearly fifty degrees outside, summer on Peloa-2, right on the upper edge of human tolerances—and Nine Hibiscus on her bridge so very far away still felt chilled, looking at all that silence and stillness. The plumes of silicate dust, rising when the wind did, ripples of white in the air like storm-whipped snow.

Sixteen Moonrise's voice in her ears: "Find out how bad it is. Locate survivors if you can."

That was an order Nine Hibiscus might have given. No matter what else they disagreed on, it was good to know that she and Sixteen Moonrise were both concerned with the Empire's people and what had become of them. That was somewhere to start, in finding commonalities that might let them work together during this war.

Shard-sight carried her out of the ships—she was glad for the pilots that they had their vacuum suits and the temperature control they maintained, and also for the updated interfaces that rode in them, keeping the collective vision active even on the ground, without the benefit of a ship's AI to route the connections through. Glad all the way until they reached the insides of the port's buildings and found the first bodies.

Nine Hibiscus was a soldier. She'd killed more people than she strictly could count—there was no way to know, for real, in space combat situations—and some of those people had been face-to-face, blood and the stink of shit and organ meat spilled and wasted, sacrifices to no one and to everyone at once. She'd worn the blood of her first groundside kill across her forehead until it flaked off, that old ritual, and had felt more Teixcalaanli at that moment than at any other time in her life. Twenty years old and crowned red, up to her knees in the mud of some half-rebelled planetoid—

—and still, seeing these bodies, she wished she could unsee them. So *many* people. Cut open, mostly: not the clean death of energy weapons, though there were some of those scars too, Teixcalaanlitzlim turned to partially blackened, partially melted corpse-friezes. But mostly, cut open. Eviscerated like the satellites. She thought, *Maybe they eat large mammals,* and almost found that idea comforting—a species that thought humans were prey was a problem, but the Ebrekti ate large mammals too, and they'd managed with the Ebrekti. But none of the spilled viscera had been chewed on. It had all just been—pulled out. Discards, then, not food.

How easy it was to begin to think like these enemies. And in thinking like them, to begin to hate them quite personally.

The group leader from *Dreaming Citadel*'s complement of Shards gestured to her companions, and to the Shard group from *Porcelain*: *We go this way, you go that way*. Her opposite number nodded. They were running silent, for safety's sake—if the aliens were still here, letting them know they had company would be a good way to get rapidly killed—relying only on their shared sight to communicate by. Nine Hibiscus was drawn along with the group comprising her people. They knew she was with them, watching. She hoped they found it a comfort, as they waded through the destruction of Peloa-2. Their Fleet Captain, witnessing as they did.

It took several hours before she began to understand what the aliens had wanted here, aside from destruction for destruction's sake. Several hours of finding another and another group of dead Teixcalaanli, days dead, building after building full of corpses. The invading force had been quite efficient in the slaughter. She'd have to check the manifests—she'd ask Twenty Cicada, he would know—but she thought there had been around fifteen hundred colonists on Peloa-2, maybe as many as two thousand. It was a *tiny* colony. It was a glorified factory floor, a place for turning fine sand full of rare crystalline additives into the kind of glass that made cloudhooks, flexible and near-unbreakable. Peloa-2 was out on the very edge of Teixcalaanli territory, too hot for most people to do more than a short engineering stint on, earn hazard pay on top of their usual contracts with the War Ministry. The only reason all these people were dead, Nine Hibiscus realized, was that these aliens understood supply lines, and what to do with a single-resource colony.

Cut it off. And take whatever it had already produced.

The central factory floor, where the tall stacks of cloudhook-ready glass had waited for their journey back through the jump-gate toward more thickly civilized parts of the universe, was pristine—and *empty*. Nothing was broken here except the machinery to produce more sheets of glass. All the glass itself was gone, as if it had turned back into silica dust and blown away.

They were hungry, then, these enemies of Teixcalaan: they wanted at least one thing. They wanted to take away a resource the Empire needed, and prevent them from ever being able to make more. They couldn't know that there were other planets that made cloudhook-glass, other deserts that had the right mineral mix. They were right *enough*: Peloa-2 had been worth colonizing when the Empire had found it because of those resources, those particular mineral additives. And in a war with the Empire, if your enemy was Teixcalaan, that resource—*any* resource that was controllable—needed to be denied. Taken away. The people here—the people hadn't mattered, in that calculation.

How the hell am I going to talk to these things, even with an Information Ministry spook? Nine Hibiscus thought, and blinked herself out of Shard-sight, back into the comforting normalcy of *Weight for the Wheel*, where no one was currently a half-empty corpse.

"Call it off," she said on tight-band comm to Sixteen Moonrise. "Pull our people back, set up an orbital perimeter around Peloa, and tell your legion to prepare for a funerary rite for a whole fucking planet."

———

Lsel Station was *little*. Little and very pretty, a turning diamond-shaped jewel set against a rich starfield, two spokes and a thick torus of decks at their middle. Three Seagrass couldn't quite imagine *living* on it—it'd be like living on a warship full-time, the biggest warship anyone had ever built—but she liked it immediately.

Liked it, at least, until the cargo barge she'd paid an extortionate price to ride on for eleven uncomfortable, chilly hours docked at the bottom point of one of those spokes and began to unload its crates of—well, whatever was in them was labeled in Verashk-Talay, and thus Three Seagrass wasn't sure if she was remembering the script for "fish" correctly or not. Freeze-dried fish? Fish *powder*? Who could need this many crates of fish powder, even out here on a planetless planet made of metal? She'd unloaded herself along with the crates, still in her Esker-1 jumpsuit, and a tall barbarian with an enormous forehead had immediately grabbed her, shoved her up against a wall, and demanded some information in Mahit's very syllabic and unpronounceable language. Three Seagrass didn't know *what* information, and also the wall was metal and hurt to be shoved into, and the cargo-barge engineer took it upon herself to stand around unhelpfully, emitting *I told you so* in every gesture.

Maybe she should have worn the special-envoy outfit.

"I'm Envoy Three Seagrass of the Teixcalaanli Information Ministry," she said, in her own language, loudly, "and you're committing a diplomatic offense. Unhand me."

The barbarian apparently knew Teixcalaanli. He unhanded her. And then he pressed some button on a flat screen he carried instead of a cloudhook, and a rather loud alarm began to go off: a bright noise, three tones repeated, like the start of a song, if the song was being played in a noisecore club in Belltown Six.

"You're who?" asked the cargo-barge engineer.

Three Seagrass waved a hand at her ears. *Can't hear you, someone's decided to set off an alarm, also that is a terrible question all considered.*

"I brought *what* here?" asked the cargo-barge captain, which was insulting. Three Seagrass was a *person,* not a *what.* She shrugged. Smiled, Teixcalaanli wide-eyed. Made sure she had control of her luggage, while the barbarian who had grabbed her said, "Don't move," in quite passable Teixcalaanli. She didn't move.

(Her heart was in her throat. If the alarm went off for much longer, she might actually get scared. Being thrown in jail on Lsel Station would be an abrogation of her duties as an envoy, not to mention that she'd never been in jail unless that terrible few hours trapped in the Ministry during the insurrection counted—she wasn't supposed to have come here at all—)

There was a commotion at the other end of the hangar. The barbarian who'd set up the alarm had summoned some more barbarians with it, it seemed like—important ones, for how the attention of all the other Stationers working to unload this barge and the other newly arrived ships had rotated their attention toward them. Three Seagrass could read the feel of the room, even when she was scared, even when it was so *loud*— that bit of her training hadn't deserted her, even outside the Empire amongst strangers. One of the newcomers waved an arm, and the alarm silenced itself.

Three Seagrass exhaled hard into the quiet. Shut her eyes for a quarter second, squeezed the lids together until she saw phosphenes, rolled her shoulders back. Thought, *Here we go, then, time to talk my way to Mahit Dzmare, even if I have to tie my tongue in spirals to get through to these Stationers.* Opened her eyes again.

And found Mahit herself standing in front of her, flanked by an old man and a middle-aged woman who looked like a hawk.

Mahit looked awful, and also rested. Still tall as ever, spare-boned and olive-pale, with the same curly hair—longer now, tendrils down the back of her neck and framing her face, brushing her cheekbones and making them even sharper, as sharp as her nose was. She no longer seemed like a strong shove would knock her sideways, sleepless and shaken; instead she looked surprised, and angry, and faintly sick to her stomach. *My barbarian,* Three Seagrass thought, which was—oh, inopportune in its fondness, entirely.

"Hello," she said to Mahit, and tried smiling like a Stationer again.

"What are you doing here?" Mahit asked her, and it was very nice to have someone speak her own language so gracefully. "Three Seagrass, I was under the impression you were an Undersecretary now, not in the habit of being smuggled cargo—"

"You know her," said the hawk-faced woman. It seemed very like an accusation. Of course Mahit would be in some kind of political mess; she attracted them. Three Seagrass was well aware of *that*, from direct experience.

"This is the *asekreta* Three Seagrass," Mahit began, and Three Seagrass found herself utterly, peculiarly delighted to be introduced. It was like they'd reversed roles, liaison and barbarian inverted, and hadn't they just, she was on Mahit's planet—station—now, wasn't she? "Patrician first-class, Third Undersecretary to the Teixcalaanli Minister for Information. My former cultural liaison."

"Most interesting job I'll ever have, being your cultural liaison," Three Seagrass added, thinking, *Except perhaps this one I'm doing now.* She bowed over her fingertips at the strange barbarians. "You have my advantage; Mahit, if you would be so kind as to introduce your—companions?"

Diplomacy was a lovely refuge. There were *rituals* for it, and none of them involved being arrested. Usually.

Mahit's expression had gone from faintly ill to a mix of chagrin and pleasure. She was so *expressive*. All Stationers seemed to be: the other two that Mahit had come in with looked positively scheming, observant and attentive and not *displeased* so much as—anticipatory.

Mahit said, "You are quite honored, Three Seagrass; these are two members of our governing Council. Darj Tarats, the Councilor for the Miners"—she gestured to the old thin man to her right—"and Dekakel Onchu, the Councilor for the Pilots.

I believe you are Councilor Onchu's problem, as you're in her hangar. Illegally."

Three Seagrass asked, with as much apology as she could muster, "Councilors. Do you understand Teixcalaanli?" (Really, she needed to learn Stationer properly, more than the amateur level of vocabulary she currently had, even if Mahit's language had noises in it that a civilized tongue disliked.)

The hawk-faced woman, Onchu, nodded. Just once. She hadn't said a word yet. She didn't need to; everything about her demanded Three Seagrass justify herself posthaste or be ejected out the nearest airlock, of which there were two in direct line of sight.

"My deepest apologies for the unorthodox method of my arrival," Three Seagrass went on, "but I needed to come to Lsel Station with absolute speed, and there was no way to circumvent the sublight travel time aside from traveling through the Anhamemat Gate instead of the usual one. I do understand that I may have inadvertently violated the treaties between our two peoples by not announcing my intentions, but trust me, I am not here in secret or for purposes that would damage our relations further."

Councilor Onchu's eyebrows were as expressive as the rest of her. They'd climbed nearly to where her hairline would have been if she hadn't shaved her head bald. "What are you here for, then?" she asked. Her Teixcalaanli was *more* than passable. "What requires absolute speed? And why were we not informed of a situation that would cause you to choose this method of coming into our territory, *Undersecretary*?"

Some things had been easier when she was simply an *asekreta*. People seemed to expect Undersecretaries of any variety to have staff, and press releases over the newsfeeds, and probably to file their intersystem travel plans ahead of time.

"I need," said Three Seagrass, figuring that clarity was the simpler part of valor, "to borrow the Ambassador." She gestured at Mahit, who had gone Teixcalaanli-still around the eyes. "She *is* still the Ambassador, is she not?"

Once he'd sealed the door to his bedroom shut behind him, Eight Antidote could pretend that he had some privacy. He knew better: there were two camera-eyes in here that he was aware of, and another one in the bathroom, discreetly pointed at the window rather than either the shower or the toilet. (*That* one was to look for intruders and people who might want to kidnap an imperial heir, not for watching the imperial heir wash himself. He hoped. Even so, he'd always showered with his back to the window and his genitals facing the corner of the shower stall.) But shutting the door made him *feel* alone.

Eight Antidote told his holoprojector to cue up an episode of *Dawn with Encroaching Clouds*. It was a serial drama with an absolutely enormous costume budget and a set that was partially built out of a real historical warship, a museum piece from four hundred years ago, the same time as when the story took place. There'd been special permission from the War Ministry for using it, during the filming. The current episode he was watching was from the fifth season of six. The fifth season was called *Sunlight Dissolves Tendrils of Haze,* and it was the part of the story where the Emperor Two Sunspot—having faced down the first-contact negotiation with the Ebrekti and returned through the jumpgate she'd fled through, only to reencounter on the other side her former *ezuazuacat,* the attempted usurper Eleven Cloud—began a yearlong campaign of attrition against the usurper's legionary ships. It was Eight Antidote's favorite part, or at least it had been before the whole insurrection and usurpation last year. Now it was harder to watch, but it made him—feel nervous, and excited, and interested, and a little awful.

Which was how he felt anyway, after talking to the Emperor herself about Nine Hibiscus on Kauraan and the new war, so it worked out.

Eleven Cloud, or the actress playing her, was in the middle of having her Fleet Captains reaffirm their vows of loyalty to her and their acclamation of her as Emperor. Which of course meant she couldn't just surrender to Two Sunspot, even though they'd grown up together and loved each other. It was a very dramatic episode, with flashback sections where Eleven Cloud and Two Sunspot were in bed together in Palace-Earth, before everything went wrong between them. The sex was pretty graphic. Eight Antidote knew that kids his age probably weren't supposed to watch *Dawn with Encroaching Clouds*, there was a no-sex-and-less-blood version of the story of Two Sunspot and Eleven Cloud called *Glass Key*, which was labeled as appropriate for crèche-school use, but the writing in it was *awful*.

Also Eight Antidote had never had any restrictions on his media accesses. He'd watched a lot of people have sex on holoproj. It seemed messy and also made people do stupid things afterward.

Probably the *yaotlek* Nine Hibiscus hadn't gotten stuck with leading an unwinnable war because of sex, though. It looked more like politics to Eight Antidote, and *everyone* had politics, even if only some people had sex. He kept thinking about what the Emperor had said: that Nine Hibiscus might be good enough to *stay alive*. Which was so different from what Eleven Laurel seemed to want him to think—that there was something so dangerous about her, and her people's loyalty to her, that it was better if she died nobly.

Well, if she died nobly, nothing like what happened to Eleven Cloud could happen to her, and to Teixcalaan through her. Her loyal legions couldn't convince her to become Emperor if she wasn't there to convince.

It seemed like such a waste to him, though. To let someone who could come up with how to find a victory on Kauraan just—*die*, because of what *might* happen. Not everything was like it had been four hundred years ago. Nineteen Adze didn't even *know* Nine Hibiscus, not really, Eight Antidote didn't think they'd met more than one time in person.

Not everything was like a holodrama, though, either. Even if the holodrama was a visual version of a novel that was a version of an epic poem that still got sung at concerts in the palace. Some things were new, and also *recent*. Like the former *yaotlek* One Lightning, and *his* loyalist legions, and how Eight Antidote's ancestor-the-Emperor had died. Maybe that was part of the answer. Not letting anyone who had a chance of being like One Lightning close enough *to* know, or like, or even stick around long enough to think maybe they should be Emperor instead of Nineteen Adze.

Instead of him, too. He didn't want to think about that.

(Sometimes, when he felt *really* awful and interested at the same time, when he was already nauseous and unhappy, he would pull up the newsfeeds from the day of the riots and look at pictures of Six Direction dying. He always wondered if he'd look like that, when he was old, when he was dying. That same expression. Probably. It was like seeing the future.)

Next time he went to see Eleven Laurel, he decided, he was going to find out how the war was going, for real.

———

It wasn't, Three Seagrass thought, the *worst* place she and Mahit had sat down together. That was probably the bunker underneath the palace, where they'd watched Six Direction die on live newsfeed. (Or maybe not: that had also been when they'd ended up *kissing*. Even if Three Seagrass had been about to cry the whole time that had been happening, and had almost certainly ruined the whole experience because of it. It had only been that one time. If Mahit wasn't going to mention that kissing had happened, she certainly wasn't either.)

Mahit hadn't mentioned much, yet. Just extracted her from both the utter disaster of Lsel Station customs and the clutches of not one, but *two* high government officials, after she'd gone and demanded Mahit *come with her*. So far, she'd come with Mahit instead. They'd walked through the hangar and out into the deck—so *many* Stationers, it was fascinating, and most of them ignoring her very pointedly—and Mahit had unerringly steered her through a maze of corridors until they'd arrived at a tiny room. A *pod,* really, hanging in a rack like a two-person-sized seed, the only thing that could grow from a metal world like this Station—with curved walls and curved couches inside to match. Mahit had keyed it open with her infopad, and it had descended from its row of other, identical pods and opened up for them. Three Seagrass had looked over Mahit's shoulder while she was calling it (they kept standing close to each other, Three Seagrass was just *used* to it from back in the City, or at least she had been, and it was simple to pick up the habit again, stand at Mahit's left shoulder like she belonged there), and thought that the transaction was a financial one.

"You have rent-an-offices on the Station?" she asked, brightly, when they were inside. The couches were a pale grey-blue, one on each wall. There was a table between them. Three Seagrass rested her elbows on it—cold metal—and wished for her Information Ministry jackets, still safely folded inside her luggage.

"They're efficient," Mahit told her, "and use-fungible. Also I can't take you off this deck. You're not really here."

"I really did come to get you, though. I'm here enough for that."

Mahit looked at her for a moment, sufficiently long to make Three Seagrass want to turn away. Instead she widened her eyes and propped her chin in her hands and made herself wait.

Finally, Mahit said, "Did *you* come? Or did Nineteen Adze send you?"

Her barbarian always did ask the clever questions.

"I came," Three Seagrass said. "I'm really not meant to be here at all. But it's on the way to where I'm going, and I *did* come here for you. Her Brilliance—well, I imagine she knows exactly where I ended up, but it was my idea."

"She knows where most people end up," Mahit said.

"She's the Emperor," Three Seagrass agreed. "And also she's herself, so, yes. I should tell you, she sent Five Agate to bother me in a spaceport bar before I left, and I hadn't filed a single travel plan with the City. She found me *anyhow*."

"Five Agate, *really*. I'm trying to imagine her in a spaceport bar."

"She wanted me to swear a blood oath that I wasn't suborned by one of the Undersecretaries of the War Ministry, it wasn't incongruous at all, she sort of—slots into whatever setting—"

Mahit had reached across the table, and now her fingertips were touching the skin just above Three Seagrass's right elbow. Warm fingertips. "Reed," she said—and Three Seagrass felt like a spike had gone right through her throat, no one called her that anymore, Mahit never had before now, but *oh,* oh—"Reed, are you in the sort of trouble you had to run away from?"

She wished she was. If she was, the next part of this story would be where the imperial agent and the barbarian stole a small fighter-ship and went off through the nearest jumpgate into the black, together. She'd always liked those sorts of poems, even if they invariably ended in tragedy.

She covered Mahit's hand with her own. "No. I'm fine. I don't even *know* Undersecretary Eleven Laurel. I'm supposed to go to war, that's all. And talk to aliens. Come with me. You're the best at talking to aliens of anyone I know."

"That's because you Teixcalaanlitzlim insist on thinking that *I'm* the alien," Mahit said, but so very gently. Three Seagrass didn't *think* she was behaving in a way that would need gentleness, not from Mahit Dzmare, but quite honestly she couldn't be sure; Mahit surprised her all the time, which was also why she wanted to take her to the front.

"You're only *almost* an alien," she told her, firmly. "Wouldn't you like to meet some real ones? And try to understand them faster than the Ministry of War can shoot them down?"

Mahit didn't answer her questions, or say yes—or even say

no. She said, "First explain why it's *you* going to war. And wearing that."

At least she hadn't moved her hand from under Three Seagrass's. ". . . It's a very expensive jumpsuit," she said.

"Are you in *disguise*?"

"Not currently!"

Mahit actually laughed, and Three Seagrass found herself smirking at her. This, *this* was what she had missed. The dizzying speed of events, the hilarious and absurd questions that nevertheless needed to be asked. She would *never* have had this in her office in the Ministry.

"I needed to get here fast, that's all," she explained. "That's why I came through the wrong gate. And several of the stops along the way were—easier if I wasn't me. Briefly. But you should see my special envoy uniforms. I could have one made up for you, if you weren't so tall." She paused. Squeezed Mahit's hand, knowing very well that she was structuring this conversation, offering and enticing, the sort of manipulation she really oughtn't be doing to someone she wanted to trust and be trusted by in turn. But she also wanted her to say yes. Needed her to, now that she'd come all this way. "I mean. If you're willing to serve as Ambassador again. Ambassador, and special political agent seconded to the Tenth Legion, via the Information Ministry."

Mahit said, "You *are* in trouble, aren't you. Or the Empire is. It's a bad war."

"How wide," said Three Seagrass, "is *Lsel's* definition of 'you'?" Unspoken, but entirely acknowledged: *Yes, it's a bad war. We don't know the nature of the enemy, we've lost multiple resource-extraction colonies, you yourself told us how bad it will be if we let these all-devouring aliens move farther into our territory. Why would the Fleet want a diplomat, when they already have warships, if this wasn't a bad war?*

Half of Mahit's mouth had twisted up, a grimace, close to laughter but suppressed. "Not wide enough," she said, and for

a moment she sounded like—someone else. The way her face
moved, too—not quite right. Not what Three Seagrass remembered. Three Seagrass needed to ask her about why she'd been
surrounded by her own government's highest officials. It was
Mahit. She was probably up to her hairline in unpleasant and
threatening politics all on her own time, if Three Seagrass
knew her at all.

(They'd really only been together a little over a week, in the
City. A week wasn't enough to know someone. But that week
seemed longer. Fulcrum points usually did. There was *before
that week*, when Three Seagrass had been an ambitious young
Information agent with a habit of spending her evenings at
court poetry salons, and a best friend out in the City who she'd
known since they'd been cadets together; and then there was
after, when she was Three Seagrass, Third Undersecretary to
the Minister for Information, and her friend was dead, and she
hadn't written a poem, much less read one at court, in more
than two months.)

"Are *you* in trouble?" she asked Mahit.

"When haven't I been?" Mahit said, and sighed, and sank back
into her couch, letting go of Three Seagrass's wrist. The loss
felt like a spark-gap, widened just too far for current to pass
through.

"Presumably you were an exemplary student," Three Seagrass said.

"All right," Mahit agreed, "I was *briefly* not in trouble, while
safely locked in an examination hall."

"And now?"

"I would have come back to the City eventually," Mahit said,
after an excruciating pause. "I think I would have. When I
thought it was the right time."

Three Seagrass waited for her. She thought Mahit had already arrived at her decision, but it was better if Three Seagrass
didn't push her while she made it a decision that could be spoken out loud. She'd pushed fairly hard already. Mahit might not

forgive her for that, later on. If this went badly for them. Or even—especially—if it went *well*. Hadn't she run off just when it seemed like the City and all of Teixcalaan had finally stopped trying to kill her and acknowledged how much it could make use of her, barbarian or not, instead? She might do it again: succeed, and then write herself out of Teixcalaan's memory and history, make herself a ghost, exiled to her own home.

Mahit shut her eyes, squeezed their lids shut. She pressed her fingertips to the wrinkles that drew themselves up her forehead, twin worry lines. "You're going to have to make this very official," she said, muffled by her own palm. "'The Ministry of Information commands, at the order of Her Brilliance the Emperor' sort of official. *The Edgeshine of a Knife, through her envoy Three Seagrass, demands the immediate presence of the Ambassador Mahit Dzmare on the Whatever That Legion's Flagship Is Called.*"

She had an *annoyingly* good grasp on exactly how Teixcalaanli communiqués were structured grammatically. It wasn't fair that she was a barbarian. She'd have made a brilliant Information agent.

"And while you're at it," Mahit went on, "*please* don't break our import-export laws again? Find a way to have been here officially all along. I would like Councilor Onchu not to find reasons beyond the usual ones to hate me."

Three Seagrass was going to have to find out what *the usual reasons* were. But she'd have a while, she thought. She'd have the three-month length of her assignment, and a battlefront. That was long enough to get to know anyone, and all their secrets. Even if they were Mahit Dzmare.

———

"The Empire is going to remember the colonist-workers of Peloa-2 as Teixcalaanlitzlim who died in combat," Twenty Cicada was saying to the assembled soldiers, standing rank on rank in the widest hangar bay of *Weight for the Wheel*—the only space on the ship large enough to assemble all nonemergency, nondeployed personnel. "Your participation in these mourning rites will make sure of it. You will carry the dead of Peloa-2 in your memory; you will inscribe their names on the weapons with which you will avenge them. The blood they spilled will not be drunk by the ground of their planet, but by the Empire that fed them, and feeds you too."

It wasn't the usual funeral oration. It couldn't be, for many reasons: a funeral for so many dead at once could only be done via the modes Teixcalaan had developed either for commemorating space-dead, or the ones for plague victims. Nine Hibiscus was glad Twenty Cicada had gone for a variant on *these citizens died in the black between the stars and we reclaim their blood sacrifice from the void*, rather than *the world is out of balance and illness obliterates our grief and their lives mercifully*. They'd had a disagreement about which one to choose. He'd made a disturbingly convincing argument that the eviscerated bodies were plague-dead and the plague was the aliens, a plague that destroyed without meaning, like a virus that killed its hosts so fast that it killed itself, too.

Nine Hibiscus didn't want that sort of idea spread to the rest of her soldiers, even if Twenty Cicada was usually right about how systems worked, even—especially—biological ones. Having an entire legion of frightened germophobes would cripple any direct engagement with the enemy that happened face-to-face, or face-to-mandible, or face to whatever horror they actually turned out to be. Neither did she want a bunch of over-eager captains breaking out the flamethrowers and biochemical sanitizing blanket bombs. The next planet they recaptured might have survivors. She wasn't willing to give up on that possibility. Not yet.

The Information Ministry spook couldn't get here soon enough, for her tastes. If she was going to be able to talk to these things at all, it needed to be soon. While she still had even the slightest shred of desire to. A war of extermination, against these aliens, would have a *great many* Teixcalaanli casualties, more than she was willing to risk, even if the first group of them happened to be someone else's legion and not her own people. But they would be her people. Her people, who had followed her out to this bleak edge. They deserved better than being bodies thrown into the machinery of a war in order to begin the breaking of its gears. So she had to figure out if there was anything there to talk to, anything worth what had happened to Peloa-2, what had probably happened to the other darkened systems in this sector.

"From this barren soil will grow new flowers," Twenty Cicada said, intent and dreamy-soft, an enticement made audible throughout the entire hangar, reverberating in everyone's cloudhook, on the overhead speakers, on the other speakers embedded in the floor, bone-conduction transmission so that a captain's voice—or an adjutant's voice, if one's adjutant could have been a great orator if he hadn't wanted to be a soldier instead, and had unorthodox religious beliefs besides—could sound inside the skull of every soldier gathered. Be *felt*, collectively. "They will be hard-won flowers—fragile petals well defended by your hands, with parasites beaten away, warmed by the sunlight of energy weapons."

The *parasites* line was definitely Twenty Cicada having feelings about plague. About *homeostasis*, and balance. Even if the rest of this speech was the usual rousing entry to a collective mourning rite—all of those soldiers would be pricking their fingers for a blood-bowl by the end of the hour, the sort of bowl she could pour out on Peloa-2's empty factory floor like a promise (and she *would* do it herself, better her than Sixteen Moonrise, it had to be the *yaotlek* who led the Fleet)—talking about *parasites* was entirely from Twenty Cicada's own philosophy and religious convictions.

Nine Hibiscus trusted him more than anyone else in the entire galaxy, and she still didn't understand why he didn't follow the usual Teixcalaanli religion. Spend time in a sun temple and bleed for luck like anyone else. He'd always kept to the religion

of his home planet instead—the homeostat-cult, in crude parlance, even though his home planet had been inside the Empire for generations. Her *ikantlos*-prime fasted and shaved his
head and filled his personal chamber with a thousand growing-
green plants, and kept the logistical flow of her ship (and her legion, and her Fleet) running in perfect systematic balance. A
person's religion was their own business, Nine Hibiscus had
always thought, but—

Parasites.

It probably wouldn't matter. Most of these soldiers wouldn't
even register the valences. They hadn't seen Peloa-2. They hadn't
seen the alien ship-spit eat up one of their own Shard pilots—
except for the other Shard pilots who had shared her death. Felt
her death, all the way down to the last merciful conflagration.
They would know. She wondered how this oration was landing
with them. The new technology made Shard pilots even closer
to one another than they'd been when she was one of them, and
they'd been close then—the closeness of people who were willing to die in starfire brilliance, as easy as breathing.

It was almost over. Twenty Cicada had reached the part of
the rite which everyone knew: the call and response eulogy-
poem that had closed almost all funerals since the time of the
Emperor Twelve Solar-Flare, when it had been written for her
dead *ezuazuacat* Two Amaranth.

"Within each cell is a bloom of chemical fire," Twenty Cicada
began, and by the time he'd finished the syllables of the line,
half the soldiers were saying it along with him, a massed voice
that made Nine Hibiscus ache with how much she loved them,
loved *all* of them, loved the hungry and clever beast they made
together, they her claws and her lungs and her eyes, and she
their guiding mind.

"All of Peloa-2, committed to the earth," Twenty Cicada said,
slurring the scansion to make it fit, "shall burst into a thousand
flowers—"

"As many as their breaths in life," Nine Hibiscus said, joining in. Her mouth knew the shapes of these words. How many times had she said them? How many lives had she commemorated in this way?

Enough. Enough to feel ancient, standing here with all of her soldiers looking up at her on the bridge, to feel heavy in the weight of all their regard.

"And we shall recall their names!"

All the soldiers together: "Their names and the names of their ancestors!"

"And in those names, the people gathered here let blood bloom also from their palms," called Twenty Cicada, and the soldiers with the copper bowls and carbon-steel sacrifice knives began to move up and down their assigned rows. "And shall cast this chemical fire as well into the earth, to join them—"

The bowl and knife came to Nine Hibiscus's left. She sliced the pad of her left thumb open, right through the scar from the last time she'd given funereal blood, after Kauraan. She healed fast. It was a good quality in a Fleet Captain.

It was probably an even better one in a *yaotlek*.

CHAPTER
SIX

. . . the problem (one of the problems) with Third Palmers is that they hate Information enough to cover their tracks on public networks. The Undersecretary Eleven Laurel was a good soldier, but the last time I fought with him we were both twenty years younger, and he's immured himself in the Ministry of War for longer than I've even been on-City. Which makes him institutional memory, especially now that I've relocated Nine Propulsion. You know the parameters, Five Agate—get me a dossier before he finishes educating Six Direction's heir and decides he'd like to be Minister of War, would you?

> —private cloudhook communication, Her Brilliance
> Nineteen Adze, Emperor of All Teixcalaan, to the
> *ezuazuacat* Five Agate, undated, encrypted

* * *

HOLOPROJ SHOW! THIRD SHIFT THROUGH FIFTH SHIFT ON *THE PARABOLIC COMPRESSION* DECK TWO TONIGHT, AND SIMULCAST TO ANYONE CLOSE ENOUGH TO TUNE IN! SHOWING THE LATEST EPISODES OF *ASPHODEL DROWNING* (YES THE NEW ONES! SEASON FIVE! WE MEAN IT! DON'T ASK WHERE WE GOT THEM!)

THANK THE GLORIOUS TWENTY-FOURTH LEGION FOR YOUR ENTERTAINMENT WHILE WE ALL WAIT AROUND WITH OUR THUMBS UP OUR ASSES

> —signage posted on multiple decks of the *Parabolic
> Compression* and other Fleet ships in the Sixth,
> Twenty-Fourth, and Fortieth Legions

THE *Jasmine Throat*, a *Succor*-class Teixcalaanli supply ship, had begun its journey out of Teixcalaanli space a good three weeks before Three Seagrass had, headed for the war with a bellyful of flash-dried cured meats, energy-pulse chargers sized variously for hand weapons all the way up to Shard cannons, apricots and squash blossoms to rehydrate or chew dried on long deployments, and gallons and gallons of medical-grade plasma suspension fluid. Your standard complement of *we don't know what this war is going to be like, but you'll probably need to eat, and shoot people, and patch up your wounded*. The *Jasmine Throat* had filed a travel plan, and obtained a transit visa for the sector of space that Lsel Station was in, and was, right on schedule, passing by the Station on its way to the Anhamemat Gate and nastier regions beyond.

Three Seagrass, who had put back on her special-envoy uniform with considerable relief the moment she was alone enough to dig it out of her luggage and strip off the jumpsuit, hailed it as it came into hailing range.

The captain of the *Jasmine Throat* was *ixplanatl* Six Capsaicin, who did not sound nearly as surprised as Three Seagrass had expected him to be when hailed by an Information Ministry special envoy and asked for a pickup shuttle off of the local not-quite-imperial, definitely-an-independent-republic-we-swear mining station. Probably he had stranger things happen to him all the time—he was a captain *and* had managed to earn *ixplanatl* rank, which meant he'd written some kind of scientific thesis in addition to qualifying himself to fly a military supply ship. A person like that surely had had more inconvenient adventures than this one. He had simply checked Three Seagrass's identity glyph against his cloudhook, determined she was in fact herself and was supposed to be headed to *Weight for the Wheel* on assignment. Then she'd sent him *Mahit's* assignment: the Lsel Ambassador to Teixcalaan, who had graciously volunteered to contribute her skills to the war effort, considering the proximity of her home culture to the front, also needed to be transported there posthaste. Three Seagrass had made the language *very* official. She hadn't needed to; Six Capsaicin shrugged, said, "What's one more warm body for twenty hours, we've got the oxygen and she can't eat *that* much, Stationers have standard bodily chemistries," and informed Three Seagrass that a transport shuttle would be arriving for her and her companion in three and three-quarters hours.

It would be very useful if Mahit would come back by then.

They'd arrived at their—agreement, or decision, inside the fungible rent-an-office, and then Mahit had said that she had some loose ends to tie up, which was entirely transparent: she had to go use Three Seagrass's offer to get herself out of whatever political tangle she'd been in the middle of. Two Councilors out of—Three Seagrass consulted her cloudhook's onboard storage memory, pulling up the dossier on Lsel Station's government— only *six*. A full one-third of the government right there in the hangar, chummily having some sort of *problem* on either side of Mahit Dzmare.

So it made sense that she'd need the time. Even if waiting for her was nerve-racking.

Waiting also left Three Seagrass at loose ends, in a place she'd never been, and what she wanted more than just about anything else, right now, was to go wandering and get to know it. She'd promised not to leave the deck with the hangar bay, and she planned to keep that promise, but—oh, it was likely a good two miles of a loop around, and full of all sorts of sights. And when would she have the opportunity to see Mahit's home again? Probably never. It'd be a waste not to go sightseeing. It wasn't even sightseeing! It was *reconnaissance*. She was designed for reconnaissance; she was Information Ministry.

She climbed out of the office-pod and arbitrarily decided to turn left down the corridor. Her cloudhook was next to useless here, aside from communicating with Teixcalaanli vessels that might be inside this sector of space. Once she'd gone through a jumpgate into a sector without a Teixcalaanli repeater station network, it couldn't talk to the City or to much else; cloudhook technology didn't cross jumpgates. Nothing crossed a jumpgate unless it went *through* a jumpgate, physically. All she had was onboard storage, her own documents, and a scaled-down, nonupdating version of the Information Ministry intranet, which entirely lacked a map of the inside of Lsel Station. (If she was *really* doing reconnaissance, she should turn on her cloudhook's geomapping function while she walked around, but she hadn't come here to be a spy. It seemed vastly impolite.)

The corridors on Lsel were wide enough to walk four abreast, and floored in metal polished by many feet to a comfortable matte sheen. The first strange thing about walking inside them was that there was sunlight. Sunlight everywhere. She'd always imagined that a station would be a closed metal box, all artificial lighting and no plants to speak of, nothing that grew. But Lsel's corridors—or at least this outer loop—had well-designed plastisteel window ports, and outside was the lovely spangled starfield, and a genuine small and cheerful sun with a pleasant white-gold light. It was moving quite quickly, that light—the station's rotational period certainly wasn't going to be anything like a *day*, more like four sunrises and sunsets in a usual human-length cycle. Three Seagrass could imagine enjoying that. All those sunrises.

The second strange thing was the people. Stationers were *tall*, and Stationers were very, very good at ignoring one another, and even at ignoring small Teixcalaanlitzlim in bright coral-orange uniforms. They didn't make much eye contact, and they slipped out of each other's way even in the more-crowded parts of the corridors with practiced ease. Three Seagrass imagined that it was a side effect of living in such a small space; they acted like they were Inmost Province City-dwellers, happy and comfortable with being crowded, and yet she knew very well that there were only thirty thousand of them on the whole Station.

It must be very strange to be one of only thirty thousand of a people. Three Seagrass thought it would feel fragile. Just these thin metal walls between *all* of you and the void.

Actually it was better if she didn't think about the thinness of Station walls; she'd make herself claustrophobic. Instead she took another turn—she was in a more inward corridor now, and instead of real windows there were flat infoscreens *displaying* the outside, which was a fascinating choice—maybe Stationers liked feeling close to the stars all the time—and found herself in a shopping district. Kiosks, mostly. She *really* needed to learn some more of Mahit's language; it took her far too long to piece out the squiggles of Stationer alphabetics into phonemes, and even then she wasn't always sure on vocabulary. Let alone pronunciation.

But half the kiosks had glyphs in understandable language right alongside the squiggles of Stationer alphabetics. Very *artistic* glyphs, more decoration than communication, and she was pretty sure the kiosk selling bottled beverages didn't mean to have their Teixcalaanli sign read HERE IS PORKS! unless she had severely misunderstood both the nature of bottled beverages and Station animal husbandry capabilities. Also the plural was terribly formed. It was probably meant to say HERE ARE RICH-UMAMI-FLAVORS. The glyphs were close enough that someone could confuse them, she guessed. Unsweet bottled beverages, then.

She approached that kiosk and smiled like a Stationer, remembering to bare her teeth. The kiosk operator didn't smile back. Maybe she was doing it wrong—she stretched her cheeks until they hurt—

"I didn't know there were guests from Teixcalaan," said the Stationer, in entirely decent Teixcalaanli. "Would you like a sample of our drinks?"

Three Seagrass blinked at him, and stopped smiling with relief. "Yes," she said. "I would enjoy that. You speak so well!"

"I took courses." He poured a small amount of his beverage into a plastic cup that looked extremely biodegradable—probably a four-hour cup, organic plastic, with a hydro-triggered decay cycle. The beverage foamed. Interesting.

"What is it made of?" Three Seagrass asked, and then drank it before he could answer her.

It tasted like *salt*. Like—alcoholic salt, and oceans. There weren't any oceans here. It was fascinating, and also awful, and she was never, ever drinking it again.

The Stationer said a word in his own language. And then screwed up his face like he was racking his brain for vocabulary, and came up with "Underwater wavy plants?"

"Kelp," Three Seagrass said. "You made beer out of *kelp*."

"Do you think it would be popular in the Empire?" asked the Stationer. "I've been thinking about an export contract . . ."

No, Three Seagrass thought. *It tastes like kelp. Blood and starlight, no one would drink that*—"Perhaps on some planets," she told him, brightly. "Teixcalaan is very large."

"Are you with a trade delegation, miss—?"

The kiosk operator had attracted several *other* kiosk operators during the conversation. They had samples of their own. How hungry *was* Lsel for trade with the Empire? Mahit had always been so adamant about preserving their independence . . .

"I am Three Seagrass," said Three Seagrass, "and I am afraid I have absolutely nothing to do with trade in an official capacity."

"A private investor, then," said one of the other Stationers, *also* in Teixcalaanli. Three Seagrass hoped her . . . cake? It seemed like cake—wasn't also made out of kelp.

"Not quite," she said, and was about to go on when there was another voice, behind her and to the right.

"What is all this, then?" that voice asked, and Three Seagrass watched all the Stationers draw themselves up to their full ridiculous heights. An authority. A . . . trade authority. She tried to remember which of the six Lsel Councilors controlled trade. It was Miners, wasn't it? But she'd met the Councilor for the Miners, the cadaverous man in the hangar. She turned around.

This was not Darj Tarats at all. This was a small, spare woman with grey bubbles of curls and high, windburned cheekbones. Three Seagrass bowed to her and waited for her to introduce herself. Safest—simplest. Let the other person lead, until you can take control of the conversation. That was one of the earliest lessons she'd learned as an *asekreta* cadet. She used to practice on Twelve Azalea. (She didn't want to think about Twelve Azalea.)

"I was not aware that a Teixcalaanli delegation had been approved to *land*, let alone wander around a public market," said the authority. "And yet here you are. I would have you understand, whoever you are, that Heritage does not allow individual trade agreements between Lsel merchants and Teixcalaanli ones."

"To be sure," said Three Seagrass. "I have no interest in violating your local laws. I assume you are from Heritage, then?"

"That's Councilor Amnardbat," said the kelp beer merchant, behind her. He sounded like he was worried he was about to be given a truly massive fine, and possibly have his kelp confiscated.

What had Mahit told her about the Councilor for Heritage, back in the City? Three Seagrass couldn't remember anything specific. Certainly she hadn't mentioned Heritage being a trade-protectionist faction of the Lsel government. "Councilor," she said. "I merely was interested in sampling local products. I am not a member of a trade concern."

"What *are* you a member of?" asked the Councilor.

It sounded rather like saying *I'm from the Ministry of Information* would be as poor a choice of stated allegiance as *I'm a traveling merchant looking for something peculiar enough to surprise even the Teixcalaanli markets*. Someone who disliked trade-that-wasn't-under-her-control this much was also going to dislike what she would doubtlessly interpret as *a spy*.

"I am on my way to the war," Three Seagrass said instead, somewhat grandly. "I am a translator and a diplomat. I will shortly be leaving on the *Jasmine Throat*."

All true.

Councilor Amnardbat was unimpressed. "Ah," she said. "I must have missed an arrival manifest." Her smile was extremely unpleasant, and Three Seagrass sincerely hoped she'd be off this Station and safely on a Teixcalaanli warship being attacked by mysterious aliens before the Councilor finished looking for that manifest which would explain how Three Seagrass had *arrived*.

"Have you paid for your drink?" asked the Councilor.

"Not yet," Three Seagrass said, as breezily as she could manage, which was getting less breezy all the time.

"It was a free small drink," said the kiosk operator, which was rather brave of him, especially since he clearly didn't know the Teixcalaanli word for *sample*. "If the—visitor?—wants a big bottle, I will charge her."

Amnardbat said, "I'll cover it. I doubt the Teixcalaanlitzlim has anything by the way of local currency."

Three Seagrass had plenty of local currency—well, not plenty, not after Esker-1 and the cargo barge bribe, but she had *some,* and this was quite insulting, but also—useful. Interestingly useful. Perhaps she could make the Heritage Councilor believe she *owed* her. "I'd appreciate that, Councilor," she said. "As I mentioned, I am only here briefly, and I had no intention of making purchases outside of our already-extant trading contracts . . ."

The kiosk operator held out a hand-sized scanner, and Amnardbat waved a credit chit at it until it made a pleasant chime. "That's done, then," she said. "Now, Three Seagrass—diplomat and translator or *whatever* you are—might I walk you back to the main transport hangar? I wouldn't want you to get lost and miss your shuttle."

You wouldn't want me to see more of your Station. Or talk to any more unsuspecting citizens. You're very angry with Teixcalaan, aren't you, Councilor. And here we didn't even annex you—"Of course," Three Seagrass said, and bowed again. "I am honored that you'd spend your time on such a simple errand."

"It's so rare that I see a Teixcalaanlitzlim on this deck," said Amnardbat, still with that very unpleasant smile. "I wouldn't miss the chance for the world. Come on, then."

———

When Eight Antidote climbed out of the tunnels and into the basement of the Ministry of War this time, Eleven Laurel wasn't waiting for him; it wasn't time for their weekly meeting. Eight Antidote hadn't finished the strategy exercise he'd been given after they'd talked about Kauraan, either—he'd looked at it, seen the complex shape of it, and left its cartographs mostly unopened on his cloudhook and kept thinking about Kauraan instead. But even so, being here without having solved his puzzle first made Eight Antidote feel guilty and worried. He *always* did his assignments. Even the unofficial ones.

But Eleven Laurel wasn't expecting him, and he was here to— maybe talk to Eleven Laurel, if he saw him, but more to watch the war with the aliens. He'd started thinking of it as *Nine Hibiscus's war,* which he definitely wasn't going to say out loud in the Ministry of War. He wasn't *dumb.*

He just wanted to see a real strategy room, with real communication with a real battlefront, and try understanding that the way he understood the puzzles and exercises. See whether the war was going badly, or well, or unexpectedly. Maybe—if he was lucky—he'd talk to someone here in the Six Outreaching Palms who would like having a maybe-someday-Emperor to show off to. That kind of thing worked on adults all the time, even if he was still eleven. It was only going to work better as he got older. He should get in some practice now.

When he passed the first set of camera-eyes that he knew about, the ones that he thought Nineteen Adze watched for him through, he waved at them and smiled, eyes wide, and went on as cheerfully as he could imagine. Walking cheerfully was kind of complicated—what he wanted to do was break into a run. Not to escape—there wasn't any escape, some official had probably already sent Her Brilliance a note about where Eight Antidote had gone this time—but to get to more populated places of the Ministry *faster*. To get away from his usual paths, and see something new.

The Ministry of War was laid out in a six-pointed star (how could it be anything else?), and a long time ago each Palm had probably lived in its corresponding sector. Now, because bureaucracy was more efficient if teams were near each other no matter who they ultimately reported up to (this was something his tutors liked to repeat a great deal, which just told Eight Antidote that they were bureaucrats and didn't like the thought of moving offices), the six spokes of the star were much harder to find one's way around in. If a person was looking for a *specific* individual, that was. Eight Antidote wanted to find the central command room. He wanted to look at a real strategy table for a real war. And all that would be in the middle of the star.

Security increased considerably as he turned toward the center of the building, which meant he was headed the right way. There were all sorts of soldiers in a variety of uniforms: the Ministry uniform, like Eleven Laurel wore, was on most of them, but Eight Antidote saw members of at *least* seven different legions as well; he recognized the diving-hawk patch of the Eighth on one woman's shoulder, and the star-shower of the First on another's, plus emblems he couldn't place immediately. The first person to stop him—four corridors and one security check that he got waved right through later—was carrying a shockstick half as long as Eight Antidote was tall, grey to match his grey War Ministry jacket. The point of the shockstick rested just above Eight Antidote's breastbone.

He probably should have been scared.

Not being scared was *fun*.

He bowed, fingertips pressed together, pushing the shockstick into his chest. Then he said, "I am the imperial-associate Eight Antidote, sir, and I would like to see the progress of our war."

The shockstick went away so fast it might as well have never been there. "Please forgive my impertinence," said the soldier, and Eight Antidote waved one hand, dismissive. *Magnanimous,* he thought. *Be magnanimous.*

"It's nothing. I appreciate your efforts to keep the Ministry secure." And then he smiled, wide-eyed, and remembered how he had made himself look like Six Direction when he'd been talking to Nineteen Adze. Tried it again. *Remember me? I'm the Emperor, just in kid shape. Just wait, and I might be the Emperor again.*

It worked. "This way, Your Excellency," the soldier said, having received some sort of confirmation on his cloudhook—Eight Antidote had seen the rapid flicker of messages behind the glass. "You are in luck—the Minister Three Azimuth, she who kindles enmity in the most oath-sworn heart—she herself is at the strategy table right now."

Which was a little more significant of a success than he'd particularly planned. He'd thought he'd just—see the strategy room, hang around, maybe meet some generals, another Undersecretary—if Eleven Laurel was there, that wouldn't be bad, he'd be showing initiative and creativity—but the *Minister of War* herself? That was—a lot. He'd met her, but only once, right when she'd arrived two months ago. She hadn't paid him any attention then, not after the obligatory good-morning-your-Excellencies, just gone in to speak with Her Brilliance Nineteen Adze. She had a poetic epithet that made her sound dangerous and frightening, but that was what poetic epithets were supposed to do.

The soldier took him into the center point of the Ministry's star. He knew that the strategy rooms were there—Eleven Laurel had explained that a long time back—all of them except for the one for the Emperor, which was in Palace-Earth instead. Everyone stared at him as he passed, trying to look confident in the soldier's wake, and wishing so much that he was taller already. He wasn't going to be taller until he was thirteen at *least.* Holographs of Six Direction only started looking like a man in his midteens. Sometimes Eight Antidote wished his genetics came from someone who was more physically impressive. At least he was going to be able to put on muscle easily and stay as agile as he was now—

The door to Central Strategy Two irised open for him at his escort's gesture, and beyond was twilight laced so thickly with stars that for a moment he thought the air had turned into a net. Then he blinked and saw the cartograph table—*huge,* wider than he imagined they could be, set into the floor instead of raised above it—was projecting four entire sectors of space at once, and that the Ministry analysts and generals had dimmed the lights to see the vector trajectories better. Minister of War Three Azimuth was at the far side of it, her hands moving in sweeping gestures, lightening some stars and darkening others. She made a fist, twisted her hand, and shook out a tiny fleet of gunnery ships from her fingertips, holoimages that she flicked out into the starscape and adjusted with minute nudges. It looked like dancing, like she was dancing the battlefield into existence.

I want to do that, Eight Antidote thought. *I want to do that more than almost anything I can think of.*

Three Azimuth was small and paler than most Teixcalaan-litzlim, with short sleek hair as dark and thick and straight as Eight Antidote's own, and narrow almond-shaped eyes. She'd taken off her jacket and was arranging the battlefield bare-armed. She had the kind of muscles that came from lifting her-self and heavier things, and putting them down again: ropy and defined. Somehow Eight Antidote always thought of her as be-ing taller. Before Nineteen Adze had become Emperor, Three Azimuth had been the military governor of Nakhar System, and Nakhar hadn't rebelled while she was in control of it, and Nakhar rebelled every indiction or so usually, according to his political history lessons. He still didn't know why she'd been the one to become Minister of War, or why Nine Propulsion had retired early, but he was pretty sure that Nineteen Adze had made a really good choice.

It took her a while to notice him. She had more ships to place first, and a whole set of supply-line vectors to adjust, her fingers plucking at the lines of light like they were the strings of some instrument. When she was satisfied, she said, "Barring our scouts locating their supply-line bases, this is where we are," and brought her hands together in a clap. The whole enormous projection began slowly to move, running its simulation.

"His Excellency the imperial heir Eight Antidote is here, Minister," said Eight Antidote's soldier. "He would like to see the war, he says."

"Well, bring the kid over, then," said Three Azimuth. "He can't see a bloody thing from that side of the room."

Eight Antidote went. He tried to skirt around the edges of the projection, but he still walked through star systems, blanking them out for brief moments in his wake, as if *he* was the aliens who were destroying Teixcalaanli communications. They were in the simulation too—a spreading blackness, like ink. There were a lot of eyes on him: all the advisors and commanders and analysts here to see Three Azimuth simulate the war were watching him traverse a starscape instead. He tried to walk as cheerfully as he had when he'd waved to the camera-eye. The camera-eyes were so much easier than so many pairs of real ones attached to people. (At least none of them were Eleven Laurel. He didn't know where Eleven Laurel was. Shouldn't the Third Undersecretary be here too?)

When he got to Three Azimuth's side—she was only a few inches taller than him, which made him feel very strange, he was a kid and she was the Minister of War—he said, "Thank you for allowing me to see the strategy simulation, Minister," in the second-highest form of politeness he knew. (Highest was for talking to the Emperor Herself, formally and in public, and he only knew that one because he'd grown up hearing it. It didn't get used much.)

"I expected you'd find your way in here eventually," said the

Minister. "You've been in the Palms enough, and kids your age get curious. I know I was. Watch."

Eight Antidote nodded, quickly, and turned to look at the simulation. Three Azimuth made a tiny gesture with one finger, and everything which had been paused began to move again, the alien darkness encroaching, the pinpoint-holograms of Teixcalaanli ships arcing through the air. Three Azimuth knew about his visits—of course she did. Did she know what Eleven Laurel had been teaching him? Did she think he was doing a good job?

Abruptly the scope of the strategy projection felt like a test, the biggest one Eight Antidote had ever taken. He watched *closely*. He hadn't seen the positioning of their fleet before, not in this detail—a single six of legions, with Nine Hibiscus's Tenth Legion in the lead, arrayed like a wave about to crest over the blank-dark systems the aliens had touched already. They held position for a long time—shifted, some ships from the Twenty-Fourth Legion coming forward, sending tendrils of light into one of those darkened spaces until it relit in dull grey, Peloa System back inside the world but—damaged? He checked the datestamp on the projection where it floated at the corner of his vision. This was all what had *already* happened. There was a brief stutter-pause—Three Azimuth opened one of her hands like a flower blooming—and suddenly all that black nothing was replaced by a force of spinning three-wheeled ships that Eight Antidote had never seen before.

They moved like they were carrying jumpgates *with* them, flickering in and out. While he watched, the entirety of the Twenty-Fourth Legion and half of the Tenth—including Nine Hibiscus's flagship, *Weight for the Wheel*—exploded into energy-cannon fire and then into scorched nothingness; or else were struck by some kind of strange liquid weapon and went blank and still. The simulation wound down. The remaining legions in the Six limped back into Teixcalaanli space through the jumpgate.

All of those soldiers would be dead. Dead *fast*. A legion was ten thousand people, maybe more—a legion and a half dead in a few days would be *at least* fifteen thousand and—

What if the aliens follow them home? Eight Antidote thought, with a spike of horror. *Follow them all the way back to us, sector after sector, and come here to the City and eat us—*

"That's enough," said Three Azimuth, and the simulation stopped. "Revert to the baseline." All the ships blinked back into existence, as if the horrible slaughter had never happened.

"Do they move like that?" Eight Antidote asked. He tried to sound calm, even though he wasn't calm at all. "Our enemy."

"I hope not," said Three Azimuth. "Otherwise we're fucked. Pardon my language, kid."

Eight Antidote decided not to respond to that. He'd heard a lot worse. "But they *might* move like that. Like they're . . . jumpgates."

"What we know is that they come in and out of visibility like they're coming out of a jumpgate," Three Azimuth went on. "Run it again—the second option, with cloaking but not asynchronous movement."

The simulation started over. It went better—sort of. If the aliens were just invisible, the Fleet ships could triangulate, pin them down eventually—but it was slow, and a lot of the Fleet died first in the process of *finding* the enemy. Eight Antidote watched as the Minister directed her analysts to push reinforcements through the jumpgates into the battlefront sector—watched the supply lines get skinnier and longer. And the constraint of the simulation was that Teixcalaan didn't know where the enemy supply lines came from, didn't know where their home planet was, or a nearby central base, or if they had a home at all or just lived in the void of space all the time. It was a *hard* constraint. It meant the Fleet *had* to go slow, piecemeal, and get ambushed while they found where the enemy was lurking.

"Doesn't look very good, does it," she said, after a good ten minutes. Waved her hand. The simulation reset again.

"Not really," Eight Antidote said, warily. ". . . There should be a better way to find them than letting them ambush *us*."

"So there should," the Minister said. "Got any ideas, or has my spymaster just been letting you solve *old* problems?"

It *was* a test. And now all of the advisors and generals and analysts and the soldier who had brought him to this room at the point of a shockstick, however deferred, and probably Eleven Laurel too (*my spymaster*, the Minister said, and Eight Antidote felt a little sick to his stomach) were watching to see what he'd do.

It turned out that there was a place you went *after* you were scared. A big, cold, bright place inside your head. Eight Antidote thought this was a good thing to have discovered.

"May I?" he said, gesturing at the simulation. "It would be easier to *show* you, Minister."

Three Azimuth had the kind of expression Eight Antidote couldn't figure out; one of those adult faces that wasn't surprise or admiration or displeasure exactly, but something else, something combined. She blinked behind her cloudhook, adjusting the simulation's control settings. It was one of the enormous ones, a pane of glass that extended from mid-forehead to cheekbone and curved around her skull to cover the ear on that side—or where the ear *would be*, Eight Antidote noticed, a sudden realization that seemed as much part of his new cold bright place as anything else. She didn't have an ear on that side. She had a burnt and twisted place where an energy weapon had gotten her ear and *melted* it.

Real combat was different than the strategy table simulations. He needed to remember that, for when he was Emperor.

He stepped to the front of the room. Took control of the simulation—it had so many more variables than the problems Eleven Laurel had been setting for him, but the program was the same. He knew how to make the Fleet ships move, and the simulation's AI would move the aliens for him, in the dark where he couldn't see.

The ships he placed flew from his fingertips like they'd flown

from the Minister's, though he knew he didn't look half as elegant as she did when she'd danced them into being. He arrayed
them in a net, carved the blank sector into cubes like he was
using a legion to lay out a garden for planting. Then he gathered a smaller force, all *Eternal*-class flagships and fast scout-
gunners, who would be mobile: if the sweeps found the enemy,
the strike force would move in to support them, fast and with
firepower. It took longer than he wanted to set up—some ships
had to stay by the jumpgate, and the supply lines were so long,
sectors long, with jumpgate delays built in. The weight of all
those eyes on him felt very heavy by the time he was ready to
say, "All right. Run it," like he was a grown *yaotlek,* a man who
made decisions.

"It's not bad," said Three Azimuth, but she didn't run his simulation. "It's not bad at all. The net pattern is smart, in fact. But
the *Eternal*-class ships don't move that fast. They won't be able
to get to where you need them with a net that *big.* We tried
it—oh, before you were born, I think. A sector-wide net pulls
the supply lines to nothing. And you've used all the legions like
one enormous legion—which has its merits, mind you, but a
yaotlek's six is six minds together, and they don't always move
as one . . ."

"You're saying," Eight Antidote said, "that I forgot about politics?"

Three Azimuth laughed. "I'm saying you did very well for
someone who's never been off-planet, let alone been a soldier."

"I wish I could see it," Eight Antidote told her, knowing he
sounded like a kid, asking for things he couldn't have, and not
being able to help himself from doing it.

"The war?" asked the Minister.

Eight Antidote had meant *the simulation he'd just designed.*
But—"Yes," he said.

"Can't let you go out there; there's only the one of you, and
Her Brilliance would be pissed at me."

"How about here?" he asked. "I can see a lot from right here next to you."

"You are a nasty little viper," said Three Azimuth, and actually *ruffled his hair*. Her hand was warm and calloused and entirely surprising. *"How* old are you?"

"Eleven."

"Blood and starlight. I was painting my toenails at eleven. All right, kid. Show up here in the morning, and we might make an Emperor of you someday."

Against the rush of satisfaction and excitement, Eight Antidote thought, *What will Eleven Laurel say to me? I should have asked him first*—and tried to hold on to that worry so he wouldn't jump up and down and look like someone who was young enough to be painting their toenails instead of learning how to run a war.

———

Mahit left Three Seagrass in the rent-an-office to arrange for their passage off-Station and into the war. Left her there because she needed to think, needed to breathe for a moment without *looking* at her, without looking at the impossibility of her presence on Lsel. She leaned her back against the metal corridor a few turns of the deck away, eyes shut, trying not to shake.

<You have good luck,> Yskandr whispered to her. <Good luck and good friends.>

I don't know if we're friends. She—needs me, or thinks she does.

<That's enough to get you away from Amnardbat.>

Briefly. And if I go, we are never going to be able to come home—no one here will protect us, you heard Tarats's offer—

<Make him a better one. You can now.> She was walking, without meaning to be walking. Following Yskandr's memory like a thread, a path he used to take: up four decks and into the vast and bustling offices of the Miners' Coalition, the engine of economic policy for Lsel. Slipping past desks and busy Stationers working at them, all the way to the Councilor's office

door. Yskandr leading her. She was letting him. *They* were doing this, and if how it was happening was the integration she had been waiting to experience, it was both wrong (she was never supposed to give up this much control to her imago, to ride inside his judgment and his momentum, to let go of her own volition so easily) and a profound relief.

Tarats's secretary, a tall woman whose name Yskandr couldn't remember and Mahit had never known, took her name and disappeared into his office. She was only gone for a few minutes.

"The Councilor will see you," she said. "He said to tell you he was expecting you."

Mahit nodded, thanked her, and strode through the door when the secretary held it open. She wasn't even moving like herself; Yskandr's center of gravity was higher. He led with the chest, like a male-bodied person would. She should stop, right now. She should pull back, right now.

<Let me get us out of here,> Yskandr said to her. <And then I'll apologize and we can get back to work at being an *us*.>

Out loud, she—they—said, "Councilor Tarats," and even shook his cadaverous, arthritis-twisted hand when he came around his desk to offer it. No bowing over fingertips here on Lsel. The old-fashioned way of greeting, instead. Hand to hand. The continuity of the flesh.

"What have you done with our Teixcalaanli visitor?" Tarats asked her. "Did you stash her somewhere, or did you space her?"

"Stashed," said Mahit, and then—oh, because she did, horribly, trust Yskandr to get her through this after all—grinned, his grin, too wide for her face, and knew her eyes were bright and gleaming-conspiratorial. "Why would I space an asset, Tarats?"

Unspoken: *I wouldn't. Are you going to? Even if that asset is me?*

And, an echo: <When I was you, Mahit, he could never look away from an opportunity. Let me make us one for him.>

"Sit down, Dzmare," said Darj Tarats. "Let's have ourselves a discussion about what you plan to do with the envoy if it isn't consignment to the void."

"Go with her, of course," Mahit said. Yskandr had a blithe-ness to him, an inexorability, which she thought he'd learned from Nineteen Adze: not her own headlong momentum but a calculating belief in his inevitable success. She borrowed it now. "You engineered a war to entrap Teixcalaan, Councilor Tarats. You and my predecessor, though he didn't want it. And the war is happening, right over our Station's head, right *through* our sector. And you have no eyes, Councilor, on that war."

"You mean to say, I have no eyes yet."

<He's unshockable,> said Yskandr in her mind. <Acknowl-edge him and keep going.>

"I mean precisely that," Mahit told Tarats, firm, serene. Re-lying on Yskandr to be serene for her, to keep her heart from racing, her throat from locking up. "I'll go with this envoy to her war, and I will be your eyes. I'll be Lsel's eyes, as I couldn't be in the City."

A long time ago Tarats's voice might have been silky, but all the weft had worn away, and the warp of the sound was harsh. "If you mean to do this for me, Dzmare, I will not have you hide from me like Yskandr did."

"My predecessor and I are in agreement on this course of ac-tion," said Mahit, which was true enough for the moment. She grinned another Yskandr-grin. The stretch was getting more comfortable. "A full and accurate account of Teixcalaan's mil-itary activities, Councilor, to the best of my knowledge and analysis. Everything."

Let me be useful again, so that I'm worth protecting.

"That's the beginning of a promise." His hands were mobile, punctuation for the shape of his words: inelegant with arthritis and elegant regardless as they gestured. "All your eyes can see and your analytic mind can interpret: good. But why would I want to watch a war, as you say, of *entrapment*? I'm not a sadist, Dzmare. I don't have any interest in the detail of Teixcalaanli failure."

She tried to not to feel Yskandr's spike of anger. Tried not to think of the scent of juniper gin, of *draw a monstrous thing to its death*. "And yet you took this meeting with me," she said. It was a gambit: if Tarats didn't want her eyes, what *did* he want?

"I did," said the Councilor for the Miners. "What else would you do for me, Mahit Dzmare, out amongst the Teixcalaanli warships? I wonder. You were very good at arraying all of the politics on the Jewel of the World to our advantage, when you had to."

Wary, Mahit asked, "What is more to our advantage than what is happening now, Councilor?"

Tarats smiled, a brief unpleasant flash. "Nothing. Nothing at all. Go to war, Dzmare. Go to war and—if there is an appropriate opportunity, of course—array the politics of the Fleet to ensure that Teixcalaan remains at war. Unable to win. Unable to retreat."

"How," Mahit began, because it was easier to ask *how* than *why,* than to acknowledge out loud that if she wanted to escape Heritage's surgeons, she would have to render herself into that hook that was meant to draw Teixcalaan to attrition and death—

<Or at least convince Tarats we will be,> Yskandr told her, vicious. Her hands spiked to invisible neuropathic fire. <I convinced him for ten years that I was still his agent entire. You're no less capable.>

Tarats was saying, "You have a little experience of sabotage yourself, do you not? I think you'll find a way." Mahit wondered what he'd do if she vomited on his desk. She felt as if she might.

"When have the Ambassadors to Teixcalaan not looked out for Lsel Station's best interests?" she managed, and thought she sounded like she was agreeing.

"Mmm." Tarats paused, like he was weighing her against Yskandr, measuring the depth of their integration, the degree to which he could trust her, given those twenty years of correspondence with her imago. She stayed still. Met his eyes and didn't drop hers.

Finally, he said, "Keep it that way. Don't you have a shuttle to catch, *Ambassador?*" he added, and Mahit felt the peculiar, disorienting surge of someone else's triumph running through her sympathetic nervous system while she herself was horrified; Yskandr, satisfied that they'd gotten away, willing to make this promise and break it.

She wasn't so sure she'd be able to. Not very sure at all.

————

Aknel Amnardbat walked Three Seagrass all the way back to the hangar she'd arrived in. It was still full of crates being unloaded, though the crates were mostly coming off different cargo barges than the one she rode in with. She'd only been on Lsel Station for five hours. Flying visit. (She could imagine herself saying that to Mahit: *Last time was only a flying visit, won't you show me around properly?* Wouldn't Councilor Amnardbat be scandalized. A Teixcalaanlitzlim, being *shown around* all of Lsel's secrets.) Said Councilor had kept up a perfect, even, impenetrable tour-guide's patter about the Station as she'd firmly and thoroughly guided Three Seagrass away from anything a tour guide would actually point out. It was masterful. Three Seagrass took internal notes, for the next time she needed to bore someone to death who was genuinely interested in the subject being used as the murder weapon.

You hate us quite profoundly, she thought, addressing the Councilor in her mind with the sort of formality used for precocious crèche-students or new cadets, a calculated and enjoyable and *invisible* insult. *Someday I will find out why.*

(Mahit, saying *Teixcalaan devours us.* But Lsel seemed quite entirely *itself* and undevoured, even if everyone seemed to understand a bit of Teixcalaanli. And her escort spoke it viciously well, like the language was a knife she'd learned to handle carefully.)

Their arrival in the hangar to meet the *Jasmine Throat*'s transport shuttle was more abrupt than Three Seagrass expected, and thus she didn't have the slightest bit of time to prepare: the giant hangar door clanked open, she spotted her baggage (just the one suitcase, she was traveling so light on this entire adventure!) waiting next to Mahit, flanked by *her* single bag on the left and Dekakel Onchu on the right—and Mahit went *white*, grey-white like she'd been bleached, as soon as she spotted Three Seagrass.

No. As soon as she spotted Aknel Amnardbat.

Whose hand was on Three Seagrass's elbow, where it hadn't been before. Who—was surprisingly strong, and *clearly* wasn't expecting to see Mahit, either, and—

Blood and fucking starlight, Three Seagrass hated working without an adequate dossier on current local conditions. Mahit could have *told her*. Mahit had intimated that she was in political hot water, but she hadn't bothered to explain what kind, and weren't they supposed to be partners?

That was an interestingly wrong thought she'd just had, wasn't it. An interestingly wrong *belief*, and she'd have to think about it, really she would; she and Mahit weren't on the same side anymore, hadn't been since Mahit had left the City. But now Three Seagrass was walking right up to her, with Amnardbat's fingers pressing indentations into her upper arm, and all she could think was *Don't run, Mahit Dzmare. Stick with me and we'll get on that shuttle and away. If you run I am comprehensively fucked.*

CHAPTER SEVEN

Revision of aptitude requirements for further study in non-Stationer languages and literatures: high scores on pattern recognition and memory capacity are no longer sufficient in and of themselves for progress beyond the intermediate levels offered to all Lsel citizens. For promotion to the advanced courses, students should also display high aptitudes in group cohesion and social integration with both peers and adults, and have already completed a preparatory (intermediate-plus) course in Stationer history and culture—preferably the same course recommended to prospective members of the Heritage Board.

—*Aptitude and Educational Requirements Handbook for*
Stationers Ages 13–18, revised edition, issued by the
Heritage Board of Lsel Station under the authority
of Aknel Amnardbat, Councilor for Heritage

* * *

Your tongue is a chrysanthemum
Because all your words are petals!
At the heart of language is a stem
That balances a thousand syllables.
Add a prefix to say MINE
Add a suffix to say WHY
Add an infix to say WHAT
And see how tongue becomes language!

—Teixcalaanli rhyming grammar, prepared for crèche-
students by Seventeen Frame, Information Ministry
(Education Division), in common use

MAHIT had let herself think she was going to get off-Station entirely clear if not entirely clean (never clean, getting away clean was an impossibility—Teixcalaan had taught her that, Teixcalaan and Yskandr, and now Darj Tarats was proving it to her again). She might manage to get on that shuttle Three Seagrass had called, and leap from an *immediate* danger into a merely probable one. She might *not* die under alien gunfire. Sometimes people didn't.

And yet, here she was, inches from the just-landed Teixca-laanli shuttle, and staring down Aknel Amnardbat herself. Who had somehow, through ill luck or profound cleverness or *both*, captured Three Seagrass.

Mahit could hear her heartbeat in her ears like rushing water, too fast and too loud. She was going to faint, or she was going to break and run for the shuttle, one or the other, and Three Seagrass and Amnardbat were coming toward her like a slow and terrible wave, too large a problem to outpace. Even having Dekakel Onchu standing right next to her wouldn't do her a bit of good—Onchu had made it perfectly clear that Mahit's usefulness to *her* was over. It had ended the moment she'd decided to not immediately mention that she'd received Onchu's secret notes to Yskandr when she'd returned to Lsel a month ago. Onchu would hand her over to Amnardbat if Amnardbat asked nicely—Pilots needed Heritage to keep approving new pilot imago-lines, since so many were being lost to the aliens out by the Anhamemat Gate. Onchu was here because she was supervising the exit of a Teixcalaanli ship from Lsel Station, and making sure it stayed gone. Not for Mahit. This little scene was all politics, and Mahit wasn't a player here; she was a spent and useless resource to everyone but Darj Tarats, who only cared enough to *let her go,* not keep her safe, and to Three Seagrass—

—who was looking at her with clear and determined and *furious* eyes as Amnardbat steered her across the hangar bay. With icy clarity, Mahit thought, *If I run, I think they may try to kill her for a spy.* And icier still: *She might be a spy, and I need to get her off my Station, and me with her.*

<You're a spy yourself, now,> Yskandr murmured, and she *ignored* him. She couldn't think about what she'd promised Darj Tarats. Not now. Not until after this, if there was an *after this* which contained sufficient time to contemplate what a person promised in extremity. What a person promised when they were half letting their imago lead them into choices they would never have made before they were part of a chain of living memory.

"Councilor," she found herself saying, surprised by the ease of her own voice, the smooth unshaking confidence she felt none of. Her own tonality, this time, not Yskandr. All her, and yet that perfect serenity. "What an unexpected surprise; it will save me leaving a message with your secretary. I've been unavoidably called away and will have to postpone my uploading appointment."

Any minute now, Amnardbat was going to say, *No, Mahit, come with me at once,* and there would be Heritage security personnel emerging from the shadows like the Teixcalaanli Judiciary's Mist agents, melting into visibility and taking her *away.* Any minute now, Amnardbat was going to say, *See? Dzmare is compromised, she has allowed this Teixcalaanli agent into our Station,* and possibly she wouldn't even be wrong. Any minute now.

"Where is it that you have been called away to so urgently?" asked Aknel Amnardbat, mild and colorless as distilled water.

"I am afraid, Councilor Amnardbat," said Three Seagrass in Teixcalaanli, "that it is my duty to reclaim the services of the Ambassador from Lsel Station to Teixcalaan." The language felt wrong to Mahit for the first time in a long time. Out of context. Three Seagrass, in bright flame-orange, Teixcalaanlitzlim-perfect, was like a cut poisonous flower in the center of the hangar. Something beautiful and dangerous that shouldn't be where it was, that would die and in its dying take what was nearby with it.

Amnardbat glanced from Three Seagrass to Mahit to the waiting shuttle, its doors open, her eyebrows raised and her mouth pursed like she'd tasted citrus-flavoring powder straight from the packet. And then she let go of Three Seagrass's arm.

I wonder if there'll be bruises, Mahit thought.

<You might get a chance to find out if you don't make any sudden movements,> Yskandr whispered, and there was something utterly filthy in how he said it that made Mahit want to hide from the inside of her own mind. Had that inflection been hers or his? Both? How hard was it going to be to tell, going forward?

Amnardbat did not speak in Teixcalaanli, even though Mahit knew she could use the language perfectly well. But she must *also* have known that Three Seagrass couldn't understand much Stationer at all. "Is that so, Dzmare? Are you headed back to the Empire, despite owing your home the repository of your memory?"

Mahit winced. "I'm—*we're*—going to the war, not the City. Councilor." That plural. She should watch her plurals. She'd meant her and Three Seagrass, surely.

Yskandr, a flicker of the younger, damaged version, less prurient, more vicious: <*We* is an appropriate singular for us.>

Mahit wished both of them would let her *think,* and also wished she hadn't wished it. She'd wanted him back so badly, when he'd been gone.

Amnardbat looked her over, and looked Onchu next to her over, too. There was a vast judgment in that gaze, and a sense of utter disregard: *Well, if you want. What use are you, anyway.* Mahit was projecting. Almost certainly. Assigning narrative where there wasn't any. She didn't seem to be able to stop. She hadn't been able to stop since the City. But then Amnardbat said, still in Stationer, "There are so many *easier* ways to commit suicide, Dzmare, than going to someone else's war."

Mahit didn't think that barb was pointed at her at all. It was for Onchu, and maybe for Darj Tarats *through* Onchu: someone else's war. A waste of Lsel's resources, again, at the mercy of Teixcalaanli whims.

If you hadn't threatened me, I wouldn't be going. I didn't mean to leave Lsel. I just came home. I came home, Councilor.

Thought was cheap. "I expect to be back, alive," Mahit said. "Anything else, Councilor?"

Now, surely, would come the security personnel, or Onchu would step in, or Three Seagrass would stop looking like she could suddenly develop telepathy and tell Mahit what to do if she glared with sufficient expression.

"Oh, go on, then," said Aknel Amnardbat, easy as anything, and waved a hand at the shuttle. "Enjoy yourself, while you've got breath for it." She gave Three Seagrass a pat on the shoulder—Three Seagrass visibly flinched. "Onchu? A word, while the Teixcalaanlitzlim and her . . . charge . . . get out of our controlled space?"

"Of course, Councilor," said Onchu smoothly. "Good luck, Mahit. And good luck to you as well, Envoy."

Onchu, at least, had bothered to revert to Teixcalaanli when directly addressing Three Seagrass. She also had the wherewithal to immediately walk away from where she and Mahit had been standing, drawing Amnardbat along with her in her wake: these little things—a Teixcalaanlitzlim, a broken Ambassador—all of that was not important when one Councilor of Lsel was having a conversation with another. It was blunt. Blunt and skillful. Mahit could imagine growing into a woman like that, if she lived so long—

The open door of the shuttle looked like a dark mouth. Mahit picked up her luggage—less than she'd taken to the City, by far—and walked into it, Three Seagrass just behind her to the left, snapping back into place like a detached limb suddenly remade. As if they had never stopped being Ambassador and liaison, barbarian and opener-of-doors. As if everything hadn't changed.

Eight Antidote woke up with the Emperor standing in the frame of his bedroom window, moonlight thick behind her. She glowed like a dream-apparition, a ghost, dressed in the white she'd worn before she'd been made Emperor. Eight Antidote wondered if he'd awoken a year ago, if the entire world he'd fallen into after his ancestor-the-Emperor killed himself would dissolve into dreamsmoke, fade to nothing. Maybe he was ten years old. Maybe all that would happen today was that he'd go see the palace-hummers in their garden, and recite poetry for his tutor, and avoid whoever the other child who had been provided for him to socialize with was. And forget—

Nineteen Adze was watching him. The world as it was refused to slip away into half-recalled snatches. He was eleven, and sole imperial heir, and yesterday he'd convinced the Minister of War to show him how to be a commander.

"I have something I want to show you," said Nineteen Adze. The weight of her eyes was very heavy. She was paying all of her attention to him right now, and he was in bed without a shirt on. Abruptly he was embarrassed, and pulled the sheet up to his chest as he sat up.

". . . Your Brilliance?" he said, trying not to sound like he'd been asleep just a minute ago. Or too much like a kid.

She came away from the window, a shadow separating. She had something in one hand. A sharp something, metal. Eight Antidote couldn't understand the shape of it. Maybe it was a knife. Maybe she was going to stab him and keep the sun-spear throne for herself and *her* heirs, whoever they would be, forever. Could he stop her? Eleven Laurel had taught him basic grappling, and he knew how to use an energy pistol, but he didn't *have* an energy pistol, and Nineteen Adze outweighed him twice over and also he was lying down and she was standing up, so she had all the advantages she'd need—

It wasn't a knife. Not exactly.

It was shaped like an arrowhead, like something Eight Anti-dote had seen in historical holos about pre-spaceflight humans and how they killed each other. But it was big. Big as a palm, and made of a dark brassy metal. The moonlight caught the edge of it. It looked rusted. It wasn't rusted. It was stained. Blood, old enough it should have flaked off. Nineteen Adze held it out to him. "Go on," she said. "Take it."

He did. It was heavy. It had been coated with some kind of thin clear lacquer, which kept the blood on. A memory, then. The tip of a spear, like the points of the sun-spear throne. Down the center of it was a raised part, like a spine, and when he ran his thumb over that ridge, he could feel indentations. He pressed down on the deepest one. A thin panel of the metal spine slid soundlessly back, and inside was—a hologram. Like the entire object was a giant infofiche stick, and he'd just broken it open.

It was an image. Very small, without any glyph annotations. But Eight Antidote could recognize it clearly. There was his ancestor-the-Emperor, middle-aged, strong, with his hair un-bound and reaching almost to his hips, sitting on a four-legged animal (*a horse*, he remembered, *that's a horse, or else a camel, but I think it's a horse*). And next to him, on another horse, was Nine-teen Adze in the uniform of a soldier in the Third Legion, no rank marks at all. Eight Antidote wasn't that good at judging ages, but he thought she might have been twenty. At most.

They were both laughing, in the holo. Like they shared a se-cret. Nineteen Adze had a long stick with a metal point on the end in her hand, and there was blood dripping down it, and blood on her forehead in the shape of the Emperor's fingers, like he'd dipped them in an enemy and pressed them there. It was the same spearpoint on that stick that Eight Antidote was hold-ing now. He was absolutely sure.

"Why are you showing me this?" he asked.

The Emperor didn't smile. She came to the edge of the bed and sat down on it instead. Her weight hardly disturbed it. For the first time, Eight Antidote thought of her as *narrow*.

Unfashionably tall, but in the full imperial regalia, she always seemed broad-shouldered, strong—but here she was, feather-light, like a ghost in the moonshine from the window. "Because I loved your ancestor, Eight Antidote. I would have died for him, in his service. See us there? I don't know anything of the next thirty years there. Not what I would do, or what he would do, or what he'd ask of me. But I already knew that I believed in his Teixcalaan. In an empire strong enough to be at peace, if only we could build that strength high enough. And we did. We did, for decades. Built it and held it."

"It didn't last," Eight Antidote said. He couldn't look at her while he said that, only at the tiny hologram-Emperor, un-stained with sheets of his own sacrificed blood. Thirty years away from that blood, and still Eight Antidote could almost see it, how it would look. It would get all over the horse.

"Nothing does," Nineteen Adze told him, which was awful: especially because she said it with such flat, resigned finality. A true thing, from the land of being a grown-up. From the land of being Emperor. "But I still believe in that Teixcalaan. When Six Direction made me Emperor in the sun temple, he entrusted that Teixcalaan to me. And to you, after me."

"I'm eleven," said Eight Antidote, as if he could make her go away by saying it. He held on to the metal memory-spear so hard his knuckles were white. The tiny hologram wavered. Stabilized.

"You're eleven, little spy," Nineteen Adze agreed, and sighed. "You're eleven, and you're *not* Six Direction, no matter what your face looks like. I made sure you didn't have to be." Her mouth twisted. "Sometimes I'm amazed that Six Direction handed me Teixcalaan after I made sure of that. After what I did to make sure of it. But I know you're not him, Eight Antidote. I know that quite definitively."

He wanted to ask her, *What did you do? What did you do to make you look like that, when you say so? What might have happened to me if you hadn't?* He couldn't find his voice.

"Which is why we won't be friends the way your ancestor

and I were friends," she went on. "And you *are* eleven. But you're involved already. A kid who finds his way into the Ministry of War and extracts a promise from Three Azimuth is a politician even if he's a kid. You know that."

"I know," Eight Antidote said, very quietly. "I'm sorry I went."

"Oh, blood and *stars*, don't be," said Nineteen Adze, brisk. "I'd rather have a clever, annoying, interesting successor than a dullard or a bore. How else are we going to build your ancestor's Teixcalaan?"

She was using the collective plural. Like they were equals. Like they were grown adults and she trusted him. It probably wasn't true, but he didn't know why she'd say it if she was lying to him or keeping him from knowing something he was too young to know.

He asked, "Aren't we at war, Your Brilliance? How can we have Six Direction's empire of peace if we're fighting these aliens?"

"We can't," Nineteen Adze agreed. "So we're going to have to win, or we're going to have to change the parameters of the conflict."

"Three Azimuth's projections make winning look—"

"Unlikely, yes. I've heard. In detail. Here's what I want you to do for me, little spy. Little successor. You hold on to this spearhead, and you look at it when you aren't sure what your Emperor wants for you. You remember what I've said tonight. And you go into the Ministry of War, and find out for me what is happening there. Find out why Eleven Laurel is so interested in you. Find out if Three Azimuth means to win this war or if she wants to maintain a permanent state of conflict. Be *you*, exactly as you have been—but pay attention."

Eight Antidote felt like his tongue had gone numb, and his fingers. His heart was thrumming. He didn't know why Three Azimuth wouldn't want to win a war. Wasn't that what Ministers of War were *for*, winning Teixcalaan's battles? But he managed to nod—how could he *not* nod?—and clutched the spearhead to his chest.

"Good," said the Emperor. "Now go back to sleep. You *are* only eleven. You get to sleep for a while yet." She reached out, touched his cheek with cool fingertips. A kind, small touch. And then she got up and left. The door to his rooms irised shut behind her with the faintest of clicks.

Eight Antidote didn't sleep at all. He watched the dawn come up instead, glittering through the hologram, making his dead ancestor look transfigured, sunlit, like a god.

After Peloa-2, there were funeral orations every few hours. Nine Hibiscus kept the old tradition of a Fleetwide broadcast on a seldom-used frequency, a recitation of the names of the dead. When the Tenth Legion wasn't in active combat, it sang its way through a thousand years of previous casualties, cycling every week and a half from the most recent fallen soldier in the Legion to the very first Teixcalaanlitzlim who had died wearing this uniform. Nine Hibiscus couldn't forget his name, or the low tone it was sung on during the litany—Two Cholla. A spear-name, all cactus needles, a name that would have sounded very fine with *captain* or *ikantlos* in front of it. Two Cholla had died a thousand years ago, at seventeen, before any titles or ranks could accrue around his name. There were a lot of names that came after his.

During active combat, the funeral frequency stopped playing its endless loop of memory and broadcast actual funeral orations, however small and paltry they ended up being. A snatch of song, the sound of blood falling into a bowl, and on to the next.

They were happening so fast because something about what Sixteen Moonrise had done on Peloa-2 had woken up the aliens and set them to full alert. They hadn't entirely engaged the Fleet yet. They were still testing the edges. The edges were mostly Sixteen Moonrise's people, the Twenty-Fourth, and a few of Forty Oxide's Seventeenth Legion who had been positioned on the far left of the Fleet's current arrangement. The enemy liked the left flank. Nine Hibiscus was beginning to think that somewhere beyond the blackout communication silence, in the dark places between this sector's thin stars, there was a *base,* or at least a large collection of ships, that she couldn't see. Somewhere to the left of *Weight for the Wheel.*

She'd expected consequences for retaking Peloa-2. It had been a statement: *We are here, this planet and these people were ours and are ours again; Peloa is inside the world. Peloa is Teixcalaan. Fuck off.* Of course there would be consequences. But somehow she hadn't been mentally prepared for the enemy—bloody stars, but she needed a better name for them than "the enemy" or "the aliens," the Information Ministry diplomat couldn't get here fast enough to tell her what they called *themselves*—deciding that attrition was the better part of valor.

After the scorched, eviscerated planetary corpse of Peloa-2, she'd been convinced that these aliens were nihilistic, resource-destroying, and covetous of territory more than power or colonization. But attrition—picking at the edges of the Fleet, at the few ships which Sixteen Moonrise had sent out to do reconnoitering—that was something else. That was something smart. Letting the vast tide of Teixcalaan find no purchase, no solid targets.

Only funerals; six so far today, two Shard pilots and the four-person crew of one of Forty Oxide's scout-gunners. She watched the replay of the death of that ship on holo. The aliens hadn't bothered with their ship-dissolving spit. They'd simply appeared, with the peculiar vision distortion that accompanied the end of their cloaking system, and tore the ship to pieces with energy weapon fire. The pilot and his crew hadn't even had time to react before they were burnt and shattered. Which, of course, meant that those three-ringed prowling alien ships could be *anywhere.*

There were too many deaths. Every time she dipped into Shard-sight she saw another one, another Teixcalaanlitzlim gone dark, felt an echo of the collective flinch, the sharpness of grief, the deeper burn of fury—*that we could so easily be lost,* how dare these enemies act with such impunity—

All that, and a scrim-afterimage of each death. She wondered how much worse it would be for the Shard pilots who had proprioception as well as visual linkage. Much worse. Almost certainly.

She was going to have to move with overwhelming force, and soon, and still *blind*—overwhelm them—wherever they were—

Twenty Cicada tapped her on the shoulder, and she *startled.* Spun on him, had her hand up to shove him in the throat and away, as if they were in a sparring ring. She hadn't reacted like that in years. He backed off, his hands up.

"Mallow," he said, so soft—her cadet nickname, when *she'd* been softer. No one else would remember it now, let alone use it to such effect. Shame was a slow surge; so was the distant fear that she was not in control of herself, or of this Fleet.

"I'm sorry," she said. "I wasn't expecting you."

He shook himself, an infinitesimal shuddering resettlement of shoulders. Straightened the collar of his uniform back to regulation-perfect. Smiled at her, a flicker of widened eyes, curving mouth. "You were listening to the funerals," he said, which was a way of forgiving her. "I would have been startled too."

"They do keep going," said Nine Hibiscus. "I should turn it off, or at least *down,* and actually get some work done."

"Our casualty rates are too high," Twenty Cicada agreed. "We can't wait much longer; losing our most adventurous and fastest ships is rotting morale, *yaotlek.* We need to—do something."

"You sound like Sixteen Moonrise."

Twenty Cicada winced. "I wish I didn't. But what we are up against is an obscenity, and our people know it. They need to stop having to see it, be hurt by it, and not strike back."

"We still don't know what's out there," Nine Hibiscus said, hating the bitterness in her own voice. "I can commit the Fleet to all-out attack, but if we go into a slaughtering field, without supplies and reinforcements—"

"They'd go for you. Everyone on this ship."

"I *know*," Nine Hibiscus said. That was the problem.

Twenty Cicada nodded, a short acknowledgment, but didn't stop talking. "Trust is not an endlessly renewable resource. Loyalty might be. For longer. Especially when we are up against something that doesn't even bother to *use* what it takes—"

"I think they do. I think we just don't understand how yet."

"I don't want to understand how what they did to Peloa-2 is useful," said Twenty Cicada, as softly as when he'd said her old nickname. "I think understanding would stain me indelibly."

How could she even answer that? She shrugged, her hands open. "I won't wait much longer. I promise."

Just until the envoy came. She was supposed to be arriving on the *Jasmine Throat,* scheduled for two shifts from now. That was only, oh, four more funerals away.

———

The inside of the *Jasmine Throat* was shocking, like being thrown into thick humidity after a long time in clear processed air. Not that there was any discernible difference to Mahit in the actual atmosphere: the *Jasmine Throat* was a spacecraft, and it was precisely climate-controlled and oxygen-regulated like every other spacecraft, including Lsel Station itself. The difference was that it was Teixcalaanli.

The walls were metal and plastisteel, yes—but covered in inlays of gold and green and rich pinks, all the formality and structure of a military supply ship layered over with Teixcalaanli symbolism. Green things, growing things, bright stars. Flowers. *Fuck,* how could she have forgotten flowers everywhere, white jasmine patterns painted on the ceiling of the hangar bay, the Teixcalaanlitzlim dressed in grey and gold Fleet uniforms, cloudhooks over every eye. No wonder she felt like she was breathing heavy air.

"Welcome back," Three Seagrass said, still a step behind her and to the left as they exited the shuttle and made their way through the hangar toward the passenger deck, that achingly familiar positioning. "Or—welcome to the war?"

She hadn't said much to Mahit the entire time they'd been in transit to the *Jasmine Throat*. Just *looked* at her, and murmured, "That was interesting," and shut up, a silent flame-orange presence, Teixcalaanli blank. They'd *both* thought the encounter with Amnardbat was going to have ended differently, Mahit suspected. And neither of them was sure why it hadn't. It made for uncomfortable company. Neither of them knew how to talk about a disaster that hadn't *been* a disaster, not without explaining to each other why it might have been disastrous. And explaining felt too dangerous to Mahit. Probably to Three Seagrass, as well.

Now, having arrived on the *Jasmine Throat* proper, with two-jumpgates-and-the-sublight-crawl-between-them's worth of travel time before they came to the Fleet—call it seven hours subjective time—Mahit realized that she and Three Seagrass were going to have to start all over again. Back to the beginning. Back to *let's assume that I'm not going to try to sabotage you* and *let's assume I'm not an idiot.*

It seemed a long distance to fall back. Especially since she was (possibly—nothing, *nothing* was decided, she kept telling herself that, or telling Yskandr that, to stave off the stabs of neuropathic pain radiating through her palms) the saboteur this time. And Three Seagrass had never been an idiot.

When they weren't thinking about Darj Tarats, Yskandr was a quiet, humming, *pleased* presence in the back of her mind: he'd never been on a Teixcalaanli military ship, neither supply-line reinforcement nor attack vessel, and Mahit leaned into his intent and curious observation with some relief. She needed that. She needed anything that would remind her that this experience was *new,* and not quite a return. Not in any sense a coming-home.

"We're not at the war yet," she told Three Seagrass. "We have half a day before the war happens to us. We should get ready for it."

"Fuck, but I missed you," said Three Seagrass, with a sort of regret that Mahit couldn't place. "Someone else who throws themselves at problems—"

Mahit could feel the ghost with them then, as abrupt and clear as any other realization of political loyalties, secret alliances: the missing third person. Twelve Azalea was three months dead and interred with the rest of the Information Ministry's fallen officers behind a plaque down on the City, an unfathomable distance away from the two of them. *The one of us who was practical at all,* she thought—and then revised. *No. The one Three Seagrass needed to keep her steady. I've never had a friend like that. Or lost one, either.*

"Tell me the problem, then," Mahit said, "aside from 'we have to talk to aliens' and 'you missed me.'" They were walking past a multitude of Teixcalaanli soldiers, all of whom seemed unabashed in their willingness to stare at an Information envoy and a barbarian.

"That's really the sum of the problem," Three Seagrass said. "Those two. The aliens are a bit more pressing. Also I *could* add that you seem to have made many enemies while you were visiting your Station—"

"That's not a *current* problem," Mahit said, as serene as she could manage.

<Ah, so we *are* going be Tarats's agent? I was beginning to wonder if you'd simply confess to her.>

Like I said before, Yskandr, if I was going to give us up to Teixcalaan, it would take a lot more than some political pressure.

She didn't feel as brave as she sounded. She knew he knew that; he was inside her endocrine system, party to the thousand messages of her neurotransmitters and her glands. He knew precisely how neatly Darj Tarats had trapped her: make sure Teixcalaan remains endlessly at war, or be subject to Heritage's plans. One or the other. So far, all she'd done was fail to mention Tarats's orders. That wasn't very *much* of being his agent. But it left all the doors of future action open. Keeping secrets always did.

"If you say it's not a current problem, fine," Three Seagrass said, dryly, and opened a door to the tiny transit chamber—hardly larger than the rent-an-office they'd been in on Lsel—which they had been assigned for the duration of the trip. It had no windows. Mahit wasn't terribly interested in seeing the distortion of space around a jumpgate, but she still felt obscurely disappointed that she wouldn't be able to. With the door shut behind them, there was nothing between her and Three Seagrass but three months of time, an envoy's uniform, and deep suspicion.

Three Seagrass set her luggage down beside the door and knelt to rummage in it. She came up again with her hands full of infofiche sticks, the simple industrial-grey plastic kind, stamped with the Information Ministry seal in cheery and threatening coral-orange.

"Surely," Mahit found herself saying, "you can't have brought along the unanswered mail. I swear I had it forwarded when I left, I've been working on it—"

She was rewarded by Three Seagrass laughing, and a brief, utterly pleasant relaxation of all the tension months apart had somehow engendered. "No," said Three Seagrass. "I don't have a scrap of mail for you. What I have is all the records the *yaotlek* in charge of the Fleet has of our mysterious and very dangerous aliens. I haven't had a chance to look at them yet. Want to see?"

<Yes,> murmured Yskandr, covetous, excited—exactly the same as Mahit was. Acquisitiveness, a certain degree of xenophilia—that showed up in both of their aptitudes. It was a central part of their compatibility. *Show me something new.*

"Let's figure out what we're learning to talk to," she said to

Three Seagrass, and took the first of the infofiche sticks from her hand, snapping it open easily between her fingers.

It was audio only. It was—*fuck,* it was like Mahit had carved a hole in the world between the space of one side of the infofiche stick and the other, and on the inside was static and screaming, or static that was screaming, or—

She felt ill. There didn't seem to be a way to turn it off. Three Seagrass had gone grey-green under the warm brown of her skin. It made her look dead, or dying. Or like she wanted to be dead, or dying.

And yet there were *different* terrible sounds in the audio recording, a stuttering shriek that was repeated three times, a lower buzz that roiled Mahit's stomach and occurred after every pause longer than ten seconds. She couldn't understand it, and it was hideous, but it wasn't noise.

When the recording was finally over, both she and Three Seagrass were breathing in hyperventilating gasps, huge snatches of air to shove back the nausea. They stared at each other. ". . . I don't know if it's language," Mahit managed, finally, "but it's definitely communication. Phonemes, or—I don't think words, it's not enough differentiation, but—maybe tone markers?"

Three Seagrass nodded. Swallowed like she was forcing back bile, and nodded again, more firmly. "Horrible sick-making tone markers. Got it. I want to cross-reference it to the readout from the ship that recorded the transmission, they were interacting with it somehow—maybe we can map which noise goes with what—"

"If either of us vomits, we should vomit in a bin," Mahit said. "Do we have a bin—are any more of these audio only?" She gestured at Three Seagrass's fistful of infofiche sticks.

"Only one was marked for audio. The rest should be visual and text," said Three Seagrass. "Open them up, and I'll go find *two* bins. This is a resupply vessel, I'm sure they've got bins."

"Possibly also bin liners. We're going to have to listen to that—a lot."

"Bleeding sunlight," Three Seagrass cursed, but she was smiling, Stationer-style: the edges of her teeth showing. Mahit felt charmed, and worried at being charmed, and utterly relieved that, given work to do, the two of them were apparently fine with one another. "Bin liners, excellent. Seven hours is plenty of time to categorize our tone markers by how many bin liners listening to them requires—"

"Wouldn't want you to look bad in front of the *yaotlek*," Mahit said. "She'll want the bin liner report straightaway. And presumably the rest of the report also."

"See?" said Three Seagrass, still smiling that almost-Stationer smile. "I knew fetching a barbarian diplomat who could learn *our* language would save me time in learning someone else's—"

She slipped out the door before Mahit could ask her the questions on the tip of her tongue: *Would you be as fascinated with these aliens as you have been with me? Considering we are all barbarians, even if I am as human as you are?*

<Better not to ask,> Yskandr told her. <You don't really want to know the answer anyhow.>

In poetry and epics, and even in statecraft manuals of the driest and most clinical kind, emperors were exempt from sleep, or ought to be, and therefore so were starship captains. Nine Hibiscus had always thought that a *yaotlek*, who was somewhere in-between captain and emperor, really ought to develop the ability to stay awake indefinitely upon receiving her spear-arc collar tabs. Practicality, however, had a notorious way of ignoring poetry, epics, *and* statecraft manuals. Like everyone else on *Weight for the Wheel,* Nine Hibiscus had a designated eight-hour shift for sleeping.

Lately, she wasn't very good at it. Which said something about Emperors, and *yaotlekim,* and the difference between being in charge of one small but powerful thing, like a starship, and a whole lot of disparate things, like a fleet full of Teixca-laanlitzlim all ready to die for the sake of the Empire, and at her command.

Nine Hibiscus had been *trying* to sleep. She had removed her uniform, and laid herself down on her bed in an undershirt and sleeping shorts, and cued her cloudhook to dim the roomlights to almost blackout. She'd even set her messages to silent save for absolute priority; if the aliens attacked *Weight for the Wheel*, she'd wake up, but probably not for anything else.

If she ever went to sleep at all, anyway. She'd been trying for a full third of her eight hours, and had gotten nowhere. All she could think about was the flashfire deaths of the Shards—about whether the new biofeedback technology was worth giv-ing half the Fleet post-traumatic flashbacks when someone half a sector away died badly. Cost-benefit analysis was antithetical to sleeping.

It was a relief when someone *physically* knocked on her door. Most likely they'd been trying to send a nonpriority message and hadn't heard from her, and now something was *happening* and she didn't have to pretend she was sleeping any longer. She raised the lights and wriggled into her trousers for a modicum of authority, and waved the door open. On the other side, look-ing apologetic, was her chief communications officer, Two Foam. This wasn't one of Two Foam's off-shifts—the bridge took careful and staggered turns, and when Nine Hibiscus was sleeping, Two Foam was usually awake—but she looked ex-hausted anyhow, even if *she* hadn't been woken up.

"*Yaotlek*," she said, "there's been a major development."

The crew of *Weight for the Wheel* called Two Foam *Bubbles*, because she wasn't bubbly at all. The nickname was ubiqui-tous; even Nine Hibiscus had to remember not to use it. In-stead she waved her inside her quarters without using any name in particular, and let the door shut behind her. Her own heart rate had kicked up; this was better than sleep, this was the shimmer-focus of *being responsible* in a crisis. "Yes? What *sort* of development that is significant enough for you to come fetch me?"

Two Foam didn't seem particularly comfortable standing in her superior officer's quarters while said superior officer found the other pieces of her uniform and put them back on. Nevertheless, she gamely directed her eyes toward the ceiling and explained. "Sir. We have one of the aliens."

"What? *Alive?* Did we capture a ship?"

Two Foam shook her head. "Dead. A Shard from the Seventeenth found it floating in vacuum after one of the . . . engagements we've been having. He lassoed it and brought it back."

Nine Hibiscus felt shaky with exhilaration; she had to exert effort to keep a visible tremor out of her hands. "Get that soldier a commendation. From Forty Oxide, if you can manage it; it should come from his own Fleet Captain. And—where is it? The alien?"

"In the medical bay," said Two Foam. "The medtechs are going to autopsy it. But I thought you might want to see it first."

"Fuck yes I do," said Nine Hibiscus, and slammed her feet into her boots. "Let's go."

Medical was two decks up and in the rear of the ship. They made the fifteen-minute walk in ten, and Nine Hibiscus took a deep, brief pleasure in how Bubbles kept pace with her, a half step behind to her left. It made her feel like something was right in the universe, and she was going to need that to deal with whatever she was about to see. She was trying not to imagine it. Imagination created biases. And besides, all she could think of was a smaller, human-scale version of their three-ringed ships, and that was absurd; they clearly *weren't* some kind of hungry ship-species that budded off smaller ships. The Shard pilot wouldn't have been able to bring one in if they had been.

This was what imagining got her. Absurdities. Comforting

absurdities. She suspected what she was going to be looking at would be *much worse* than anything she could come up with—

But it wasn't.

Which was awful.

Laid out on the table the medtechs usually used for surgery, which had been stripped of its standard padding and cushions designed to hold a human body in place, pared down to flat metal, was something that looked like an animal. Not even a horrible animal. Just a new one.

They'd stripped it of its clothes, which were a deep red tactical-weight cloth and looked well made—someone would analyze them later, though the fact that it wore clothes at all was significant. But now, now was for the creature itself. Nine Hibiscus stepped close, close enough to see that it would have towered over her by a foot and a half at least when it had been alive and standing. The naked alien had four limbs, like most bipeds. The rear two were thick and short, powerful in the thighs below a long torso; the front two were overlong by human standards, with four-fingered hands that ended in blunt claws. The claws were capped, decoratively, in some kind of bright plastic shot through with silvery wires. *Those might be a piloting interface,* Nine Hibiscus thought, fascinated, and then kept looking, scanning up the body. The skin was mottled—it could have been trauma, or vacuum-chill, but she thought it was coloration, spots and blotches—and the neck. The neck was *wrong*.

Too long. Half as long as the torso, a neck for bending and tearing, flexible, muscle-ridged, leading to a head that was all jaw, mouth open in death, a dark tongue hanging over carnivore teeth, jagged and massive. The eyes faced forward, like a human's eyes, and were sightless, clouded, the left one burst open during whatever dying had happened to it. Predator's eyes, like a human's.

The ears were cups set far back on the skull, and faintly furred. Somehow that was the worst thing about it. Those ears were like the ears of the soft almost-cat pets from Kauraan, that purred and bred in the air ducts and annoyed Twenty Cicada. And they were on *this* thing, this otherwise hairless scavenger thing that was killing her Fleet.

"Is it a mammal?" Nine Hibiscus asked. She knew how to kill mammals. They had fairly standard physiologies. The heart, for example, was in the chest.

"It's not an insect or a reptile," said the medtech. "Probably a mammal. A male-sexed one." He gestured; Nine Hibiscus noted the penile sheath and nodded. "I'll know more when we open it up."

"Well, then, open it up," she said. "Figure out how it works, so we can know how best to stop it from working."

INTERLUDE

THIS is not the first time this has happened. The place: the depth of Bardzravand Sector, close enough to the Anhamemat Gate that the discontinuity of jumpgate space begins to distort vision. Human eyes—and other eyes, any eyes that function on the old clever model of refraction and reflection, that assembly of light on a retina into image flaring between one neuron and the next—they cannot see what a jumpgate does to space-time. There is an inability to assemble the light into any coherent image. A collapse of meaning.

That discontinuity shivers, shudders, spreads. A portion of it sections off, and moves. A ripple thrown into the black, the afterimage of a stone landing in water. The half-caught reflection of a school of fish, glinting once as light glances off their scales, and then—moving together, angling—gone, unseeable.

This is not at *all* the first time this has happened, and the last time it did—the last time it did, in the aftermath Dekakel Onchu held the hand of her terrified and half-dead pilot and imagined how the shimmering black between stars could resolve into hungry, lamprey-mouth rings. Could devour the entirety of an imago-line before there was any chance of preservation of memory.

The last time, there had been no steady flow of Teixcalaanli military vessels through the Far Gate. Onchu had hoped that, if Darj Tarats was using all of Lsel Station as bait for Teixcalaan, drawing the Empire through and past them into the maws of those ring-ships—she'd hoped at least she wouldn't have to deal with any more ring-ships eating her pilots.

Hoped, and is now denied even that.

The message comes in bright and hot, a desperate, breathless cry over long-range broadcast: *They hide in the jumpgate, they LOOK like the jumpgate, they're after me, I'm not fast enough—*

And Onchu, sitting in the nexus of Pilot's Command, for her the true heart of Lsel, no matter what Heritage believed about their room-repository of imago-machines—Onchu, sitting there, has to ask her pilot to not come home. To not lead that hungry thing that Tarats thinks could devour an empire back to the fragile shell of Lsel Station. It is the worst thing she's ever done. When she dies, she will die thinking of it, like a splinter finally reaching her heart after years of worming its way through flesh. Over that long-range broadcast, she says: *Go through the jumpgate. If they're chasing you make them chase you.* Dzoh Anjat—her pilot's name, or that pilot's imago's name, in these moments she slips, she has known so many of her people, in all their iterations—*I am with you. Lsel is with you. Take them through the jumpgate and hope the Empire is on the other side to catch you. I'll be listening—*

She does not receive an answer aside from a positional ping. A small shift in that discontinuity around the Far Gate. Dzoh Anjat and her pursuer, gone over. Gone entire.

Dekakel Onchu is very good at listening, and she stays by her instruments for hours and hours. She never hears from Dzoh Anjat again.

(Dzoh Anjat, obedient and patriotic, going to her death, but not the death she expected: Teixcalaan is on the other side of the Anhamemat Gate, yes, but Teixcalaan sees the three-ringed maw of one of their enemy's ships and cares not at all for one small patrol-craft smashed in the conflagration of their energy-cannon fire—cares not at all, and may not have even seen, or noticed, or thought to look. Only to keep themselves safe from what appears, to the member of the Seventeenth Legion who sees that rippling discontinuity materialize, to be a flanking ambush.)

And Dekakel Onchu cannot hear the singing of the *we*, not at all. Not how the extinguishing of the voices on that ring-ship does not alter the volume of the song, but only its shape. She thinks language, after all.

She thinks language, and finds herself ragged with tears, waiting for voices that will never come to her, not once while she is alive.

CHAPTER
EIGHT

. . . despite his three-indiction stay amongst the Ebrekti, Eleven Lathe neglected to provide the Empire's scientists with much in the way of physiological information. His *Dispatches* is a work of philosophical and moral exploration, and perhaps a person cannot be expected to provide both a spiritual exegesis of living amongst aliens and an accurate description of their physical habits, development, diet, and morbidities—but the sheer weight of absence in the text of much practical information means that readers of the *Dispatches* are far more acquainted with Eleven Lathe's mind than they are with an Ebrekti body—or an Ebrekti anything-at-all. We sent a poet where we ought to have sent a team of *ixplanatl* researchers.

> —introduction to a scholarly commentary on *Dispatches from the Numinous Frontier,* composed on commission by the *ixplanatl* Two Catenary, chief of medical ethics at the Twelve Solar-Flare Memorial Teaching Hospital

* * *

```
>>QUERY/auth:ONCHU(PILOTS)/"re-implantation"
>>There are no records including "re-implantation" in the
    database. Please refine your search and try again.
>>QUERY/auth:ONCHU(PILOTS)/"imago repair"
>>237 results found. Display? Refine search?
>>REFINE/auth:ONCHU(PILOTS)/"surgical" OR "post-
    traumatic"
```

>> 19 results found. Displaying in alpha order . . .
   —record of queries made to Lsel medical research
   database by Dekakel Onchu, 92.1.1–19A
   (Teixcalaanli reckoning)

ON the other side of the last jumpgate between them and the
war was the Fleet. Or at least six legions' worth of the Fleet, and
a swath of support ships, darting between the hulking elegance
of the larger destroyers and flagships and gunners. The array
of them all ate up the visible stars. There weren't many stars to
start with. Mahit knew this sector of space, though she'd never
been to it before; it was resource-poor, Teixcalaanli-controlled,
and Lsel Station kept a watch on it and did little else.

It was also where Darj Tarats had first noticed the aliens she'd
just spent a nauseating six hours listening to, over and over
until she was sure she'd *dream* that sequence of static and metallic squalling in auditory afterimage. This was the sector that
had disappeared sufficient numbers of Lsel pilots to make a
pattern that first Tarats and then, later, Dekakel Onchu could
notice. Notice, take note of, and use. And nevertheless there
weren't enough stars here. No stars, no *sky* like on the City
or any other planet, and only an enormous amount of Teixcalaanli firepower to steer by.

They were very beautiful, all those ships. Mahit's childhood had been full of breathless horror biopics about what the
Fleet could do to a planet (not a *Station*, never a Station, always
a planet, always far away, but it was easy to extrapolate), and
equally breathless serial dramas about life *on* a Teixcalaanli
legionary ship, all uniforms and poetry contests off-shift. Fuck,
but she'd devoured those like sugar pastilles. She could probably still explain the plots, the convoluted love stories and the
politics and multiseason faction-swapping and here she was, and
even after all that had happened in the City three months ago,
she still felt *doubled*. Vertiginous and falling. The self that

experienced and the self that evaluated, wondered, *Is this when I feel real? Is this when I feel like a civilized person?*

And the self that sounded like Yskandr, dark and amused: *Is this when I forget what being a Stationer feels like? How about now? Now? Are we still Mahit Dzmare?*

She had imagined the Fleet, and feared it, and admired it, and seeing it was still a profound discontinuity.

Three Seagrass had no such problems. She had effortlessly infiltrated the affections—or at least the interest—of the *Jasmine Throat*'s comms officer, and now that they were in hailing range of the Fleet's flagship-of-flagships, the *yaotlek* Nine Hibiscus's very own *Weight for the Wheel*, she leaned over his shoulder and took control of the transmission.

"This is Special Envoy Three Seagrass aboard the supply ship *Jasmine Throat*," she said. "Hailing the flagship *Weight for the Wheel*—you called for the Information Ministry, I believe?"

There was a long pause, longer than the time it would take for the transmission to cross the sublight distance between the two ships. Mahit imagined that other bridge: Were they surprised? Annoyed? Had they even been *warned* about the advent of Three Seagrass?

At last, a transmission came back: an arch tenor voice, smooth and completely unaccented, as if whoever was speaking had learned Teixcalaanli from newsfeeds, or was a newsfeed anchor himself. "Welcome to the Tenth Legion, Envoy. This is the *ikantlos*-prime Twenty Cicada, acting as adjutant for the *yaotlek* herself—she regrets being occupied at the moment and unable to greet you properly."

"Formality," Three Seagrass said smoothly, "is for the imperial court; this is a battlefield. I look forward to speaking with the *yaotlek* whenever she has time to spare. We'll be on board shortly, adjutant—we'll come in with your supplies on the *Jasmine Throat*'s shuttle."

"We?" asked that voice, and Mahit thought, *Well, so much for this being simple.*

"We!" Three Seagrass agreed, enthusiastically. "I've brought a consultant linguist. She's a barbarian, but don't hold it against her. She's *brilliant*."

And then she cut the connection on the adjutant. On the man who was the second-most powerful person in the entire Tenth Legion. Mahit couldn't decide if she was horrified, proud, or simply, deliciously, *hideously* intrigued. She watched Three Seagrass straighten up, flash a wide-eyed Teixcalaanli smile at the comms officer, and crack her spine, leaning back with her hands laced together behind her. *Getting ready*, Mahit thought. *I should, too.*

"Consultant linguist, mm? Is that what I am now?" she asked.

Three Seagrass shrugged, one shoulder and one hand in brief motion. "If you'd rather be the Lsel Ambassador to Teixcalaan, I can reintroduce you when we get there." She brushed Mahit's wrist with warm fingertips as she passed by, and Mahit followed her easily, thinking of flowers that turned toward sunlight, and less pleasant tropisms—gravity wells, the attraction of insects to rot. "Which reminds me, Mahit—if you want to be the Lsel Ambassador, *do* you have the authority to negotiate with our screaming aliens on behalf of your Station?"

<I don't see why not,> Yskandr murmured to her. <No one else is going to, and you're right here.>

Oh, fuck it, why *not* be an ambassador *and* a diplomat—be *useful* again, have authority and room to use it and use it for Lsel as well as for Teixcalaan—do something more than escape and be Tarats's corroding agent. Do *something*.

The supply shuttle in the *Jasmine Throat*'s hangar was being loaded with practiced efficiency—grey-metal case after grey-metal case heaved inward by a small assembly line of Teixcalaanlitzlim. Three Seagrass and Mahit joined the line, as if they were cargo themselves, though Mahit doubted they'd be tossed bodily inside.

"Of course I have that authority," said Mahit. "No one *un*-Ambassadored me, Three Seagrass, no matter what the Councilor for Heritage implied."

"She didn't," said Three Seagrass, sounding quite interested indeed, and slipped inside the shuttle. Over her shoulder she added, "Imply that."

Fuck.

Mahit said, "Well, that's unexpectedly pleasant, all considered," and didn't go on any further. She didn't want to—she *couldn't* tell Three Seagrass that she was here to spy on the war for Darj Tarats, in order to escape Aknel Amnardbat's surgeons. To do worse things for Darj Tarats, if there was an opportunity. She couldn't. So she got into the shuttle instead, settling amongst the supply crates and strapping herself into some freefall-control webbing. There were similar webbings on all of the walls, the floor, the ceiling. It was an efficient, well-designed ship. It must make a hundred of these short hops in a month—

"Quite," said Three Seagrass, all edges, interest and wariness and a sort of invitation deferred: *We can play, Mahit, even if we don't play just now, if playing's what you want.*

The shuttle door sealed behind them with a hiss of vacuum, and Mahit shut her eyes against acceleration.

———

It took too long to approach *Weight for the Wheel*—longer than Mahit expected, given how huge the flagship was. It had seemed very close from the bridge of the *Jasmine Throat*. Now it was growing larger and larger through the small viewport inside the supply shuttle until it was horizon and sky and ground all at once, a solid wall of ship that seemed to be the entire visible universe. A solid wall of ship with a discontinuity, a maw, black and wide, a hangar bay—and *that too* was too large and growing larger all the time, gaining color and dimension as the shuttle approached it. A hangar bay which could contain not only this sizeable supply shuttle but hundreds of tiny triangular ships, arrayed in *racks* awaiting their pilots, and other large vessels besides, and still have room for at least ten shuttles the size of this one—a hangar bay with a ceiling as high as some *buildings* had been, in Palace-Central down on the City.

They landed with hardly a shudder, and Mahit was on a Teixcalaanli warship for the first time in her life.

The shuttle doors opened immediately, and as Mahit and Three Seagrass released their webbing-harnesses, they were swarmed by enterprising Teixcalaanlitzlim: soldiers in stripped-down and functional uniform, grey and gold coveralls with reinforced patches at the knee, their name glyphs and the insignia of the Tenth Legion on the left shoulder. Swarmed, and ignored in favor of the supply crates. It was like being inside an enormous machine that had absolutely no interest in you, since you weren't shaped like the sort of object the machine preferred to ingest and spit out again on the other side.

Three Seagrass flashed her a smile, lightning-quick widening of the eyes, the barest hint of white teeth. "Ready?"

"As I'm going to be," said Mahit, and just as she had once before, stepped off a shuttle and into Teixcalaanli space to see what was waiting for her there.

The hangar was busy—this shuttle wasn't the only one being unloaded—and there were so very *many* soldiers. The Fleet was enormous. Mahit thought of the thirty thousand Stationers on Lsel and how that had once, when she was a small child, seemed like a very large number of people. There were probably three thousand Teixcalaanlitzlim on this flagship. Maybe more. And at least ten ships this size only on this battlefront—there was Lsel entire, rendered in Teixcalaanli battle flags. And so many other ships besides, all over the galaxy, on the other side of nearly every jumpgate. Some of the soldiers were obviously injured—one ship in this hangar was scorched almost black, partially *absent*, and the people climbing out of it were bleeding, or burnt, or being carried on stretchers by efficient medical personnel.

<That's what a ship looks like after it gets brushed with energy-cannon fire,> Yskandr murmured to her, horrified and

fascinated, as horrified and fascinated as she felt herself. <That's what these aliens can do to this fleet—no matter how many soldiers there are in Teixcalaan, all ships burn the same.>

All ships burn the same, Mahit thought, echo, stutter-thought—and then Three Seagrass tapped her lightly on the shoulder, gesturing across the crowds with her chin, pointing out that they had clearly, clearly been *expected.*

She and Three Seagrass had been sent an escort, and that escort was waiting for them. A man and a woman, each in *full* Fleet uniform instead of the hangar-worker coveralls. The man was tall, terrifyingly thin, and had shaved his head absolutely bald; the first bald Teixcalaanlitzlim that Mahit had ever seen who wasn't also old. The woman was all the same color all over, an electrum shade, hair and skin only fractionally different. She wore a Fleet Captain's sunburst on her shoulder, and Mahit wondered for a moment if this was the *yaotlek* herself—but no, it couldn't be Nine Hibiscus, this woman's legion insignia was different, the glyph for *Twenty-Four* turned into a stylized parabola. Not this legion's Fleet Captain, but on this legion's flagship nevertheless—and coming to greet the Information agent, too—

Mahit didn't have much time to wonder about internecine competition between the legions making up the attack force; she was a fractional step behind Three Seagrass, feeling utterly drab and barbaric in her jacket and trousers next to that spot of flame-coral and everyone else's perfect Fleet uniforms, and the two-person high-powered welcoming committee wasn't waiting for them to get close. They were coming to meet them in the middle of the hangar. It looked like it was the woman's idea—she strode forward, long ship-circumnavigating strides that ate up the space—and the man shot her a look of absolute unbridled *displeasure,* so quickly blooming and gone again from his face that Mahit wasn't entirely sure she hadn't imagined it. He followed after, catching up in the space of four steps.

They coincided beneath the glittering curve of a bank of those triangular fighter ships. Three Seagrass bowed to the two Fleet representatives over her fingertips, a deep but not servile greeting, and Mahit imitated it, right down to the angle. She was a barbarian, but she was also supposed to be here, wasn't she? She was. Supposed to be surrounded by all the swarming might of the Teixcalaanli military, too huge and too complex to be seen all at once.

<Breathe,> murmured Yskandr, and Mahit did, one long breath as she straightened up.

"The envoy, and the linguist-diplomat," said the man, that same arch tenor voice that had emerged from the comm—this must be the adjutant, the *ikantlos*-prime Twenty Cicada, and wasn't *that* interesting, that a man who looked so very un-Teixcalaanli aside from the perfection of his uniform—unfashionably, *worryingly* thin, bald—this close Mahit could tell that he didn't even have eyebrows, he'd shaved them off, and Teixcalaanlitzlim were usually so *proud* of their hair, wore it long and braided or long and loose—and yet, here he was, second in command of the lead flagship of a Teixcalaanli imperial war.

What sort of yaotlek *has this man as her second?*

<An interesting one—look at his hands, Mahit, see the tattooing on the wrists? He's a homeostat-cultist.>

There were tattoos, just barely visible under the sleeves of his uniform. Green branching things, fractals. *A what cultist?*

<In a minute—pay attention, Mahit.>

The woman had not bowed. "I see that the Information Ministry has sent Nine Hibiscus one very young woman and one barbarian," she said, ice-clear. "A *fantastic* showing. I'm sure the two of you will be of profound help to her."

Twenty Cicada said, in murmured perfect formality, "The Fleet Captain Sixteen Moonrise of the Twenty-Fourth Legion," and gestured, as if he was displaying her as a curiosity. "Our honored guest today."

Sixteen Moonrise failed, with deliberation and malice aforethought, to match Twenty Cicada's utterly polite tense usage. "Let's get on with it, shall we, adjutant? Now you've got the spook and her pet all picked up, show me to what we all came here to see. The body."

"The body?" asked Three Seagrass, as if none of this byplay mattered at all.

"The body," Sixteen Moonrise said, "of the things you're here to talk to. How good is Information at raising the dead?"

"It isn't *my* specialty," Three Seagrass said.

"The *yaotlek* is expecting all of us in the medical bay morgue," Twenty Cicada confirmed, ignoring all insinuations of necromantic powers. "We do have a body to show you, Envoy; it doesn't talk, but it ought to show you something. Shall we?"

Ring composition, Mahit thought, *around we go. I've only just arrived, and it is time to see a corpse—at least it won't be your corpse, Yskandr.*

<A man can only die so often,> said Yskandr, which was hideously funny. Mahit had to work to keep her face still. It wouldn't be useful, just now, to make the Teixcalaanlitzlim think that the barbarian talked to invisible ghosts inside her head. Invisible, blackly hilarious ghosts. That wouldn't be useful at all.

This time there was no elevator down into the basement of the Judiciary, no knot of *ixplanatlim* in red huddled around a body, and no modest sheet covering the corpse. Mahit arrived in *this* morgue just as a medtech lifted two enormous lungs out of the splayed-open barrel of an alien rib cage and bore them off to be weighed and measured, tested for oxygenation, for cause of death, for whatever else Teixcalaanlitzlim tested alien body parts for. The rib cage, eviscerated of lungs, gaped like naked wings on either side of the alien's long neck. Behind it, looking down at it like she could read fortunes in its hollowness, was the *yaotlek.* Mahit knew her by her sunspear epaulets, but she was also quite precisely what Mahit had imagined a *yaotlek* to look like, if that *yaotlek* wasn't the unlamented One Lightning, he of the near-usurpation three months back.

Nine Hibiscus was large and sleek, solid muscle under a generous curve of fat: all hips and smooth outcurve of belly, broad shoulders and broad chest, thighs like the steady steel T-bars that constructed station decks. She looked like someone who could never be moved. She looked like it would take months of searching for an actress who perfectly suited when some Teixcalaanli holoproduction did an epic about this war; Teixcalaanli central casting couldn't have done better.

The first thing that came out of Mahit's mouth, seeing her, was "That alien did not make those sounds from that throat, *yaotlek*," as if she thought direct clarity would prove her usefulness beyond reproach of barbarism.

"Five points for drawing the obvious conclusion," said Nine Hibiscus, in a smooth, attentive low alto that reminded Mahit of nothing so much as Nineteen Adze's calm and terrifying precision. "Are you a xenobiologist, then?"

"The spook brought a pet," said the other Fleet Captain. Sixteen Moonrise. Nine Hibiscus looked at her with what Mahit suspected was deep dislike under multiple layers of propriety and projected authority.

"I am not a xenobiologist," Mahit said, deciding that Sixteen Moonrise's opinions of her were unlikely to become *less* hostile if she answered the *yaotlek*'s question. "I am Mahit Dzmare, the Ambassador to Teixcalaan from Lsel Station, and Lsel Station's diplomatic authority in this sector."

"The Ambassador is a linguist and translator," said Three Seagrass. "*I'm* the spook." She paused, entirely for effect. "We're here to help."

The adjutant, Twenty Cicada, made an entirely remarkable noise, like he'd drowned a laugh and swallowed its corpse. Three Seagrass either neglected to notice or neglected to care. She went on, saying, "It is exquisite to make your acquaintance, *yaotlek.* I, and the Information Ministry, are grateful for the opportunity to be of service in this first-contact scenario. What a fascinating throat this alien has."

"And yet," said the *yaotlek,* "your linguist-translator-ambassador is entirely sure that it cannot have made the sounds on our transmission. However fascinating it may be. Care to explain? For my edification, and for the Fleet Captain Sixteen Moonrise, of course." When she looked at Sixteen Moonrise, she smiled enough to show a tiny flash of teeth, and Mahit's mouth went metallic and dry at the sense of *threat.* A Teixcalaanli general who would bare her teeth while smiling. All energy, all danger.

<She's *very* good,> Yskandr murmured, and Mahit agreed with him. Nine Hibiscus was exquisitely in command, even when surprised, as she had clearly been surprised by Sixteen Moonrise. Mahit suspected she hadn't even known the Fleet Captain was on board her flagship until she'd walked into this makeshift morgue with Mahit and Three Seagrass.

—who was in the middle of saying, serene and direct, "After extensive audio analysis of the samples you sent to the Ministry of Information, we believe that the sounds on the transmission are tonal markers, not specific speech—and unless this alien has got vocal cords made of synthesizers and a theremin, it can't have made them by itself."

"You could dissect it and find out, though," Mahit added. "To be certain that it isn't capable of producing sound via oscillating magnetic fields."

"You've dissected the rest," added Sixteen Moonrise. "You might as well look at its neck. Since I'm here, I'll stay and watch. It's my soldiers who are being killed by these things most imminently, after all."

"If I'd known you were on board the *Weight for the Wheel,* Fleet Captain," said Twenty Cicada silkily, "more than two minutes before you met me in the hangar bay, I would have made sure you also were invited to the autopsy."

Mahit couldn't turn around to see Sixteen Moonrise's reaction, and having it occur behind her made her feel peculiarly exposed, her skin prickling with the crawling sensation
of being watched, even if she wasn't at all the focus of the
watcher. She wanted to see. This tangle of Fleet Captains
was—significant, important; if she and Three Seagrass were
going to be useful enough to survive this war, she had to understand it.

<You're still thinking like we're trying to get away from
Councilor Amnardbat,> Yskandr whispered to her. <Useful
enough to survive this war? It's not that bad. Yet.>

Yet, Mahit thought. *But it's politics, and I need to understand—*

<The shape of it. Who wants Information here, and who
doesn't.> And then Yskandr slipped away from her, a banked
fire just out of reach, like some fish streaking silver-sided into
the shadows of the hydroponic tanks.

Sixteen Moonrise, whatever her expression, was saying,
"Swarm, I had always believed better of you—*Porcelain Fragment
Scorched* docked four hours back, and I have been cooling my
heels all unknown to the adjutant of our *yaotlek?*"

Twenty Cicada—*Swarm.* Mahit remembered what Yskandr
had said to her, when she'd caught sight of his tattoos. *Homeostat-
cultist.* With the name of an insect. A *pervasive* insect. Teixcalaanlitzlim weren't supposed to have names which were animals, at
all. Did insects not qualify as animals? She'd always assumed
they did.

Nine Hibiscus watched the squabble with that same threatening impassiveness that seemed to be endemic to her, and then
set her hands down on the metal autopsy table heavily enough
to quell any further sniping. One on either side of the alien's
head, as if she could crush it between her palms. "Stay, Sixteen
Moonrise. See the inside of our enemy. The medtech will fill
you in on what you've missed. Now. *You*—" She pointed at Three
Seagrass with her chin. "I want to know if either you or your
barbarian linguist can talk *back* with these tonal markers you say

you've identified. That's the whole point of you. Figure out how to talk to these things before I decide they're not worth the trouble of talking to."

"What's your broadcast system like?" Three Seagrass asked, bright and effervescent, as if this would be no trouble at all. Mahit knew better. They'd barely started interpreting the sounds on the transmission, spent half of their interpretation time too nauseated to think, breathing in gasps against the wrongness of those sounds. They might be able to say something to the aliens, but it was almost certainly going to be a wrong thing, a half-formed and misshapen utterance, distorted by human tongues and human minds.

<But it might draw them in close,> Yskandr murmured, and she thought, *Bait*.

Just like Darj Tarats had used Lsel as bait for Teixcalaan.

Just as she herself was bait now—for Three Seagrass, for this Fleet. If she acted as Tarats's saboteur. She didn't know how she *could*. She didn't—

<You don't want to.>

I don't want to be bad at my job on purpose, Mahit thought, a vicious little stab of a phrase, and felt Yskandr's answering query of *Oh? And your job is first-contact protocols now?* as a stabbing pain from elbows to fourth fingers and her own voice in her own head. They were so very close now. And still the places they were misaligned bloomed into pain.

"We can prepare a transmission to be intercepted on the frequency they used," said Nine Hibiscus to Three Seagrass. "Once you have a transmission to send. Bring it to me first. Twenty Cicada will show you to your quarters and to the communications workroom."

That was some sort of a dismissal. The next gesture the *yaotlek* made, calling the medtech in his red scrubs over and Sixteen Moonrise to stand by her side and watch, was another. Mahit bowed deep over her fingertips, and found herself distressed all

over again by the comfort of knowing that gesture was appropriate again, here. At how easily she'd been scooped up out of
the Station, slipped easily into the politics and pleasures and
poisons of Teixcalaan. At how much she wanted to be useful,
and how much she hated that wanting.

The throat of the alien peeled open under her medtech's scalpel like a perfectly ripe fruit. Inside Nine Hibiscus could see
the usual sort of muscles, still sluggishly oozing red. Oxygen-
ated blood. It hadn't been dead very *long,* this alien, and wasn't
that disturbing, if she thought about it too deeply—this thing had
been alive, and hungry, and acting with its own inexplicable intelligence, less than half a day ago, and if it wasn't cut open like this,
it could have been *hiding,* pretending, lying in wait to spring—

Sixteen Moonrise, persistent at her left elbow, leaned in and
peered at the flash of the scalpel blade as it sliced the muscle free
and revealed something that looked like a trachea, ribbed and
rubbery. "It looks like a normal throat," she said, and Nine Hibiscus wondered how many throats her fellow Fleet Captain had
dissected personally.

"Open it. At the top, where the larynx should be," Nine Hibiscus said, and her medtech did.

There were laryngic membranes, all right. A large but—from
what she could remember from basic anatomy, aeons ago at the
Fleet academy in her first year—standard sort of arrangement.
Folds of alien flesh at the top of the alien trachea, all very regular and mammalian-standard: closeable to keep food out of
the airway, capable of vibrating to produce sound when air was
forced through them. Nothing that looked like it could produce
those machine-screaming resonant noises from the intercepted
recording.

Sixteen Moonrise said, "Go lower. Where the trachea
branches into the lungs. It has lungs, right?"

The lungs were resting in metal basins across the surgery-cum-autopsy room, on a shelf. Nine Hibiscus pointed at them. "It *had* lungs. Two of them."

Whatever political game Sixteen Moonrise was playing, coming onto her flagship and invading her medical labs, it seemed to have paled before the possibility of having *come up with a good idea*. Nine Hibiscus wondered if she'd aimed for a medical career before she'd joined the Fleet, or was just the sort of ghoul who watched autopsies and studied the inner workings of bodies for her own amusement. "Go lower," she repeated, and her eyes were wide in a satisfied grin.

Nine Hibiscus nodded to her medtech, and he did as Sixteen Moonrise was suggesting, splitting the tube of the trachea open so it lay nearly flat, a ridged strip of stiff flesh. Where it began to divide, there was something—a bony structure like another voice box, surrounded by what looked like a deflated balloon connected to a whole series of muscles Nine Hibiscus definitely did *not* remember from basic anatomy.

"A *syrinx*," said Sixteen Moonrise, with profound satisfaction. "Birds have them. Your spook and her pet are wrong, *yaotlek*—this alien can make all sorts of horrible noises with that thing."

The balloon around it must be the part that vibrated, Nine Hibiscus thought, and the muscles were what held it at appropriate levels of tension. With a certain delicious squeamishness, she reached into the alien's throat and stretched the membrane between her fingertips. It was strong and thick. Her fingertips were red.

If this had been her kill, she'd have smeared the blood on her forehead in victory. But she didn't deserve that yet.

"Cut it out," she directed the medtech. "With as many of the muscles as you can keep. And preserve it. I suspect my spook and her pet"—that, for Sixteen Moonrise's benefit, an acknowledgment, a sidewise appreciation of the other Fleet Captain's skill at predicting autopsy results—"might want to use it to make some of those noises themselves."

"So you *are* trusting the Information agent," said Sixteen Moonrise. They'd come away from the table to let the medtech do his work. Nine Hibiscus hadn't washed her hands yet. There was something satisfying about having *touched* the alien and not being dead, or dissolving. Some small part of the mystery of them undone. They died. They died and bled and cooled and were peculiar but entirely understandable as collections of organs. Just meat, like any other dead thing.

"Why shouldn't I?" she asked Sixteen Moonrise. "And if you tell me *because she's a spook,* I will have to revise your intelligence downward, and that would be a shame. Specifics, Fleet Captain."

Sixteen Moonrise refused to bristle, which Nine Hibiscus gave her some credit for. She said, "You have no idea who she is or where her loyalties lie, except perhaps *to Teixcalaan.* She's not Fleet. This,"—she gestured at the alien, the medical bay, the whole *situation*—"is Fleet work. I never imagined the hero of Kauraan would want to bring in outsiders to prosecute a war. With all due respect, *yaotlek.*"

"I'm not a hero," Nine Hibiscus found herself saying. "I'm a soldier. And Kauraan was won by soldiers, using the best possible intelligence I could procure. I don't deny my people resources, Fleet Captain. I *provide* them. The Information agent will get us what we lack, without exposing my people—or yours, or Forty Oxide's, or anyone's—to these aliens any more than is strictly necessary."

"The Fleet has an intelligence service," said Sixteen Moonrise, and left it there, hanging between them like a challenge. *Why haven't you gone to the Third Palm, O yaotlek, if you are so concerned with providing adequate resources?* She didn't need to say it. Nine Hibiscus could hear it very well in the silence of the room, interrupted only by the occasional squelch of alien fluids coming from the medtech at work behind them.

"We don't do first contact," she said, as if that was an adequate answer. "Information does. And there's only *one* spook, Sixteen Moonrise. Far more controllable than a squadron of Third Palmers."

A flicker of some emotion behind those pale eyes. Nine Hibiscus wondered if she'd given Sixteen Moonrise too much information about her own distaste for the Fleet's intelligencers. That would only be a *true* problem if the Fleet Captain of the Twenty-Fourth was *herself* a Third Palmer, or had been, before she became an officer—she *had* to check her public records. Or have Swarm do it. But they'd been so busy.

"One spook and one barbarian," said Sixteen Moonrise, eventually. "A spook I could understand. One with an agenda that includes foreigners who were involved with *starting* this war? That, *yaotlek*, disturbs me. She's from Lsel Station. Lsel Station is the little independent entity that told us about these aliens in the first place—"

"And brought down One Lightning, yes," Nine Hibiscus said.

"One Lightning, and Minister Nine Propulsion along with him."

Minister Nine Propulsion, Nine Hibiscus's patron and mentor, her political protection. Sixteen Moonrise was implying that Nine Propulsion hadn't *retired*—but that she'd been implicated in the coup, been pushed out and replaced. "I'm sure the former Minister is enjoying her retirement," Nine Hibiscus said. It was so difficult to imagine Nine Propulsion doing something like getting involved in an attempted usurpation. She'd always been so careful, a watchful eye in the City, steady enough that Nine Hibiscus had felt she could always take appropriate risks and be backed up.

"*Retirement* is an interesting way to put it," said Sixteen Moonrise. "Half the Ministry turned over, *yaotlek*, that's not *retirements*." That was a goad. She was trying to get Nine Hibiscus to complain about the new Emperor, about the new Minister of

War, Three Azimuth, the very people who had given her this command—

(Who had sent her out here to defeat an impossible force with only one six of legions, half of which had signed on to Sixteen Moonrise's little letter of insubordination. Which suggested—unpleasantly—that Sixteen Moonrise was *right*, and she was being punished for being Nine Propulsion's protégé, and Nine Propulsion *had* been in on the attempted usurpation, after all—)

And if she said any of that, she'd be playing into whatever political game Sixteen Moonrise had brought with her from the Ministry to the front lines. She'd be admitting that her own loyalties might not be to the Empire, or even the Ministry of War. She refused to be entrapped like this. "A new Emperor has new military priorities. And Three Azimuth deserved the promotion. To tell you the truth, Fleet Captain, I hope I do as well as Nine Propulsion has, when my time in the front lines is done."

Let Sixteen Moonrise think she hadn't picked up the insinuation of Nine Propulsion's disloyalty. Let her think she was simpler than she was.

"With your record, I can't imagine otherwise," Sixteen Moonrise said, which was vicious. Nine Hibiscus could hate her. If she didn't need her and her Twenty-Fourth Legion to win this war, she could hate her quite a lot.

"That's a lovely thing to say," she told her, and smiled with the edges of her teeth showing.

Sixteen Moonrise matched her: that sliver of tooth-bone like a threat. "What I'm trying to convey, *yaotlek*, Ministers all aside, is that I don't trust anything that came from Lsel Station. And attached to a spook just makes it worse."

There was some agenda here, a deeper and more unpleasant one than a rivalry between Fleet Captains. Sixteen Moonrise wanted the Third Palm involved with this war. She wanted it very, very much. And that meant someone in the Ministry or the rest of the palace wanted political-officer attention on what Nine Hibiscus was doing.

"I do appreciate your candid opinion, Fleet Captain," she said. "And be assured, I will keep as many eyes on the spook as are necessary. Let's see what sort of work she does for us. I'll reserve my judgment."

"As you like," Sixteen Moonrise said. "I believe your tech has extracted the syrinx, *yaotlek*. Fill it full of air and see if it screams for you before you let the spook have it."

And with that, she saluted, spun on her heel, and left Nine Hibiscus alone with the dismembered corpse of their enemy, which had begun to stink of decomposition.

The adjutant Twenty Cicada did not escort Three Seagrass and Mahit to whatever quarters were prepared for them. Instead he mentioned, in an offhand fashion Three Seagrass recognized intimately—the precise air of a person who had to deal with vastly more complex logistics-management problems than this present one at *least* four times a day—that while their quarters were reconfigured for *two* beds instead of one, the pair of them could get straight to work.

"Envoy," he said, as they followed him through the busy, fine-kept corridors of the *Weight for the Wheel,* being watched with unabashed curiosity by all sorts of Fleet personnel, "your cloudhook should have a map of the ship now that you're aboard. You and Ambassador Dzmare have the communications work-room until twenty-two hundred hours—and the *yaotlek* will want some sort of result at that point." He glanced back over his shoulder with a sharp smile, a narrow movement of the eyes and the corners of the mouth. Smiling looked odd on a person who lacked eyebrows and hair. Three Seagrass had never inter-acted with a person who took homeostasis-practice so *seriously;* most people with an unusual religion were less pointed about

reminding you of it. She was . . . interested, she decided. Interested in how this man had come to his high place of power,
while looking ever so not-quite-civilized. But eyebrows or none,
Three Seagrass suspected Twenty Cicada knew his master Nine
Hibiscus well enough to have meant what he said: the *yaotlek*
would want a report at the end of the evening shift, no matter
how late that shift ended or how well matched it was with the
yaotlek's own sleeping schedule.

"She'll have it," Three Seagrass said, and bowed *very* deeply
when Twenty Cicada took this promise as sufficient collateral to
nod to the both of them and disappear off at an angle on some
business of his own—not an errand boy, that one. Not someone who usually escorted stray Information agents around the
ship. Not that an adjutant would be—

And oh, there was the map, gleaming in tracery over her
cloudhook. Four decks up, toward the bow. Easy enough.

"Follow me," she said to Mahit, who was being *very* quiet. Un-
usually so, especially after she'd been all flashfire forwardness
in the medbay. Had Fleet Captain Sixteen Moonrise spooked
her? Three Seagrass didn't remember Mahit spooking easily.
But spooked or not, she followed, close at Three Seagrass's left
shoulder, their habitual positions all reversed. The ship map
overlaid on the right side of her vision was easy to follow—
someone, probably Twenty Cicada, had highlighted their
destination with a small glowing star—and they moved up
three levels of the enormous flagship without incident. On
the fourth, though—oh, *there* was the security-conscious Fleet
that Three Seagrass had always been taught about in Information briefings.

It came in the person of a serenely massive Fleet soldier, his
hair in a neat queue, his energy pistol—all right, energy *pistols,*
plural—holstered with elegant threat at each hip, who barred
the door that Three Seagrass's map required them to pass
through on their way to the communications workroom. This

soldier held out a hand, palm flat and authoritative, and Three
Seagrass lurched to a stop, with Mahit just behind her.

"You are both out of uniform," said the soldier. "Her especially." He indicated Mahit with his chin. "What is your business
on this deck?"

"I am the envoy Three Seagrass, seconded here by the
Information Ministry," said Three Seagrass, with some
annoyance—wasn't her envoy's suit uniform uniform *enough*?
But perhaps this soldier had never seen one. "And this is Ambassador Mahit Dzmare. Do check your manifests, sir, we're
on our way to the communications workroom on the *yaotlek*'s
orders."

The soldier blinked through some search function on his
cloudhook, found whatever he was looking for, and then made
her and Mahit wait. She could feel Mahit's nervous energy like
a thrumming power generator at her side, and yet her barbarian continued *not saying anything*. After an interminable fifteen
seconds, the soldier pressed his fingertips together in the most
cursory of acknowledgments, and waved them through. "To the
left, Envoy. Ambassador," he said, as if there had been absolutely
no reason to stop them.

It happened again approximately two hundred feet down the
corridor, the instant they'd passed out of visual view of one
soldier and into the purview of the next. Three Seagrass was
unpleasantly reminded of the Sunlit of her childhood, before
the algorithmic reform, back when they would ask you the
same questions if you'd switched *jurisdictions*, no matter how
many jurisdictions you passed through. This soldier was shorter,
brisker, and visibly horrified at Mahit's lack of propriety: her
complaint about *you are both out of uniform* was accompanied by
an encompassing hand gesture, shoulder to foot, as if to suggest,
*What is a nice envoy like you doing with a jacket-and-trouser set like
that?*

Three Seagrass expected Mahit to take point on this one, to
give the explanation of who they were as confidently as she'd

introduced herself to the *yaotlek* in the medical bay. But she *didn't*. She raised her eyebrows at Three Seagrass until Three Seagrass repeated what she'd told the last soldier, suffered through the waiting as the soldier consulted her cloudhook, and then breezily waved them onward.

The third time, at the door of the communications workroom itself, was just *insulting*. The previous impediment was *still in view,* and doing absolutely nothing about informing her compatriot that the two people standing in front of her had reasonable and assigned business behind the door she was guarding so assiduously.

"You're—" the soldier began.

"Out of uniform, yes," Mahit snapped, at last—snapped with a fluid and vicious intonation Three Seagrass didn't remember her using back in the palace. Something in the tone, the deep and bored *dismissal* of the problem at hand.

I wonder what Yskandr Aghavn sounded like when he was pissed off, she thought, and didn't like thinking it.

"If you would *check your records,*" she added, before Mahit could say anything else.

"There's no need to be so abrupt, Envoy," said the soldier, which didn't help: if this one knew who she and Mahit were, why under every single bleeding star wasn't she letting them into the workroom?

"We have orders to be inside that workroom," Mahit said, with that same silky viciousness, her Teixcalaanli note-perfect. "Orders from your *yaotlek.* For the safety of the Fleet and the apt and skillful prosecution of this war."

She was, Three Seagrass realized, quoting one of the Reclamation Songs—"Song #16," one of the more obscure ones because it was so *long* and thus difficult to memorize. *The apt and skillful prosecution of this war.* Fifteen perfect Teixcalaanli syllables, with a caesura in the center. Fuck but it was a continuous heartbreak that Mahit Dzmare had been born a barbarian—

But would she have liked her as well, if she hadn't been?

The soldier acting as doorkeep took her sweet time checking her records, though Three Seagrass thought she saw a flush on her dark cheeks—embarrassment, or even shame, to be so effortlessly put in her place by a barbarian. Mahit should be proud of herself.

She was about to say so, even—they were finally inside, with a delicious profusion of audiovisual and holorecording equipment arrayed like a bouquet of flowers for their use, and the door shut quite firmly against the doorkeepers outside—but Mahit went straight for the audioplay controls. She had the infofiche stick with the intercepted alien noises on it in her hands, and Three Seagrass absolutely didn't have time to tell her that this particular audioplay looked like it was preset to full volume repeater before she broke it open and the familiar, completely hideous noises flooded the room—from every direction. The repeater was surround-sound, there were speakers in every wall, the horrible static-singing *sounds* were hitting her from every angle instead of just one—

They were getting into her *bones,* Three Seagrass thought, right before she threw up. The noises were getting into her bones and would sing in there forever, and she was going to die of nausea—

It stopped. Three Seagrass retched again, helplessly (how brilliant; the first thing the envoy does is vomit on the floor of the flagship, fantastic work on her part), and waited for the waves of queasiness to ease back.

"—sorry," Mahit said, thinly. Three Seagrass looked up. Ah. At least she wasn't the only one to have vomited on the floor. But Mahit had found the off switch for the audioplay. Two and a half minutes of that—the length of the recording—would have left the both of them incapacitated, not just embarrassed.

". . . We forgot the bin liners," she managed, and Mahit looked as if she would laugh if it was something her innards found advisable.

Instead, she swiped the back of her hand across her mouth, grimaced, and said, "That was worse than when we listened to it on the shuttle. *Much* worse."

"That audioplay is set to repeater. All input is retransmitted through every speaker in every wall in here."

Mahit considered this information, coiled and still, evaluating it—like she was *tasting* it, or maybe she was only tasting the sourness of her own mouth, like Three Seagrass was. Then she said, "We need a live alien. Not a corpse."

"I don't disagree, but—what makes you bring that up just *now*?"

"I think," Mahit said, "that if a whole lot of them make those noises in a circle—like the speakers did—it amplifies. A reinforcing sound wave. Infrasound, not just what we can hear. I wonder if they know it makes us ill."

"I suspect they do," Three Seagrass said, as dryly as she could manage while looking around for *some* sort of cloth to wipe up or at least cover two persons' worth of sick. "They've met a lot more live *us* than we have live *them*. Everybody on Peloa-2, for example."

"All the more reason we need a live one," said Mahit. "The one in the medbay was a mammal. Even if they're scavenger mammals, weren't we the same, a long time ago? And they have to be talking in more ways than just *this*, this noise—"

"Some way we can't hear. A sign language, or—pheromones, or—" There were a lot of cabinets in this room, and *none* of them had anything absorbent in them—just banks of electronics.

"Or structural skin coloration that shifts in patterns, I don't know. Anything, really. Probably not pheromones, pheromones would be more tonal markers, for mammals. I think. Comparative zoology is not my specialty."

"All right. A live one. Maybe we can make this message good enough, even if it's just tone-shrieking into the void, that they'll send over someone we can see." Three Seagrass opened another cabinet, and shut it again in frustration. "Give me your jacket," she said.

"Why?"

Three Seagrass sighed. Mahit was *brilliant,* and was solving this entire puzzle just like she'd hoped she would, and yet she couldn't recognize why Three Seagrass needed something made out of *cloth.* "To clean up with, unless you feel like working surrounded by un-bin-linered stomach contents?"

"Why *my* jacket?" Mahit said.

"Because *mine* is a uniform, which at least *some* of the Fleet on this enormous ship recognize as a uniform, and yours is a very nice and very absorbent piece of cloth. We should get you a uniform yourself, really. I'm sure they have some without rank signs, or I can try to adjust one of mine to fit you if you'd rather look like Information. It'll save us time later, in the hallways . . ."

She trailed off at Mahit's expression, which was as complicatedly hurt as it might have been if Three Seagrass had hit her across the face.

"I'm not a Fleet member," said Mahit, too evenly, too sharply. "Nor am I a special envoy of the Information Ministry."

"If you're worried about insubordination for wearing a Teixcalaanli uniform, I'll take responsibility?" Three Seagrass tried, puzzled as to the severity of Mahit's reaction. All right, she was being slightly awful about the jacket, she wouldn't have wanted someone to suggest *her* jacket be used as a rag—

"Of course you'd take responsibility," said Mahit. "That's always been your job with me, hasn't it? Opening doors and taking responsibility and being an *exact legal equivalent* for your barbarian. Since the very beginning."

"I didn't mean that," Three Seagrass said, shocked. She hadn't. It was a stupid, flippant suggestion, that was all, not some kind of—assumption that Mahit couldn't decide for herself what she should do. "*Stars,* Mahit, we'll use my jacket instead, forget it."

She shrugged out of one sleeve, was halfway through the

next, apologetically turned away, when Mahit said, as narrow and distantly cold as Three Seagrass had ever heard her: "You didn't mean it. But you *said* it, Reed."

Her nickname, polished and sharpened to wound. In that mouth, which had not known to say it when Twelve Azalea had still been alive.

She snapped, "You *think* I said that, because you can't hear anything but one of us saying *you aren't a Teixcalaanlitzlim* whenever we speak to you." Snapped, and regretted snapping, and at the same time felt that brutal and brittle glee she always had at getting right down to the meat of some argument, some *problem,* and sinking in her teeth, ready to tear.

"Don't you?" asked Mahit. "Say that." She was very still, very calm. Three Seagrass thought of snakes, of spiders, of all the creatures that stung when threatened. "You remind me I'm a barbarian all the time. Now, in the City before—and not just you, Three Seagrass, the soldiers in the corridors too, but at least they have the honesty not to pretend that I'm anything *but* what Teixcalaan thinks I am. You? You want to give me *uniforms* and make me *useful* and have a clever almost-human barbarian to show off on your arm—you decide that you want me and here I am, you decide it'd be useful if your barbarian exercised diplomatic authority and so I do, you decide I need a uniform so we don't get stopped in corridors and you don't think about what it'd look like if you dressed me up like a toy Teixcalaanlitzlim—"

"I asked," Three Seagrass said, and she *had* asked, hadn't she? She'd asked every time. She was almost sure she'd asked, she'd never given Mahit *orders,* she wouldn't, the idea was absurd. But Mahit ignored her and kept *going,* like words were an infection she was squeezing from a wound.

"And you'd have liked it if I'd stayed with you in the palace, wouldn't you have? You could've had me all this time to amuse you and not had to come all the way to a *war*—"

Before she could stop herself, Three Seagrass said, "Would

that have been so awful? You staying with me." Distantly, she thought it'd be absolutely terrible if she started crying. She'd never cried in arguments. Not since she had grown big enough to leave the crèche. Mahit did all sorts of things to her that she'd never expected, made her feel all sorts of new and complicated kinds of *everything,* including—apparently—hurt and miserable. All she'd done was suggest that a *uniform* might make things simpler, and now they were going to have this fight, which felt awful and unfixable and like Mahit had been saving it up, waiting for the inevitable point where she couldn't stand Three Seagrass any longer and did *this* to whatever it was they had between them.

"No," said Mahit. "It wouldn't have been terrible to stay with you. Which is why I *didn't.*"

"That makes no sense."

Mahit had sat herself down at the central conference table, and now she put her face in her palms and hid her eyes from Three Seagrass. The last time they'd been around a conference room table, they'd stopped a usurpation with poetry. Now they couldn't even write a *message* together, because they were having the most useless, incomprehensible, horrible argument Three Seagrass could remember having since her ex-girlfriend Nine Arch had broken up with her in the middle of exams during their second year of *asekreta* training.

"It *doesn't* make sense," Three Seagrass said again, louder. "It doesn't. I'm sorry about the uniforms, and the jacket, and I won't mention it again, but you aren't being—"

"Explicable? Understandable? *Civilized?*"

"Fuck," said Three Seagrass, hearing as she said it how her voice had gone narrow and high, uncontrolled. "If you didn't want to come with me here, you didn't *have to.*"

Mahit took her hands down and looked Three Seagrass straight in the face. It felt like her gaze had weight, weight and edges, a sudden revealed landscape of places to cut oneself open on. Again Three Seagrass found herself wondering what of this person was Mahit Dzmare and what was Yskandr Aghavn, and if all the ruinous confusion between them now was born of Mahit's precious imago-technology—or if she'd *never* understood her. Not really. Only pretended to.

(Only pretended, like they were pretending they understood something of these aliens and their incomprehensible language that hurt humans to hear.)

Three Seagrass dropped her eyes first.

Mahit said, "Reed," softly, and Three Seagrass looked up again, heliotropic, compelled.

"Yes?" she asked.

"When you figure out why I *did* have to come with you, we can talk again."

". . . again, *at all*?" There was something horrible in the idea: that she'd gone so far wrong that she wouldn't even have a chance to keep going, keep trying. That there was some flaw in everything that was invisible to her. (She *didn't know why* Mahit couldn't have stayed on Lsel. Politics, of course, but there were other avenues than this mad gambit of a trip to the edge of a war to get out of *politics*. Mahit hadn't told her why. She *knew* she hadn't told her why, she'd avoided telling her quite deliberately, and now she was somehow supposed to figure it out—)

"We have work to do," said Mahit, which wasn't an answer at all. "We need to get one of these things to think this Fleet is worth talking to."

They did have work to do. And less than six hours until the *yaotlek* would want that work. And yet Three Seagrass felt like she couldn't think through the urge to cry, or grab Mahit by the arm and *shake* her until she explained. Until she stopped being—

Oh, say it, Reed. To yourself if no one else.

Uncivilized. Refusing to participate, like an animal or a child. The silence between them dragged onward, endless and misshapen, as if gravity was off-kilter, the great engines of *Weight for the Wheel* shifted out of true, the universe undoing itself from its expected course. The room smelled of acidic vomit. Three Seagrass didn't know what to say. Everything she'd said so far had made things worse.

She sat down at the table, two chairs away from where Mahit was. It was better than her other option, which was storming out of the room. She *needed* Mahit. And she needed to do the job she'd set herself when the request for a special envoy came in to the Information Ministry. She should never have been allowed to be here; almost everything about her being here was unauthorized. Aside from the fact that she was very, very good and that she'd found the smartest person she knew to help her with the linguistics and the culture shock of first contact, and that *technically* she had the requisite rank in the Ministry. But if she didn't manage it—

If she didn't manage it, she wouldn't have a career. Also, probably, a whole lot of Teixcalaanlitzlim would die at the hands of these invaders, considering what they'd done on Peloa-2 and how the *yaotlek* was clearly having political problems with one of her Fleet Captains. Of which she had only five, hardly enough to prevent an alien attack force from spilling through the jumpgate and into Teixcalaanli space *proper*. A *lot* of dead people, if Three Seagrass didn't figure out how to talk to aliens. Which was more important than her career. If less immediately stomach-churning.

And here was Mahit, waiting for her, or waiting for—something. The gulf of silence felt uncrossable.

She crossed it anyway. "Start with the third sound," she said. "The one they make when they're approached too closely. And combine it with—oh, the last one, the one that they made when they were chasing *Knifepoint*. I think that's a victory sound."

"*Approach-danger* plus *hurrah-we-win*," Mahit said, dry as dust. "Could be worse. I hope we're right about *hurrah-we-win*, otherwise we're saying something like *approach-danger* and *we're-going-to-chase-you.*"

"Do you have a better idea?" asked Three Seagrass, and was more gratified than she could bear to think about when Mahit nodded, and they began to get to work in earnest.

CHAPTER
NINE

You'd like him. You'd be proud of him. And every time I see his face I think of yours, and your voice, and what I might have had to guide me. And every time I think of your voice I think of the monstrous creature that might have whispered to me with it— and if I had that creature I would have your ghost, and listen to it—so all in all I suspect I have done right, and my longings are my own to bear. But that's being the Illuminate Majesty, isn't it? You always said so. I wish you'd believed it.

> —the private notes of Her Brilliance the Emperor
> Nineteen Adze, undated, locked, and encrypted

* * *

This is a terrible idea. What animal doesn't come back from a long hunt hungry for scraps? But you don't want to hear pretty Teixcalaanli rhetoric, do you. You want something direct? How about this: every Fleet officer I've ever met would get greedy enough to take a little detour into Station-conquering if they were bored enough and had the opportunity of legal proximity. Fuck off about this and give me another year to work. You'll get your precious isolation.

> —from a letter written by Ambassador Yskandr Aghavn to
> Darj Tarats, Councilor for the Miners, received on Lsel
> Station 101.2.11–6D (Teixcalaanli reckoning)

EIGHT Antidote came into the Ministry of War through the front door, like he was supposed to be there. Like he'd won the right to be there, which he guessed he had. Three Azimuth had told him to come, *and* Her Brilliance had—well, she'd given him the strange charge of the spearpoint in the middle of the night. The spearpoint and the command: *Find out if Three Azimuth means to win this war.* He was still chewing that over, the idea of it like a raw place in his mouth where a baby tooth had fallen out and a new one hadn't come in yet. Whatever it meant, though, he had double permission to come in the front way instead of from the tunnels. (He'd hidden the spearpoint in the drawer where he kept his shirts, a bright heavy secret, nestled amongst the greys and the golds and the reds.)

Eleven Laurel was waiting for him just inside. Eight Antidote abruptly remembered that he hadn't even *touched* his problem set puzzle, and wondered if there was time to turn around and pretend he had ended up here by accident. There wasn't, and anyway, running off was what a kid would do, so he wouldn't.

"Hello, Undersecretary," he said, and bowed over his fingertips, inclined just *so* far, like he was greeting an equal. It felt squirmy and wrong and *great,* to presuppose that he and the Third Undersecretary of the Ministry of War, his teacher and his elder by fifty years at least, was someone he didn't have to bow very far to.

"Cure," said Eleven Laurel, warm and *pleased* with him. Eight Antidote was blushing by the time he stood up. He hated being so obvious. He shouldn't be this obvious. "I think you will enjoy today," the Undersecretary went on. "We have just received some intelligence from the Twenty-Fourth Legion, and the Minister of War thinks you, my young friend, ought to get to see it analyzed."

"I'd like that a very great deal," Eight Antidote said, trying to remember who was in charge of the Twenty-Fourth Legion. Not *yaotlek* Nine Hibiscus—it had been the *Tenth* at Kauraan, the Tenth was the dangerously loyal one—but another woman, with an astronomical aspect to the noun half of her name. He'd done just one exercise with the Twenty-Fourth as part of a puzzle,

a long time ago, back at the very beginning of when Eleven
Laurel was teaching him. But he knew the Twenty-Fourth was
one of Nine Hibiscus's *yaotlek's* six, her complement of legions
to work with on the edge of the battlefront.

"Not from the Tenth?" he asked, following Eleven Laurel
through the warren of the Ministry of War. "That's interesting."

"A good observation, Cure," said Eleven Laurel. "No, our
intelligence is straight from Fleet Captain Sixteen Moonrise,
on fast-courier relay through the jumpgates. She *very* much
wanted the Ministry to have this information right away. I'm
extremely curious myself as to what it is she wants to show us."

Sixteen Moonrise. Eight Antidote had to remember the name
this time; at least he'd gotten the astronomical part right. But
it'd be much easier to remember her name now that she wasn't
a collection of holographs on a strategy table and instead a Fleet
Captain who went above, or *around,* her *yaotlek's* command in
order to send intelligence to War back in the City.

For the first time, Eight Antidote wondered if Nine Hibiscus
knew that there were elements in the Ministry that had sent her
to war hoping she was going to die in it. He figured she *must.*
She wasn't stupid. No one who could command loyalty like that
was stupid. They couldn't be. He was pretty sure. But maybe
she was the kind of person who thought that loyalty protected
her, that since all her soldiers loved her so very well, and she
loved the Empire (she must, if Nineteen Adze had made her
yaotlek), then the Ministry of War would love her and protect
her as well.

That seemed like the kind of mistake a person who relied on
loyalty would make. He'd have to remember not to make it,
when he was Emperor. Loyalty wasn't transitive. It didn't move
up and down the chain of command smoothly. It could get cut
off, or rerouted. Especially if someone else powerful was inter-
vening in the movement of *information,* like Fleet Captain Sixteen Moonrise was right now.

Eleven Laurel didn't take him to one of the strategy rooms

this time. They went up an elevator in the center of the Palms instead, and through a series of very secure checkpoints staffed with Fleet soldiers, into what must have been Minister Three Azimuth's very own office. It was covered in star-charts: beautiful ones on the walls, artist's renderings of Teixcalaanli space, with pride of place behind the Minister's desk taken by a vast and glimmering mosaic in a frame, dark crystal slices and golden pinpoint stars made out of glass pieces smaller than Eight Antidote's littlest fingernail. It was a famous piece: *The World,* it was called, or sometimes just *Teixcalaan,* a map of everywhere the Empire had touched as of two hundred years ago when it was made by the artisan Eighteen Coral. Eight Antidote had seen it in holo, and on infofiche, but never before in person.

It lived behind the desk of the Minister of War. Of course he'd never seen it in person.

There were maps *everywhere,* though. On the large table in front of that desk, some holographic and some paper ones too—on the desk itself, in piles—pinned to the walls next to and overlapping the famous and artistic renderings.

Minister Three Azimuth sat amongst her cartography like a bird in a well-lined nest, her cloudhook glowing silver-white and translucent over the wreckage of her melted ear, her hair a smooth dark cap. Eight Antidote swallowed, his throat feeling suddenly thick, and quickly looked away from her to the other Ministry officials seated around the table to her right and left. There was Undersecretary Seven Aster of the Second Palm, the master of supply chains, and his staff, immediately recognizable by how the hands in their shoulder patches had their fingers pointing to the left; next to him was Twenty-Two Thread, the Fifth Palm, the armaments chief, who had come to give a presentation on new sorts of spaceship engines to Eight Antidote's ancestor-the-Emperor two years ago. Eight Antidote had fallen asleep while she was talking. But he'd been a little kid then. He wouldn't do that kind of thing now.

Eleven Laurel's own staff were waiting for him on the other

side of the table; two women Eight Antidote didn't know, both wearing patches figured with downward-pointing hands for the Third Palm, on their shoulders next to their rank sigils. And two empty chairs. One for Eleven Laurel—and one for him. He sat down. Like he belonged. Like he wasn't eleven years old.

At the end of the table, opposite the Minister, was an empty space where the Emperor would have gone, if she'd been invited. Presumably, if whatever was about to be discussed was important enough, she *would* be. (Probably. Unless the Ministry of War was hiding something from Nineteen Adze—but that was what he would have to watch for, wasn't it? Being careful, paying attention. That's what he'd been asked to do, in the middle of the night.)

"Eleven Laurel," said the Minister, nodding welcome and then looked right at him and said, "Your Excellency Eight Antidote. Thank you both for coming. I'm going to play a transmission from Fleet Captain Sixteen Moonrise now. It came in on fast courier a few hours ago, priority communication."

Eight Antidote was profoundly grateful that the room lights dimmed when the transmission started, so no one could see that he was blushing, his cheeks hot, just from being addressed directly by Three Azimuth with his entire formal title. It was embarrassing and *ridiculous*. Lots of people called him *Your Excellency*, and he didn't usually blush at all.

In holo, Fleet Captain Sixteen Moonrise of the Twenty-Fourth Legion looked like a statue in a plaza, visible only from the waist up in full three-sixty-degree reproduction and hovering above the table. She bowed over her fingers—or she had, about six hours ago. Six and a half. It took at *least* that long for a transmission to cross all the jumpgates between the battlefront and the City, even on fastest courier and being bounced across sectors by the strongest repeater stations. Wherever she was, six hours ago, had been dim and metal-walled. Some ship. She was alone.

"A message for Minister Three Azimuth," she said. "Priority. Security code Hyacinth." She was speaking softly, just loud enough that her recorder could catch each syllable but not loud enough for anyone to overhear her. Eight Antidote had never heard of security code Hyacinth before. He glanced at the faces of the adults around the table; they showed no obvious surprise or consternation, only attentiveness.

"The Fleet has obtained the corpse of one of our enemies and conducted an autopsy on the alien. A formal report of the autopsy will arrive from *yaotlek* Nine Hibiscus's medical team in due course, I'm sure, and I am equally sure that it will be accurate but brief. I myself observed the conclusion of the autopsy. The aliens are mammalian, likely to be scavengers, and carnivorous or omnivorous based on their dentition. More significantly, however, the *yaotlek* invited a special envoy from the Ministry of Information to be present at the autopsy as well. The envoy brought with her a foreign national from Lsel Station. I have enclosed a visual image of the Stationer. It is my belief that Lsel Station may be attempting to exert diplomatic influence over the decisions of *yaotlek* Nine Hibiscus via the person of the Information envoy, whom Nine Hibiscus has commanded to initiate first-contact protocols. The Palms should be aware of the possibility that Information may contain compromised individuals, or that the Stationers may be infringing on Teixcalaanli sovereignty. In sending this message I perform my duty as a sworn officer of the Fleet. May Teixcalaan and the Emperor endure a thousand thousand years. End security code Hyacinth."

The holo ended, and Sixteen Moonrise vanished as if she'd never been. The lights came back up. Minister Three Azimuth sat back in her chair, her fingers laced together in front of her chest. She did not look like someone who had just been told that there was a foreign diplomat conspiring with a rogue Information agent running loose around the battlefield of a thus-far-unwinnable war. Eight Antidote would like to look that confident someday. And she was small, not much taller than him, and yet she appeared every inch the master of all six Palms, the encompasser of the Empire's military mind. She blinked behind her cloudhook, and a two-dimensional image of a tallish woman in a foreign-cut jacket and trousers, high-cheekboned and curly-haired, replaced the holo of Sixteen Moonrise above the table. The image was fuzzy at the edges, the angle strange. Eight Antidote thought it had been pulled off a security camera. But he knew that face. He'd seen that face splashed across newsfeeds over and over after Six Direction died. He'd seen it close up, too: in one of the garden rooms in Palace-Earth, the *huitzahuitlim* garden, where he went to watch the hummer-birds sip nectar and fly only as far as their invisible netting allowed them. She'd spoken to him then.

"So," Three Azimuth said. "What do we think of the former Ambassador from Lsel Station, Mahit Dzmare? She, if you re-call, of the heartfelt plea that we notice the alien threat, the one broadcast right before the Emperor Six Direction's death. The one who gave us the direction of our war. Since that esteemed individual is who has just shown up on *Weight for the Wheel*."

In the garden, surrounded by the buzzing red-and-gold wings of the tiniest birds in Teixcalaan, Dzmare had made him a strange offer. She'd said to him, *You're a very powerful young person, and if you still want to, when you are of age, Lsel Station would be honored to host you.* And he'd known better, right then, as he knew better right now, than to say yes: she'd been lost, and drunk, and sad, and still trying to find an angle of influence. So he'd shown her how to get the *huitzahuitlim* to drink nectar from her palm, and then sent her away.

He wondered what she'd learned from that night. And what had driven her first away from Teixcalaan and then out to the battlefront itself.

Eight Antidote sat up straight, and paid *attention*. This con-versation was one he'd have to bring back to Her Brilliance the Emperor. *Even little spies have secrets,* he thought to him-self, and was surprised by the degree of his own satisfaction at the idea.

The Ministry of War didn't like Mahit Dzmare, it turned out.

Or at least—some of them didn't. She was a barbarian, that was just *true,* and Second Undersecretary Seven Aster (who was new—as new as Minister Three Azimuth, as new as the Emperor Herself) mostly seemed to dislike her because she was a barbarian and was out on a battlefront unsupervised, while possibly having diplomatic authority. That didn't seem to be Dzmare's fault, though. She couldn't help being a barbarian, or that the Information envoy had brought her along—unless she'd somehow *made* the envoy take her?

The last Ambassador from Lsel Station, Yskandr Aghavn, had seemed like the sort of person who made people do things they never expected. Eight Antidote hadn't known him, except for knowing the shape of his face and how much his ancestor-the-Emperor had enjoyed his companionship. Aghavn either hadn't liked kids that much or had better things to do than talk to one. But he'd been in the palace all the time. He'd been friends with *everyone.* Until he'd died.

Maybe all Lsel Ambassadors were like that.

Eight Antidote was still considering whether being good at making people act in ways they usually wouldn't would be helpful or unhelpful on a battlefront when Eleven Laurel said, "Minister, my chief concern with Dzmare has nothing to do with her barbarian origins—it is to do with her effects on situations around her. Her destabilizing effects."

"Go on," said Minister Three Azimuth. "As you keep reminding me, Undersecretary, you were here when Dzmare was involved with the unfortunate circumstances surrounding our Emperor's ascension to the throne, and I was not. Is there something specific about her activities then that you think is *indicative?*"

"You were very busy on Nakhar, I'm sure you didn't have time to notice these small things," said Eleven Laurel, which seemed to Eight Antidote like an innocuous statement that really didn't deserve Three Azimuth's quick displeased expression. She *had* been on Nakhar, and military governors were busy by nature, almost as busy as emperors. "Dzmare—and the forces that she either allied herself with or who found her useful—ignores all protocols. She ignores all *history*—she, like Aghavn before her, just slides blithely in and does what she believes is necessary, and if the institutions of our Empire are disregarded, our processes dissolved or lost—what is it to her?"

Three Azimuth's face was very still. "My dear Undersecretary," she said, "I assume you are talking about the early retirement of my predecessor Nine Propulsion."

Eight Antidote was suddenly aware of how much *older* Eleven Laurel was than Three Azimuth. He wondered how many Ministers of War he'd served, and if the number was big enough to keep him from even being concerned when the current Minister . . . implied he wasn't loyal to her? Was that what was being said here? He felt like he was watching a conversation that had been going on for a long time, long before this meeting.

Eleven Laurel exhaled on a resigned sigh, all of the deep wrinkles in his face settling deeper. "Minister, it is not *Nine Propulsion* who concerns me—I hope she enjoys her retirement, of course, but she isn't Minister now, is she?—it is how much our Emperor trusts us here in War, now that she is gone and the *yaotlek* One Lightning has been sent off in disgrace. And how much Her Brilliance trusts creatures like Dzmare, or Information envoys, or *anyone* but her Fleet, on Fleet business. That's all, Minister."

"That's never *all*," Three Azimuth said, and Eight Antidote, trying to think through what Eleven Laurel had just said—did Nineteen Adze really not trust War? *while* War was defending all Teixcalaan from incredibly dangerous aliens?—practiced keeping his face as still as he could, as serene as a grown-up, calm as someone who wasn't trying to put all these pieces together.

The Emperor had sent *him* to spy on War, though. Hadn't she. Maybe that meant Eleven Laurel was right. He didn't know how he felt about that. Didn't know at all, except that part of how he felt was scared.

————

The message they came up with was eleven seconds long, and made up of four sounds spliced from the intercepted recording, repeated twice over. As far as Mahit could understand, and based on the best of her ability to communicate in sound waves that made her nauseated, it said something like *approach-danger—contact-initiated—hurrah-we-win*, in sequence, and then—using their newfound unpleasant knowledge about how the alien noises increased in potency when they were layered on top of each other—played *contact-initiated* from two opposite directions at once, and then added *hurrah-we-win* on top of that. Then it repeated again from the start. She wasn't *sure* that what she and Three Seagrass were saying was *come talk to us in person, it'll work out great*, but she also wasn't *not* sure, and that was—well, it was the best they were going to do with this limited data set. Perhaps the message would get them more noises to work with, even if it didn't get them a live alien negotiator.

They'd finished it, and the instant it was done, all of the fragile peace between them shattered like a glass dropped on the floor. Three Seagrass was sullen and silent and uncomprehending, and Mahit was exhausted. She had never wanted to have that fight—

<That's not true,> said Yskandr inside her mind, where his voice was almost exactly like hers, like her own thoughts were being operated by an external force, coming to the top of her mind with alien suddenness. <You've been wanting to have that fight since the oration contest at Six Direction's banquet, when you saw how effortless being Teixcalaanli was for her. Poetry competitions and all her glittering friends, and how much she *likes aliens*. You wanted to have it. You were just hoping you wouldn't *have* to.>

She hated when he sounded like he knew everything, like twenty years of extra experience and sleeping with the Emperor of all Teixcalaan—both current and former versions thereof—made him an expert on how she felt. But then, he was inside her endocrine system. He *knew* how she felt, because he felt it the same—and they were getting closer all the time. More integrated.

Her hands hurt, that sparkling ulnar nerve pain. Her head hurt, too, like she'd been trying not to cry for a long time.

I want her to see how she hurts me, she said, in the privacy of her own mind, while Three Seagrass put their message on a fresh infofiche stick and sealed it with her wax sealing kit, the flame-orange wax the same color as her perfect, infuriating uniform. *I want her to—notice, when she does, without being told.*

<She's a Teixcalaanlitzlim, Mahit. They don't. Not unless you tell them, over and over, and even then . . . >

A slide, sense-memory and longing, the strange mirrored room of their shared mind reflecting a shard of time: the shape of Nineteen Adze's shoulder blades, delineated in the palest light of early morning in Palace-East. How Yskandr had felt a terrifying, sweet tenderness—felt it on some morning not too long before Nineteen Adze had let him, with her full knowledge and acquiescence, be murdered. Let him asphyxiate under the watchful eyes of Ten Pearl, Minister of Science. And yet the sense-memory remained, even through death and botched imago-surgery. Mahit looked at Three Seagrass and felt an echo of that tenderness, an echo of that betrayal.

She's not going to kill me to save her Emperor from corruption, she thought, pointedly.

<I wouldn't underestimate her,> Yskandr murmured. <Not if I were in your place.>

You are in my place.

<She likes Mahit Dzmare, not Yskandr Aghavn. If she likes any part of us at all, after what we've said to her.>

"I'm going to present this to the *yaotlek*," Three Seagrass said, light and chilly, and tucked the infofiche stick into the inner jacket pocket of her uniform. "I'll make sure to point out that it's more than half your work. Thank you."

As if they'd never been anything but brief colleagues working on a difficult problem. Mahit felt as if she had broken the world, and hated herself for feeling that way—Three Seagrass, *asekreta* and patrician first-class, Third Undersecretary to the Minister for Information, special envoy to the Fleet . . . she wasn't *the world*. Mahit had done fine without her on Lsel, had missed her only as much as she'd missed Teixcalaan, which was enormously and with aching frustration.

<The world, the Empire,> Yskandr whispered, that single word in Teixcalaanli.

The right order of things, Mahit whispered back, which was just another shading of pronunciation. That was what felt broken. How she had wanted the world to be.

"I assume," she found herself saying, "that if it works and they do respond, you'll let me know."

Three Seagrass looked at her, a glancing, miserable expression, and dropped her eyes again. "Of course," she said, too fast. "And I'll— When they respond, I want you to hear it."

It almost sounded like *I want you to help me.* It would have been better, Mahit thought, if she'd actually said that. But Mahit hadn't particularly left her any room to do so, had she. She'd said, *When you know why I had to come with you, then we can talk.* And she hadn't meant, *When you figure out the political situation on Lsel Station,* she'd meant—

She'd meant, *When you understand that when the Empire commands, I can't say no.* She'd meant, *When you understand that there's no room for me to mean yes, even if I want to.* She'd meant, *You don't understand that there's no such thing as being free.* Free to choose, or free otherwise.

So all she said out loud was, "Good. Until then, Three Seagrass."

Three Seagrass didn't reply. She slipped out the door of the communications workroom like she couldn't wait to be gone, and left Mahit alone to try to do something about the remains of the vomit and find her way back to the quarters they were supposed to share. All those corridors between her and that limited safety, and her here without the benefit of a uniformed Teixcalaanli liaison to open all the doors, dispatch all the guardians. She'd crippled herself, on this Fleet flagship, farther away from anything she could have ever called home than she'd ever been, for the sake of—what, exactly? For wanting an understanding that she—or at least the part of her that was Yskandr, and it was hard to tell the difference between them now, about this—wasn't even sure Three Seagrass was capable of *comprehending*, let alone having?

What was the *point* of this?

Mahit had thought she'd known, but now she wasn't sure.

———

The adjutant *ikantlos*-prime Twenty Cicada, Three Seagrass discovered, was *ubiquitous*. She hadn't gone much farther into the deep corridors of *Weight for the Wheel*—aiming, by cloudhook map, away from the audio processing room and toward the general area of the bridge in hopes of encountering either the *yaotlek* or someone who knew where to fetch her from—when he simply materialized out of a three-way passage nexus, like the ship itself had manifested him.

There's never been a ship AI that took human form, Three Seagrass reminded herself. *That's a holodrama plot. And besides, he's touched physical objects where I could see him do it. He is definitely a real person.* Nevertheless she felt sufficiently—oh, sufficiently a lot of things, but mostly exhausted and unhappy and brittle-bright, ready to snap—that being surprised by Twenty Cicada was downright spooky. Then she remembered that Fleet Captain Sixteen Moonrise had called him *Swarm*, which was a fascinatingly nasty nickname for someone who had a fascinatingly untoward name: an *insect* for his noun signifier. Swarm, though . . .

"You're everywhere at once," she said to him. "Aren't you."

The light in the corridors of *Weight for the Wheel* was directionless; it made Twenty Cicada's shaved head gleam, olive-gold like patina on old coins. He seemed to consider this statement, tilting his head ever so slightly, like he was calculating a vector of attack. Three Seagrass was going to have to look him up when she had access to the Information network again; she wanted to know everything about his military record. Had he flown Shards? Been in hand-to-hand combat? Or had he always been a logistics and operations officer, arranging the movement of ships and supply lines across jumpgates under the peculiar spiritual guidance of his balance-obsessed religion?

"I'm where I should be," he said.

"I have the message we prepared for the *yaotlek* to broadcast," Three Seagrass told him, trying not to wince over the *we;* she needed to not think about Mahit right now. She'd been doing so well! Not thinking about her. She wasn't going to start now. She needed to pay attention to what was happening right in front of her. "Is she on the bridge?"

Twenty Cicada made a gesture with one hand that could mean *certainly* and could mean *I assume, if you like.* It showed off the edges of his homeostat-cult tattoos, slipping out from the cuffs of his uniform in pale green fractal shapes. He was frustratingly difficult to read; too strange and too exactly-Teixcalaanli-soldier at the same time.

"Walk with me," he said, instead of giving her a proper answer, and Three Seagrass decided that she would.

They did not turn toward the bridge. Three Seagrass dismissed her cloudhook's navigational function with a blink; it kept sending her small alerts at the corner of her vision that she really ought to have turned left, and now it had to recalculate her route, and she could do without *that* sort of petty annoyance.

She set it to record her movements and build a new area map instead—as she had *not* done on Lsel Station, and what did it mean that she was willing to conduct surveillance mapping of one of the Empire's flagships and not a foreign sovereign state?

It says, she thought, deliberately, like pressing on a bruise, *that you trusted Mahit Dzmare too much.*

Twenty Cicada led her down two levels of the ship. He was not talkative, exactly. He asked *questions,* but not like an interrogator or an *asekreta* would. She couldn't put her hands on his goals. They were slippery.

"Have you seen what these aliens do to human beings?" he asked. "I believe Nine Hibiscus sent along some of the holo-recordings of what we found on Peloa-2."

She had. Three Seagrass had glanced through them and felt nothing: *Oh, look, another war.* Someone else's atrocity, far away on the edges of the known world. But she was very close to those edges now. "They like evisceration," she told Twenty Cicada. "An interesting preference for mass casualties. Messy."

"Wasteful," he said, correcting her.

"What, because it takes too much effort to pull out the entrails on every single human being? You saw the claws the dead one has; it can't be *that* inefficient for them to do."

Twenty Cicada said, "The dead creature was a scavenger, or its presentient ancestors were—that mouth, the eyes on the front of the skull—and yet it left all those guts to rot. *That's* wasteful."

They'd come to a heavily sealed door, airtight enough that Three Seagrass wondered for a moment if she was about to be unceremoniously spaced through an airlock. Twenty Cicada stepped close to it, let it read his cloudhook: the clear glass over one eye flowing full of tiny grey-gold glyphs, like a storm boiling up over the City. It opened—and behind it was *heat,* and warm wet air, and the scents of soil and growth and flowers. A hydroponics deck. Three Seagrass followed him inside with a gratitude she had not expected to feel: her skin *drank* the moisture, starved for nonprocessed air. She wanted to luxuriate in it. A place on this ship that felt like—like *Teixcalaan,* like the Jewel of the World. A garden heart. She took deep breaths. The drag of humidity in her lungs was delicious.

Twenty Cicada had much the same expression as she did, she suspected: a blissed relaxation of all the tension in his face. This was a place he loved—of course he did, how could he not—which meant, of course, that he'd brought her here to use it as a setting, a frame for the argument he was making to her. A place powerful enough to be worth a detour, rather than bringing her and her work straight to the *yaotlek* who had ordered it done. This argument must be *deeply* important to him.

She'd listen. She'd rather have the second-in-command of a Fleet flagship try to manipulate her with humidity and the amazing scent of rice, sorrel, and lotuses growing in hydroponic pools than think about Mahit Dzmare.

"How many people do you feed?" she asked, following Twenty Cicada to the edge of one of the terraced pools. The effect was like standing on a balcony: they leaned on the fine-wrought metal railings of a catwalk, looking down into green.

"The capacity is five thousand," Twenty Cicada said. "On emergency rations, for three months. With *Weight for the Wheel*'s usual crew numbers, we're entirely self-sufficient, at better than subsistence levels."

"And enough flowers for every deck," Three Seagrass added. "All those lotuses . . ."

"As I said: *better* than subsistence."

Beauty, then, was part of his definition of self-sufficiency. Three Seagrass had always thought that homeostat-cultists weren't supposed to like *anything* overly pretty or overly ugly, but this hydroponics deck was—gorgeous. And so were all the lotuses. Every color: blue and silver-pale, white and the sort of pink that looked like sunrises.

"What are the casualty rates looking like?" she inquired, after a moment of deliberate quiet, the both of them breathing the thick air like nectar. "Aside from Peloa-2. *Our* casualty rates."

"Don't you know?" He lifted the place where his eyebrow would be, under the cloudhook, as if to indicate her Information-issue dress.

"We're not omniscient by virtue of being in the Information Ministry, *ikantlos*-prime. And even if we were, there's a difference between reading reports and hearing from a soldier on the front."

Twenty Cicada made a small, considering noise: a click of the tongue against the teeth. "Omniscience is somewhat crippled by lack of omnipresence, I'd agree. And—too high. That's what our casualty rate is. Too high, for a Fleet that is waiting to decide what to do next, who has not yet found the source of these enemies, despite our best scouting efforts throughout the sector."

We don't know where they grow, Three Seagrass thought. *We don't even know what the garden heart of their home would look like, except that it wouldn't look like this deck, this place that Twenty Cicada values.* "You'd prefer action," she said.

"My preferences are hardly the point, Envoy. I merely— dislike waste, and wasteful things."

And you think these aliens are—offensive. Your word for "offensive" is "wasteful." Three Seagrass wrapped her fingers around the railing, felt the slick dampness of the metal. "What would you ask them? If they do answer our message and come to talk to us."

This time, the noise he made was not so considering. "What makes you think they're going to want to *talk*? No matter how clever you and the Lsel Ambassador have been in your sound-splicing—oh, *bloody stars,* one of them's gotten into the rice again."

"One of what?" Three Seagrass started, but Twenty Cicada had already swung his hips up over the railing and landed with a splash, water up above his knees and soaking the pants of his uniform. He waded with purpose and annoyance—paused, entirely still, like an ibis waiting to spear a fish with its beak—and ducked to grab a small dark shape from amongst the stalks of rice.

It squalled. He held it out at arm's length, by the scruff of its neck, and brought it back to her as if it was an unpleasant trophy. "Hold this," he said, and shoved it through the bars of the railing for Three Seagrass to grab.

"It's a cat," she said. It was. A black kitten, by the size of it, with enormous yellow eyes and the usual needle-claws that kittens had, all of which were now sunk into Three Seagrass's jacket sleeve, and her skin underneath. It was also dripping and damp, and unlike any other cat she had heard of, didn't seem perturbed by the water.

Twenty Cicada clambered back onto the dry side of the balcony. "It *was* a cat," he said darkly, "several thousand years ago before it became an arboreal pest that lives in the mangrove swamps on Kauraan. An arboreal pest that has *escaped into the air ducts of my ship because someone on the down-planet team thought they were cute and brought back a pregnant one.*"

The kitten climbed onto Three Seagrass's shoulder. It was very sharp. It also was much better at holding on to her than she remembered kittens being, the last time she'd been close to a kitten, in the sitting room of some patrician's poetry salon back in the City. That kitten had been fluffy, pale, and uninterested in sitting on her shoulder. *This* one had very long phalanges, like the fingers of a human being, and a sort of thumb that was quite nearly opposable. "They're in the air ducts," she repeated, dumbfounded and delighted.

"They, like me, are *everywhere*," said Twenty Cicada, and sighed so as not to laugh. "And they shouldn't be in here. They're not native to the hydroponic ecosystem and their waste products have too much ammonia. You can have that one."

"What am I supposed to do with it?" Three Seagrass asked. "I have a report to give to the *yaotlek* Nine Hibiscus—I can't keep a kitten."

"It won't stay with you long. Just take it *out* with you and leave it on a deck that isn't this one. And don't worry about Nine Hibiscus. I'll give her your message."

"Will you?" Three Seagrass asked, knowing that what she was asking was closer to *ought I to trust you, now that you've shown me how little you think these enemies are worth talking to at all?*

"Nine Hibiscus asked for it," said her adjutant, as if this fact rendered the universe entirely simple. "So I'll bring it to her. I always know where she is."

He could have gone straight to Nineteen Adze right after he left the Ministry of War. There was no reason not to: it wouldn't be suspicious. Eight Antidote *lived* in Palace-Earth, same as the Emperor did, and he went to see her all the time. And he did have—well, not *actionable* intelligence, like people talked about in spywork holodramas, but *useful information* of the kind that Her Brilliance had specifically asked for. He could have walked right in.

But it felt wrong. It felt like—oh, like being a tattletale, not a spy. Like being someone else's ears, instead of his own person, making his own decisions. He *would* tell her about Ambassador Mahit Dzmare and Fleet Captain Sixteen Moonrise, of course. And—maybe, probably—about Eleven Laurel's concern that Her Brilliance didn't trust the War Ministry. He'd even tell her today. But first—well. First he wanted to really understand, for himself, what he'd learned.

Which was why Eight Antidote had walked into the lobby of the Information Ministry, announced himself with *all* of his titles, and asked the nice *asekreta* trainee who was staffing the public information desk to find him someone who could spare a half hour to explain rapid communications through jumpgates to the future Emperor of all Teixcalaan.

"It's for my education," Eight Antidote had said, extremely cheerfully, and the trainee had actually stifled a conspiratorial giggle behind her hand. *Yes,* he thought. *You're helping the heir to the Empire with his homework. Keep thinking that.*

He only had to wait a little while, and he kept himself amused by looking at the way the Information Ministry presented itself, so different from the Six Outreaching Palms: clear and clean, serenely white marble walls coupled with ever-present coral-colored accents, like the sleeves of their *asekretim* had bled into the architecture. Coral inlay on the floor, done in a carnelian-stone mosaic of an enormous chrysanthemum framed by smaller lotuses. *Eternity,* Eight Antidote remembered from some very long-ago tutoring session, when he'd been extremely small, hardly older than a baby. Everybody learned flowers first. *Chrysanthemums are eternity, and lotuses are memory and rebirth, which is why the Information Ministry sigil has got both. They like to think that they know everything and always have and always will. Or at least that's what Eleven Laurel would say.*

He wasn't sure what *he'd* say. Yet.

The person who showed up to talk to him was a round, broad-shouldered man with an open sort of face, the kind of face that seemed friendly even when it wasn't. A good face for an Information Ministry employee.

"Your Excellency," he said. "I understand you would like to discuss interstellar communication?"

Eight Antidote made himself look like his ancestor-the-Emperor, composed his mouth and eyes into that same knowing, interested, serene expression that had made Nineteen Adze flinch back from him in surprised recognition. He was getting good at it. It worked even on people who hadn't known his ancestor so well; it was an *adult* expression, and people got nervous in a useful way when he made it with his kid's face. "I would, very much," he said. "If I'm not taking up your valuable time, *asekreta*—I'm terribly sorry, I didn't catch your name?"

"One Cyclamen, Your Excellency," said the *asekreta*, "and I have the honor of being the Second Sub-Secretary of the Epistolary Department of the Ministry of Information, which means

I am the person who spends a great deal of time on the intricacies of interstellar communication through jumpgates—a process, Your Excellency, which is so very automated and regular that my time is absolutely most valuably spent on informing you about it. Would you like to come into a conference room?"

One Cyclamen was amazingly obsequious, and in such a way that Eight Antidote felt more flattered than annoyed. He wished he could learn *that* skill. "Yes please," he said, and wondered what the camera-eyes of the City would think of him now: following an Information agent into a white-and-beige conference room. No holographic strategy tables here, no star-chart outlines of the universe. Only a holoprojector at one end of a regular sort of table, decorously turned down to a low flicker of light. The chairs were too big for him. His feet didn't touch the floor, so he tucked them up under himself, sitting cross-legged. It was better than letting them swing. He felt steadier.

"How does a message get to the Jewel of the World from thousands of light-years away in just a few hours, Second Sub-Secretary?" he asked, in tones of high politeness, as if he was speaking to one of his tutors. "And can it go faster than usual? Or slower?"

"In the most technical sense, a message cannot go faster or slower than it can be routed through a jumpgate, Your Excellency," said One Cyclamen. "The jumpgates are our sticking point. Forgive me—you do understand how they work, do you not?"

"If I get confused, I'll tell you," Eight Antidote said, and folded his hands together to make a cup for his chin, looking up at One Cyclamen intently. *Everyone* knew how jumpgates worked. They were like narrow mountain passes: the only way to get from one side to the other was through the aperture. Except instead of two pieces of land with a mountain range dividing them, one side was a sector of space and the other side was a completely *different* one, which could be anywhere. There wasn't a *connection* between the sectors, except for through the gates, and some sectors of Teixcalaanli space, well . . . no one knew exactly where they were in terms of vectors away from the Jewel of the World. But you could get there, just as easily as you could take the subway out to Plaza Central Nine, if you knew which jumpgate to go through.

And if you didn't, you'd have to crawl at sublight speeds across the galaxy, hoping to run into where you meant to go before you died. Jumpgates were why the Empire worked.

One Cyclamen was talking, and had been talking for several seconds, and Eight Antidote wasn't sure if it was good or bad that he had apparently learned to look like he was paying attention when he wasn't.

". . . electronic communication is essentially transmittable at faster-than-light speeds—practically instantaneous!—via our signaling stations within a sector, and has been for hundreds of years. But only physical objects can go through a jumpgate, and only nonphysical ones can be transmitted via the imperial signal service. You see the problem?"

"Someone has to carry the message on an infofiche stick through every jumpgate between its origin and destination."

"Yes! Which is why I have a job, Your Excellency, incidentally. Or—why my job exists. The Epistolary Department staffs the jumpgate postal services. We're the only Information workers who fly spaceships—though they're quite short little flights, back and forth through the jumpgate with the mail, and most of them are automated these days."

Eight Antidote nodded. "Unpiloted ships."

"It's a very simple routing algorithm," One Cyclamen said, shrugging. "No reason to use a person unless it is a rush job or the jumpgate is very tricky or heavily trafficked."

A rush job, like Sixteen Moonrise's. Had Information passed the very message that was so anti-Information? Did Information *read* the physical messages, or did they merely arrive, a pile of infofiche sticks, like the worst possible heap of unanswered palace mail? Eight Antidote imagined a *sack* of the things, or a series of crates, and was a bit horrified at the idea of so *many* messages all at once.

He didn't ask how a rush job got scheduled. That would be too—obvious. And he was being a spy today. (It was possible that once a person started being a spy, they were going to be one forever, which was definitely something he would need to think about later.) What he asked instead was, "Does Information process *everyone's* mail? From all of Teixcalaan?"

One Cyclamen paused. There was a faint line between his eyebrows, a tension line, like he'd just remembered that he was talking to an imperial heir and not any crèche-kid doing an enrichment project. "We don't *process*," he said. "We *transmit*. Unless ordered to do otherwise by Her Brilliance the Emperor, of course. But I'm sure that's not what you meant, Your Excellency—perhaps you wanted to know if there were other mail carriers?"

"Are there?" said Eight Antidote, and waited. The waiting was another adult trick. A Nineteen Adze trick. She did it to him all the time: made him answer questions while not knowing why she'd asked them, and learned what he was thinking by how he answered, whether he wanted her to or not.

"Aside from the Fleet, which carries its own orders on its own ships . . . no official ones," One Cyclamen said, "but any vessel moving through a jumpgate can carry a message with them, of course. And then there are sector-wide mail services, a great number, some governmental and some private businesses— would you like a list? I can have one prepared and sent to your cloudhook."

He wasn't about to turn down information, even if it wasn't information he currently could think of any actual use for. Except for that moment where One Cyclamen had said *the Fleet carries its own orders on its own ships*. Had Sixteen Moonrise's message come in that way? "I'd like that," he said. "Thank you." Then he paused, as if he was suddenly remembering another question, and leaned forward on his elbows, smiling wide-eyed—*I'm eleven, I'm small, I'm harmless, I'm doing my homework*—and asked one more question. "Has anyone ever— delayed jumpgate mail? Or captured it, or changed it, or sent it through other jumpgates than the ones it was routed to?"

One Cyclamen laughed. Eight Antidote thought it was the kind of laughter that was meant to cover being uncomfortable. "Like pirates, Your Excellency? Mail pirates?"

Eight Antidote shrugged. *Maybe. Go on. Tell me how this process can be fooled, or accelerated, or stopped.*

". . . Historically, there have been a few incidents, of course, but we try very hard to prevent them. And truly significant messages go through on Fleet ships, of course, just like the Fleet's own orders; diplomatic communiqués, imperial proc- lamations."

There. "Because Fleet ships have right of way through jump- gates."

"Quite so, Your Excellency. If something needs to move fastest, it will be on a Fleet ship. But do be assured that the Information Ministry doesn't lose your letters."

"I would never think that," Eight Antidote said, cheerfully. That tension line in One Cyclamen's forehead deepened. "Thank you so very much for spending time with me and an- swering all these questions!"

"Of course. Giving out information—well, that's what we're *for*, here in Information."

Yes, Eight Antidote thought. *That's what you're for. And I won- der how many of your jumpgate postal offices Sixteen Moonrise skipped right over when she sent that message to the Minister of War. I bet it was most of them. And Eleven Laurel doesn't mind that kind of circumventing protocols. Not when what's being circumvented is the Information Ministry.*

———

If she stayed on this ship for much longer, Mahit thought grimly as she turned one last corner and finally arrived at the sealed door of the quarters she and Three Seagrass had been assigned, she was going to have to find some way to requisition a cloud-hook. For navigation's sake, if nothing else. *Weight for the Wheel* was a tenth of the size of Lsel Station, and many thousands of times smaller than the Jewel of the World, and yet here neither her nor Yskandr's knowledge of place sufficed for not having to ask, humiliatingly, for directions. More than once. At least she'd been headed *away* from the more restricted decks, instead of into the ship's heart: no one asked her why a barbarian was alone, so far away from barbarian territory.

<Either that, or the ship's AI updated itself, and you show up as a legitimate passenger,> Yskandr said to her. He sounded as pissed off and frustrated as she felt. She wanted to throw something. Break something. Break something *lovely*, some gorgeous piece of Teixcalaanli décor she could knock off a table and shatter. Maybe there would be one inside the quarters. (How she was going to share a room with Three Seagrass, after what they had done to each other, she wasn't thinking about right now. It wasn't the current *problem*.)

On the touchpad-lock next to the door was a piece of sticky disposable plastifilm, which read *your password is VOID*: the Teixcalaanli glyph shaped like a giant hollow circle. For a moment, Mahit wasn't sure what she was supposed to do if her door-unlocking code was already expired—and then she realized it was a preset. An easy glyph to draw, to unlock your room before you could change the code. She unpeeled the plastifilm and drew a VOID on the touchpad, and the door hissed open.

Silhouetted against the light from the room's single lamp was a tall, narrow figure. It took a step toward Mahit—

She had dropped to her knees on the floor before she quite knew why, a flare of whiteout-panic—and then she was rolling, rolling *toward* the figure, getting her feet under her and throwing herself at the figure's legs in a headlong tackling leap. They collided. Her shoulder spasmed like she'd hit it with a hammer—or a knee—and the person she'd hit fell heavily over her, grunting, their palms striking the floor in a slap. *Where's the needle?* Mahit thought. *I have to get away from the needle, it's poison—*

Whoever it was rolled down her shoulder and somersaulted to their feet, leaving Mahit in a heap on the floor, scrambling *away,* waiting for the sharp prick and the end of everything—

<Stop it,> Yskandr said, as loud in her mind as if he'd been next to her and shouting, <you're not dying, you're not in the City, this isn't Eleven Conifer. Stop it.>

You're not dying. How many times had she said that to him, in the middle of the night, when he'd woken them up from dreams of asphyxiation?

"—You do *not* take surprises well," said the intruder, and Mahit shoved her hair out of her eyes and managed to look up, focusing.

She had just attacked Fleet Captain Sixteen Moonrise and come out rather the worse for it. The Fleet Captain looked entirely unperturbed, not a hair out of place. Mahit felt her face go dark with an embarrassed flush.

Just because I was ambushed in my apartment once shouldn't mean I react like this every time I'm surprised by someone in a room, she thought miserably, and got nothing but Yskandr's rueful and sympathetic acknowledgment in return.

". . . No," she managed. "I don't. My apologies, I didn't intend to—assault you. Fleet Captain."

A slim pale gold hand appeared in front of her, offering, and Mahit took it. Sixteen Moonrise pulled her up to her feet. "It's quite understandable," she said. "I didn't know you'd been in combat, Ambassador Dzmare. I ought to have left a note on the door. But I did want to talk to you alone."

"I haven't been in combat," Mahit said. "I—oh, for fuck's sake, I failed the physical combat aptitudes by *eighteen points,* I've never been near combat."

"One hardly needs good aptitudes to have ended up in

situations where combat *happens,*" Sixteen Moonrise said, dismissively, "and regardless, you have good instincts. Shall we sit down?"

Mahit's mouth tasted of adrenaline, bitter and metallic, and she was shaking very slightly; there seemed to be no plausible way, barring another attempt at bodily force, to remove the Fleet Captain from the room. And the first attempt had been bad enough. She glanced around, looking for something to sit on, or at, and found that there was a small folding desk which had already been pulled down from the wall, and two stools, one on either side of it. Sixteen Moonrise must have been here for a while. She'd had time to prepare. Probably she hadn't expected Mahit to get horribly lost in the ship and had gotten bored enough to investigate the furniture—Mahit was being hysterical, even in the privacy of her own mind. What limited privacy her own mind had, anyway.

She sat. Gestured at the other stool. *Welcome to my office, such as it is.* And folded her hands tightly together in her lap, willing them to stop shaking.

"I imagine you're wondering why I've been waiting for you," said Sixteen Moonrise, taking the opposite seat. Mahit nodded, a rueful bit of acquiescence. Sixteen Moonrise folded *her* hands—on the table, where Mahit could see them. Mirroring. Establishing rapport.

I can't handle an interrogation, she thought, miserably, *not now.*

<Pull yourself the fuck together,> Yskandr told her, <even if she's a Third Palmer, or trained that way, and I think she might be—they're the military spies, the interrogators—she's a soldier, and she needs you for something. Pay *attention,* Mahit.>

Mahit took a breath. Settled back on her pelvis, straightened her spine. She was of a height with Sixteen Moonrise, at least when they were both sitting down. "From your reaction to Special Envoy Three Seagrass and me," she said, "I would expect nearly anything *except* you waiting for me, Fleet Captain. What was it you said—*the spook and her pet?*"

"I did say that," Sixteen Moonrise agreed, easily enough, and didn't apologize for it. "She is a spook, and you are—or you certainly were brought here as—her pet. I imagine she told you all sorts of things about how your presence could ensure a diplomatic voice for the Stations in whatever negotiations she ends up conducting with our enemies, yes?"

Not quite, Mahit thought. *That would have been transparent. This is Three Seagrass. Transparency is beyond her. Beyond us both.* She lifted one hand from her lap, tilted it back and forth—maybe yes, maybe no, go on.

"Mm," Sixteen Moonrise said, an evaluating noise. "Why *are* you here, Ambassador Dzmare? I imagined you'd want to be shut of Teixcalaan, after being involved in that mess in the capital three months ago."

"I like challenges," Mahit said. "I'm a translator. Who *wouldn't* want to be involved in a first-contact scenario?"

"Nearly everyone who has ever been near an alien," said Sixteen Moonrise. "I don't believe you, Ambassador Dzmare. Glory-seeking naïveté does not match up with the woman who *started* this war for us. Your broadcast before Six Direction's death was masterful, by the way. You horrified me, and I don't horrify easily."

"With all due respect, Fleet Captain, it was the aliens who started this war. I alerted the Emperor to it. I considered it an act of good citizenship."

"You're a barbarian."

"Barbarians," Mahit said, imagining Three Seagrass's face the whole time she was saying it, "are human beings; good citizenship in the face of existential threats extends beyond the boundaries of sovereignty. Or at least that is what we barbarians are taught, on my Station."

It wasn't. Mahit had never been taught anything of the kind. But it made Sixteen Moonrise's electrum-colored eyes widen, not a smile and not a grimace—but a veritable *hit*. And it was a useful lie.

Sixteen Moonrise exhaled through her nose, as if in exasperation. "Let me put it this way, Ambassador," she said. "I've watched your work on the newsfeeds during One Lightning's idiotic little usurpation attempt, which the Fleet really could have done without, by the way. You're too smart and too much of a politician to be here only as the envoy's pet—and you're already having difficulties with the envoy, aren't you? I notice she isn't here, and you aren't on the bridge with the *yaotlek*. Not to mention that your precious Stations are right *next* to this sector, which is full of aliens with ship-dissolving spit. One jumpgate away. That's not very far at all."

"I've seen the holographs of Peloa-2," Mahit said. "Is it so strange that I'd want to be part of stopping what is happening here? And yes, stopping it from reaching my home as well?" She wasn't going to talk about Three Seagrass. It was bad enough that Sixteen Moonrise, who was clearly no friend to either of them, had noticed that there was something *wrong* between them, and noticed from only the evidence of an absence. She wasn't going to confirm it. Not now, not ever.

"It's not strange," said Sixteen Moonrise, lifting one shoulder in a shrug. "It's merely—interesting. You show up in the most fascinating places, Ambassador. And you seem to be quite convinced by the envoy's argument that *talking* to our enemies will deliver the halt to hostilities you so reasonably desire."

"You think otherwise?"

"Oh, I reserve judgment until an attempt is made," said Sixteen Moonrise, and for a moment Mahit could see how she would be as a commander: the sort of person who evaluated, and evaluated, and then *struck,* a flurry of orders and decisions, no hesitation. "But I have lost twenty-seven soldiers in the past week, and I am beginning to be sick of funeral hymns. I have what I would consider perfectly reasonable doubts about the envoy's efficacy. And yours—at first-contact negotiations, at least. You may be a very skillful barbarian, Mahit Dzmare, and you may have wrapped the Information Ministry around your finger like a satellite caught in orbit, but you're no Emperor Two Sunspot. And these things aren't the Ebrekti."

Mahit found it within herself to laugh—it wasn't her laugh, exactly, it was some sort of self-mocking amusement that belonged mostly to the younger, half-dissolved Yskandr, his flashfire arrogance and bravado. "They're worse than the Ebrekti, based merely on their noises—did you know those sounds function as a self-reinforcing amplifying sine wave when played from different directions, Fleet Captain? I thought not. And I am certainly much worse than Her Brilliance Two Sunspot. As a negotiator, and as a person with weight on the world. I would never compare myself to an Emperor of all Teixcalaan."

It felt good to say. To be vicious in her own despair, to display the wound of her desire in full: *No, I will not be Teixcalaanli, I am incapable, I know, let me hold the bleeding lips of this injury open for you to see the raw hurt inside.* To say, *I would never compare myself to one of you,* with full consciousness that she would, and had, and could not stop.

Like a reflection, a shard of memory, hers or Yskandr's, too blurred to discern: Nineteen Adze saying, *It's a shame you're not one of us—you argue like a poet.* Or had that been Three Seagrass? She couldn't tell. She wished she could. It might mean something, if she could remember if that had been her or Yskandr, the now-Emperor or the *asekreta,* wishing for her—for them—to be otherwise than they were.

"Ah," said Sixteen Moonrise. "And yet you have willingly tried to bring them to a negotiating table."

"I use," Mahit said, feeling very tired and very cold, "what skills I have available."

"As does your Station, I see. What skills, and what people."

And she doesn't even know for certain that I'm a spy, Mahit thought. Here for herself, and her Station, surely—and here also for Darj Tarats, in payment for how he would spare her from Heritage's scans and knives. Her eyes were only her own until she made her first report back to him. And once she did that—once she did that, she might have to choose whether or not she would be a saboteur as well as a spy, to keep being spared.

<This one,> Yskandr told her as her fingers went numb—as her *forearms* went numb, to the elbow, she'd thought they were getting better, but this was worse, much worse than it had been in a while—<this one doesn't need to *know* to have already decided. For her, all barbarians are spies and saboteurs, if they're somewhere as secret and sacred as a Teixcalaanli flagship of the Fleet. How could they be otherwise?>

"Would you prefer we sent fighter ships rather than ambassadors?" Mahit asked the Fleet Captain. "We have a few. Not nearly so many as Teixcalaan, of course."

Sixteen Moonrise looked at her, considering and expressionless. "There may be a time, Ambassador, that we need every ship we can find," she said. "At that time, I'll remind you of what you've said to me. And until then—well. Good luck, with the envoy and the aliens and the *yaotlek*. I assume Stationers believe in luck?"

"When we need it," Mahit said.

"You'll need it," said Sixteen Moonrise, and left Mahit at the worktable alone, vanishing into the hallway as if she had never been lying in wait for her at all.

Mahit put her face in her numb hands, numb elbows on the table, and pressed the heels of her palms against her eyes. The last thing she wanted to do was cry. She didn't have time to cry. She had to think about why Sixteen Moonrise—a Fleet Captain, out of place, drifting through a flagship not her own, sneaking into the rooms of Information agents and barbarian ambassadors—would have wanted to challenge her, test her motivations, warn her—if it was a warning and not a threat—of how little the Fleet wanted to talk to these aliens. How much they wanted to kill them instead. How inconsequential the desires of Information agents, barbarian ambassadors, and even *yaotlekim* might be against the long weight of habitual violence that was the Teixcalaanli legions.

When she exhaled, hard through her nose, trying to expel all the spent air from her lungs and start again, her jacket rustled—like it was full of paper

(like the jacket she'd worn in the City had been full of ciphertext instructions for how best to start this war and prevent Lsel from being devoured by Teixcalaan)

(it had crackled the same way)

—and she reached into her inner jacket pocket and came up with *The Perilous Frontier!* A graphic story exactly the size of a political pamphlet. She'd forgotten she'd bought it.

<You forgot to take it out of your jacket, that's even more distracted than *I forgot I bought it.*>

Aknel Amnardbat was very distracting, Mahit told Yskandr. *At the time.* And then, finding herself hoping for a distraction that was neither tears nor Aknel Amnardbat, she opened it and began to read.

Graphic stories had never been of particular interest to Mahit as a literary form—they'd always seemed unnecessarily hybrid, not quite holoproj, not quite still art, not quite prose. And as a child—all right, as an adult as well, and continuously—most of what she read when she had time to read for pleasure was in Teixcalaanli. *The Perilous Frontier!* was in Stationer. Drawn by Stationers, and written by Stationers, *for* Stationers. How old had the kid at the kiosk been who sold it to her? Seventeen at most. Mahit hadn't been any good at being seventeen. She wouldn't have known what to do with an artist collective writing graphic stories if one had been tossed at her head, when she was seventeen.

Reading it—Volume One of an as-yet-incomplete cycle of at least ten—felt more like an anthropological exercise than anything else. The protagonist, Captain Cameron, a pilot from a long imago-line of pilots, was on the first spread in the midst of getting into nasty trouble trying to fly through an asteroid cluster, apparently aiming for an abandoned mine and some other character trapped in it. Mahit didn't know if she was supposed to know what was going on, or if there was some sort of Volume Zero she'd missed. Yskandr was no help: graphic stories hadn't been youth-culture fashion when he'd been young at *all*. Mahit found herself grasping for the background, the referentiality and citation, that she'd expect in a Teixcalaanli text, even an unfamiliar one—and didn't find it.

<It figures,> Yskandr told her—all the older Yskandr, amused, world-weary, faintly intrigued, <that the one thing we'd have to read would be Stationer-native art written by teenagers who haven't taken the aptitudes yet. Go on. Turn the page. I want to see what happens next.>

What happened next was Captain Cameron dodged an ice-comet, flew in close to an asteroid large enough to have an atmosphere of its own, practically a planetoid, and searched grimly through the snow that atmosphere was producing for a person named Esharakir Lrut and the secret archive of ancient Lsel documents that she had apparently hidden in said abandoned mine. Lrut was drawn thin, attenuated, an exaggerated version of how someone might look if they were much younger than their imago, and also had eaten nothing but protein cakes for months. It was impressive art. Mahit couldn't imagine sitting still for long enough to draw all of this, in *ink,* by hand—and make it look so evocative, without any colors at all.

Esharakir Lrut had been hiding documents to preserve them in their original forms. Cameron was there to rescue her, or the documents—and the majority of the middle of the story was Lrut arguing that yes, she would come back, and *with* the documents, but that Cameron had to promise to support her versions rather than the official, Heritage-sanctioned ones, when they got back to the Station. Otherwise she wasn't going anywhere at all. She'd stay in a mine, on an asteroid, in the snow, and wait for someone else to agree to defend the memory of Lsel.

<This is amazingly subversive,> Yskandr said to Mahit.

<Anti-Heritage by way of being *more Heritage than Heritage.* And teenagers wrote this?>

Wrote and drew, Mahit thought. *I guess there's a reason it's the same size as a political pamphlet, after all.*

<Perhaps we're not the only ones who have reasons to dislike Aknel Amnardbat.>

I haven't been home long enough to know why artist kids would be angry—

And even if Mahit had, she wouldn't have ever been friends with these people, who made art out of ink and paper, about Stationer memory, Stationer art, Stationer politics. She'd always spent her time with the other Teixcalaan-obsessed students. Writing poetry. Imagining the City. *The Perilous Frontier!* was as alien to her as—oh, not *quite* as alien as the beings that had made the sickening noises she and Three Seagrass had been trying to work with, but almost. Or felt that way, at least.

<Good thing you didn't give her your jacket,> Yskandr said. <This would be hard to read with the pages stuck together with vomit.>

Mahit winced, and shut the book. *I don't want to talk about Three Seagrass.*

<Or think about her, but you keep doing it.>

Mahit pictured Three Seagrass reading *The Perilous Frontier!* all despite herself, and wished her imago was less *right* about what she thought, and how it made her feel. But he felt it too. More and more all the time.

[begin security code APOLUNE] Wreath: other hands here than those of the Emperor are at work: the information I coded Hyacinth is only half of what I suspect. Watch for patterns, like you taught me. There are barbarian minds shaping Teixcalaanli policy, and we don't know what processes they have set in motion. Such things are outside our capacity to easily grasp. The story squirms away and takes incomprehensible forms. Prepare our Minister for rapid and decisive action. I will maintain contact. I remain, as ever, your Ascent. [end security code APOLUNE]

> —encrypted message received by the Third
> Undersecretary of the Ministry of War, Eleven
> Laurel, from the Fleet Captain Sixteen Moonrise
> of the Twenty-Fourth Legion, 95.1.1–19A

* * *

Here's a question for you, Tarats: how many *other* imago-lines might our esteemed colleague have compromised? Are we prepared to suffer a plague of Dzmares, right now, while Teixcalaan fights a war of your making over our heads and we wait to see if the Dzmare we *are* plagued with is of any use at all? Tell me that. And if you can reassure me that I can requisition a new set of pilot imago-lines to replace the ones I am losing, day by day, without worrying about their integrity—well, then, I imagine I'll owe you a drink.

And I don't usually owe people drinks.

—private message, handwritten and hand-delivered from
the Councilor for the Pilots to the Councilor for the
Miners, 95.1.1–19A (Teixcalaanli reckoning)

NINE Hibiscus was on the bridge when the enemy sent their ships close enough to see. There was that, at least. She hadn't needed to be fetched. When the slick grey three-wheeled rings—*two* of them, a large ship and a small one—appeared out of the black in a shimmer of discontinuity, just at the farthest edge of *Weight for the Wheel*'s visual range, she was right there, as shocked as anyone else. They hadn't come so close before. Which meant they could have come this close all along, and hadn't—an idea that made her skin crawl even as she held up a hand, arresting, and said, "Hold."

They'd been playing the envoy's message on open channels for seven hours, bouncing it off the back side of Peloa-2 and deeper into the alien-controlled area of the sector. Even so, Nine Hibiscus was surprised by having someone answer. If this was an answer, and not an attack force, right here at the heart of her Fleet, as sudden as a shockstick pressed abruptly behind the ear in the dark.

Two ships could mean anything: an advance scout, here to prove that they *could* in fact materialize right beside a Teixcalaanli *Eternal*-class warship like *Weight for the Wheel* without anyone noticing their approach; or a diplomat and an escort, one big and one small; or even an attack strike, if they had some weapon even more destructive than the corrosive semiliquid net that had eaten her Shard pilot. Two ships was *not enough information*.

"Captain," said Five Thistle, and then corrected himself hastily. "*Yaotlek,* they are still coming closer, I have our energy cannons locked on their vector of approach."

They were all staring at the ring-ships, all her soldiers, all her officers, as if their own eyes could make the ships legible just by seeing. The weight of human attention on an inhuman problem. Nine Hibiscus's heart thrummed, adrenaline-shimmer. Her chief weapons officer had just slipped and forgotten her rank, called her by the name he'd always known her by, when their enemies had been understandable, manipulable, predictable.

Every last person on this bridge was waiting for her to make a decision. Attack, or hold. Hope that the Information Ministry's agents were as clever as they seemed, and that no matter how alien and vicious, these aliens were people that could be spoken with—or obliterate them before they could get any closer. She couldn't stop thinking about the Shard that she'd had shot down. How that pilot had begged to die before she was eaten. How every other Shard pilot she could hear had begged with her, their biofeedback full of terror and blanked-out shock. The echoes of that shock, still rebounding.

And yet. And yet, she'd called for a special envoy. She'd gone to Information, rather than to the Third Palm, who had never liked her methodology with *humans,* let alone what she might want to do with aliens. Information had prepared a message. And after that message was sent, something had *changed.*

"Hold," she repeated. "Wait for my signal. Two Foam, are you recording on all open channels?"

"Yes," Two Foam said. "Nothing yet but Fleet unencrypted chatter and our outgoing alien message—I've got it muted on pickup in here to preserve our ears, but it's loud as you want outside."

"Tell me if it changes," Nine Hibiscus said. "The *instant,* if it changes. Five Thistle, stay on that vector and wait for me."

The ring-ships spun. They were closer. Nine Hibiscus noticed how tight and shallow her breathing had become, and inhaled through her nose, out her mouth, old calming exercises from her first year as a Fleet cadet. They hadn't worked very well for her then and didn't work very well now. The smaller ring-ship had shifted in front of the larger one. They spun in different directions, like the shells of electrons around an atomic core, a probabilistic cloud, difficult to see. The smaller one was darker. There was a red tinge to its grey-slick metal. Blood on a deck floor that hadn't been cleaned properly. A stain.

Almost, she dropped her hand and told Five Thistle to fire. Almost.

"I have something," said Two Foam. "They're playing our message back at us, *yaotlek*. It took me a minute to understand—it's the same message as we sent, so I didn't realize—but it's amplified, like a sine wave reinforcing. Louder."

Bleeding stars, but I hope the envoy knew what she was saying when she sent that, Nine Hibiscus thought, *because they're saying it too. Only one way to find out, though.*

"Get the *Reflective Prism* on the comm," she said, and was reassured at the serene command in her own voice. *Reflective Prism* was the nearest of the Tenth Legion warships to her own position, and she needed someone within the arc of audio interference of the ring-ships. "Tell Captain Twelve Caesura or his comms officer to play the envoy's message *too*. Aim at the enemy. Let's let them know we hear them. And for fuck's sake, if anyone fires a weapon, I will *space* them."

"Understood, *yaotlek*," Two Foam said, her hands busy in the air, her eyes already tracking back and forth in micromovements, fast enough that she looked as if she was having a seizure instead of manipulating the communications universe of the Fleet that her cloudhook was projecting for her. The entire bridge felt like an extension of Nine Hibiscus's own skin, that shimmering intensity which was *her people* paying attention to her, hanging on every word, waiting for her to show them the way out of this impossible situation just like she'd done in so many impossible situations before.

Right now she thought she might manage it. Might. Sunfire and space willing, she might just manage it. If she kept moving. Which meant she needed to keep the aliens talking.

"—Someone get the Information people up here, *now*," she added, feeling her mouth stretch into a barbarian parody of a smile. "Go. Go. Eventually we're going to need to say something else than what we've got, and *I* can't make those noises, people. Move."

———

The Kauraanian kitten didn't like being carried in any way Three Seagrass could come up with carrying a kitten. Holding it by the scruff of its neck seemed rude, especially since she didn't exactly know when she was going to get to put it down, and cradling it like it was a human infant made it puncture her with all of its many, many claws.

Eventually, she stopped carrying it and let it sit on her shoulder instead, which it seemed to enjoy. There was still some puncturing involved, but it was less malicious and more stability-oriented. She still had no idea what to do with it. There was absolutely no way she could bring it to the room she was supposed to share with Mahit, and she didn't want to go there anyway. Not yet. Maybe not at all.

In the City, this would be when she'd find herself a decent bar and an interesting stranger to amuse herself with for a while. Maybe there were bars and strangers on Fleet ships. (There would absolutely be strangers. Possibly a stranger would like a Kauraanian kitten. Three Seagrass could hold out hope!) She asked her cloudhook to direct her to the nearest location that was both recreational and *not* a fitness and training facility (she could think of nothing she wanted to do less than *exercise*, stars), and followed where it led her.

Which . . . wasn't a bar. Exactly.

It probably would have been a bar, if it wasn't on a Fleet ship. There were tables, and music—something Three Seagrass dimly remembered had been popular last winter, with a lot of synthesizers in—and dimmer lighting than in the corridors, and lots of strangers, and even some food that wouldn't have been out of place in a bar: fried noodles, maize kernels soaked in spices and vinegar, cassava chips. What there wasn't was *alcohol*.

No getting drunk on your off-shift, apparently. Not on the Fleet's credit chip, at least.

Everyone was sober, which meant everyone turned to look at her when she walked in. It was fairly gratifying. Three Seagrass could imagine the picture she made: Information envoy in coral-orange, the brightest uniform in this sea of Fleet grey-and-gold, with a kitten on her shoulder. An absurd picture. Possibly a threateningly absurd one.

"Hi," she said, brightly. "What kind of food is the best here? For me, and also for this—creature."

There was a resounding silence. Three Seagrass waited for it to shatter. It always did. Curiosity and interest would win every time, if she was just patient enough and expressed sufficient bravado.

Still, the ten seconds of détente were excruciating. Then, a woman who had been sitting alone along the not-a-bar—she was wearing the rank sigils of a *cuecuelihui*, a specialist officer of some kind—said, "Hot-fried noodle cake. Why have you got a cat, Envoy?" and the whole room relaxed.

"The adjutant gave it to me," said Three Seagrass, and took the empty seat beside the *cuecuelihui*. "Do you want it? It seems very friendly. If—sharp, on the ends."

"No," said the *cuecuelihui*, "I definitely don't want a Kauraanian kitten," and held out her arms for it.

Three Seagrass felt a sharp pang of recognition: this person knew exactly how to take control of a conversation, combine surprise and confusion and generosity to engender rapid trust. How nice! Someone trained in basic interrogation! Like finding a lost *asekreta* sibling on a Fleet ship. She coaxed the kitten off her shoulder and let it settle on the *cuecuelihui*'s knee, where it transformed itself into an ovoid of contently vibrating black fur and claws.

"I'm Three Seagrass," she said, once freed of animalian en-
cumbrances. "Are you serious about the noodle cake, or are you
trying to make the Information spook look bad via capsaicin poisoning?"

"I'm serious about the noodle cake, unless you're especially
sensitive to capsaicin poisoning, Envoy." The *cuecuelihui* sketched
a bow over her fingertips without dislodging the kitten. "Fourteen Spike, of the scout-gunner *Knifepoint's Ninth Blooming*,
Tenth Legion. We don't poison spooks unless necessary."

Knifepoint's Ninth Blooming was the ship which had brought
back the transmission of hideous alien noises. Maybe Three Seagrass had picked the right recreation area after all, even if there
wasn't any alcohol to be served. She said, "Thank you," in two
formality-modes higher than what she'd been using before, and
watched Fourteen Spike figure out *why* she was being thanked.
It didn't take that long. Definitely a trained negotiator. A spy,
even! A Fleet spy, but that hardly mattered.

"You're using that recording," said Fourteen Spike. "The one
Knifepoint took before we got chased back here. Good fucking
luck, Envoy. I speak five languages and that stuff isn't language."

Three Seagrass nodded. "I've noticed," she said. "But Information makes a habit of speaking to the unspeakable, so one
has to try, no?"

"Better you than us."

"*Five* languages. What do you use those for on a scout-
gunner?"

There was an art to this. Like playing a *amalitzli* game against
a new opponent, gauging skill and speed, but all with words. It
was what Three Seagrass was *for*. It was—so much easier than
thinking about Mahit Dzmare.

Fourteen Spike shrugged, a fractional amused motion, and
said, "Talking. We do that. Even in the Fleet. It isn't reserved
for spooks." She had begun petting the Kauraanian kitten, and
it purred like it wanted to be a starship engine when it grew up.

"Oh, I've heard that the Third Palm of the Fleet is very good

at talking," Three Seagrass said, matching that shrug exactly—
and was surprised, delightedly surprised, when Fourteen Spike's
face went still and quiet and cold.

"Not just the Third Palm," she said.

"Forgive my ignorance," Three Seagrass told her, and left her
the opening to explain herself. She suspected Fourteen Spike
wouldn't be able to resist. She'd touched some nerve, some place
of pride at the core of her, and she'd defend it, and Three Seagrass would know something new.

"We're the Tenth Legion, not Third Palmers," said Fourteen Spike. "We don't need political officers to get our missions
done, if you understand me. Envoy."

Unspoken but obvious: *We don't need Information, either.* And
more importantly: the Tenth Legion under Nine Hibiscus really, really didn't like being ordered around by the Third Palm
of the Ministry of War.

Which was run by Eleven Laurel, he of the *have you ever spo-
ken to him* interrogation in the spaceport bar back in Inmost
Province. He whom the Emperor Herself was worried about.
Fascinating.

"Oh, I think I have an idea," said Three Seagrass. "Forgive
the insinuation. We are, of course, only the Information Ministry, and can't possibly know *everything.*" She smiled, deliberately wide-eyed. "I think I'd like that noodle cake. And if you
don't mind—and it isn't classified, naturally—I'd love to hear
more about your missions."

If she played this right, she could stay here all night being useful, and not have to talk to Mahit at all until the morning. It
made her feel guilty and faintly ill—she didn't avoid problems,
she really didn't—but right now, a not-bar with a useful Fleet
contact was just so *very* much easier. Than everything.

———

Mahit lay flat on her back in the dark and tried to feel the ship
around her, the great engine of it, the hum of live machinery.

Her face was a foot from the ceiling. After she'd finished read-ing *The Perilous Frontier!* there had really been nothing else to do but go to bed. She'd taken the higher bunk, both out of deference to Three Seagrass if she ever came back to their as-signed quarters (it was miserable climbing a bunk-ladder in the dark, everyone knew that), and out of wanting what comfort she could get from enclosure. If she ignored the drop to her right side, the distance to the floor, she could be inside her own sleep-pod on Lsel, safe.

Not that she'd been safe there. But the habits of memory created all kinds of false harbors. Narrow, confined spaces to sleep in, suspended inside the complex shell of metal that was a Station—or a ship, even a Teixcalaanli one—were *correct*. They felt right. She reached up and brushed the ceiling with her fingertips—and found them numb still, waking to shimmering prickles when they touched its surface.

Neuropathy. It happened more often now. Or—it surprised her more often now, how it could sneak in even when she wasn't trying to work with her imago. With either version of her imago. She was going to have to learn to live with it, wasn't she. As a permanent part of herself.

A sensation of sorrow, from very far off: not even a thought, but an emotional echo. How she herself wanted to cry, and didn't want to want to, and felt also that Yskandr was—sorry, wished that there was an otherwise life for them, where this wasn't hap-pening—

<You're projecting, Mahit. Also wallowing.>

It is very late at night, and I am on a Teixcalaanli warship, and I have fought so badly with my friend that she won't come back to a room I am in. Also I am an exile twice over, once from my home and once from Teixcalaan, which could never have been my home. And my hands hurt. I have every right to wallow.

<You're not an exile,> Yskandr said, and there was a chilled finality to the way he said it that made Mahit want to press him further, like she'd press on a bruise.

How are we not?

<You bought us Lsel, with what you promised Tarats. And if you make up with your friend, you have Teixcalaan—anywhere in all of Teixcalaan.>

Anywhere in all the world, in the language they both so habitually spoke in the privacy of their mind—the language which was neither of their own, but was the Empire's. Mahit couldn't seem to find a way to stop. It was the language they both thought in best.

I didn't buy us anything. I made myself a spy, that's all. Someone else has my eyes: Darj Tarats sees through me. No promises of any reward. And he'll want worse than spywork if I tell him about the conflict between the yaotlek *and Fleet Captain Sixteen Moonrise. There's his sabotage. Turn them against each other fully, paralyze this Fleet, make Nineteen Adze have to commit more legions to the war, ones that aren't at each other's throats. It wouldn't be that difficult. Sixteen Moonrise is looking for levers, and I'm a likely one.* She left the rest of it alone: she didn't want to talk about Three Seagrass with Yskandr any more than she wanted to talk about Three Seagrass with Sixteen Moonrise. Which probably meant she didn't want to *think* about Three Seagrass, considering that Yskandr was right here inside her head with her.

<I can hear you,> he said, dry and distant. <And you're not anyone's eyes *until* you report back. Not anyone's eyes and not anyone's saboteur.>

Is that how you justified not returning to Lsel? If you couldn't report, you remained your own person? How fragile a peace that is, Yskandr. And here you said we weren't in exile.

<Exile isn't something self-imposed.>

He was *wrong* about that, Mahit thought, exile happened in the heart and the mind long before it happened to the body that moved in space, across borders—and thinking this, thinking *no,* felt the neuropathic pain spike in her hands, right down the ulnar nerve through the elbow, like a punishment. Except it hurt *him,* too, it hurt them, they were one person, and the neurological damage from Aknel Amnardbat's sabotage was neither of their faults. Even if it spiked when she found one of the jagged edges between their integration.

As if I knew how to send a message to Tarats from the heart of the Teixcalaanli flagship anyhow, she said, which was a sort of apology. An offer: can we put this away, for now, given all the rest of the circumstances we find ourselves in?

And a response—a flush of warmth all through her, a sense that perhaps she could sleep. A *gentle* sort of tiredness, like a gift from her own endocrine system. She shut her eyes. Curled on her side, facing the wall, her hands folded tight against her chest, protective. Breathed out.

And was startled to full, adrenaline-sharp consciousness when there was a loud banging on the door.

Her first thought was that Three Seagrass had come back after all—but she'd left the plastifilm VOID password-note on the door's touchpad, and she hadn't changed the password itself yet. Three Seagrass could have let herself in. This was someone else. Mahit swung herself off the edge of the bunk, finding the lower bed with her toes and stepping lightly down onto the floor. She wasn't dressed for this—the loose culottes and tank of her pajamas were not in any sense official, nor in any sense Teixcalaanli—

<Put on a jacket, yours is still over the back of the chair,> Yskandr told her, and she was utterly grateful. The jacket helped. It had some structure to it. *The Perilous Frontier!* was a weight against her ribs.

Whoever it was hammered on the door again. Shouted— muffled through the airtight metal—something that sounded like *Envoy! Ambassador!*

There was absolutely no point in pretending she wasn't here, and opening the door wouldn't make her any less safe than keeping it closed: this was not the Jewel of the World, or Lsel, or anywhere else Mahit had ever been. This was a Teixcalaanli warship, and there was nothing outside it but airless void, far closer than it was on a Station. Ships were smaller. Ships weren't *peoples,* even if they were societies. There was no disappearing into a ship, even a ship carrying five thousand. (Especially a Teixcalaanli ship: Mahit hadn't found the camera-eyes yet, but she knew they were here, watching—even without Sunlit behind them to analyze and follow and adjust.)

She opened the door. There was a soldier there, a man of medium height and a fashionable Teixcalaanli military haircut— low hairline accentuated by the sharpness of how he'd pulled his hair back into its queue, the tight fishtail braiding. "Ambassador," he said. "The *yaotlek* wants you and the envoy on the bridge immediately. I am to tell you that your message worked, and she needs another one right away."

The thrill that spun up her, thighs to vagus nerve to throat, was *victory,* as sharp and sweet as anything she could remember: it had *worked,* they had *figured it out,* the aliens were talking back. Mahit knew she was grinning, Stationer-smile, all teeth— knew it by the way that the soldier recoiled slightly, and didn't care. She deserved this. She and Three Seagrass had *established first contact,* and everything else—their fight, Sixteen Moonrise, Darj Tarats, the *whole war*—didn't matter at all. Not this minute. "That's fantastic," she said. "That's—brilliant, really."

It might be the most *significant* thing she'd done in her entire life. The list of people who had established a communicative relationship with a previously uncontacted spaceflight-capable alien species was now, in total, the Emperor Two Sunspot (and whatever aides she'd had, of course), Three Seagrass, and Mahit Dzmare. It was terrifying. It was *amazing.* She felt on the verge of hysterical, delighted laughter, or tears, or—she'd never dreamed of this, astrobiology hadn't been an aptitude she'd even tested for, and linguistics had always been about *human beings,* but—*oh.* It had worked.

"Where *is* the envoy?" the soldier asked, interrupting Mahit's excess of internal delight and sending her just as easily crashing down into the humdrum, miserable reality of having driven off her only friend (if friends were even a category that Teixcalaan-litzlim could fit into, and that was the horrible crux of everything, wasn't it).

She shrugged.

"Wasn't she also assigned to these quarters?" the soldier continued, obviously checking some kind of manifest on his cloudhook.

"Yes," said Mahit. "But she is out, currently."

"It's 0200 hours," said the soldier, puzzled, and then lifted one shoulder and put it down again, as if implying that, well, Information agents must keep very peculiar hours to go along with the rest of their very extensive peculiarities. ". . . Um. Do you know when she'll be back? The *yaotlek* wants you *both*. Immediately."

"I'm sure she does," Mahit said. "But what *you* have, sir, is me. I suggest you use your surveillance camera-eyes and your cloudhook's search algorithms to find the envoy—try bars, or some sort of park or recreation area with flowers, if a ship like this has them—she likes those—while I put on clothing that is appropriate for the bridge. I'll be a moment." She took a step backward into the room, and the door, no longer commanded to remain open by her proximity, slid shut in the soldier's face.

<Bars and recreation areas with flowers?> Yskandr asked, mildly incredulous.

Mahit remembered *deliberately*, which was a skill she'd only really understood since acquiring an imago, even though all Lsel children were trained in the basics of how to do it, in anticipation of future need: to recall, very specifically, an event from one's own life which was the automatic reference point for a present action or feeling. To show, in such recall, how you thought, the patterns of your mind, so that your imago could learn them and follow them and engrave them deeper with their own overlays. A pathway to joint neuroplasticity. Mahit called up the gardens of Plaza Central Four, the taste of green-colored ice cream, the scent of crushed grass under Three Seagrass's folded and napping arms. Called up, too, Twelve Azalea telling her that this sort of trouble was *exactly* like the trouble Three Seagrass had always gotten into, when they'd been trainees together. Slumming in garden parks, ice cream for breakfast after terrible, dangerous, interpersonal adventures.

<You miss her,> Yskandr murmured.

Mahit did. Mahit did, *hugely,* and wished she didn't.

<That soldier won't wait for you forever,> Yskandr went on, taking in whatever Mahit's missing of Three Seagrass meant for him, for them, and placing it aside while there were more immediate problems. Like he'd placed aside the question of *exile.* They were getting good at compartmentalizing. <He'll find her, too. They've got cameras in every corner. Get dressed. Put on whatever you have which is—*sharp*. Pointed. Clean lines. I know you have that sort of outfit.>

I have a formal dress that is that outfit. She'd brought one, and only one—a long black thing, architectural in design, a dress that was all angles and no drape, collarbone-exposing, with sleeves to the wrists. She'd brought it to the City, too, and had never worn it there. She'd never worn it at all.

<Not that. Something more—practical.>

Yskandr, do you even know what clothing types for female-bodied people are?

<You know, so I know. Or I know what you know, and also something about slightly out-of-date court fashion in the City.>

Both of them were better with Teixcalaanli style, then. On Lsel Mahit wore what *everyone* wore, which was trousers and jackets and various undershirts or undertunics, mostly grey and black and white.

<White,> Yskandr told her. <All white, if you can.>

Like Nineteen Adze.

Well, she could do worse.

<Much worse.>

When Mahit opened the door again, in white trousers and asymmetric draped shirt and a short, Lsel-style cropped jacket (she'd had to leave *The Perilous Frontier!* in the other one, there wasn't room for it in this iteration), the soldier was still there, exactly as he had been. He blinked at her for a very long moment. She wondered if he *was* thinking of Nineteen Adze, the *ezuazuacat* Nineteen Adze, in her pristine white suits, before she'd been soaked in blood and rendered suitable for the sunspear throne.

"Have you located the envoy?" Mahit asked him, lightly.

"Not personally," said the soldier. "The ship has. Are you ready now, Ambassador, or is there anything else you need to do?"

If he was thinking of Nineteen Adze, thinking so wasn't making it difficult to be snide and impatient toward the barbarian.

"Show me," Mahit said. "Quickly. I imagine the aliens won't wait for very long before they decide we don't know how to say more than *hello*."

————

Walking onto the bridge, Three Seagrass experienced a moment of debilitating psychological vertigo: standing next to the *yaotlek*, right behind the comms officer's station, was a tall woman all in white with short dark hair, poised and utterly in control of herself. She was *aware* of the process of understanding what she was seeing: not, of course not, the *ezuazuacat* Nineteen Adze, her once-possibly-patron and definitely-now-Emperor. Impossible, for three reasons. The Emperor couldn't have gotten here from the City so quickly (Three Seagrass was *intimately* acquainted with the fastest route by now, and really, what a mess it would have been to get an imperial vessel through some of those ports!); no one was deferring to this woman, as they all would be if she *was* the Emperor; and, well. She was Mahit Dzmare, not Nineteen Adze at all.

The curls of her hair just brushing the collar of her white jacket. That was Mahit, entirely.

And yet Three Seagrass felt as if she had been punched in the solar plexus, breathless and knocked back with superposition of imagery. Whatever game Mahit was playing, it was one with high stakes—

Why, for the sake of every sun and every bleeding star, had she had that stupid fight with Mahit? And not come back to their quarters? She wanted to be *in on this*. She should have been in on this. Instead, here she was, late to what might be the most important act of communication in her life, in yesterday's uniform, which had both Kauraanian kitten hairs and hydroponic waterstains on one sleeve. Having stayed up through a sleep shift talking to Tenth Legion soldiers and avoiding everything else but fried noodle cakes until an on-duty member of the Fleet had come to fetch her posthaste to the bridge.

Looking at her Ambassador, already here and at work, dressed in perfectly designed white—it made her chest ache. Which was inconvenient. At best.

"*Yaotlek*," she called across the bridge, pitched to carry and to be as respectful as possible. "I apologize for my tardiness—there was an episode with a kitten—but I see you are already in the Ambassador's capable hands."

There. That was an opening. It was even possible that Mahit might forgive her, a little, if she kept positioning them both as absolute equals. That seemed to be the crux of the whole miserable mess.

Nine Hibiscus turned toward her, but Mahit did not—Mahit bent her head close to that of the comms officer (Three Seagrass consulted her cloudhook, and pulled up the officer's name, *Two Foam*, ikantlos *first-class*, and a whole string of service records which she really didn't need right now, the War Ministry's internal user interface for personnel lookup was utterly clunky compared to Information's, but at least she'd gotten access to the ship's network at *all*), and made a quick gesture in the air, as if she was drawing an orbital arc with her fingertips. Two Foam nodded to her.

"Behold your handiwork," said the *yaotlek*, and Three

Seagrass left off staring uselessly at Mahit and looked instead at her very first glimpse of their *live* enemy.

Or at least their enemy's ships, presumably with live enemies inside them, rotating slowly at the edge of *Weight for the Wheel*'s visual range, rings on rings. A small ship and a large one. Three Seagrass thought they were peculiarly beautiful. Like the ringed mouths of cave-dwelling fish. An inhuman, somewhat disturbing beauty, but beautiful in symmetry at least. And if they liked symmetry, and were mammals, and had *decided to talk back*—well, then, she'd manage this, wouldn't she. Of course she would.

"What have we been saying back to them?" she asked Nine Hibiscus, walking by her, the comms officer, *and* Mahit to stand by the curved plastisteel windows, four layers thick between her and vacuum, only vacuum between her and the aliens.

"That we heard them play our message back—and then, since I didn't have either you or the Ambassador, Envoy, for a good twenty minutes, Two Foam and I switched to visual composition. If they can hear us and they want to talk, then they can see images that we transmit on the same channels." Nine Hibiscus had come to stand next to her, a large solid form, immovable, like a star that satellites could orbit around. Three Seagrass wished rather a lot that she'd spent a little less time trying to get rid of the kitten and feeling sorry for herself, and even a little less time talking to Fourteen Spike about how impressive the *yaotlek* was, and a little more time *going to the bridge,* even if Twenty Cicada had obviated her of the direct responsibility. Since Fourteen Spike was *right* about the *yaotlek* and her impressiveness. She was the sort of person who made you want to do what she asked, before she asked it.

"Images are easier than trying to speak their language with my extremely limited and machine-mediated vocabulary, yes," Three Seagrass agreed. "And the aliens do have eyes that seem to work in the usual fashion, based on the autopsy. What's the visual?"

"Two Foam is drawing it," Nine Hibiscus said. "Your Ambassador is helping. She's a decent hand at orbital mechanics, which is interesting."

"She was raised on a space station."

Nine Hibiscus lifted one shoulder, suggesting that living in space did very little to guarantee that a person knew how space worked. Three Seagrass assumed that was valid. Then the *yaotlek* said to her, "Envoy, before we send this message—you and the Ambassador *are* willing to meet face-to-face with these things, yes? Given appropriate military escort."

"Are you inviting them onto the ship?" Three Seagrass asked, as blandly as she could manage while thinking, quite vividly and nauseatingly, of all those holoimages of the disemboweled people on Peloa-2.

"Certainly *not*," said the *yaotlek*.

"Without much more substantive communication," Three Seagrass said, warily, "I would prefer not negotiating on *their* ship. No matter whether I am with the Ambassador, a military escort, or you yourself. It shows a certain weakness." Also, she didn't trust those pretty cave-fish mouths, spinning in space: she had already had enough of the physical effects of these aliens and their noises to last several lifetimes, and that was without whatever resonant capacities the material of their hulls provided.

"Funny," Nine Hibiscus said, "the Ambassador said the same thing, nearly word for word. Don't think we're such rubes at negotiation, Envoy, just because we're the Fleet. We're sending you down to Peloa-2. And presumably, they will also send down their representatives. Or at least that's what Two Foam is attempting to draw."

Down amongst the eviscerated. *Delightful*. "Let me see," Three Seagrass said, and braced herself for being near enough to Mahit to brush one of those pure white sleeves in apology.

Mahit didn't say hello. But she did shift slightly, so there was room around the holodisplay Two Foam was working at for Three Seagrass to see properly. The comms officer clearly knew how to draw: she'd sketched two little humans, and two aliens that looked very like the dead thing in the medical lab. Below the two humans and the two aliens was a static flat image of Peloa-2, captured from real holo. As Three Seagrass watched, the aliens and the humans descended on parallel arcs, the orbit Mahit had sketched with the gesture of one hand, and stood facing one another on the surface of the planet. They were extremely out of scale. Neither humans nor evisceration-prone aliens were several thousand feet in height, even when engaged in critical negotiations.

"You need to put the ships in," Three Seagrass said. "Ours and theirs. So it's clear that we want to talk specifically to the ones right out there." They were still spinning, those three-wheeled rings. Spinning and not moving yet, just transmitting louder and louder self-reinforcing renditions of the message Three Seagrass and Mahit had written. *Come talk. Come talk. Come talk. For our mutual benefit.*

Mahit nodded. "She's right. Both ships, and when they get to Peloa-2—when *we* get to Peloa-2—do you know the symbol for volume? For increasing volume?"

Two Foam looked at her as if she'd said something in her own incomprehensible language, instead of a perfectly under-standable Teixcalaanli sentence. "The glyph for *crescendo*?" she asked. ". . . If you *want* me to draw that, I can . . ."

Mahit's face acquired a particular amused, arch expression that Three Seagrass didn't think she'd ever possessed back in the City. Again, she wondered if what she was seeing was the *other* person, the other Ambassador from Lsel Station, dead and machine-reborn Yskandr Aghavn. (And worse, in terms of the inconvenient timing of the realization: she felt a sudden spike of hope that it wasn't *Mahit* that she'd had this terrible fight with, but Yskandr, and everything could still be put back the way it had been. That would be nice, wouldn't it. Most things turned out *not* to be nice, so perhaps she should immediately forget she'd thought of it.)

All Mahit said was, "That has eleven strokes and doesn't even look like a sound wave, *ikantlos,* of course not the glyph for crescendo. Let me show you." And instead of sketching an orbit in the air she made a gesture with one cupped hand, moving across space: a small curve, a larger one, a larger one still. Like a cone of sound.

"Oh," said Two Foam. "*Volume.* Absolutely."

Three Seagrass really needed to get Mahit a cloudhook so she could move holoimages around, but bloody stars, she hardly needed one, did she? Two Foam drew exactly what she'd described: three cupped curves, increasing in size, being emitted from the aliens and the humans once their silhouettes were standing on the surface of Peloa-2. Like they were talking to each other.

"That's good," Three Seagrass said. "I like it. Anything else, Mahit, or should we transmit?"

Transmit, and get ready to go down there. We're not going to have time to make up. Maybe that's easiest.

"We've kept them waiting long enough," said Mahit. "Send it. And let's see how much audio playback equipment we can make portable, and does the Fleet have exceptionally strong antiemetics?"

"You'd have to ask medical," said Two Foam.

"Someone ask medical," said Mahit. "I can't talk to anyone. I'm not a *citizen.*" And she smiled, terrifying and far too beautiful with all those teeth exposed, gesturing to her entire lack of cloudhook.

———

"I'm disappointed in you, Cure," Eleven Laurel said, and Eight Antidote cringed so hard he almost fell off the bench he was sitting on and into the reflecting pool in the garden outside Palace-Earth. Which would have been hideously embarrassing, and bad aquaculture besides. *Splash,* one wet kid and a lot of ruined water lilies, smashed pink petals.

"I don't like being snuck up on," he said, which was true and also not a good response to being surprised by a teacher who was *disappointed*. But he'd really thought he was alone.

"Pay more attention, then," said Eleven Laurel. "You're easy to spot, right out in the open like this, and you're not watching your blind spots. Do they not teach you *anything* in Palace-Earth about your own defense?"

"I'm eleven," Eight Antidote said. "I know how to kick a male-bodied person between the legs and bend anybody's arm back far enough so that they scream, but I don't have much body mass or height leverage, and also the entire City watches me. Haven't you seen the camera-eyes? If I get kidnapped, the Sunlit will kidnap me right back."

"I certainly hope they would," Eleven Laurel said, and came around the bench to sit next to Eight Antidote. All of his very long limbs folded up too much; the bench was too high for Eight Antidote and too low for him. His knees stuck up. "It would be a bad time in Teixcalaan indeed if the Sunlit let the imperial heir *stay* kidnapped."

Eight Antidote wondered if that was some kind of threat. It felt like it might be, but he didn't understand the shape of it, or why he was being threatened right now, in this way. Was Eleven Laurel implying the Sunlit were *currently* not trustworthy, or that they could become so, if Eight Antidote continued to be disappointing? Either version was bad. Either version was *frightening*.

He asked, "Why have I disappointed you?"

Eleven Laurel sighed, a long, deliberate release of breath. "When a person—young or old, seasoned or brand-new—is brought into the sort of meeting like the one you were party to, Cure, a meeting in which one Ministry is suspicious of the motivations of another one—and then that person chooses to go directly from the Ministry that had hosted them to the Ministry under suspicion, direct and brazen—well, that person must either be very young, very stupid, or very untrustworthy. Or all three. I am hoping that it isn't all three, in your case."

"You followed me."

"As I was saying, you're not watching your blind spots very well. You're a fair sneak, Your Excellency, but you light up the entire Palace when you walk in a Ministry front door in broad daylight. Especially the Information Ministry."

Eight Antidote liked being called *Cure* a lot better than *Your Excellency*, but maybe he didn't deserve an affectionate use-name right now. He'd made a *dumb* mistake—apparently—the worst kind of mistake, the kind you don't know is a mistake that you *could* make, so you can't avoid it. He said, "I guess you wouldn't have liked it better if I wriggled in through the Information air ducts instead."

Eleven Laurel cleared his throat like he was pushing away a laugh. "No," he said. "I wouldn't have liked that any better. I'd have liked that worse—then I'd *know* you were trying to be surreptitious. You've at least managed the benefit of my doubts by being obvious. Now. What did you tell Information about what you heard at War, Your Excellency?"

"Nothing," Eight Antidote said, and tried to make himself sound offended, insulted, and not let his voice go high and whiny like a baby's. "I *cross-checked,* Undersecretary, to improve my understanding of communication over interstellar distances. So I could better understand what I heard at War."

"That does sound plausible," Eleven Laurel said, and then said nothing more.

Eight Antidote knew this trick; knew it from Nineteen Adze, knew it from his tutors, knew it from how he'd tried to use it himself on One Cyclamen just an hour ago. It was the trick where he was being invited to get himself in trouble by continuing to talk, by explaining *more,* to make how uncomfortable this conversation was go away. He wasn't going to fall for it. Not this time. (And if he was actually really upset that Eleven Laurel was manipulating him like this, like he was an *asset* and not a *person,* well, he never should have expected otherwise; people like him didn't *have* friends, even grown-up friends, and

also he wasn't going to cry. Or even sniffle like crying was a possibility.)

"Are there any other ways I've disappointed you?" he asked,
instead.

Eleven Laurel patted him on the shoulder, a brief touch that
almost felt parental. "Not yet. *Try* to watch your blind spots,
would you? It'd be nice to see you live to be Emperor."

And then he stood up, brushed his trousers clear of dust
with his hands, straightened his already-straight cuffs, and
strode off through the gardens. Eight Antidote was about to call
after him, *That's not the way out,* but thought better of it. Either
Eleven Laurel wanted to wander through the lily-maze, or he
didn't, and Eight Antidote didn't owe him any help. He got up
himself—kicked a clod of dirt into the pool, which he knew was
self-indulgent and environmentally irresponsible, and he didn't
care one bit—and headed, finally, to talk to Her Brilliance the
Emperor. If he was going to get accused of spying by someone
he thought had *liked him,* he should actually do some spying. And
he was sure Nineteen Adze would want to know about the Lsel
Ambassador appearing, suddenly, on the site of the battlefront.

And maybe about Eleven Laurel implying to Minister Three
Azimuth that the Emperor Herself didn't trust the Ministry of
War. Telling her that would serve him right.

INTERLUDE

DEKAKEL Onchu is not the sort of person who stands on ceremony, or bothers with *channels of communication* when she could achieve the same results by simply taking advantage of her own authority. She is the Councilor for the Pilots; her imago-line is the oldest imago-line on Lsel Station. Sometimes, if she is tired enough, she dreams fourteen generations back: the great calculations for maneuvering what had been a ship-world to a point where it could forever be still, a home for all its travelers at last. She never remembers the numbers when she wakes, but she remembers being someone who knew how to find them.

That is all the authority she will ever need to walk directly into Aknel Amnardbat's office without appointment or announcement. She has questions she wants answered, and she will have her answers now. There will be no further slippery avoidance regarding *sabotage*. There will be no further waiting for semidisgraced ambassadors to decide to finally admit what Dekakel had suspected to be true all along. And there will be no chance for Councilor Amnardbat to neatly slip away and refuse to talk to her fellow Councilor, like she had in the cargo bay when Mahit Dzmare had so unceremoniously been allowed to be nigh-on kidnapped by a Teixcalaanli envoy.

Amnardbat is behind her desk. She has the grace to not look surprised when Dekakel walks through her door; perhaps her secretary managed to send her a warning message. Dekakel does not sit down, even when Amnardbat gestures at the chair opposite her own. Sitting down would imply a certain equality between the two of them that Dekakel no longer feels.

"Councilor," says Amnardbat. "How can I help you?"

"You can tell me why you let Dzmare get onto that shuttle when you'd convinced her you wanted her here badly enough that she came to *me* for rescue. Let's start there. *Councilor.*"

Aknel Amnardbat has a face that settles easily into serene and confident distaste; the bubbles of her curls and the pleasant high arches of her cheekbones are accustomed to the look she gives Dekakel now. "I don't care what happens to Dzmare," she said, "as long as she isn't on this Station. I don't care one bit, as long as that imago-line isn't here, twisting whatever it touches. If that Teixcalaanlitzlim wants her, she can *have* her."

Dekakel doesn't let herself be shocked. *That imago-line.* Aghavn and Dzmare. *Twisting whatever it touches.* No wonder Amnardbat had sabotaged Mahit Dzmare: she'd wanted to kill the whole *line,* and that line was only one imago-machine strong, if you didn't count Tsagkel Ambak, and Dekakel doesn't—she wasn't an ambassador, she was a negotiator, and a long-gone one. Aghavn's reticence in returning to Lsel had made sure of that. Sabotage, and let the Empire deal with the wrecked remains of an ambassador; it'd probably kill her its own self.

"And if she'd stayed on-Station? What would you have done with her then?"

"Why does Pilots care what Heritage does with an imago-line? You are out of your jurisdiction, Councilor Onchu."

"Pilots always cares what Heritage does," Dekakel snaps, "since Heritage holds our imago-lines as well as everyone else's—tell me, Aknel, that you aren't making unilateral decisions about line corruption and suitability, tell me that true, and I will walk out of here and leave you be."

"I'm the Councilor for Heritage," says Aknel Amnardbat. "My mandate is to preserve Lsel Station. Are you questioning that mandate, or my adherence to it?"

"That wasn't *no.*"

Amnardbat looks at her, and deliberately, slowly, and with intent—shrugs. "Someone, Councilor, needs to make decisions that preserve not only our lives, and our sovereignty, but our sense of ourselves as *ourselves*. That's what Heritage is for. That's what I'm doing."

"And if Dzmare were to come back?" Dekakel isn't sure why she asked that; she's fairly certain that Mahit Dzmare is going to die at war, along with a great many Teixcalaanlitzlim.

"Then I'd want to carve that machine out of her skull, Dekakel, and space it, and see if there was anything left of her worth keeping on-Station if she woke up. Poor woman. I do take a little of the blame—had I given her another imago rather than Aghavn's, perhaps her xenophilic obsession could have been ameliorated."

"Why didn't you, then?"

Amnardbat sighs, put-upon. "*Someone* needed to be a sacrifice to the Empire, and her aptitudes really were outrageously green for Aghavn's imago. Might as well be her. And it gets them both off our decks, Councilor."

Chilled, Dekakel asks one last question: "Is there any other line you've done this to?"

"Is there a line you'd recommend?"

Dekakel will remember the easiness with which Aknel Amnardbat answered her for a very long time; the easiness, and the way she abruptly knew she couldn't trust any imago-line that this woman had touched to be unaltered. How clearly she saw what Amnardbat was, in that moment: a person who so loved Lsel Station that she'd replaced her ethical responsibilities with the appalling brightness of that love, and didn't care what she burned out to preserve it.

CHAPTER ELEVEN

Industrial Employment Opportunity SILICA-2318A—Temporary Relocation—Hardship Bonus Pay—Four-Month Rotations. An opportunity for glassworkers, manufactory employees with management experience, and natural resource specialists (particularly those Teixcalaanlitzlim with extraction and/or arid-landscape experience) is available for imperial citizens willing to relocate to the Peloa System for at least four months. Hardship bonus pay conditions derive from planetary temperature extremes, but Peloa-2 has no indigenous predators or known disease vectors. Contraindications: asthma, reactive airway disorder, heat sensitivity, prior episode of sunstroke . . .

—job posting on Teixcalaanli central government jobs
board, to be reposted every month

* * *

And am I made to die? / To lay this body down / to let my trembling
mem'ry fly / into a mind unknown?
Our home in deepest shade / well-caught by pilots' knots / the bril-
liant regions of the dead / where nothing is forgot!
Soon as from flesh I go / what will become of me? / eternal memory
bestowed / will now my portion be.
And woken by the Station, bound, / I from my body rise / and see my
successor glory-crowned / within our star-flamed skies!

—Lsel vernacular folk-harmony song, unknown origin,
possibly pre-establishment of the Station

HER first desert, even without the anticipation of attempted negotiations with murderous and incomprehensible alien life, was intoxicating. It stretched all around the landing site in an endless wave of bone-white silica sand, unmarked by water or by vegetation save for one copse of small, wide-crowned grey-green trees near the buildings that the Teixcalaanli refinery workers had lived in before they had all died. Those buildings were white, too. Sun-bleached. Even the sky had all the color leached out of it, reducing it to a hazy blue-pallor vault.

Mahit had never been on a planet as hot as Peloa-2. She'd never *thought* about planets as hot as Peloa-2, certainly not as places people might actually live. Temperatures this high were on the edge of human tolerances. If there had been a heat anomaly of this intensity on Lsel Station, half of the Stationers would be preparing for emergency evacuation because of radical life support system failure. The soldiers on *Weight for the Wheel* had warned her and Three Seagrass before they'd all boarded the atmospheric-descent shuttle: take extra water. Drink even if you aren't thirsty. If you're down there for more than eight hours, take salt pills. Try to stay out of direct sunlight.

Mahit had thought they were being melodramatic, trying to tease the Information agent and the barbarian, City-born or eternally foreign: neither one the sort of people who would know how to deal with inclement environments, *of course*. But they weren't teasing. The air on Peloa-2 was dry enough it sucked the moisture from her tongue in the space of a breath. The light seemed to have both weight and weightlessness all at once. She felt a pressured sort of heat, sunlight on her skin but also the *air itself*, so hot, making her respiration deeper, her heart slower, as if the gravity on this planet was twice as high as it truly was—and at the same time, she felt drunk. Featherlight. Like she could walk forever into the bright desert of Peloa-2 and come back unharmed.

And then the wind changed, and the smell of charnel drifted

toward her and Three Seagrass and their small escort of Fleet soldiers: the dead colonists, rotting in their factory buildings. The leavings of the creatures—the people, Mahit was going to think of them as people for the duration of this encounter— that they were here to meet.

She'd never been on a planet that all of Teixcalaan had held a funeral for before, either. She suspected none of them had: not her, not Three Seagrass, not their small escort of ground-combat specialists, bristling with black-muzzled energy weapons.

She'd had no time to talk to Three Seagrass alone, hardly enough time to do more than prepare a sequence of short recordings in what they believed was the alien language. A repetition or two of *hello-we're-here* and *hurrah!* and something they suspected might be *back-the-fuck-off*—since their intercepted transmission had included something that might have been that, right when the aliens had noticed *Knifepoint* but before they had begun to chase them. They'd also found time to locate a very large, but still portable, holoprojector programmed for graphic representation, since one could only go so far with approximately six vocabulary words, that weren't words as much as tonal markers for feelings, anyhow.

Whatever she and Three Seagrass were going to do about what had happened between them would have to wait until this meeting was done.

"You're the better draftsman," Three Seagrass said, her voice a curl of smoke in the heat, wavering and distant. Mahit wondered if heat distorted sound or if she was simply experiencing a mild auditory hallucination. "If they want to talk in pictures, I'll give you my cloudhook so that you can draw."

"All right," Mahit said, and then—because she didn't want to go into this conversation raw, with nothing but work between the two of them to hold it together—and because the desert was so beautiful and horrible at once, the stretched-out shimmer of it—asked, "Are all deserts like this?"

Three Seagrass shook her head. "I've never been anywhere like this," she said. "The deserts I know are—red rock, plateaus and carved-out mountains, flowers. The south continent back home. This is a *sand* desert. It's—"

"It makes me want to walk out into it," Mahit said, as a confession. As a single offering: *I will try to trust you, on the very small things at least, if you try too.*

"I know," said Three Seagrass, and she really sounded as if she did. As if the desert heat pulled at her that way, too. "Guess what, Mahit? We get to. A little. The meeting site is fifteen minutes away."

They'd picked a plateau, a flat place where the dunes drifted less and where it was possible for their escort soldiers to erect a canopy to provide some shade. Mahit had expected a piece of high-albedo tarp and some tent-poles, from what the soldiers unpacked, moving with practiced speed—but when the canopy was unfolded, and she and Three Seagrass and all their battery-powered audiovisual equipment were positioned underneath it, she saw that the underside of the tarp was patterned in silver and pink and gold-shot blue, lotuses and water lilies, a woven fabric sewn to the light-reflective plastic. A piece of the City spread out here like a traveling palace.

<Teixcalaan does not neglect symbolism,> Yskandr murmured to her, <even in deserts.> Mahit had *missed* that, she realized, or Yskandr had, or—it didn't matter which of them. Having symbolic valence encoded into the smallest action was familiar, and comforting, even if she wished it wasn't—even if that comfort was just another sign of how Teixcalaan had reordered her mind, her sense of aesthetics.

"Did you bring this from the City?" she asked Three Seagrass, gesturing at the cloth.

"I wish I had," said Three Seagrass, "it's rather brilliant. No, I got it from Twenty Cicada."

Mahit wondered when *that* had happened. At what point during the long night they'd spent apart, not sleeping—was she doomed to sleep deprivation *every* time she spent more than a day surrounded by Teixcalaanlitzlim?—had Three Seagrass been given a piece of Teixcalaanli propaganda encoded in a beautiful tapestry? *Here is water, even in the desert. We are a people who bring flowers.*

<You should have been a poet,> Yskandr said again. <Poets sleep more than political operatives.>

Not in Teixcalaan they don't, Mahit thought, and got electric laughter spiking up and down her ulnar nerves in response.

"It's good," she said to Three Seagrass. "Whether it was his idea or yours, I think it's going to be effective, at least if they come from systems with plant life . . ."

She trailed off. There was something coming up the other side of the plateau.

They moved in a hunting lope, a stride that covered ground, even when the ground was the uncertain footing of sand. Their shoulders rocked forward with each step; powerful, heavily muscled. There were two. They had not come with an escort. Mahit's first impression was of black-keratin claws on their hands, of terribly long and flexible necks that ended in muzzled heads, round ears that were faintly furred. Their skins were spotted, variegated patterns, and they towered two feet above human heads—three feet over the smaller Teixcalaanlitzlim, like Three Seagrass. They wore pale grey tactical uniforms, built for deserts, and no visible weaponry. They looked like nothing she'd ever seen. They looked like people. They looked like those claws were all the weapons they'd need.

Every opening word Mahit could think of dried up in her mouth, as if the heat had stolen not only her saliva but her speech.

Beside her, Three Seagrass straightened her shoulders and set her jaw as if she was about to speak oratory in front of the Emperor. Mahit knew the shape of her like this, the focus that meant *performance*, and wondered when she'd learned to recognize it so well, how she knew *this* about Three Seagrass and not much else. Not enough else.

"Play the *hello* noise, Mahit," she said. "You'll know when."

And then, as if she was meeting a functionary from some other Ministry, and not a foreign creature that stood shoulders and many-toothed head above her, Three Seagrass walked to the edge of the shade canopy, barely five feet from the aliens, pressed her fingertips together, and bowed over them. Mahit reached for the control-datapad for their audio projector— hoped it would work, that it hadn't been fried in the smothering heat, or impregnated with gumming sand. Her fingertips ghosted over the pad's surface, summoning up the right terrible noise. She didn't press hard. It was like holding the trigger of an energy weapon; the slightest motion was all that was necessary—

"I am Envoy Three Seagrass of the Teixcalaanli Empire," said Three Seagrass to the aliens, one hand pressed first to her chest—*I am*—and then flying up in an encompassing gesture to take in the canopy behind her, laden with its woven flowers. *And this is mine, this is what I represent.* "I negotiate on behalf of Her Brilliance the Emperor Nineteen Adze, the Edgeshine of a Knife, whose reign shatters all darkness."

Nothing Three Seagrass was saying would be understandable to the aliens. That was what Mahit was for, right now. She pressed her fingers to the datapad, and played *hello*, all of the sickening static scream of it.

The aliens went very still. One of them glanced at Three Seagrass, and then pointed with its chin at the projector setup. The other one looked there, too. Mahit wished she could read anything about their body language. They hadn't moved forward or back. Were they puzzled, intrigued, angry? It was worse than trying to understand the understated delicacy of Teixcalaanli facial expressions. Worse by a *lot*. She knew they were communicating, but she couldn't tell how. Not audibly. Maybe they *did* communicate by scent, or by ear positioning, or something else she'd never imagined. She was a linguist at *best* (more like a diplomat-poet with pretensions, she'd never taken a xenolinguistics specialty, she'd had all of Teixcalaanli language to play with and back then she hadn't thought she'd ever need anything else), and if the aliens didn't have words to decipher . . .

The second one opened its mouth and made the *hello* noise, without any benefit of amplification or audio processing. The first alien, the one which had pointed at the audio equipment, joined it. The same noise, reverberating. On *Weight for the Wheel*, Mahit and Three Seagrass and all of their escorts had been stuffed full of antiemetics, the best that the medical bay could locate, and she *still* felt twistingly nauseated. The *vibrations*. The static noise of them, in her bones. It really was infrasound, with all of infrasound's physical horrors. But all right, all right, they heard *hello* and they said *hello* back, two sharp-toothed maws wide open. Their tongues were as spotted as their skins.

Mahit looked at Three Seagrass and shrugged as if to say, *Now what?*

Three Seagrass caught her eyes. Held them with her own: a wild intensity, a semihysteric *giddiness*. Mahit remembered it from how she'd looked right after the first time someone tried to kill Mahit in front of her, back in the Ambassadorial apartment in Palace-East, so very far away. A sense of *watch me—here we go*.

Three Seagrass took a breath, the kind that expanded all of her narrow chest and belly: breathed not only for oratory but for something even louder. And, exhaling, began to *sing*.

"Within each cell is a bloom of chemical fire," she sang, bell-clear alto, a voice for calling lost people home, a carrying voice, meant for distance. "Committed to the earth, we shall burst into a thousand flowers—as many as our breaths in life—and we shall recall our names—our names and the names of our ancestors—and in those names blood blooms also from our palms . . ."

It was the Teixcalaanli funeral poem. The one Mahit had heard arranged in a hundred different ways, spoken or sung—the one she'd read the first time in a textbook in a classroom on the Station, marveling at *chemical fire* and the idea of flowers made of blood. But she'd never heard it like this. Three Seagrass had made it sound like a war chant. A promise. *You spilled our blood, and we will rise.*

Also it was *fucking* clever. Not the alien sort of resonant vibrations, but a very human version.

<Showing them that we can talk, too, and have language,> Yskandr murmured. <She's more than clever. That was masterful. I see why she's worth how upset you are.>

Three Seagrass was gesturing with one hand, beckoning Mahit forward. She went, as if pulled—the heat still made her dizzy, and she wondered if the aliens felt it, or cared, and what their home planet was like climatewise—and took up the position that still felt exactly *correct:* Three Seagrass at her left. The two of them arrayed in front of an insolvable political problem. (The two of them, and the ghost of Twelve Azalea like an echo, an imago who would never exist. That thought was like a fishhook through her lip, a sudden and capturing pain.)

"You know the song?" Three Seagrass murmured. Mahit nodded. She knew it well enough. "Good," said Three Seagrass. "Let's see if we make them get sick when we make resonant sound waves, too."

Mahit hadn't sung with another person in years. Poetry was different. She could recite, she could declaim—but singing wasn't something she *did,* by habit or inclination. It had a strange intimacy to it that she hadn't expected. They had to breathe together. They had to *pitch* together. And all the while the aliens stared at them, blank and evaluating, with their killing claws peacefully at their sides. They didn't vomit. Mahit was glad; she didn't want to get possibly toxic alien on her skin, and she was so *close* to them. They smelled like—animal, and something else, a dry herbal scent she'd never smelled before.

It wasn't a long song, the funeral poem. Mahit was still gasping after it was finished. The heat lived inside her lungs now, and her throat felt raw. She swallowed, but there was no saliva to wet her mouth with.

The left-side alien made a low, crooning noise that Mahit had never heard before. The sound was metallic, machine-liquid like a synthesizer, but clearly, clearly organic. It made her ache just behind her sternum, as if her heart was racing out of control. The right-side alien came two loping steps closer, and now she knew her heart *was* racing, familiar adrenaline-spike of visceral fear. She was going to faint, or scream. Three Seagrass's shoulder brushed her shoulder. They were both shaking.

<Stop it. Hush. If you're going to die, you'll die because this thing ripped out your organs, and not for any other reason.> Yskandr was a *balm,* a clear secure place in her mind, something *hers*—as was the sudden rush of shivery warmth that ran through her, her imago playing games with her endocrine response again, but oh, right now she was grateful for any feeling that wasn't externally induced.

The alien pressed one of its claws to its chest, as Three Seagrass had done. And it gestured behind itself, even though there was nothing behind it to gesture at, no canopy and no escort of soldiers. And then it made *sounds*. Almost reasonable sounds. Almost, Mahit thought, *words*. A spitting, consonant-heavy, pitched syllable sequence, but one she thought she could imitate. Even though she was going to have to sing to do it.

I should have taken lessons in holding pitch, she thought. And tried, like she'd tried the very first time she'd been in a Teixcalaanli language class, to make the unfamiliar sounds she'd heard with her own mouth.

———

Nine Hibiscus had never been very good at waiting. It was why she'd been a Shard pilot, back at the beginning of her service in the Fleet: Shard pilots tumbled out of warships like glittering knife-sharp glass, unhesitant, and most of the time they didn't know they were going to be deployed until right before it happened. No delays, no effort to make herself hold still, to stay in calculating abeyance until the right moment to strike. That skill, she'd had to learn. She'd learned it well enough to be captain, then Fleet Captain, and now *yaotlek*—but that didn't mean she *liked* it.

Down on Peloa-2, four of her people—plus an Information agent and a barbarian diplomat, but *four of her people,* first and foremost—were either being dismembered by aliens (worst case) or being subject to heatstroke-inducing temperatures while waiting for negotiations to proceed (best case). And she could do nothing but wait—wait, like she was waiting for her scout-ships to find some base the aliens were using, off to the left where Forty Oxide's people were being picked off, little by little, death after death and funeral after funeral; wait, like a just-graduated cadet expecting word about their first posting in the mail—wait and watch the larger of the two three-ringed ships spin menacingly at the very limits of her visual field on the bridge. The smaller had gone into the Peloa System, just like her own shuttle had. They were experimenting with parity, as if this was a negotiation between two groups of humans and not an attempt at communicating with a species which seemed to be driven only to devour or despoil, one or the other . . . but which still had technological capabilities as good as or better than any Teixcalaanli warship.

Nine Hibiscus *hated* waiting, in situations like this. So she did exactly what she'd always done, from the time when she'd been a cadet: she made sure that there was nothing on fire on the bridge, literally or metaphorically, and likely wouldn't be during the next two hours—and went to invade Swarm's personal space, so that they could wait together.

On *Weight for the Wheel* his personal space was the adjutant's suite, two rooms on the exact opposite side of the ship from her own: the idea being that, if some enemy weapon took out the captain in her quarters, her adjutant might survive to act in her stead. Nine Hibiscus knew the way there as well as she knew the way to any place in the galaxy. Furthermore, she had the door codes, unless Twenty Cicada had changed them again—

He hadn't. His door opened up for her like he and she were precisely the same person, and Nine Hibiscus was hit in the sinuses with the scent of *green*. That very particular smell: the richness of plant life, alienated from flowers: vines and succulents and anything else Twenty Cicada could convince to grow with next to no help from water. He used his *own* water-ration for his garden. That, too, he'd been doing since they were cadets together. No waste; no excess. Not for her Swarm.

So said his religion, anyhow, and she suspected he'd do it anyway, even if homeostasis didn't request it of him. That was the difficulty of Twenty Cicada: determining where the devotion to an entirely minority religious practice stopped and the person began. If there was a space between the two concepts at all.

He was sitting in the middle of the floor, cross-legged, a halo of holograph analyses arced around his head, transparent enough to show all the green creeping up the walls through each image. Most of them were views of ship systems she knew, instant familiarity even seen backward: the readout of energy consumption and life support systems from the entirety of *Weight for the Wheel* was pinned in its usual place about a foot above his forehead, so that everything else he wanted to look at could spin around it. A still point like a crown.

Also, curled in his lap like a puddle of space without stars, was one of the pets from Kauraan. It seemed to be asleep. He was petting it.

"I thought you hated them," Nine Hibiscus said, dryly. "Was all of that complaining about ecosystem disruption for show, then?"

Twenty Cicada looked up at her, and dismissed most of his work holos with the hand that wasn't petting the small void on his knee. "I do hate them," he said, smiling. "But this one likes me, and what am I going to do with the things, space them? It's not their fault they exist."

She came to sit next to him, knee to knee. There always seemed to be more oxygen in one of Twenty Cicada's garden rooms. (Not seemed: there *was*. Plant respiration. She'd checked the readouts once. It was a fractional difference, but real.) The Kauraanian pet lifted its head and opened yellow eyes. It made a noise like a badly tuned stringed instrument, stood, paced in a tight circle on Twenty Cicada's lap, and settled down again. "I didn't think you'd *space* them, Swarm," she said. "But this is cuddling."

"It yowls if I don't," Twenty Cicada said, perfectly bland, and Nine Hibiscus laughed. For a moment she felt very young: transported more than a decade back. To some ship where she'd been of use, and so had he, and she had never thought of not sleeping for the sake of her Fleet.

"Ah, well, then I assume you'll have to keep it," she said, and stroked its fur herself. It was very soft.

"Nothing from Peloa-2 yet?" Twenty Cicada asked, just as neutrally as he'd explained his sudden affection for the pet.

"If there was anything, I wouldn't be here, would I?"

"I know you wouldn't," he said, and waved off the insinuation with a falling gesture of one hand. "Better question, *yaotlek:* how many hours until we go down to pick up their corpses and the doubtless ruined remains of my favorite wall hanging?"

Nine Hibiscus blinked. "Why do the envoy and the Stationer have *any* of your wall hangings, let alone your favorite?" The object in question was a tapestry of pink and blue-gold lotus flowers, in the highest City style. It usually hung in Twenty Cicada's bedroom, which meant Nine Hibiscus hadn't seen it since he'd bought it and shown it off to her. There were other, presumably less-favorite wall hangings all over his quarters: everywhere there wasn't a plant. For someone who hardly ate and who divested his own personal self of all but the most severely correct trappings of his job and his authority—just the uniform, no hair and no skin-pigments, the *essence* of a Teixcalaanli Fleet officer distilled—Twenty Cicada surrounded himself with a riot of color and aesthetic luxury. He'd explained it once: it was one of those balances that the homeostasis-worshippers could practice. Excess and asceticism at once.

"I thought the envoy would need something lush to stand in all that desert with. If she doesn't get herself eviscerated before the enemy has time to notice symbolism."

". . . If the enemy is *capable* of noticing symbolism," Nine Hibiscus muttered.

Twenty Cicada shrugged. "I'm sure they have *some*. But I doubt they care for ours."

"Why give the envoy your flower tapestry, then? If you're just expecting us to go down and retrieve partial envoys and partial tapestries in another three hours."

"Three hours. Longer than I'd wait, *yaotlek,* but you're the one who gets to make decisions." There was something in his expression, in the shape of that phrase, that made Nine Hibiscus want to wince. Yes—she was the one who made decisions, and she didn't much like it when her adjutant disagreed with them, especially when he went along with her anyway. When he placed so very much weight on his trust in her.

"There are other luxuries on our ship we could have given the envoy that weren't your *favorite* tapestry, Swarm," she said. "If you wanted to set her up to use symbolic valence provided she could get these aliens to recognize what a flower *is*."

He scratched the Kauraanian pet behind its ears. It emitted a purr like a very small starship engine. "I could have," he said, "but why would I send anyone out on one of your missions, Mallow, without the sharpest knives and the most beautiful examples of our culture I have to give? If we are trying to talk to these—*things*—then we're *trying*. Entirely."

Which was precisely what made her want to flinch. He didn't want to talk to them, or even make the attempt to, but she had set their course and here he was devoting their resources to that course, no matter what sacrifices were required. She wanted to apologize, but that wasn't something she did. It undermined both that trust and the authority it gave her. Instead she nodded. "If we go down there to fetch the envoy and our people back and there's nothing but rent tapestry pieces and entrails, I will give you an absurd service bonus next time we're on leave in the Western Arc and you can go buy a *larger* one, with more thread count."

"In such a situation, *if* we survive long enough to go on leave, *yaotlek*, I'd quite appreciate it."

"Your confidence is overwhelming."

Twenty Cicada cast his eyes up toward the ceiling, which had been well colonized by a creeping net of green, laden with tiny white flowers. "You've seen their firepower," he said. "And we both know ours. This is going to be a very bad, very long war, and while the prospect is the furthest thing from what I'd wish for, I don't think you or I will be the last set of *yaotlek*-and-adjutant to lead it."

"We haven't died yet," she said. "Despite the best efforts of a great many people."

"*People*, yes," Twenty Cicada said, correcting her. "If it was people in those solvent-spitting ring-ships, I'd be negotiating with you for just *how* large my service bonus should be. But they're not people. Perhaps the envoy can turn them into people, but she's just one Information agent, and she is *very* young. As is her Stationer companion. You know who that is, don't you?"

"Mahit Dzmare. The one who was on the newsfeeds when One Lightning was pulling that incredibly stupid stunt at the end of the last Emperor's reign. I know."

"Good," said Twenty Cicada. "Because Fleet Captain Sixteen Moonrise *definitely* knows who she is, and if I have her dead to rights—and I almost always do—she'll find a way to use Mahit Dzmare, or what she represents, against you."

Nine Hibiscus hummed through her teeth. "You think Sixteen Moonrise is that aggressively opposed to my leadership?"

Twenty Cicada shook his head, blinked to have his cloudhook call up a holoimage of *Weight for the Wheel* as a flattened schematic map. There was a tracery in electrum-silver threaded through a *very* large number of the decks. "She's been haunting us," he said. "I've tracked her. I don't think it's exactly that the Fleet Captain of the Twenty-Fourth is opposed to you, Nine Hibiscus. I think someone in the Ministry is. And she's a very effective agent for their purposes. She knows as much about the aliens as we do, for example. As much as anyone save the envoy and Dzmare. And if she wasn't trying to find out more, she would have gone back to the *Parabolic Compression* half a day ago."

"So she's a spy?"

"So she's a spy whose eyes should be trained outward and which have been turned inward by someone else's hand," Twenty Cicada said. Which was gnomic, even for him. But Nine Hibiscus thought she got what he was gesturing at. Sixteen Moonrise had, after all, spent the first five years of her recorded Fleet career as a political officer on the same *Parabolic Compression* she captained now. And political officers were placed on the orders of the Undersecretary for the Third Palm—the Ministry of War's internal intelligence service.

"You think she's *still* Third Palm. Not just served there as a cadet."

Twenty Cicada smiled, one corner of his mouth twisting. "I think that the Third of the Six Outreaching Palms would like to snatch you back into a more controllable orbit than the one you're on, and that Fleet Captain Sixteen Moonrise is as good a pulling-hook as any."

"Swarm, she *isn't* my type."

He snorted. "No, you like them with more flesh and more masculinity, I'm well aware. Not that kind of hook. The kind that keeps you distracted enough from our real enemy out there that you make mistakes. And we can't afford mistakes. Not in this war. Not if we don't want to learn how to sing funerals for a great many more planets than Peloa-2."

"Consider me warned," Nine Hibiscus said. "And get her off my ship, would you?"

"I can *try*—" Twenty Cicada began, and then both his cloud-hook and Nine Hibiscus's went off with a sharp chime: priority message. Something had come back from Peloa-2 after all.

————

Of course, he had to wait. Emperors were busy all the time; this was the nature of Emperors, his ancestor had been exactly the same. Eight Antidote only ever had seen him at events or late in the evenings or once, memorably, at dawn, when he showed up to Eight Antidote's bedroom and took his hand and they went walking in the gardens, like they were parent and child instead of ancestor and ninety-percent clone. He'd been very small then. His ancestor-the-Emperor had plucked a nasturtium and woven it into Eight Antidote's hair, a red one, and then when he'd said he liked it, a yellow one and an orange one, and he'd worn them until they rotted and he had to be washed.

That was a long time ago, even for someone who was only eleven.

It was almost midnight by the time Nineteen Adze was available to see him, and at that hour, she wanted to see him in her own suite. She'd sent an infofiche-stick message to say so, one of the clean white ones that no one else used but her, waiting in the mail slot outside Eight Antidote's room like he was a grown person who got mail. He broke the seal open, and the holo glyphs that spilled out were simple and inviting: *Come by, if you're still awake.* And then her signature glyph, the same one which was on the infofiche seal. No titles.

Well, they were sort of family. And also she'd shown up *in-side* his bedroom without even asking, so just signing a message *Nineteen Adze* wasn't that weird. (It was weird. It was one of those small things that made Eight Antidote wonder when a person stopped being a child entirely, and started being something else.) He put the opened infofiche stick into the drawer of his desk, so he could look at it again later, if he wanted to. If he wanted to think about how simple and clear and friendly that message had been, later.

The Emperor's suite was where his ancestor had lived, and the Emperor before him, and a whole lot of other Emperors also, but that didn't mean it looked the same as it had six months ago. His ancestor-the-Emperor had liked lots of small, beautiful objects, and bright colors, blue and teal and red, and there had been a plush woven rug on the floor of the front sitting room, with lotus-flower patterns woven in by hand, a gift from the Western Arc families. Nineteen Adze was different. Nineteen Adze liked *books*. Codex-books, not just infofiche; books and also stones, slices of rock that you could see the light through. She'd lined the walls with cases for them. That lotus-woven rug was hanging on one of the walls instead of being on the floor, so you just saw the bare tiled flagstones, the marble and its patterns that looked like imaginary cities. The floor had been here as long as Palace-Earth had.

The Emperor Her Brilliance Nineteen Adze, She Whose Gracious Presence Illuminates the Room Like the Edgeshine of a Knife, was sitting on a couch, reading one of her books. She looked up when Eight Antidote came in, and patted the arm of the identical couch catty-corner to hers. "Come sit," she said. "I'm sorry to keep you up this late, but it was the only time we could talk with relatively low chances of emergency interruption."

Eight Antidote sat. The couches were upholstered in bone-white velvet, with tufted backs, the indentations set with grey-and-gold disks. He always worried he'd spill something on one of them. "It's all right, Your Brilliance," he said. "I know emperors don't sleep. I should get some practice while I can."

She didn't smile. He wished she had. Instead she put her book down on the glass end table between the two couches—it was something Eight Antidote had never read, by someone named

Eleven Lathe—and looked him over, eyes still narrow and neutral. There was a tiny line between her eyebrows which wasn't always there.

"What would you like to tell me?" she asked, which wasn't at all the question he'd expected. It meant he had to choose.

He could start with Eleven Laurel in the garden. That would be telling the Emperor that War and Information—or at least parts of War and Information—really didn't like each other. But she probably knew that already, and also it would mean revealing how *he* felt about Eleven Laurel threatening him—and he didn't want to start with that. Not with the Emperor. It would sound like he was *complaining,* and asking her to fix it, and he didn't want Nineteen Adze fixing *his* problems.

He opened his mouth, and what came out was, "The Ambassador Mahit Dzmare is on *yaotlek* Nine Hibiscus's flagship."

Nineteen Adze clicked her tongue against her teeth. ". . . How did you learn *that*?" she asked.

"The special envoy from the Information Ministry brought her there," he said. That wasn't exactly an answer. It turned out it was very hard to be a spy, when it came time to tell the secrets you'd learned. It turned out you really, really wanted to keep them for yourself. But at least the fact that Dzmare had been brought along by an Information agent seemed like the sort of additional information he really ought to share.

"Of course she did," said Nineteen Adze, and Eight Antidote couldn't decipher her expression at all. Whatever it was, it wasn't surprise. "What else do you know about the envoy?"

At the strategy meeting in War, *no one* had liked the envoy, but he wasn't sure whose dislike was real and whose was inter-Ministry rivalry. There had been a lot of inter-Ministry rivalry, especially between the people who were left over from Nine Propulsion's administration (like Eleven Laurel and the Fifth Palm undersecretary, the man who controlled armaments and research) and people who had come in with Three Azimuth, or at least at the same time she had, and were still learning their jobs and deciding where their loyalties would go. So he didn't know anything about the envoy, not for real. Except—

"The Fleet Captain Sixteen Moonrise doesn't trust her," he said. "Doesn't trust her maybe because of Mahit Dzmare, but maybe because she just doesn't."

"Sixteen Moonrise of the Twenty-Fourth. Did you know, little spy, that she used to be one of Eleven Laurel's students, too?"

Eight Antidote shook his head. (Of course Eleven Laurel had had students before him; there was no reason to feel jealous of some grown-up faraway Fleet Captain. But he did: squirmingly jealous and a little ashamed. *Was* that how the Emperor thought of him, now? As Eleven Laurel's student? Did he want her to think of him that way? Even if Eleven Laurel had threatened him, made him wonder if the Sunlit would protect him, made him wonder if Nineteen Adze didn't trust her own Minister of War?)

"She was," Nineteen Adze went on. "A good one. The Third Palm was sad to lose her to command, I believe. Mm. Tell me *how* you discovered this dislike you mentioned, and then I think I ought to send you to bed. It's going on for moonset. Have you been sending messages to the Fleet yourself, and hearing back?"

"I'm not that enterprising," said Eight Antidote, and liked how saying that made Nineteen Adze's eyes crinkle up at the corners, like she was laughing, silent and appreciative.

"Not *yet* you aren't. Go on."

He tried to remind himself that the Emperor had sent him into the Ministry of War, that she already knew what he was doing there, that he wasn't betraying anyone's secrets except possibly Sixteen Moonrise's, and certainly none of his own. But it was still hard to start. Hard enough that Nineteen Adze tapped her fingertips on the couch arm, once, a little patter of impatience that made Eight Antidote want to apologize for *everything,* and then resent her for being able to do that to him. It wasn't *fair* that he had a child's emotions, a child's endocrine system and sympathetic nerves, and that children reacted to authority figures in very predictable ways he had studied with his tutors. It wasn't fair at all.

Finally, he said, "She sent a priority message—fast, the kind that overrides the jumpgate mail protocols, I think it came through on a Fleet courier—from the Fleet to Minister Three Azimuth. And in that message—the Minister played it for all of the Palms and their staff, and me, I guess—the Fleet Captain pointed out that all the, um. What happened two months ago—" (They hadn't talked about it. He didn't *want* to, not really, it was easier to just call it *what happened* and be done, instead of saying *when my ancestor made you Emperor and died on live newsfeed for the sake of Teixcalaan*.) "That Mahit Dzmare was involved in that, and now she was out on the battlefront, and that this was probably not good at all, and Information was involved."

"Oh, little spy," said Nineteen Adze, "you are *very good* at what I asked you to do, aren't you."

He wasn't sure that was a compliment. "Do you think she's right?" he asked. "The Fleet Captain. I only met the Ambassador once, so I can't tell."

Nineteen Adze hesitated—the first time, Eight Antidote thought, that he'd ever seen her hesitate and not do so deliberately, for effect. "To be perfectly clear with you," she said, at last, "I haven't decided. And I'm not sure what *I* think matters as much as what Three Azimuth does. If you get a chance, you should try to find out."

He *had* to tell her, now. Or—ask her, if he didn't want to tell her about what Eleven Laurel had said in the garden. He at least had to ask. (Asking was a way of not telling a secret. That was a useful thing to know.)

"Your Brilliance," he said, very careful, trying to frame the question right, "do you think Minister Three Azimuth would disagree with you?"

The Emperor looked at him, long enough for one slow eyeblink. He swallowed. His mouth was dry. She asked, "On the matter of Mahit Dzmare, or in general?"

She was treating him like his questions mattered. He tried not to feel either nervous or grateful, and felt both things anyway. Took a breath, and in breathing decided he *was* going to tell her about what Eleven Laurel had insinuated. Not that he had threatened him. Just that he'd . . . threatened Minister Three Azimuth, who could probably take care of herself. "In general," he said. "Because—in that meeting, when we heard the recording, Eleven Laurel kept talking about the *old* Minister of War. Nine Propulsion. And how she'd *retired*. And about how you might not trust the new Minister, either."

"*Did* he now," said Nineteen Adze.

Guilt was a squirming uncomfortable feeling in Eight Antidote's stomach. Eleven Laurel was his *teacher,* and here he was—doing this. He nodded, though. He couldn't lie. Not right after he'd told the truth, anyway.

"The technician's garden of the War Ministry grows all sorts of flowers, little spy," the Emperor said to him. "But especially the sort that poisons. That's what a weapon is, Eight Antidote. A poison flower. Whether it's dangerous or not depends on who is holding it."

"I don't understand," Eight Antidote said, just as guilty, and now *embarrassed* for not being able to decipher the allusion. "Not without knowing who the poison flower is supposed to be."

Nineteen Adze laughed, which made him feel worse. "All of them," she said. "But gardens need outside grafts, sometimes, to keep them healthy. Ask your biology tutors about that, if you have time while you're finding out what Three Azimuth thinks about Mahit Dzmare."

The outside graft had to be Three Azimuth. Maybe that meant Nineteen Adze *did* trust her. Or—thought that she'd be good for War, which wasn't the same thing at all—

He nodded. "I'll try," he said, because he guessed he was the Emperor's spy before he was anything else except the Emperor's heir. And he could figure out the rest later. He wasn't *stupid*. He read all kinds of poems. He'd find one with poison flowers, and figure it out.

————

By the time Mahit's voice had gone completely—a heat-struck rasp, wrung out from attempts at singing and the strangling moistureless air—she and Three Seagrass and the alien, who they were calling Second (as opposed to its somewhat taller and much quieter companion, First) had a mutual vocabulary of approximately twenty words. Most of them were nouns, or things *like* nouns. Nouns were easy. One pointed at an object, and said its name, and then the alien said *its* name for the object, and thus they'd acquired *energy pistol* (or at least "weapon"), *shoe, water, sand,* and what was either *flower* or *picture* or *shade*, depending on whether Second understood representational objects, and to what degree.

They also had some verbs, but none of them made much sense. There was *drink*, or what Mahit hoped was *drink*, but could have been *consume, internalize,* or even *perform an action on command*—Second used the pitch-growl sound of that word when it wanted her or Three Seagrass to repeat what it was saying. Maybe *drink* was for both water and for concepts. *To take in.* Their other verbs were not much clearer: something which might have been *fly, land,* or *pilot a spacecraft,* and something else which was probably *stop*. Though that sound wasn't necessarily a verb. It could have been just the negation sound, *no* and *zero* and *not that*. Or a threat: *don't continue, or harm will come to you.* Second had raised its claws to them twice. Once when Three Seagrass had stepped quite close to it, and offered an open palm—Mahit had thought of poison, of contact poison, of all the ways Teixcalaan could seep through the skin—only to be met with bared teeth, that noise, and claws at her throat that made her skitter backward, pale as glass. And the other time, when one of their soldier escorts had come out from under the shade of the tapestry to bring them more water. Both First and Second had made the *no* sound, then, and followed it with a resonant scream that made that soldier gag and drop the precious water to spill in the sand.

Mahit wished that she could convey the concept of *waste*, seeing that dark puddle vanish, drunk up by Peloa-2's silica dust. But she couldn't even get close. The aliens had watched the water disappear, too, but they didn't react to it in any way she could understand, any way she could hook onto, emotionally *or* linguistically. Was their whole planet desert? Were they used to loss? Did they even *have* the concept of loss?

The other problem was that as far as either she or Three Seagrass was able to tell, they weren't learning a language. They were learning a pidgin. There was no alteration in form, pitch, or volume of any of the words they'd put together when they were used in different contexts. None of the verbs related to objects. None of the verbs had *tenses,* or referred to the future or the past, completed or uncompleted actions. They were all pinpoints, unrelated to everything surrounding them. Even more frustratingly, they had not in the slightest been able to establish the concept of *names.* Of selves, at all. No pronouns, no name signs, nothing. No *I.*

Mahit thought, with exhausted irony, *And how wide is the Teixcalaanli concept of "you"?*—that question she'd asked Three Seagrass so very many times in the City. No way to ask it here. If these aliens had a concept of *you,* it was entirely opaque.

Worst, though—worst was how First and Second communicated, *obviously* communicated, and used absolutely no sounds to do so. Not the resonant vibrations and not these pidgin syllables. Soundless and perfect accord. Whatever language they were learning, it wasn't the language the aliens spoke.

And whatever language it was, Mahit couldn't do it any longer. She couldn't make sounds in *Teixcalaanli,* let alone sing; she thought that if she tried again, even with water poured down her throat, she might faint.

<Hold on,> Yskandr murmured to her, sharp instruction like a stone in her mouth to suck on even though there was no moisture. It gave her enough presence of mind to turn away from Second—not turn her back on it, no, never, the idea was atavistically horrible—but to turn *away,* and reach to touch Three Seagrass's shoulder, and rasp, "We're going to have to come back. It's too hot. I can't *think,* and if I can't think, I can't think fast enough to keep them from deciding we're evisceratable—I know that isn't a word—"

Three Seagrass nodded. She was flushed and grey at once, and not sweating as much as she should have—Mahit tried to remember the symptoms of incipient heat exhaustion and figured being unable to remember them was a symptom in and of itself. "They don't look terribly well either," she said, hardly audible. Her voice went in and out like an unturned radio channel, as hoarse as Mahit's was. "This planet is bad for *everyone* except—except *sand.*"

"We're not done," Mahit said. "We don't know *anything* yet."

"A meeting is not a negotiation if it is singular," said Three Seagrass, which was obviously a quotation from *some* Teixcalaanli text that Mahit had never read—it was a perfect fifteen-syllable line with a caesura in the middle. An Information Ministry instruction manual, maybe. Those would probably be in political verse.

". . . Yes," she said, "but we need to convince them of that."

Three Seagrass grimly straightened her shoulders in agreement, and turned to face Second again, who looked—exhausted. Possibly. It was hard to tell; Second's white-and-grey-spotted skin didn't show bloodflow or sweat. There was nothing to *read.* But Mahit thought its head hung lower on the great curve of its neck, and she was *sure* its round, faintly furred ears were pulled back against its skull in some sort of distress.

Years of oration had given Three Seagrass some natural advantages over Mahit on maintaining volume and pitch even when her voice was a wreck. She sang *fly/pilot-a-spaceship/land* and pointed at herself, Mahit, and their escorts—made a collective gesture like gathering all of them into her cupped palm—and then pointed up. Sang *no/stop.* Mahit hoped it was *no/stop,* and not *back the fuck off.* Because otherwise they'd said something like *we're never leaving and neither are you.*

Second looked at her for a very long, very still moment. Mahit thought about how some animals looked carefully at prey before striking; the lizards that lived in the City, plant-eating and enormous, who tilted their eyes just like Second was tilting its eyes at Three Seagrass—and then *lunged.* (Mahit had never seen one herself, only holorecordings; they were kept out of the palace grounds and she had hardly had time to go exploring, she'd hardly had time for anything—the very idea of the water-rich air on the Jewel of the World seemed impossible now, a place where lizards could grow to such size on plants alone—)

<You're drifting, Mahit,> Yskandr told her. <Don't faint. I probably can't stop you, and I am absolutely sure it would be a faux pas.>

She bit her tongue, deliberately and hard. It helped. Second hadn't lunged and eaten Three Seagrass after all. It was backing off. So was First; they moved in their terrible and perfect silent communication.

"Quick," Three Seagrass rasped. "The holoprojector—play the sequence where we leave and come back."

Mahit caught up the controls again. Her hands felt very distant from the rest of her. She could wish for neuropathy, neuropathy was better than dissociation—

<No it isn't. Play the *fucking* recording.>

She cued the visual. Two little alien silhouettes and two little human silhouettes, retreating away from the image of Peloa-2 back to their respective ships . . . and then a pause, while the planet rotated a quarter-turn (Peloa rotated *slowly,* it would still be *day* when they came back, the killing sun would still be here), followed by the same aliens and the same humans coming back down again.

While it was playing, Mahit added the resonant-scream noise of *victory-hurrah!* over it. Do this, and we all benefit. Listening to it was like suddenly drowning in nausea. The antiemetics were wearing off. Or she was just not all right. Or both.

<Both. But look.>

The alien they had been calling Second opened its maw and echoed the same noise. The whole world was a resonant chamber. Mahit needed to not vomit. Not until the aliens had left—

They didn't turn their backs on her and Three Seagrass as they went. They loped *backward,* seemingly as comfortable with that direction of locomotion as they had been with coming forward. Mahit wondered about their hip joints. Wondered if they could move sideways, if they could *slide,* imagined the disconcerting rapidity of that sort of travel. Thought, dizzyingly, of how their ships winked in and out of the void, there and then not-there, secret and revealed.

And then they were gone, disappeared over the crux of the dune. Whether or not they'd come back—whether or not she and Three Seagrass had accomplished anything aside from learning a few words in a pidgin language without *tenses*—was entirely unclear.

Three Seagrass vomited first, before Mahit could turn off the holo and the audioplay. Vomited and went down on her knees with dry heaves afterward. Mahit dropped the controls and found herself, operating on complete instinct, all arguments and irrevocable conflicts between them rendered *profoundly* unimportant, crouched protectively next to her in the sand and in the hot silence. Her hand came to rest on Three Seagrass's spine, gentle and steadying, until the physical convulsion was over.

". . . That could have gone *much worse,*" said Three Seagrass, when she could. She straightened up. Wiped her mouth with the back of her hand. And didn't try to get away from Mahit's touch, not at all. "Look, Mahit—*nobody died,* not even slightly."

CHAPTER
TWELVE

Minister Three Azimuth, I have taken the opportunity to review precisely how you accomplished the pacification of Nakhar System, and I begin to see in detail why you are so unfortunately called "the butcher of the Nakharese mind" by the sort of people who resort to petty doggerel. Your accomplishments are impressive in both their efficacy and the precision of their cruelty. I have preserved recordings for later consultation, if necessary.
> —personal communication from Undersecretary Eleven
> Laurel to Minister of War Three Azimuth, 35.1.1–19A

* * *

When you traveled with him, my dear, when you were young and did all those great deeds in the dirt by his side, how did you breathe from being near him? How did you hold on to yourself? If you've a bit of advice for a barbarian, entranced, you know I'd appreciate it. I'll buy the drinks.
> —note from the Lsel Ambassador Yskandr Aghavn to the
> *ezuazuacat* Nineteen Adze, handwritten, preserved
> in the private files of Her Brilliance the Emperor
> Nineteen Adze, undated

HER Brilliance the Emperor Nineteen Adze had said to him, *If you get a chance, you should try to find out what Three Azimuth thinks about the Ambassador Mahit Dzmare.* Not what Fleet Captain Sixteen Moonrise thought of her, not what the Emperor Herself thought of her, not what his dead ancestor-the-Emperor had thought of her or her predecessor in the role of Lsel Ambassador, a man Eight Antidote primarily remembered for how often he'd been in the palace, how easily he'd become a normal, everyday presence—but what the Minister of War thought about the Lsel Ambassador, right now.

And then she'd left it up to him to decide if what the Minister of War thought was something the Emperor *should* disagree with. A poison flower in someone else's hand.

It seemed like a much bigger and harder task than he was capable of. (He could get it *wrong*. What would happen if he got it wrong? He didn't know, and not knowing was frightening in itself.)

But that wasn't the first problem. The first, biggest problem was that he didn't know how to get close to the Minister of War at all. There was no way he was going to find out what she thought by looking up official documents about Teixcalaanli-Stationer relations, and the legal status of Teixcalaanli military passage through Stationer space, which was what he'd tried first. Also, attempting to read legal documents about the difference between *freight supply* and *personnel supply* and *full armaments of war,* as applied to various sorts of ships with various sorts of cargo, during various situations of more or less hypothetical nature, had done very little for him but give him a headache and the conviction that when he was Emperor, he was going to pick a Judiciary Minister who liked reading this sort of stuff and would do it *for him.*

He was pretty sure that relations between Teixcalaan and Lsel Station were what his tutors would call *normalized but fraught,* though. Teixcalaanli vessels could move through Stationer space, and Teixcalaan bought a *lot* of Stationer-refined metals, but Stationers needed more immigration papers than Eight Antidote had previously thought existed to come live in the Empire, and Teixcalaanlitzlim couldn't live on the Station at all. Ever.

He'd looked at the star-charts. Almost every battleship that was headed to the front was moving through Stationer space, from the jumpgate they shared with Teixcalaan to the jump-gate they *didn't*. The jumpgate that had the war on the other side of it.

And none of this was going to help him unless he could fig-ure out how to get Three Azimuth alone. Alone, and to trust him with her real opinions.

He really, really wished he was older. If he was older, he could—oh, enlist in the Fleet, or something. Be the Minister's cadet-assistant. But there were probably a lot more Fleet cadets who were more suited to that job than he was, and less polit-ically fraught to pick. It wouldn't work, even if he was four-teen and of enlistable age instead of just-eleven-last-month. Also it'd be transparent. Why would Eight Antidote make himself Three Azimuth's assistant unless he *wanted* something from her?

There had to be another way. A not-official way. A way of be-ing in the right place, a place that all the camera-eyes and City-algorithms and Sunlit would think was *how the world should be* if he was in it, and that place needed to be where Three Azimuth was, too. Which meant that he needed to figure out what kind of places Three Azimuth spent time in, without her knowing he wanted to know.

Being a spy was *difficult*. Eight Antidote sighed, and got up from his desk and its many, many infofilm transparencies with legal regulations printed on them. He was really tired of sitting still. Outside his windows it was already late afternoon, and he'd done nothing with his day but homework and trying to investigate Lsel Station, and he thought if he looked at any more documents he might throw something. (If he was a kid, for real, and not himself, he guessed he would go *play outside*. Or some-thing. He wasn't really sure what a person did while playing outside if it wasn't *amalitzli*, and you needed a whole team for *amalitzli*.)

Instead of trying to locate an imaginary *amalitzli* team, he stretched his arms above his head as far as he could reach and bent forward from the waist in a standing pike stretch. Put his hands on the ground and jumped his feet backward, *thud,* and held the plank for a whole minute until his arms burned. Calisthenics counted as homework, and they felt good, too.

He was in the middle of trying to do a one-handed push-up, a trick he'd never managed yet (puberty and its accompanying muscle development couldn't get here soon enough, in his opinion), when he had the idea. It was like feeling his mind go *click,* information falling into place, like solving one of Eleven Laurel's strategy puzzles.

A person who was as fit as Three Azimuth definitely had to do physical work to stay that way, especially if she was also the Minister of War.

And the War Ministry had a gymnasium with *much* more equipment than the one in Palace-Earth. Including a shooting range. And Eight Antidote really had been meaning to practice his targeting, like Eleven Laurel had told him to. He was behind on that, now that he was thinking about strategy so much. It would be very easy to run into the Minister there, he bet.

He was so pleased with himself that he didn't mind at all when his push-up attempt failed spectacularly and dumped him on his face.

———

Three Seagrass had never been debriefed by an officer of the Teixcalaanli Fleet before, let alone a *yaotlek.* It was extremely novel. It was also much less frightening than being debriefed by an *ezuazuacat* who was less than six hours away from becoming Emperor. After Nineteen Adze, almost everyone paled in comparison, no matter how much this particular *yaotlek* looked like she'd walked straight out of a holodrama casting call for *yaotlekim.*

Almost everyone. She'd been absolutely terrified of the aliens.

If they counted as people, they beat Her Brilliance Nineteen Adze for intimidation hands down.

She was going to remember those claws for a *long time*. The claws and the teeth and how very close they had come to her skin. Everything else about Peloa-2 was blurring into a haze of heat exhaustion and mental overwork. They'd *talked* to the aliens, though. She and Mahit had. They had *managed it*. Even if they hadn't done a damn thing to stop or slow down the war, they'd *done it*, and Three Seagrass was going to fly on that for as long as she could. She felt delicious. And hysterical. And absolutely delighted to be standing in front of Nine Hibiscus, Mahit at her side, explaining what they had done and how.

It helped that she'd been given several large glasses of water, and had remembered to drink them in slow sips so she didn't bring them right back up again. She'd had to remind Mahit about that. Deserts weren't something that Stationers trained their diplomats for. Which wasn't surprising. (What had been surprising was Mahit's hand on her back, in the sun and the sand, the sheer *comfort* of being touched and acknowledged, the opening up of possibility: perhaps she hadn't fucked everything up between them irrevocably after all! . . . Perhaps. But even *perhaps* felt shimmering, gorgeously amazing. Like everything did right now.)

They'd been scooped off the shuttle with enormous, near-secretive haste. She'd caught a brief glimpse of Twenty Cicada in the enormous hangar bay, and expected him to show up to the briefing, to reclaim his tapestry, if nothing else—she'd folded it up ever so carefully and shaken out the sand first—but he hadn't. It was only the *yaotlek*, and the comms officer Two Foam. No adjutant and no accusatory and disparaging supernumerary Fleet Captain Sixteen Moonrise, either. Interesting. When Three Seagrass was less dehydrated and less exhilarated, she would examine the political situation on *Weight*

for the Wheel with the attention it obviously deserved. Later!
Neither dehydration nor exhilaration made for decent analytic
capabilities. The Information Ministry taught cadets a whole
list of altered states not to be in while evaluating a situation,
and Three Seagrass did *try* to remember her training.

The water she'd drunk made her able to talk. Even sing one
of the absurd pitched-consonant words that they'd picked up
from the aliens in demonstration for the *yaotlek*, though Mahit
was so much better at making those noises that Three Seagrass
had begun to plan a scheme in which she taught her how to
have some halfway-decent breath and pitch control, pass on the
lessons she'd had as a crèche-kid in how to project from the
diaphragm when orating. But no amount of water got her and
Mahit past the very simple, very structural problem that was
threaded through their magnificent success: they had twenty
words, and not a single one of them was much use to ask, *Please
hand over your war criminals who murdered our colonists, and also
cease from contemplating attacking any of our systems closer to the
heart of the Empire. In exchange, we will try really hard not to point
our very large energy weapons at your spaceships.*

They were going to need a lot more meetings to get to that
point. If it was possible to get to that point. Three Seagrass wasn't
half the linguist Mahit was, and she still knew that they'd been
speaking—singing, rather—some kind of sketch of a language.
Less of a sketch than the tone marker vibrations, but still a sketch.

"... no *pronouns*?" asked Two Foam, the comms officer, who
was also clearly more of a linguist than Three Seagrass. She and
Mahit had been talking about grammar for the last five minutes,
and Three Seagrass was both enjoying Mahit's easy comfort in
explaining, her command of technical Teixcalaanli vocabulary
effortless, and enjoying the opportunity to exchange *blood-and-
sunlight-these-scientists-can-you-even-believe* glances with the *yaotlek*
herself. She'd need Nine Hibiscus to keep liking them—to like
them at all, possibly, she hadn't had time to figure out how the
yaotlek figured in the spread of *happy that Information was here* to

Sixteen Moonrise—if they were going to get a chance to keep talking to the aliens. Or to make the right *kind* of decision to stop talking.

Stars, she just needed allies out here in the middle of the Fleet. Any allies she could get. Three Seagrass *liked* being in foreign environments—what Information-trained person didn't—but she was exquisitely aware that she didn't know the rules here, the shape of the relationships between ship and ship and their commanders and soldiers. No civilian would. (And yet it was still easier than dealing with the aliens—)

". . . the larger difficulty is that there's no *time* in the language we're acquiring," Mahit was saying. "No tenses. No causality; I'm not sure there's a way to ask a question, let alone offer multiple options or convey consequences. It's as if they were talking to us like we were very young."

"Maybe they think we are," said Nine Hibiscus. "Or that you two are. Possibly they send their young to negotiate with hazardous foreigners."

"What, because they think younger members of the species are more expendable?" Three Seagrass asked. It was a very interesting idea. Except it didn't make sense with how First and Second had looked. "If so, then their adults must be *very* large. The two that came down to the desert were—oh, as big or bigger than the one you were autopsying, *yaotlek*."

"So either all their soldiers are neonates . . ." Two Foam began, consideringly.

". . . or they have another language we still can't hear," Mahit finished for her. "An impenetrable language."

Three Seagrass didn't think Mahit knew that she'd quoted Eleven Lathe's *Asymptote/Fragmentation* just then. As far as she was aware, Mahit still had never read Three Seagrass's favorite poet-diplomat, who had lived six years amongst the Ebrekti and come back still human, his tongue loosened and made strange, his poetry full of images Three Seagrass had never quite been able to comprehend. *The motion of a swift is an impenetrable language,* he'd written, attempting to describe the shifting, protean hierarchies of how the Ebrekti moved and ran, their predatory herds, the physicality of their social behavior. It was so strange to hear Mahit say the same words and not know— she was almost sure she didn't know—the deep resonance of them. The echo of Teixcalaan's history with what could not be understood, what was too alien to stay with long. Eleven Lathe *had* come home, after his long exile. And written, after he was home, in language worth remembering.

"If their language is impenetrable," said Nine Hibiscus, serene in command, serene in *instruction,* "then go around it."

Mahit opened her mouth, probably to explain all of the ways that that command would be next to impossible to achieve— and she wouldn't be wrong—but it was the wrong thing to say, and Three Seagrass knew that order was as good as permission to *keep trying to talk with the aliens*—so she opened her mouth, too, and said, "Of course, *yaotlek.* We'll be back on Peloa-2 in nine hours for the next rendezvous," and bowed so deeply over her fingertips that her queue of braided hair brushed the floor.

"See to it that you are," the *yaotlek* said—and then, softer, went on. "Sleep first, if you can. If you both keel over of heat-stroke or exhaustion, Twenty Cicada will write up the most irate report he is capable of, and I will be honor-bound to read all of it."

She waved one of her wide-palmed, well-fleshed hands in dismissal. Three Seagrass had to stop herself from grinning, all Stationer-like, and scaring the comms officer. They'd get their next diplomatic meeting. And they'd get some *time* now, before it. Time where—if she and Mahit didn't have another stupid, horrible, miserable fight—the two of them could think through the politics of what they were trying to do.

And whether or not it matched the politics of what Mahit's Station wanted her to do—

But if Three Seagrass brought *that* up, they would absolutely have another fight. Or—have another iteration of the same fight.

No. Better to think of Mahit Dzmare quoting Eleven Lathe as if his words belonged in her clever mouth.

It wasn't that Three Seagrass was *unaware* that she was allowing herself to not acquire information about her associate's loyalties and plans, information that might be vital, all for the sake of her own emotional peace. Really. She was *extremely* aware. But possibly being aware would be enough in and of itself: if she knew she was missing information, her analysis of the situation could account for its lack. She'd always managed that before. She just had to imagine Lsel Station's influence on Mahit as a kind of negative space that still had gravity. Diplomatic dark matter.

Her metaphors were getting more extraplanetary every hour she spent on a Fleet ship. That might be a good sign for her poetry, or just exactly the opposite. Cliché wouldn't help her, even if it was scenically appropriate cliché.

After she'd sent the envoy and her politically complicated companion away—after that, and before she had a real chance to think about what they had brought her (half a negotiation and a lot of unanswered questions, not anything solid enough to put weight on), Nine Hibiscus took stock of the bridge of *Weight for the Wheel,* and the Fleet beyond it. She was not in a position she liked.

Six legions. A single *yaotlek's* six, far too few to fight a war with no current goals but attrition and jumpgate defense, no enemy strongholds to overwhelm. Two of those legions— the Seventeenth under Forty Oxide and the Twenty-Fourth under Sixteen Moonrise—already weakened with guerrilla-warfare casualties, ships lost at their edges to the marauding three-ringed enemy vessels. *Three* of those legions (the aforementioned two and the Sixth under Two Canal) chafing at her authority, being driven by politics originating somewhere in the Ministry of War, politics Nine Hibiscus couldn't see clearly from where she was. One Information agent, who was effective but possibly compromised, and one linguist-ambassador, who was certainly a barbarian with barbarian desires, even if they coincided with the Fleet's at this particular moment.

Supply lines stretched over too many jumpgates.

A funeral for an entire planet.

An enemy that might, or might not, be open to negotiation. That might, or might not, understand the *concept* of negotiation.

And a visiting Fleet Captain, that selfsame Sixteen Moonrise of too-many-recently-killed-in-action-soldiers and undermining-Nine-Hibiscus's-authority as well as the Twenty-Fourth Legion, who was haunting her flagship like a rogue AI haunts a comms system.

Not in a position she liked at all. At least her people here on the bridge were still hers, and doing their jobs exactly as they were supposed to.

Eighteen Chisel, the navigation officer, had come up to stand next to her. He was almost as broad as she was: a barrel of a man, with a gut that looked soft and was nothing of the kind. The sort of soldier who was built for endurance, and who had somehow ended up being the most competent celestial mechanic she had ever encountered even after he'd spent the first fifteen years of his service as ground operations infantry. (He'd had the navigation aptitudes down pat, he'd told her once, over drinks in the officer's mess. He'd just wanted to feel the weight of soldiering first, before he spent all his time staring into the stars.) She turned to him, a fractional motion, a gesture—*go on, report*.

"*Yaotlek*," he murmured. Low. This wasn't for everyone, then. This was something he wanted to tell her quietly, so she'd have a chance to react. To decide how to react. She nodded to him to go on.

"One of the scout-ships—the *Gravity Rose,* with Captain Eighty-Four Twilight in command—is reporting on narrow-cast that they've found something. Something that looks like a home base for these things we're fighting."

A DESOLATION CALLED PEACE

Nine Hibiscus's heart thudded against her chest wall like she was being rocked by cannon fire. "Planet, station, or just a really big ship?" she asked, equally soft. "And where?"

"Planet," said Eighteen Chisel. "Planet and one satellite, both inhabited. Lots of civilian traffic, like a proper system would have. Eighty-Four Twilight didn't give me much detail, just that the ships are definitely in the same style, but not military. Or don't look it. The place is—out, far out. Past where Fleet Captain Forty Oxide's stationed the Seventeenth. But that's why the angle of attack they're using is coming from that direction." His smile was tight, wired, glittering-sharp. "I think we have them, *yaotlek*. I think if we could get Five Thistle over there with the number of nuclear scatterbombs in our hangar bay . . . well, we could blow them out of their sky, at least in that system. Send a message."

"If we can get there without them seeing us," Nine Hibiscus said. The scatterbombs would do exactly what Eighteen Chisel was imagining. They would, yes, blow *anyone* out of their sky. And then they'd poison that sky, and the planets below it. The scatterbombs were deathrain. A last resort. Almost never used where people *lived*—because after them, people didn't live there anymore. She'd only used a scatterbomb barrage once, and that had been against another ship, safe in the blackness of space. The idea of using them on the aliens was—

She liked it too much, was what. Liked it too much, too fast. Such a simple solution. So much easier than the rest of the situation she'd been detailing for herself.

"Tell Eighty-Four Twilight to get the *Gravity Rose* out of there," she said. "Quiet and quick. Make sure she knows I don't want to let the enemy know we know where they are. I want to make the most of this, Eighteen Chisel. Plan it *right*. Keep it quiet here, too. For now."

He nodded again and went back to his console. Satisfied. Anticipatory. (And wasn't she the same? Anticipatory? *Eager?*)

And then she thought again of Sixteen Moonrise, somewhere

in the bowels of her ship, wandering and watching with
an agenda of her own, and decided that some things, some
things—well, some things even other Fleet Captains didn't need
to know about until their *yaotlek* decided they needed to know.
She wanted Sixteen Moonrise off *Weight for the Wheel*. Now. So
that she would have time to plan at all.

————

The Minister of War was extremely good at push-ups. Also
handstand balances, lunges, punching a bag of sand, and running very fast without getting out of breath. Eight Antidote had
watched her do these things in sequence three times now from
his perch on the balcony level of the Outreaching Palms' training gymnasium, and was beginning to despair about the pros-
pects of his own physical fitness.

When the Minister rounded the corner of the track again,
moving away from him in even, quick strides, her cheeks flushed
red and the scar of her ear flushed redder, Eight Antidote sighed
and headed down to intercept her. Not by running, of course.
Even if he could keep up with her—and he wasn't *unfit*, his genetics were pretty good for basic athleticism, it was just that
mostly he never ran anywhere—he didn't want to talk to her
while panting. It seemed undignified. Also embarrassing. And
he really didn't want to be embarrassed in front of Three Azimuth, to a degree which was unexpectedly overwhelming.
So instead he took himself over to the mats where she'd been
doing the calisthenic portion of her training cycle and began,
gamely and not without a certain dizzy thrill, to try to figure
out a handstand balance himself.

He could do a *handstand*. If he sort of—threw himself forward onto his hands and kicked up, and squeezed his core
muscles together very hard so he didn't overbalance. But he'd
never done a *balance*, going from kneeling on the ground,
palms flat to the padded matting, and *unfolding* into the air. It

was much harder. He was sure he was missing some vital instruction. He kept getting partially up and then collapsing, or tipping over. But that was the point. Of *course* he was missing vital instruction. That was what Three Azimuth was going to give him.

"Kid," she said, and he tried very hard not to startle, and only succeeded in falling out of his latest attempt onto his back with a thump. The Minister of War was staring down at him, her breathing fast but regular from her run, an expression of complete amusement on her face. Eight Antidote refused to cringe. He *wanted* her to be interested in him. Amusement was a sort of interest, right? And it *was* funny that he kept falling over. (He was blushing anyway, which was *dumb* of him.)

"Good morning, Minister," he said, from his prone position. "I think I'm not very good at balances."

She sat down beside him, a graceful fold to crossed legs. Her eyebrows had climbed halfway up her forehead. ". . . You're quite spectacularly bad at them, in fact," she said. "Why are you trying to do push-handstands when you're too young to have even started the Fleet training regimen?"

"I saw you do them," said Eight Antidote, and sat up—it was too embarrassing to be flat, he couldn't handle that and keep talking—"and I can do a normal handstand fine, so . . ."

Now she *did* laugh. He thought it was kind laughter. He hoped it was. (It was so inconvenient and awful that he *liked* the Minister of War and wanted her to like him too.) "So you thought you'd try, with your little arms. You are a dangerously ambitious child, Your Excellency. I'm sure you know that."

Eight Antidote made his face as still as possible and said, "I have been told so. Though not in such direct terms before just now."

"*Stars*," said Three Azimuth. "I don't know how they raise children in the palace, but they've done a number on you. All right. What do you want with push-handstands, aside from trying something you don't know how to do?"

"To learn how to do something I don't know how to do," Eight Antidote said. "You do them. You're the Minister of War. They must be useful."

Three Azimuth *sputtered* with snickering, a delighted and uncontrolled noise. (Maybe that meant he was getting somewhere?) She said, "Not everything I do is useful, kid. The office does not confer *usefulness* on my morning gymnasium routine."

"What does?" he asked.

She paused. Thought about it. (Let him see that she was thinking about it.) "It keeps me strong and agile, even at this desk job. And I know it well enough that I can do it without thinking too much, so it's easy to maintain. That's why it's useful to me. Here. Come on, let me show you *one* of the things you're doing wrong. Start again, hands on the mat."

He started again. Hands flat on the mat, his legs tucked under him, balanced on the balls of his feet. Three Azimuth made a considering sound. And then she touched him—her hands over his hands, pressing his fingers apart and his palms into the mat. His mouth went dry. "Make your hands stars," she said. "All the points spread out, and stars have heavy gravity pull, right? That gravity sinks your palms into the mat. *Press*. And *then* bend your elbows—good—lean forward—and put your knees on your elbows."

What? Eight Antidote thought, utterly confused, and then tried anyway—hopping, his ass in the air, trying to land his knees onto his bent elbows.

He missed. The momentum took him into a forward roll, which at least let him come up to sitting and not flop over again.

"Sorry," he said to the Minister of War.

She shook her head. "Hilarious, but not bad for a first try. Next time, one knee and then the other. And hold *that* balance before you try pushing up to a handstand. Got it?"

He nodded. He didn't get it, but he thought he could probably figure it out—

"Now. What *else* do you want, kid, besides free lessons in

strength exercises? You've been up in the balcony for my whole workout."

Really, he needed to learn how not to blush. But it was so *hard,* when he got caught. And when it was Three Azimuth that caught him. He'd really thought he'd been quiet, unobserved, careful, and yet—

"I wanted to ask you about the Lsel Ambassador," he blurted out, not knowing what else to do or how to talk to this woman *at all.* "Um. I met her once. And I don't—I wanted to know what you thought of her, because I'm not sure, and at that meeting— thank you for allowing me to be there, Minister, I meant to say—"

She'd gone quite still, like a bird about to dive, prey-seeking. He shut his mouth. Swallowed against the dryness there.

The Minister ran a hand through her own hair, pushing it back in slick black strands from her forehead. "Did Eleven Laurel tell you to ask me that?"

"No," Eight Antidote said. *Not Eleven Laurel. The Emperor, the Edgeshine of a Knife.*

"Are you lying to me, Your Excellency?"

He shook his head, a fast harsh motion.

"Be sure you don't lie to me. I'll find out, Your Excellency. I'll find out eventually." Her voice was slow, serene, utterly determined. He felt hypnotized. Terrified. "Tell me, now: did Eleven Laurel put you up to this little scheme?"

"I swear," Eight Antidote said, "he didn't." He wasn't sure what he'd do if Three Azimuth asked him who *had* put him up to it. He wasn't sure she'd believe a lie, wasn't sure if telling the truth would be the beginning of an unfolding disaster like what had happened with the last Minister of War, Nine Propulsion, during the—insurrection—that had ended his ancestor-the-Emperor's reign. Who wasn't Minister of War any longer. Who had sided—probably, Eight Antidote wasn't sure, everything about three months ago was confusing and he'd been *ten* then, not eleven, and hadn't been told a lot of information—with the *yaotlek* One Lightning in his usurpation bid. Which was probably why the Emperor Herself had brought in someone from very far away, like Three Azimuth. Her *external graft*. But—he was *spying* on the Minister, for the Emperor. Would letting Three Azimuth know that Nineteen Adze had sent him here somehow start a new civil war? He could see ways it might. Ways that the strategy table which was the City and the palace might shift to land in that hideous outcome. If Three Azimuth had been brought in to be *loyal* and now she thought the Emperor didn't trust her, she might do anything. Anything at all.

But Three Azimuth didn't ask him *who sent you?* She'd only wanted to know whether it had been Eleven Laurel. Who was supposed to be her subordinate. She wanted to know if Eleven Laurel was using Eight Antidote to find out things from her—

Abruptly he wondered if Eleven Laurel had already found out things about her that she didn't want him to know. She'd called him *my spymaster*. Spies didn't just gather information. Spies sometimes held it over people's heads, to get them to do what they wanted.

Three Azimuth seemed to have decided he *wasn't* lying to her while he was thinking. She said, "All right. I think Ambassador Dzmare is one of those people who destabilize whatever situation they find themselves in, Eight Antidote. This is my professional opinion. I'm giving it to you so that you begin to learn what these people look like. What they behave like. Are you listening?"

He nodded. Kept quiet.

"You'll meet them all over Teixcalaan, as you get older," she went on. "Here in the palace, in the City, on whatever ship you serve on, if you join the Fleet. On every planet and at the heart of every disaster. There's always at least one. These people can have the best of intentions or the worst. They may be clever or remarkably stupid, barbarian or citizen . . . but what they always, always are, Your Excellency, are people who put themselves and their desires before the needs of Teixcalaan. Who haven't any sense of real loyalty. They shift and change."

". . . And Dzmare is one of them?" he managed to ask.

"You think about it. She comes here, she upsets the whole sugar-crystal-fragile peace between the Ministries, shows up in newsfeeds, writes a poem or two, and gets her patron made Emperor—not that Her Brilliance was a poor choice, Her Brilliance was a *perfect* choice, and I'd swear to that in a sun temple with blood from both wrists at once—and then she goes away again. But here she is, popping up on a battlefield, and immediately I have one Fleet Captain sending secret reports about a possible breach in the loyalties of another Fleet Captain? Of a *yaotlek,* no less? That Dzmare is a disruptive person. Whether she means to be or not."

Eight Antidote said, without quite knowing why he said it, "How did you learn to recognize her? People—like her. I met her in the garden, when she was here—she liked the palace-hummers. She was drunk, I think. And sad."

Three Azimuth nodded. "She might very well have been. Both drunk and sad. She was a barbarian at court. She doesn't seem like a person who bears Teixcalaan ill will, not directly. It's all right, kid, that you didn't think about her this way. I only do because it's been my job, for a long time, to notice those people and the situations they create."

"Is that what the Minister of War is for?"

"Stars, no. The Minister of War is for making sure Teixcalaan's military supremacy continues without end or interruption. Finding disruptive persons was what I did when I was the military governor of Nakhar System."

Nakhar System, which Eight Antidote knew hadn't rebelled even once while Three Azimuth had been its governor. Nakhar System, which usually rebelled every seven years or so, and always had, before Three Azimuth arrived.

Before Three Azimuth had noticed the disruptive people, and had made sure they couldn't be disruptive any longer.

———

Mahit remembered this sensation—the feeling of being swept along from moment to moment in a bright haze of exhaustion, bravado, and culture shock: it was how she'd ended up feeling every time she'd been immersed entirely in Teixcalaan. It was as pervasive on a Fleet warship as it had been in the imperial palace, and as intoxicating; as if there was a contaminant in Teixcalaanli air as pervasive and mind-altering as the heat of Peloa-2. She felt like she was flying. Untethered. She had just negotiated, as much as it was possible to describe what she had done as *negotiating,* given the limitations of language, with incomprehensible beings—

<The aliens or the *yaotlek*?> Yskandr murmured. He was flying, too—all glitter-shot laughter, the ghost of her sabotaged imago clearer in the blend of the three of them than he'd been in days.

Both, Mahit told him, as the door to the assigned quarters she shared with Three Seagrass hissed shut behind the two of them. Right now she was still vibrating, still gloriously triumphant and terrified at once. But alone in this room with her former cultural liaison, her partner-in-negotiation, who understood nothing and everything about her—she could see the approaching drop. The point where there would no longer be anything she *had* to do, and the silence and stillness of exhaustion would come down on her like the sudden hand of gravity.

Three Seagrass said, loud in the hush of a room where the only noises were the churning of *Weight for the Wheel*'s air-purification systems, "Thank you."

Which wasn't what Mahit had expected at all.

"For what?" she asked, turning toward her. Three Seagrass was still grey through the cheeks, hollow-eyed, all tension and suppressed giddy hysteria. Heatstruck and half drunk on success.

"You sang their own sounds *back* to them," Three Seagrass said. "I wouldn't have thought of it. Not that way. Not that *fast*. And look what we did. *Think* of it, Mahit. No human beings but us right here have ever spoken that language, ever before today. Just us."

Am I human, then? Mahit thought, bitter-sharp, and shoved the question away, unwanted. Couldn't she enjoy this? Couldn't she feel the same victory that Three Seagrass was feeling?

<Just this once,> Yskandr said. Or she said, to herself. She wasn't sure. It was hard to tell, when she wanted so much to be *allowed* to keep being immersed in the bright spinning perfection of accomplishment, to stave off the inevitable crash a little longer . . .

"I still think we're just picking up some kind of pidgin—they talk to each other, and we're not hearing it—" She didn't even know why she wasn't agreeing with Three Seagrass. Why she had to keep qualifying their work. They weren't in front of the *yaotlek* now. She didn't need to justify a further round of negotiations, or report honestly on her failures, or—

"Mahit," said Three Seagrass, quite intently.

". . . Yes?"

"*Hush.*" She stepped close, close enough that Mahit was abruptly aware of the shape of her body, the space she took up in the air, the scent of her dried sweat. And then her hands were in Mahit's hair, pulling her down in an arc to be kissed.

Mahit thought she made a sound—some noise that was a strangled word, half expressed—but Three Seagrass's mouth was warm and open under hers, and she kissed like she meant it, not an offer or a question but a claim; all desire, not the coming-together of exhaustion and grief that their first and only prior kiss had been, deep under the City, waiting for Six Direction to die in a sun temple, sanctified in front of all of Teixcalaan. This was—

<This is how it is. How it was, for me. Yes.>

Her hands had found Three Seagrass's shoulder blades, the curve of her waist, the ridge of her hipbone that fit exactly into Mahit's palm. The precise way that Nineteen Adze's larger hipbone had fit into Yskandr's larger palm—the doubling was intense, almost violent, a surge of desire like a pulse or a punch between her thighs. Distantly, she wondered if sex would be different now that she had an imago with male-bodied memories—decided it didn't matter, it was going to be *good*— and in deciding, realized that she'd already committed to whatever this was going to be. That she wasn't offering or asking either, but saying yes. (Like Yskandr had said yes, first to the Emperor and then to Nineteen Adze—and look where that had gotten him—but oh—and it didn't matter that they hadn't talked about their argument, it didn't matter at all, she wanted to never think of anything again, except for desire, except for triumph, except for being wanted—)

Distant, as desire-choked as she felt: <That's the way we fall— being wanted.>

Yskandr was probably right, and Mahit didn't care.

Three Seagrass broke the kiss with a slow sucking bite to Mahit's lower lip, and Mahit caught her breath on a whine, all unintentional.

"I was going to ask if you *actually* liked people of my gender and sex," Three Seagrass said, breathless, "but I don't think I need to."

Mahit shook her head. Her mouth was as dry as it had been on Peloa. She could feel her heartbeat between her legs, racing-hot.

"Good," Three Seagrass said, and kissed her again—swarmed up against her, small breasts pressed into Mahit's own, a thigh insinuated between her thighs. Mahit rocked against her, shifted, aligned her pelvis to shove her own hipbone against the seam of Three Seagrass's trousers. Three Seagrass gasped and bit Mahit's collarbone. She was hot through the fabric and Mahit was viciously, delightedly sure that when she got her hand between her legs she'd find her dripping wet.

"—Do you always get like this after you've won something?" she asked, and Three Seagrass bit her again, and *laughed*, and pushed against her hip in steady motions.

"Only when I've won something with someone like you," she said.

Almost, Mahit asked, *Only barbarians, then? Only sufficiently alien partners?* Almost, but it was better—easier—to kiss her again, to feel the expanding, dizzying memory of Yskandr kissing someone as much smaller than him as Three Seagrass was to her, the Emperor who had opened up under his mouth like Three Seagrass was opening under hers—to feel that doubling and willingly allow it in. (Six Direction's hair had been longer, and grey-silver, but the texture when Mahit wound her fingers into Three Seagrass's queue and disarrayed it was completely the same.)

"Come on," she said, when the kiss dissolved from lack of available oxygen, "come on, I'm not going to fuck you standing up—"

"That bed's tiny." One of Three Seagrass's hands had gotten under her shirt, cupped her breast, teased expertly and distractingly at the nipple. "There's a perfectly good floor right here . . ."

"I'm not *that* kind of barbarian," Mahit said, and found herself laughing, too, and pulling away long enough to squirm out of her jacket, pull her shirt over her head. The air of their quarters on bare skin raised shivery gooseflesh down her arms, over her ribs. The air, and Three Seagrass's eyes on her.

"You're not," Three Seagrass said, dark and intent, "but I am."

And then she had dropped to her knees in front of Mahit, fluid and easy motion. She pressed her open mouth between Mahit's legs. Wet heat through fabric, her tongue already mobile and seeking—Mahit thought, *Blood and starlight,* said, "Fuck, yes, please," didn't care that she'd cursed in Teixcalaanli, that she was only thinking in Teixcalaanli, that she and Yskandr were both explosively, devastatingly lost—sank a hand into Three Seagrass's hair and pulled her in, tight.

INTERLUDE

IN all the vast reach of Teixcalaan, it is an honor for a young person sworn to the Six Outreaching Palms to be selected as a medical cadet for the Fleet: the Fifth Palm, medicine coupled close with research and development, is the second-most difficult placement to achieve within the Ministry of War. And thus it is a greater honor still to serve on an active battlefront before the completion of one's mandatory years of training, and perhaps a further honor yet to be allowed, under no supervision but the watching eyes of *Weight for the Wheel*'s security cameras and biohazard containment detection algorithm, to clean up the remains of an alien autopsy.

Six Rainfall, two and a half indictions old, young enough to still have acne at his temples that he judiciously scrubs at with astringents each morning before putting on his uniform, is—by his own intimation but also by the evaluations submitted quarterly by his superior officers—quite good at his assigned tasks. He is the sort of soldier-to-be that might be headed for command of a medical bay of his own, in sufficient time. *A person who takes both scientific and health-conscious initiative,* his last supervisor had written—and that, amongst other factors, had put him here, transferred from one of the Tenth Legion's smaller ships to the flagship itself.

Currently, he has set his cloudhook to talk to his audiophonic augments and is playing his favorite new album quite loudly into the bone-conduction points in his skull while he cleans the lab and carefully packs away various alien parts in cryostorage. He's three months out of date on the shatterharmonic music scene, which is what he gets for signing up for a two-year stint with the Fleet without any ground postings, but he'd snagged this album off of an entertainment vendor at the last big jumpgate station they'd stopped at between Kauraan and this back-of-beyond killing field. It's the latest release from All Points Collapse, who are, in Six Rainfall's opinion, the shattermost of shatterharmonicists, and next time he takes leave, he's going to make sure it's on a planet where they're touring live. The harmonies sing in triplicate in his skull, and he hums along with them as he packs alien bits into appropriately labeled containers and carries them into the cryostorage unit. He's wearing latex gloves, of course. *And* a breathing-mask filter. That's standard for disposing of *any* autopsy remnants, and alien autopsy remnants obviously require strict protocol adherence.

Six Rainfall is good at protocol adherence, except for his tendency to play music when he's working.

The alien is disturbing. It has had its rib cage opened up like deeply unpleasant bloody wings, and its head nearly disarticulated from its overlong neck, all the vocal folds exposed and dissected. Six Rainfall has never seen a dead alien before. Or a live alien before. He peers at it, half to feel the squirming atavistic fascination of being disturbed, and half because he's quite genuinely interested in it. He tilts its heavy skull back to get a good view of the dentition; the lolling blue-black tongue splotched with pink; the sporelike structures in the oral cavity, white fungal tendrils extending down from the soft palate—

The sporelike structures in the oral cavity which *definitely* were not described in the autopsy report that Six Rainfall read with great and extremely specific attention before he came in here.

In his ears, the shatterharmonics are a glittering fall, and they do what they have always done for him: make him feel brilliant and fearless and serene in his curiosity.

It's not *exactly* a bad idea, what he does next. It's only a bad idea because he is so sure it was a good one, and because he moves so quickly. Of course he needs to take a sample of those spores—of course he needs to confirm that they are in fact fungal infiltrates, and if they are, immediately report them to his superior officer and from there on up to command, who need to know if the aliens-who-are-their-enemies are not mammals at all, but instead—and here Six Rainfall engages in a surprisingly accurate fantasy, though he will never know it—vessels of some sort of fungal intelligence.

His hand, appropriately gloved, in the maw of the enemy. His fingers encounter the spore-tendrils, and break them off. They're friable. Easy to aerosolize. Fungal infiltrates are. Always have been. These especially, though Six Rainfall doesn't know it. These hardly ever need to be as solid as they are now—to grow outward, questing unhappily for somewhere new to dwell within, for an end to silence and rot, for escape from the ruin of a home. Six Rainfall pulls his prize out of the alien's mouth, thinking with a sick and excited worry that he is so very glad of his breathing mask, so very glad indeed, because these things are probably emitting spores all over the place now that he's broken them off. He's going to have to put the whole medbay under contaminant/containment protocol. Right after he gets this stuff under a microscope—

He doesn't notice, pulling the spores out of the alien's mouth, that the sharp cutting edge of its teeth—carnivore's teeth, scavenger's teeth—slices right through his glove, and right through the pad of flesh at the base of his thumb. It doesn't hurt. It is too sharp to hurt—a tiny, perfect incision that Six Rainfall ignores entirely. He has a microscopic analysis to perform.

It *is* fungal, under microscopic analysis. Not a fungus Six Rainfall knows, but he's hardly a mycologist. Mycologists are usually *ixplanatlim,* and what Fleet soldier has time for that kind of training? You have to write a *thesis,* and Six Rainfall would rather be patching up soldiers any day. But he thinks this is a fungus. It's not anything *else,* at least, which means it is *utterly* worth transmitting up the command chain. He takes quick holoimages with his cloudhook connected to the micros-copy scan, and composes a brief and breathless missive, the sort of thing that doesn't even need an infofiche stick. It just says PRIORITY MEDICAL: ALIEN CORPSE IS GROWING ALIEN FUNGAL INFILTRATES, SEE ATTACHED and goes straight to the cloudhooks of everyone associated with medical on *Weight for the Wheel*, plus Twenty Cicada, who Six Rainfall thinks of only as *the adjutant*. Twenty Cicada has put himself on *all* of the ship's priority message lists, which Six Rainfall does not know about but would find supremely annoying to imag-ine if he did: *stars*, so many interrupting messages all the time, it'd be distracting as anything.

Because Twenty Cicada is on all those message lists, he *almost* arrives to the medbay in time to change what happens next. Al-most. But not quite.

Six Rainfall leans in to get a better look at the microscopy, spin the holo around, and see if he can get a more complex and clear idea of how the fungal spores grow; it looks like a fractal, like a neural net, and he's really very curious. He lifts a hand to spin the holoimage in the air, and feels something hot and liquid drip down his wrist.

Red. Blood. His blood.

He stares at it. He thinks, *I don't remember being hurt.*

It hurts now. His thumb. His wrist and fingers. A kind of burning. Like noticing the blood has made it hurt.

He pulls the glove off. It is *full* of blood. His hand is thickly coated with red. It looks wrong. The blood looks wrong. Blood shouldn't be as—thick as it is, like all of his clotting factors have gone wild. He's horrified. He is pretty sure he's in shock. His breath comes in tight wheezing gasps.

He turns his hand around. The cut is below his thumb, and it gapes wide open, the lips of it spread with white fungal struc-tures. Just like those that he has put under the microscope. They're growing out of him.

They're *growing.* More of them bloom from the wound, fast

enough that he can watch. His skin splits at the edges of the cut to make room. That hurts, too, inside the larger hurt. The low strange burning. How he can't get a breath. There's a *nest* of infiltrates, inside his thumb—he lifts his other hand to try to tear it out, try to get it *out of him*—

They break easily. But they keep blooming. There's more. They go deeper. They're in his veins, his arteries—choking them with white along with the red. *That'd explain the clotting factor problem,* he thinks. He gasps. He wonders if they're in his lungs or if he's just having an anaphylactic exposure reaction, and then he is on the floor, and then there is—

(a chorus, like distant screaming, like the music still playing on his audioplants is echoed and made strange, full of voices that no shatterharmonicist had ever sung, some reaching noise, singing *we*—)

—absolutely nothing.

CHAPTER THIRTEEN

If the traveler has the opportunity to stop in the Neltoc System and sample the cuisine of the Neltoctlim, this guide recommends it with enormous enthusiasm. While the flavors of Neltoc cuisine may be milder than those found in other culinary destinations or in the best restaurants on the Jewel of the World, that mildness is misleading: it reveals an opportunity for appreciation of the deep complexity of balancing salt and sweet, bitter and earthy, which each individual bite of the Neltoc specialty meal-style allows— one tiny composed dish at a time. Leave at least three hours for your restaurant experience, and think (as does this author!) that maybe those homeostat-cultists have a point about balance . . .

> —from *Gustatory Delights of the Outer Systems of Launai*
> *Sector: Another Guide for the Tourist in Search of Exquisite*
> *Experiences* by Twenty-Four Rose, distributed mostly
> throughout the Western Arc systems

* * *

Please confirm that the shipment of fish cakes was in fact a shipment of fish cakes, and did not contain any *other* unauthorized imports besides one Teixcalaanlitzlim. And revoke that captain's trade permit on the grounds of possibly bringing in contaminated items; it suits the situation.

> —note from the Councilor for Heritage, Aknel
> Amnardbat, left on her secretary's desk with
> the rest of the incoming mail

IT was possible—just barely, for a woman of Nine Hibiscus's size and easily recognizable distinction of rank, but possible—to *surprise* someone on *Weight for the Wheel* with the sudden presence of their commanding officer, in a place they had never intended to encounter her. The trick to it, really, was in the Shard programming she had long ago refused to have stripped out of her cloudhook: she could, if she was careful, slip into the collective vision of every Shard pilot on the flagship, and triangulate the location of the person she very much wanted to find through three hundred pairs of eyes. (If that many Shard pilots had their cloudhook programming operational at one time, and if she could handle the multiplicity of vision for long enough to make it useful.) It was like standing on the bridge and cycling through all of the camera-eyes, but—faster. More mobile.

Her Shard pilots knew about it, of course. She would never have been willing to borrow their eyes if they hadn't been asked, and signed on, and knew to turn their Shard programming off if they didn't want her to accidentally see some private or personal moment. It helped that she had no access to their shared proprioception—her cloudhook couldn't handle the new technology without being upgraded, and besides she'd probably have to plug herself into a Shard to get even close to the necessary processing power. But that lack of bodily access—she suspected that helped, when she asked if she could see through their eyes. Most of her pilots let her watch the ship through them when she needed to. It was one of the ways that they trusted her; one of the ways that their trust felt like a bright and blooming explosion of shrapnel in her chest, whenever she considered it too closely.

Now she used them—dipping in and out of Shard-sight at the intersections of corridors, trying not to get dizzy or run into anyone while her visual perception was elsewhere—to be where Fleet Captain Sixteen Moonrise was intending to go, before she got there.

Nine Hibiscus wanted to make her flinch. And then she wanted to very gently kick her off her flagship and back onto the *Parabolic Compression* where she belonged, and where her Third Palmer spywork habits would be somewhat confined. Keep her far away from Nine Hibiscus's plans—whatever they ended up being—to deal with the alien homeworld the *Gravity Rose* had found. But even more than wanting to be able to keep secrets when she chose to, Nine Hibiscus was anticipating Sixteen Moonrise's expression of strangled distress when she would be surprised. Anticipating it sharply enough that she knew she was letting her teeth show in her smile as she hurried down her ship's corridors and elevator shafts, command deck to hydroponics to crew mess to—

—a tumbling vector of stars, the taste of panic-bile and metallic adrenaline in the back of her throat, her vision consumed by the vast arch of an alien ring-ship, slick metal and rippling distortion, *too close too close too close* and then the stars again, that Shard—wherever they were, and she hadn't meant to slip out of the set of pilots who were safely on the *Weight for the Wheel*, off-shift—managing to pull back hard enough that they skirted asymptotically *up* from the ring, up, away—

Nine Hibiscus could feel her heartbeat in her wrists, her throat, the membrane of her diaphragm. Her heartbeat, or that Shard pilot's, and this was *without* having a Shard and the updated proprioception programming. Just from visuals. No wonder some of the Shard pilots were calling this new programming the *Shard trick*.

Flicker-vision: Shard pilots on her ship, in the mess, in the hydroponics deck, in the fitness facility, an echoed sense of strain—psychosomatic, surely—as that pilot bench-pressed heavy plates away from his chest. Her heart still racing.

The wheel of stars, too fast.

Did they all feel this? All the time?

The wheel of stars—and fire, a flash of heat, of sick-sweet

panic (*there goes the engine, oh*—), vision clouded entirely with red, red-to-white, and—

Gone. Blackness. Nine Hibiscus swallowed. She was hanging on to a wall, somewhere in a passage between Deck Six and Deck Five. She was entirely herself. That pilot had—had swept up away from the enemy ship, avoided a crash, and been shot from behind while in the process of moving through that escape arc. A little flash of fire, and nothing ever again.

Did every Shard pilot feel every death, if they were paying attention?

Gingerly, she reached through the programming one more time. Returned to the strain of the weight lifter. If he'd seen that death, he wasn't reacting in any way visible in his field of vision. She swapped again. There was a Shard pilot with his programming on in the Deck Five mess, and he was sitting at one end of a long communal table, and at the other end, casual in shirtsleeves, her uniform jacket slung over the back of her chair, was the Fleet Captain Sixteen Moonrise, engaged in cheerful conversation with Nine Hibiscus's own soldiers.

The spike of fury Nine Hibiscus felt was blinding-intense, like a shockstick blow to the solar plexus. Worse than watching that death—more disorienting for having just seen it. She didn't even know which Shard had just died. Or how many more just like it would die today. And here was this—intruder, this underminer, this woman who was not with *her own* legion, her own people, but too concerned with infiltrating Nine Hibiscus's people, her Fleet, her *place,* to be tending to the soldiers of the Twenty-Fourth that were hers by right—that this person would be *eating* with the Tenth Legion instead—it was the sort of rage that would make Nine Hibiscus stupid and careless. She let it happen to her. Let it wash through her, and then imagined it like the core of a ship engine, lodged in her chest, an animating force, secret and dangerous and shielded, under control.

She still wanted to get Sixteen Moonrise off her fucking flagship. That, at least, she could have some influence over.

When she walked into the Deck Five mess, it was nevertheless savagely gratifying that her people stood up to greet her when they noticed she'd come in. She grinned at them, wide-eyed and performatively incredulous—*All this for me? Come on, go eat*—and waved them back to sitting. They went. The conversation stayed at the same comfortable volume. Her soldiers were still hers. For now.

Sixteen Moonrise had been clever with her choice of seats: there were no open ones next to her. Nine Hibiscus took one in the center of the long table instead, and met the eyes of her Shard pilot for a long, shared-and-doubled moment of vision. She felt him turn his Shard programming off, for both their sakes now that they were in the same space. That doubled vision snapped away, and there was an echo, a feeling like she'd almost been breathing in time with him and now she wasn't. A mild version of feeling his sibling-pilot extinguished in fire. She inclined her head to him, fractionally. Wished she could ask him about the programming, about—side effects.

And then she didn't say a starfucked thing. She let Sixteen Moonrise keep talking, as if there was nothing wrong with what she was doing at all, and served herself a helping of rice noodle laden with soybeans and chili oil from the communal bowl in the center of the table. Soldier food. Warm enough to keep the vacuum out of your bones, or make you feel like it might.

She chewed and swallowed a few bites, feeling the energy of the table shift around her, reorient toward her presence. She licked her lips, chasing the last of the oil's numbing heat. "Fleet Captain," she said, convivial, "your crew must be very appreciative that you eat with them down in the mess. You *do* do this on the *Parabolic Compression*, don't you? Or is this only because you're our guest?"

Sixteen Moonrise's electrum-shaded eyes blinked behind her cloudhook, a slow and faintly reptilian opening and shutting.

"When my crew invites me," she said. A nasty, insinuating answer: *she* was invited, both here and on her own ships, and Nine Hibiscus merely waltzed in and took a chair, disturbing her people's privacy away from the eyes of their superior officer.

"A treat for you, then," Nine Hibiscus told her. *How rarely you must get invitations, to need to be specifically invited.*

"I'm honored by the Tenth's hospitality, *yaotlek*."

"We are by all measures hospitable," said Nine Hibiscus, and the soldier on her left laughed—*good*—and then cut herself off from laughing—less good. Nine Hibiscus wanted so very much to know what sort of conversation Sixteen Moonrise had been having here, to make her people so wary of free expression.

"I've found you so. Though it's hardly your reputation."

Nine Hibiscus raised one eyebrow. Blood-soaked *starlight,* she wanted this woman off her ship. "What *is* the reputation of the Tenth amongst your Twenty-Fourth, then?" she asked, melted-glass calm, harnessed-reactor-core calm.

Sixteen Moonrise shrugged one shoulder. The curve of her mouth was vicious and irreproachable in pretended innocence. "Insular," she said. "Devoted."

If Nine Hibiscus asked *to whom,* she knew what the answer would be: *to you, yaotlek.* And now she knew the shape of Sixteen Moonrise's distaste for her—or at least her masters' distaste, the Third Palm's distaste—knew it *without* bothering to ask. It wasn't that she was hesitating on the edge of a full, apocalyptic commitment to battle with the aliens. That had been a sop for the ambitions of the Fleet Captains of the Sixth and the Fourteenth, to get them to sign on to Sixteen Moonrise's letter of proto-insurrection and concern. It wasn't even that Nine Hibiscus had brought in Information to do the work that the Fleet shouldn't have to do—though she suspected that decision hadn't helped. It was that Sixteen Moonrise—or the Third Palm—or the Ministry of War in its entirety, a truly disturbing idea she could not entertain without feeling suddenly ill—thought that she was a risk to the Empire. That her

ARKADY MARTINE

people—their trust, their confidence, their willingness to die for her—would die for *her,* and not for Teixcalaan.

(Or would come to think of her as Teixcalaan. Something like that might have happened to One Lightning. And what had he made of it? A botched usurpation, a chaotic transition— she would *never have*—but if Minister Nine Propulsion *had* been in on the usurpation, there might be reasons the Third Palm thought Nine Hibiscus, her protégé, might try something similar.)

She said, "Hardly insular, Fleet Captain. We're eating with you, aren't we? And have been for . . . mm. How long *has* it been now, since you arrived? Days?"

"My adjutant, Twelve Fusion, is a commander I would trust with the *Parabolic Compression* for as long as is necessary for me to be elsewhere, " Sixteen Moonrise said. She sounded a little edgy, a little nervous. *Good.*

"Naturally," Nine Hibiscus said, and took another bite of noo- dles. Her tongue was numb, a fire-lash. "What, if I might pre- sume to ask"—the highest of polite forms, so polite as to be insulting—"is necessary for you on the Deck Five mess? I'm fascinated. Does the *Parabolic Compression* lack rice noodles?"

Now her soldiers *did* laugh, and more freely. She felt savagely possessive of them. *So what if we are ourselves. We're the weight that turns the wheel.*

"I like your spice mix in the oil," Sixteen Moonrise said, ut- terly bland. "I might ask you to lend me this deck's chief cook, for a day or so."

She was lodged in them like a burr. She didn't *want* to leave, and she was willing to let Nine Hibiscus know what she was thinking, which meant—*fucking* Third Palmers—that she was confident in her belief that Nine Hibiscus knowing wouldn't matter—

I wonder if I am supposed to die out here, she thought. *I wonder if Sixteen Moonrise is supposed to die too, in the mouths of our en-*

emy. *Collateral damage her masters are willing to countenance—if it means destroying me as well—*

(And who is going to win the war then, with all the Fleet Captains dead like my Shards are dying?)

"When we can spare such a necessary person as Deck Five's cook," she began—and then her entire cloudhook lit up with the red and white flare of an emergency message.

There was only one person on *Weight for the Wheel* who had accesses high enough to override her settings, spill a communiqué across her eyes without her granting permission first.

Mallow, Twenty Cicada's message read. *Medbay is under contamination protocols. I am inside. There is a fungal bloom from the corpse of our enemy. A medical tech is dead. It ate him. Acknowledge.*

She was on her feet, one hand held up to stop any questions from the table. Her eyes flickered as fast as she could, calling up her messaging system, subvocalizing into it. *Swarm, why are you inside?*

A long ten seconds. *I didn't know better. Come see. I don't seem to be dying yet.*

I have Sixteen Moonrise, she wrote. Waited. Waited. Waited. She existed in a blank abeyance of panic, fear shoved so deep into her chest she felt perfused with it, existing alongside it.

And then: *Starlight, Mallow, bring her along. Might as well.*

Eight Antidote dreamed of *disruptive persons* and woke up with the images of the dream still hanging around him like a sticky miasma, a fog-wrapped morning that no amount of sunlight could entirely get rid of. He was formlessly upset, entirely sure he'd done something very wrong and equally certain that he *hadn't*, not in the waking world: he'd only dreamed it, and the dream was fading. Fading, but not gone. Only gone to scraps.

He'd spent two whole days in the Ministry of War, coming

back to Palace-Earth only to sleep, shadowing Minister Three Azimuth. Maybe that was enough to give anyone nightmares.

He'd followed her out of the gymnasium to the shooting range, and let her correct his aim like she'd corrected the position of his hands on the padded gym mats—and followed her back to her office, and simply, easily, *magically*—had not left. He would have left if she'd told him to. She just kept not telling him to.

She let him watch her discussion with the other Palms—Six, engineering and shipbuilding; Two, logistics—even her discussions with Eleven Laurel, who looked at Eight Antidote, curled on the Minister's window seat, chin on his laced fingers on his knees and watching everything he could watch—with a complex expression, neither pleasure or displeasure. He had fixed the same expression on Minister Three Azimuth, with a leading pause she didn't fill—and after that had ignored Eight Antidote like he was a throw pillow placed on the window seat for improving the décor. He tried not to feel hurt.

Late on the first day, closer to the end of the afternoon, Eight Antidote had brought the Minister a coffee. She'd laughed at him, and ruffled his hair, and told him that she didn't drink coffee and that he was not an office aide.

He drank the coffee himself, and spent the rest of the evening wired and jittery and hugely terrified, hugely excited, when Three Azimuth began receiving reports that the Information agent and Mahit Dzmare—Mahit Dzmare, creature of *disruption*—had gone down to the dead planet of Peloa-2 and established first contact with the alien enemy. None of the reports were code Hyacinth. So all of them had to be aboveboard, simple chain-of-command reporting. Coming in on Fleet ships through the jumpgate postal system, standard courier, six hours of delay between message and receipt. Nothing like what the Fleet Captain Sixteen Moonrise had done, when she warned the Minister about the Information agent's existence in the first place. Nothing secret.

It got—stranger, after that. Stranger being there, stranger listening. Suddenly all of Three Azimuth's meetings were with members of the Science Ministry who studied xenobiology or the sort of Fleet soldiers who very calmly discussed *acceptable casualty rates in an emergency situation*. They stretched on into the night, not stopping to eat or drink or rest—and why hadn't she sent him away, what did she want him to *see*, why was he staying, anyway?

An Ebrekti expert came in, close to midnight, and had a polite shouting match with the acceptable-casualty-rates woman about how long a first-contact experience could be allowed to go on before someone needed to do something to make sure nobody was dead, and Three Azimuth sat there, watching, making notes. Eight Antidote kept staring at the burnt hole where her ear had been and wondering how she'd been injured so badly. Thinking of which of these people were *disruptive* and how he'd know if they were.

It had been the darkest, coldest part of the night when he'd gone home, walked across the gardens and into Palace-Earth, shivering in his thin jacket. Gone home, fallen into bed, slept. He didn't remember *those* dreams, but he knew he'd had them. And even so, he found himself walking through the dew-glittering grass back into the Ministry of War the next morning just after sunrise. Back into Three Azimuth's office. He folded up small on the windowsill again, and some Fleet cadet brought him grapefruit and lychee juice for breakfast, and he listened. Listened, while Minister Three Azimuth received a message on fast courier from the *yaotlek* Nine Hibiscus herself, and watched it with only him, Eleven Laurel, and two of her own close staff in the room. (He shouldn't have been there. He didn't leave.) He'd never heard Nine Hibiscus's voice before, only seen her image on holo, and it was strange to know she sounded like a person, not a threat or a puzzle to solve, just a woman with an easy, confident cadence to her speech and an urgency right behind the reserve with which she reported that her scouts had found an alien planet, a home—one of probably many, but a home—of the enemy that was eating her legions.

Listened, while Three Azimuth and Eleven Laurel calmly discussed historical precedent for massive planetary strikes. He knew of some. They were from eight hundred years ago, or more, when Teixcalaan had been—vicious. Uncompromising in stamping out rebellions.

Eleven Laurel had said lightly, "There are very good reasons the Fleet has shifted to a negotiation-and-subordination modality, Minister, which I know you're well aware of, considering Nakhar . . ."

And Three Azimuth had answered, "Massive planetary strikes on *people* waste resources and goodwill, and create eternal enmity between new-integrated systems and Teixcalaan. As you said, Undersecretary: Nakhar is an excellent example of the success of negotiation and subordination. Do you have some reason to believe I'd revise my methodology so drastically now that I've become Minister? Her Illuminate Majesty appointed me to this position for good reasons." It sounded like a warning.

"So she did!" Eleven Laurel agreed. "And for *very* good reasons—I *am* ever so well acquainted with your work on Nakhar. What was it they called you? The butcher of the Nakharese mind? So interesting to find out that there is something even a person with such an elegant epithet finds morally objectionable."

Eight Antidote was sure he was not supposed to be hearing this. He was equally sure that Eleven Laurel meant him to hear it, meant him to think that only *he*, Third Undersecretary Eleven Laurel, was trustable in the Ministry of War. That Three Azimuth had done something as governor of Nakhar that was so very wrong that she could be—pressured (blackmailed?) with only the casual mention of it. That Eight Antidote should return to being only Eleven Laurel's student. (Like Fleet Captain Sixteen Moonrise had been Eleven Laurel's student?)

Disruptive persons, he thought again. And then, *What happens to them afterward, once Three Azimuth knows who they are?* Nothing good. Nothing he wanted to examine too closely.

And at the same time, he wanted with a stupid heartfelt instant want to *defend* her. Hadn't her methods—however butcherlike—*worked*?

Did he want them to have worked, if it meant she'd do the same sort of thing again, to a whole planet?

Three Azimuth sighed, a delicate and annoyed sound. "The question is, Undersecretary, whether these enemies are people for whom *morally objectionable* applies."

"We have only Information finding out," Eleven Laurel said, with elegant distaste.

"Information and a barbarian diplomat. I'm not pleased about it either, trust me."

Eight Antidote had had to say something then. He couldn't stay quiet, not when they were considering a first-strike planetary destruction. He didn't know *what* he wanted to say, only that he wanted them both to know he was there and listening.

"Why aren't we—I mean, why isn't the Fleet doing the negotiation?" he said. He knew he'd slipped when he'd said *we*. Knew he'd been in this office too long. It was awful, to know all that and to still realize it was a useful slip to have made, aligning himself with the two of them. He was going to learn something now. He missed thinking that mistakes were just mistakes. Since he'd become a spy, he felt bad about good things as much as he did about errors.

"The kid has a point," said Three Azimuth. "We *could*—if we used the Shard trick, get one of your own people down in that negotiation, Undersecretary—"

Eight Antidote, confused, thought, *the Shard trick?* Just as Eleven Laurel shook his head, harsh negation, all of the lines on his face that Eight Antidote used to think were friendly going savage and frowning. "I don't think that discussion is happening in front of an appropriate audience," he said.

Which meant—which meant that Eight Antidote had just heard something he wasn't supposed to hear *at all,* even more than he hadn't been meant to hear about *the butcher of the Na-kharese mind.* Something worse. Something stranger. *The Shard trick.* Something that was faster than fast couriers? He was waiting for Three Azimuth to shut Eleven Laurel down; she was his *superior,* after all, blackmail or no blackmail, and she'd seemed like she was really interested in the idea—

But all she did was shrug one shoulder a little, and nod, and no one talked about Shards or joining the negotiations again. It was back to endless meetings with Logistics, and Armaments. Supply lines. How to move weapons through jumpgates without breaking too many treaties at once.

Like the Minister of War wouldn't cross Eleven Laurel at all. Which was *backward.* Like Eleven Laurel was the one who could identify *disruptive persons,* and had decided that the Minister herself, and maybe Eight Antidote too, were some of them.

That night Eight Antidote had crept back into his room in Palace-Earth and gone to bed straightaway, even though it was still hours before midnight. He wished he hadn't. Less sleep would have meant less time to dream.

———

As she approached the medbay, every protocol subroutine in *Weight for the Wheel's* ship AI shouted alerts into Nine Hibiscus's cloudhook: STOP—DO NOT ENTER—DANGER—BIOLOGICAL HAZARD on endless and unrhyming repeat. It was far more jarring than a normal safety message. Those had *prosody.* This was . . . this was for being shocked and disturbed and terrified, and for being *warned away,* shaken out of normalcy by monosyllables. Nevertheless she approached the vacuum-sealed medbay doors. Sixteen Moonrise was following her, as avid as a vulture, and she felt full up with the weight of knowing that the alien enemy *did* have a home she could reach and attack, if she was willing to risk the ships and the loss of life.

Afterimage, too fast to do more than kick her heart rate up another few notches: that Shard-death by fire, the hideous *relief* she had thought she'd felt from the pilot—but that had to have been her own projection—*emotion* didn't travel through Shard-sight. Or at least it never had before.

She peered through the heavy glass window set in the center of the medbay doors. It was her only view into whatever the fuck was happening to Swarm.

He'd shut himself off, closed down everything like the medbay was experiencing an outbreak of hemorrhagic fever. She assumed an alien fungal bloom that had killed at least one of her soldiers was an approximate equivalent to a hemorrhagic fever. If it spread like one, Twenty Cicada was already dead, even if he hadn't finished dying yet.

Aloud, not caring if Sixteen Moonrise heard her, she called up her messaging system again and sent him a quick inquiry: "We're here. What's going on inside?"

"Well," said Twenty Cicada, using the medbay's intercom service—he must not be dying very *hard* yet, if he'd turned on the two-way communication inside that was meant for just this sort of emergency, infectious disease on the inside of those doors and a healthy ship on the outside—"currently I feel fine, and there is no one in here but one dead alien and one dead medical cadet—Six Rainfall, I think. He's got fungi growing out of a wound on his hand."

"You've turned on the purifiers, and none of the air in there is getting recycled back into the ship, right?"

"*Yaotlek.* Mallow, my dear, you *know me.* Of course the purifiers are on outgas cycle. We'll make up the oxygen in about three days from the hydroponics decks."

My dear was worse than *Mallow*, as a sign of how concerned Twenty Cicada was about his own life expectancy. Fuck, but she didn't want to lose him. And she really didn't want to lose him where Sixteen Moonrise could see her grieve. "I never doubted," she told him, wishing she could *see* him. "Tell me about the cadet."

". . . Well, he found the fungus before it killed him, and he had time to send all of medical a message about it with microscopic analysis holos. That's how I knew to come—I'm on that message list. So it's *slow,* whatever it is that killed him. From what I can tell—and trust me, I am not doing what this poor child did and sticking my hand in the alien's mouth—the original locus of fungus is growing out of its *brain.* The alien, I mean. Not Six Rainfall."

Sixteen Moonrise said, ". . . Like a fungal herniation through the ethmoid bone? Into the oral cavity?"

"Quite exactly, Fleet Captain," said Twenty Cicada, faintly sepulchral through the intercom. "Are you, perhaps, a biologist by training?"

"I never have had the pleasure of serving in medical," said Sixteen Moonrise, which was not *no,* and also Nine Hibiscus despised her entirely for being useful as well as herself. "But if the fungus was living in its brain, that is how it might emerge to spore. A pressure downward, first through the ethmoid bone and then through the soft palate. The alien did have a soft palate, I recall."

Nine Hibiscus interrupted her. "How did the cadet die?"

"He cut himself," Twenty Cicada said. "And got the fungus in the wound. But I think it was anaphylaxis that killed him. Not the fungus itself. It's—not very widespread. And he is cyanotic."

One more question. The one she really didn't want to ask. "And you?"

"No cuts, no anaphylaxis," said Twenty Cicada, brisk and brief. "In a moment or two I'll have a better readout on whether these things are aerosolizing or not—the ship is running me a particle diagnostic, it's crude but it'll tell me something—and the fungus isn't very happy."

"Happy," Sixteen Moonrise said, flat.

"It's been robbed of its host," Twenty Cicada told her, "and it doesn't much like living in Six Rainfall. Or at least in Six Rainfall's bloodstream. It is wilting as I watch."

"Perhaps it'd like his brain better."

Nine Hibiscus turned on Sixteen Moonrise and took a step into her personal space. Used all of her weight and size to *loom*, to make a point of her authority. "We are not cutting open the skull of one of our dead," she said, "to do *experiments*. Alien fungi or not."

"I was hardly suggesting such a thing, *yaotlek*," Sixteen Moonrise said, and managed to sound affronted.

"What were you suggesting, then?"

"That this fungus likes neural tissue, and is stable there. That our enemies might have sent this one as a *trap*. A bomb. A sacrifice. That you should check your spook and your spook's pet for anaphylaxis—or fungal infiltrates in the brain. And your adjutant, as well. *Yaotlek*, I am not attempting to challenge you on your ship—I am *frightened* of what this might mean. Take it seriously, for the Empire's sake if not your own."

She could sound so very sincere. Cold, and sincere, and far too likely to be right to be dismissed—either from *Weight for the Wheel* or from this conversation.

"My own adjutant, as you've noticed, is inside the contaminant field," Nine Hibiscus said. "I cannot take it more seriously than I am doing right now."

Sixteen Moonrise nodded—and pushed onward. "And the Information officer? And the escort team you sent down with her? They could already have died. And already be spreading the fungus *outside* the contaminant field." Nine Hibiscus thought she must be the sort of Fleet Captain whose command was always laced through with the intimation of threat. The *Parabolic*

Compression would be an exquisitely tuned ship—tightened to snapping.

Through the intercom, Twenty Cicada said, "I doubt it, Fleet Captain. I have the results of the particle assay, and it *isn't* aerosolizing at detectable levels. Whatever it does, that's not how it spreads best. Be reassured."

Nine Hibiscus couldn't have sounded that calm or that comforting. Not from the other side of the medbay door. "Swarm," she said. "Confirm that you mean you are *unlikely* to die of fungal infection?"

His laughter was sudden, strange. "Unlikely to, yes. But I'm not coming out of here until six hours have passed and I am *sure*. Besides, the Fleet Captain's right, my dear—the *asekreta* should know about this development."

"If she doesn't already," Sixteen Moonrise said, darkly, and Nine Hibiscus could imagine, quite clearly: the bodies of *asekreta* Three Seagrass and her barbarian xenolinguist ambassador, filmed over with mold, hours dead in the quarters she had assigned them—and worse, the bodies of her soldiers, haphazardly placed throughout *Weight for the Wheel*, each a locus of infection. If it did spread. But it hadn't spread to Twenty Cicada—yet—

"Time to find out," she said. "I'll have them brought to the medical deck, and we'll see."

Everything else would have to wait until afterward.

———

Mahit woke warm—blood-heat warm, sharing-space warm, the deep primal comfort of being wrapped around another living person in a small space. There was no moment of confusion, no sensation of *let me feel this a little longer before I think about how I got here*: she knew at the first flicker of consciousness exactly where she was. She was curled around Three Seagrass in the lower bunk of their quarters on the Teixcalaanli flagship *Weight for the Wheel*: her knees behind Three Seagrass's knees, her face pressed into the loose dark tangle of Three Seagrass's hair, her naked hips a cup for Three Seagrass's naked hips. Her hand curled over Three Seagrass's rib cage, pulling her close. The sweet *used* ache between her thighs.

Oh, Mahit knew *exactly* where she was, and exactly what they had done, and how much she had enjoyed it, and how at the moment of orgasm, with half of Three Seagrass's hand inside her, almost to the knuckle, she had seen in an explosion of gold the blurred faces of Nineteen Adze and the Emperor Six Direction and remembered an entirely different physical experience of climax. And how she—hadn't minded that, either, just found her way back to herself enough to press Three Seagrass into the mattress and see if Yskandr had known any tricks for oral sex that she hadn't figured out herself.

<Only by virtue of having twenty years on you, Mahit,> he murmured to her now. <I don't think anyone is complaining about your current technique.>

It was amazing how prurient he could sound in the privacy of their own mind. She was *blushing,* hot-faced, glad that Three Seagrass was either really asleep or pretending to be asleep the same as she was, so that she didn't have to explain.

It would have been nice if they could stay right here. And not have to explain anything. Or figure out just how bad of an idea this had been.

Reed, she thought, as deliberately as she would direct a thought to Yskandr, *if you weren't compromised before in the eyes of all these soldiers, you will be now.*

And Yskandr murmured back to her, <You're just as compromised, Mahit. However will you explain *this* to Darj Tarats?>

Just like that, all vestiges of desire vanished: she felt cold and clear and faintly nauseated, like she had been plunged into icy water and released again. She had managed to not think about what she had promised Darj Tarats for almost a whole twenty-four hours, lost in culture shock, disappointed fury, first-contact protocols, heat exhaustion, and really good sex—in that order. It had been very nice, not thinking about Darj Tarats, and how her eyes were his eyes now. How she was a *spy* here, embedded in this ship like a shrapnel shard, working her way slowly through to its heart. How she was a spy, and had been commanded to be a saboteur as well, even if she hadn't figured out what to sabotage exactly—

<Everything,> Yskandr murmured. <That's the problem. Tarats wants—to see Teixcalaan, to know it so well that it can be led to its own destruction . . . >

He'll like this, then, Mahit thought, deliberate and bitter. *Look how much Teixcalaan trusts me. Admittedly, she's not an Emperor, so you're still a little ways ahead.*

She could *feel* how she'd hurt him, feel it in the hollowness of her own chest, the ache of grief as vivid as tears. She tried not to be sorry, and was sorry, and didn't know if she was sorry because she'd hurt him or because she was hurt, too. One more thing that integration therapists never warned you about: having two people's heartsickness to evoke with a misplaced slice of self-recrimination.

<I failed Tarats when I bargained our imago-technology away to Six Direction in exchange for peace,> Yskandr said, finally. <And I failed Six Direction too, in the end. Mahit—*do better than I did;* the line of us should amount to something worthwhile.>

She'd never heard him so clearly describe the shape of his own despair, his own sense of self-hatred. It was like looking into a mirror that went on forever, a hole in the world abruptly made real. She was afraid when she asked him, quiet in the vault of their mind, hesitant: *Darj Tarats would like Teixcalaan to smash itself against these aliens until they are both dead. I could tell him about Sixteen Moonrise—and then sabotage our negotiations on Peloa-2—I could get us all killed. Should I?*

<Oh, Mahit,> Yskandr said. <How the fuck should I know?>

And because he had said that, her eyes were leaking tears when Three Seagrass turned over in her arms and pressed cool fingers to her cheek, tracing the wet.

"Surely," she said, "you don't regret me *this* much?"

She sounded *devastated,* which was not at all what Mahit wanted. She wasn't sure what she wanted, but it wasn't this: Three Seagrass looking like Mahit had *hit* her, just by weeping.

"No," she said, and hated how her voice sounded thick and choked. "No, it's not *you,* Reed, it's not you at all, I—"

Words took too long, and were all in Teixcalaanli anyway. She kissed her instead.

It was still a good kiss, and Three Seagrass continued to be very good at *kissing* (when she wasn't having an existential crisis over watching her Emperor commit ritual suicide on empire-wide holocast, at least). When they broke apart, Three Seagrass was tucked easily against Mahit's shoulder, like they were designed to fit together.

"So," she said, brisk and bright and with a gentleness that reminded Mahit terribly of Nineteen Adze (or reminded Yskandr of Nineteen Adze, which was probably closer to the truth), "if it's not *me* you regret, Mahit, what is it? We did so *well* yesterday."

"We did," Mahit agreed. "We did, and we have such a long way to go, and—"

"Don't tell me you're doubting your own capabilities. *You* figured out how to sing to them. We really need a name for them besides *the enemy,* don't you think?"

"—Probably, yes, and no, I'm not doubting my own capabilities, I'm—" She stopped. Her tongue felt like lead in her mouth. All of the neuropathic pain was back in her hands, a continuous sparkling flare, like being pricked by glass splinters. She didn't know what to do, and Yskandr didn't know what to do, and Three Seagrass was going to keep hurting her like she had yesterday, keep thinking of her as *my clever barbarian* and not as Mahit Dzmare, no matter how many times they kissed, and there was no such thing as safety and no such thing as going home.

"Mahit?" Three Seagrass asked, and cupped her cheek in a narrow palm. "I don't like using interrogation techniques on gorgeous people I've just slept with, but you're *worrying me* and also not providing me with much to go on, and eventually the training just kicks in."

This was almost certainly a horrible, delicious, and representative example of Information Ministry humor. It was funny. And it was everything, absolutely everything, wrong with how the two of them were going to be together, and Mahit was tired. Tired of—

<Eventually,> Yskandr murmured, whisper-thin, <we fall. It doesn't hurt, really. The falling.>

Only the sudden stop at the end?

Electric laughter, and more of that hideous, grief-stricken hollowness flooding her chest. Her hands hurt so *badly*.

"If I was," she began, shutting her eyes and turning her head away from Three Seagrass so that there was nothing but that gentle touch and the hot darkness behind her eyelids, "if I was being the sort of agent of Lsel that I ought to be, considering how I managed to arrange to let you steal me at all, I should be trying very hard to *not* do well at talking to the aliens."

Three Seagrass made a clicking noise with her tongue. "Lsel Station would prefer an endless war?"

Mahit sighed. "No," she said. "Darj Tarats would like Teixcalaan to waste itself to exhaustion against . . . whoever these people are. What Lsel Station entire wants is a much more complicated political analysis, and we're certainly not happy with all of these beautiful warships going over our heads in a continuous stream. But Darj Tarats is who I am supposed to be working for, when I'm not working for you."

Honesty was awful, and it was an intense, full-body relief at the same time—a tension released. *I guess we're both compromised now, for good.*

<You're out on the edges of the world,> Yskandr murmured. <Maybe it's—maybe it's the right place to be compromised.>

Three Seagrass kissed her cheek, a quick and sharp brush of lips. "You are *fascinating*, Mahit. Someday I want to know why you decided to tell me that. I'm good in bed, but I'm not *that* good."

Mahit found herself laughing, despite all her better instincts. "Because, Three Seagrass, I don't think I'm going to do what Darj Tarats wants me to. And—someone should know. That I thought about it first."

"That doesn't make a whole lot of sense, but I'll think about it," Three Seagrass told her, and disentangled them enough to sit up. "Come on. Let's get breakfast and get ready to go down to Peloa-2 again. Since you've apparently decided to *not* commit sabotage?"

"Apparently," Mahit said, and reached for her discarded bra, which had ended up tangled in the springs of the upper bunk sometime in the previous evening's scramble.

"*Excellent*," said Three Seagrass. "Also, you're *really pretty* naked. Just so you know, before you put your underwear on again."

Mahit stared at her while she grinned a creditable Lsel-style grin, and then got up, stretching her hands above her head and arching her back, giving Mahit an excellent view of all of the muscles in her shoulders, the curve of her spine, the fall of her hair unbound. She was still staring when Three Seagrass picked up, with that same covetous curiosity that she'd had when stripping Mahit out of her clothes, the slim volume of *The Perilous Frontier!* that Mahit had left on the fold-out desk in her hurry to get dressed for their first trip down to Peloa-2.

". . . It's Lsel literature," she found herself saying, and hated that she sounded apologetic about it.

Still naked, Three Seagrass sat down at the desk and opened it up. "Who drew it?" she asked.

"I don't know," Mahit said. She'd pulled the covers up over herself, wrapped her arms around her knees. She felt like she was preparing to be hit, and she didn't even know *why*. *She* hadn't drawn it. "A teenager. I bought it from a kiosk on one of our residential decks—"

"You have lots of kiosks," Three Seagrass said, absently, turning the pages. She read fast. "One of them tried to sell me kelp beer. It was horrible."

Kelp beer *was* horrible. "Some people like it," Mahit said. When had Three Seagrass found time to be accosted by a kelp beer salesman? Before or *after* she'd run into Aknel Amnardbat?

"Mm. I'd rather this—the line art is really very well done, and this Esharakir character—"

"What about her?"

"She reminds me a little of you. I think. I have to read the rest, to decide."

"We have time," Mahit found herself saying. "It's not long. Come back here, if you're going to read it? The bed's more comfortable than the chair."

———

The dreams started with the twisted, melted flesh of the Minister of War's ear, except it wasn't the Minister of War, it was Mahit Dzmare in the gardens, and it was all of her face. All of her face, and the tiny beaks of the palace-hummers dipping into the wet, twisted ruin of it, drinking. Like a person who had been exposed to a nuclear shatterbomb strike and was melting of poison. Was poisoning everything she touched.

In the dream she said his own words back to him. He remembered that part. She said, *They don't even have to touch you to do it*, and was covered with birds, and burnt and slippery with lymph, and then she wasn't Mahit Dzmare at all but one of their enemy, one of the aliens, long neck and strange spotted skin and predator's teeth—and not burnt. Not at all.

Not burnt, just very carefully holding one of the palace-hummers in its long-fingered hand, delicate except for the claws, and in the dream Eight Antidote remembered thinking that surely it would eat the bird, remembered being killing-afraid, panicked-afraid, and trying to ask it not to while it preened the tiny feathers with the crystalline-laced clawtip of its index finger.

There were worse things after that, but he couldn't remember them right. Just the sense that he had done something terrible, and knowing it was something that he'd done in the dream.

He got up. Showered—facing away from the cameras, as usual—dressed. One of his spywork outfits: grey on grey. He almost looked like a normal kid. Almost. Kids maybe wore colors. He didn't really know. He pulled his hair back, combed it straight and even, and tied it with a silver and leather cord. If he didn't look like a kid, maybe he should just look like a spy. He had a grey jacket, a long one with layered lapels, a grown person's jacket, and it matched well enough.

He was going somewhere. He realized that in the middle of pulling the jacket on, and decided to sit down and decide where, before he left. It wasn't going to be the Ministry of War. He thought he might scream if he did that again, and that was both babyish and *not helpful*.

He knew a little bit about Mahit Dzmare. Not very much. But a little bit. And he had watched her speech on the newsfeeds, the one that happened right before his ancestor-the-Emperor had died, the one that had started the war. He'd watched that a lot of times. And he had—oh, he had *disruptive person* rattling around in his skull, making him feel strange and a little sick. (Was *he* a disruptive person? Could a person become an Emperor without being a disruptive person?)

But Mahit Dzmare wasn't alone, when she'd been here in the City—and she wasn't alone now, when she was out conducting first-contact negotiations on a Fleet warship. She was with the same person both places. And that person was the Third Undersecretary for Information, Three Seagrass. Or—Special Envoy Three Seagrass. Same person. And Eight Antidote didn't know much about her, at all. And she was a lot easier to think about than a planetary first strike.

The rumor was she'd written the song the rioters who were still loyal to Emperor Six Direction sang during the attempted usurpation. The one that went *released, we are a spear in the hands of the sun.* The one that got stuck in Eight Antidote's head all the time, and probably in the heads of a lot of other people too.

She was a poet, Three Seagrass. Before she was a—whatever she was now.

He called up a public search on his cloudhook for her work. There was a lot of it. She hadn't written anything—or at least anything public—in the past two and a half months, though, and he really didn't want to sit around reading poetry all morning. He'd end up feeling like he'd have to write an essay about it afterward, and submit it to one of his tutors. And it wouldn't explain much about her; it was all from—*before.*

There were other searches he could run. He was Eight Antidote, His Excellency, associate-heir to the sun-spear throne of Teixcalaan, after all. He was all of that, even if he was eleven, and his cloudhook had a *lot* of accesses. Probably more than he knew about. Probably more than he'd ever thought to use, or knew existed.

He queried the general records office for every public activity Three Seagrass had been recorded as doing in the last month. The general records office had a very annoying interface—it was part of the Judiciary Ministry, apparently, or at least it was a Judiciary glyph that spun in midair while the office's AI decided whether or not he was allowed to know what Three Seagrass did in her free time. He wondered if the Sunlit used an interface like this. Probably not. They had their own ways of seeing.

Three Seagrass hadn't done a lot of things, it turned out. Not in the past month. She spent money in restaurants. She had her uniforms dry-cleaned, which *everybody* did. She didn't buy anything strange or big or connected to aliens, and she didn't write any messages that went off-planet (or at least she didn't write any *personal* messages that did—the General Records Office didn't keep track of what Information sent in or out. Which was probably good. Probably. Even if Eight Antidote wished he could see into Information's records of who Three Seagrass had been talking to). What she did do had happened all in an eighteen-hour period right before she left the City: she got reclassified as a special envoy, withdrew most of her savings and added them to an account that was *definitely* Information property, ordered a whole lot of new uniforms, and left from the Inmost Province Spaceport as supernumerary cargo on a medical transport called the *Flower Weave*.

And then she was gone. Gone, and vanished to the other side of all the jumpgates between here and the aliens she'd decided to talk to.

Eight Antidote knew where he was going now. The *Flower Weave* made a circuit of close-in jumpgates to the Jewel of the World—its captain was really weirdly meticulous about noting all of them—and it was back in Inmost Province Spaceport right now.

A medical transport captain would not have an agenda about the *palace* or inter-ministry competition. A medical transport captain wouldn't know anything about aliens, or disruptive persons. A medical transport captain would just tell Eight Antidote what his impressions of the envoy had been. And that was what he needed. He needed to figure out if *he* thought it was a good idea that this envoy and Mahit Dzmare were talking to the aliens Three Azimuth had sent a whole *yaotlek*'s six of legions out to kill instead.

CHAPTER

FOURTEEN

QUARANTINE PROCEDURES FOR CONTAGIOUS DISEASE: WHAT YOU NEED TO KNOW! It is most important for Stationers to listen to the staff of the Councilor for Life Support Systems and to trust their judgment rather than your own during a quarantine event. However, it is very unlikely that you will ever need to! The last quarantine event on Lsel Station occurred five generations ago. Nevertheless the imago-lines of medical personnel who assisted in keeping almost every citizen of the Station safe have been carefully preserved and live amongst us now. Don't be afraid! A minor illness like the common cold, or a fungal infection like ringworm, while contagious, is unnecessary to quarantine, and happens to everyone . . . even Life Support staff. If a more serious disease outbreak occurs, you will receive detailed instructions. A sample follows . . .

> —pamphlet distributed by the Medical Safety and Health
> Board of Lsel Station, under the aegis of the Councilor
> for Life Support Systems

* * *

TRAVEL ADVISORY: There are currently no travel advisories for Teixcalaanlitzlim within the Empire. Please expect and plan for minor delays as military transport receives priority at jumpgate crossings.

> —announcement on holoproj at Inmost Province
> Spaceport, rotating/repeating

WHEN Eight Antidote had been small, he'd had minders, like any child: people to keep him from falling into a water garden or eating an infofiche stick or something else very stupid that really little kids did all the time. But he hadn't had minders for a while now. He had tutors, of course—though since his ancestor-the-Emperor had died, the tutors were more of something he *went to* when he wanted, rather than something that happened to him every day—and he had all of the camera-eyes of the City.

Camera-eyes couldn't stop him from deciding to get on the subway and go to the spaceport. They'd keep track of him—and now that he was on his way, he found that kind of reassuring, because there were *a lot* of people in the Jewel of the World once you got on the subway, and they all seemed to know where they were going and weren't distracted or overwhelmed by anything they saw, which felt absurd. *He* was distracted and overwhelmed. There was just so *much*. He knew the palace complex as well as he knew the shape of his own knees, and he'd mapped out warship trajectories for sectors six jumpgates away, and *still* the City felt very loud and very—well. Very *much*.

But he was going to the spaceport. And the City's eyes would track him. That was, for the first time in a long time, *nice*.

The subway had signs, and Eight Antidote knew the map—who *didn't* know the map?—and even if he didn't, his cloudhook would. The subway, he decided, made sense. Loud, fast-moving, uncomfortable sense, but sense. If he waited on this platform or that one, the timetables would show when the next train would arrive, and where it was going, and it *did* arrive then, and went where it was supposed to. That was the subway algorithm doing its work. He switched lines twice—terrified the first time, gleeful the second. He could do this. He absolutely could. It was so much easier than being in Three Azimuth's office that he didn't even mind when people walked in front of him and almost tripped him because he was too short for them to have noticed.

And then he was in Inmost Province Spaceport, and he wasn't sure he could do it after all. The subway was one thing. The spaceport was another thing altogether. There were even more people, and they were milling around looking at arrival and departure holos, clutching suitcases or pushing baggage carts taller than he was. The vaulted ceilings of the spaceport took all their conversations and made them into a wave of noise, a clattering that got itself mixed in with the cheerful holo jingles of food kiosks, all trying to get him to buy SNACK CAKES: LYCHEE FLAVOR! as well as SQUID STICKS: JUST IMPORTED! He felt sick to his stomach. He usually loved squid sticks, and right now he thought he was going to scream, or maybe cry, because everything was so *loud,* and he never really wanted to eat anything ever again, squid sticks included. How was he going to find the *Flower Weave* in all of this?

He ducked into a quieter side corridor, where people were moving in one direction or another instead of wandering around without any patterns at all, and sat down on a bench. He wanted to pull his knees up to his chest and hide behind them. But that was what a really little kid would do. He tried to think. He was the ninety-percent clone of the Emperor Six Direction, who was supposed to have been one of the most intelligent Emperors who ever started out as a soldier, so he *should be able to think of something.*

When he did think of it, it was so obvious he felt even stupider and more like a dumb kid than ever. He turned on his cloudhook's navigation function, and cross-referenced the berth number the *Flower Weave*'s absurdly bureaucracy-happy captain had filed when he arrived. His cloudhook chimed, soft enough that only he could hear, and lit up a navigational path from his position (which was apparently in Auxiliary Spaceport Corridor B, Tulip Terminal) to the *Flower Weave*'s berth, all the way over in what his cloudhook was calling Nasturtium Terminal. The path in front of him glowed a comforting white, everything limned in the color right before dawn on a cloudy

day. Eight Antidote struck out across the spaceport floor, trying
to look confident and comforted and like a man on a mission.

Nasturtium Terminal was clearly for ships that were headed
out-system, through jumpgates. The entire feeling of it was very
different than Tulip Terminal: Tulip Terminal had been full of
Teixcalaanlitzlim, going *everywhere,* short hops and long ones,
on-planet or up to a satellite or on a cruise around the Jewel of
the World's local planetary systems. Nasturtium Terminal had
tourists, sure, but it also had a lot of grown-ups looking very
seriously at their travel manifests and visas for out-Teixcalaan
trips, and businesspeople with crates of wares, and a few col-
umns of Fleet soldiers in their perfect uniforms, new cadets
heading out to their first postings. Looking at them made Eight
Antidote straighten his spine and square his shoulders as he
walked. His illuminated cloudhook path took him right by an
Information Ministry mail kiosk, staffed by two *asekretim* who
looked hardly older than the Fleet cadets. Operating interstellar jumpgate mail must be the sort of thing people got assigned
to when they weren't trained enough to be useful anywhere else.

Eight Antidote stopped and watched them work. It didn't
seem difficult, what they were doing. They took the infofiche
sticks that were brought to them—they came in bins about the
size of the wastebasket in his bathroom—sorted them (probably by destination, or at least by jumpgate they were supposed
to go through first on the *way* to their destination) into different bins, and then handed off the bins to other Information
Ministry workers who had pilots' uniforms on, except in Information cream-and-orange. Boring. Eight Antidote would *hate*
to have this job. It only got interesting when a non-Information
person, someone in perfectly normal clothes except for the
Judiciary-grey armband she wore, came and stood at the little
window on the side of the kiosk and handed over what looked
like a very *official* infofiche stick. That one didn't go into a bin.
That one made one of the *asekretim* leave the kiosk, special infofiche in hand, and vanish off to hand-deliver it to what Eight

Antidote guessed was a very fast courier indeed. The other *asekreta* wrote out a receipt.

He was trying to decide if he was going to let the *Flower Weave* be for a minute and go ask the receipt-writing *asekreta* about who was authorized to request fast messages from *this* side of the jumpgates leading away from the Jewel of the World, when the entire spaceport seemed to explode with noise: not chattering, shouting Teixcalaanlitzlim, but the shrill, incessant scream of an evacuation alarm.

———

In some of the older ethics manuals that Three Seagrass had once spent an excruciating semester of her time as an *asekreta* cadet reading, there was a persistent fear that extensive emotional—or, stars forbid, *physical*—contact with non-Teixcalaanlitzlim would produce a state of irredeemable contamination in the Teixcalaanlitzlim who had experienced the contact. Taking an elective course called Philosophical Shifts in Teixcalaanli Xenocontact had seemed like a good idea during the registration period, but also that had been the semester she'd registered *drunk*, at four in the morning, from an Information kiosk on the Jewel of the World's southern continent, where she had been practicing cultural immersion, if cultural immersion could be measured by her success at infiltrating music scenes she didn't even like. Mostly she remembered being bemused at those old manual writers, some of whom recommended prophylactic doses of both antibiotics, sun temple services, and social isolation if close contact had accidentally occurred. Three Seagrass had thought, as a very frustrated and no longer even slightly drunk cadet, that those writers were absurdly old-fashioned. What citizen of the Empire couldn't hold their own against the paltry cultural contamination of a nonimperial civilization? And anyone who fucked someone with a social disease had bigger problems than irreversible contamination. Problems like *fucking someone who came from a planet without adequate public health*.

Currently, standing unpleasantly nude next to Mahit Dzmare in a decontamination shower in *Weight for the Wheel*'s medical facilities, she was beginning to wonder if the Fleet had taken those old manuals to heart. Maybe they hadn't read anything written on the subject in the past five hundred years. She was also wondering if there were pruriently placed camera-eyes in their quarters.

Shivering in the chlorine-laced water, she said, "This was not what I had in mind for the morning, Mahit," and was very profoundly gratified when Mahit laughed, even if the laughter was forced and angry.

"On the Station," she said, "we don't require new lovers to get quite this *clean*."

"On your Station you don't spend hours talking to apparently infectious aliens before taking new lovers, unless I am entirely wrong about your native culture."

Mahit shook her head. Her curls, dripping wet, reached almost to the top of her shoulders and she kept shoving them back out of her eyes. "You're not wrong—about that. And if we're full of alien fungus, I don't know how a decon shower is supposed to help."

Three Seagrass didn't know either. It certainly hadn't been what she expected, walking out of the room they'd shared once she'd finished reading *The Perilous Frontier!* and discovered there were nine more volumes and made Mahit promise to get her them if she had any possible method of doing so. They'd dressed, and headed out with the intention of immediately keeping their scheduled second rendezvous with the aliens, back in the terrible heat of Peloa-2.

So Three Seagrass had *in no way* anticipated being grabbed by Fleet soldiers in full isolation gear and spirited away into the medbay, where she and Mahit were unceremoniously stripped and decontaminated while hearing only the edges of *why* this was necessary. The dead alien in the autopsy room had bloomed with fungal infiltrates, apparently. At any moment, perhaps she and Mahit would do the same.

Three Seagrass had her doubts. She felt exactly as uninfiltrated as before. At least by fungi. (When she wasn't being thoroughly distracted by having chemical disinfectants sluiced over her in chilly waves, she was *quite* aware of how she had been thoroughly infiltrated by Mahit's clever fingers, and by the strangeness of the narrative pattern of her graphic story. But there was absolutely *nothing* sexy about a decontamination shower. This moment was, in fact, the least attractive Three Seagrass had ever felt while being naked and near someone she'd had sex with.)

Besides, she was far more concerned that at any moment she and Mahit would miss their prearranged appointment on Peloa-2, and what would be worse than fungal parasitism running rampant through the Fleet was insulting your enemy by being late to a negotiation so that there wasn't *time* for fungal parasitism to run rampant through the Fleet, due to most of the Fleet being dissolved by ship-eating alien weaponry.

The shower finally turned off, and its sealed door unsealed. Three Seagrass exhaled, hard. She was very wet and very cold and *very* clean, and she needed to be on a shuttle *right now*. But on the other side of the shower door was the *ikantlos*-prime Twenty Cicada, not wearing any isolation gear at all. He was, however, wearing *clothes,* which gave him a substantial advantage over the two of them.

"Adjutant," Mahit said, mildly. She was not trying to cover herself with anything, even her hands or the angle of her hips. Three Seagrass wondered about nudity taboo on Lsel Station, and then decided there was very little point in wondering about that *right* this moment. Mahit had gestured to Twenty Cicada's lack of filter-mask or plastic plague gear, and was asking, "Are you no longer concerned that we might be emitting—what was it—spores, then?"

"I find it extremely unlikely that you are emitting anything, Ambassador, Envoy," said Twenty Cicada, "but if you are, it's no more than I've already been exposed to. I was the one who found the body of the medtech, after all. Damage, if there is any, has been done."

Mahit said, "Why are we suddenly concerned about fungal contamination? The aliens we were speaking with—or trying to speak with—were perfectly healthy. No visible fungi."

"Not *visible*," Twenty Cicada began. "Internal. If they had any. And I am beginning to think they might have—but it was dormant, in the skull cavity, the neural structures." He looked like he was willing to go on for a long while on the subject. He looked like a man who had been quietly frightened and quite alone for some time, and who would talk about anything if allowed to. Three Seagrass remembered how deeply at home he had been in the garden of hydroponics at the heart of his ship, and thought, *Isolation protocols must be terrifying to him. To think that he might lose access to all of that—be an infective agent—it would ache like the oozing sap of a cut flower-stem.*

And then: *Maybe I'm still a poet after all.*

She interrupted him before he could give Mahit much more of his stored-up lecture on the fungi which apparently lay secret and safe inside the bodies of their enemies until those enemies died. She said, "*Ikantlos*-prime—we have to go down to Peloa-2. We promised we would be there. And I quite genuinely do not know what the aliens will think—or do—if we promise one thing and give another."

"I know," said Twenty Cicada. "I'm going with you. I'm flying the shuttle."

"Your *yaotlek* doesn't want to expose anyone who hasn't been exposed yet," said Mahit, cool and calm, like an offered hand: *I'm sorry for what your people are doing to you.*

"Quite," said Twenty Cicada. "But also, I insisted. I want to ask them questions, Ambassador. I want to show them *this* and ask them *what it's for.*"

He held up a sealed clear plastic cube in one hand. Inside it was a branching fractal structure of white. The shape of it was, Three Seagrass thought, quite similar to the pale green patterns of the just-visible homeostat-cultist tattoos on his wrists. It rattled when he shook the cube.

————

The alarm went on forever. It was loud and high and unignorable, and it didn't stop, and everyone but Eight Antidote apparently knew what to do about it. All of Nasturtium Terminal had transformed into a river of people, hurrying out the exits, while the entire spaceport seemed to scream, endlessly. *Something is wrong. Something is wrong and you're in danger.* They were probably evacuating. Eight Antidote should evacuate too. But his feet felt rooted to the floor. He was a tiny rock the river of Teixcalaanlitzlim flowed around. What if the alarms were going off because he'd run away into the City and everyone was going to miss their flights and trains and *everything* because the City was looking for him? What if it was all his fault?

What if it wasn't, and it was a real alarm, for a real problem, and no one knew where he was and whether he was safe? That was worse. That was—he'd been so *selfish*—and everyone was moving so fast—he wasn't a rock anymore, he was a pebble, tumbling in the flow of people, being pushed and shoved as they tried to get to the exits of the terminal and away from the noise. Someone hit him with their backpack, and he fell down. Someone stepped on his belly, and it *hurt,* and he curled up into a ball like Eleven Laurel had taught him. Covered the back of his neck with his hands, protected his face and middle. He didn't have enough air to cry; it had all been squished out of him by the person who'd run across him like he was part of the *floor*— and another person tripped over him and *fell* and scrambled back up again—

If he stayed here, he was going to get trampled.

He tried to remember that cold, clear place he'd gone to, back in the Ministry of War's strategy room. The place that happened after you were afraid. He didn't know where that was. He was *so scared*. That place wasn't real right now.

A hand grabbed his arm. Yanked him up to his feet. A voice said, "Fucking *kids*—gonna get yourself killed like that—"

And he was stumbling forward, inside the river of people now, not an obstacle but one of a thousand parts of the water that flowed, and he had no idea who had grabbed him and helped him up. They were as lost as he was.

They spilled out of Nasturtium Terminal back into Tulip Terminal like a flood. Eight Antidote saw that all the exits to the subway were blocked by spaceport security—flanked by a rising number of Sunlit in their blank gold faceplates, threatening and reassuring at once. Out here in Tulip Terminal, the shrieking alarm had words in it: had *please proceed to an outdoor location* and *there is no immediate risk to life or property* and *please do not attempt to access the subway at this time* mixed in with the high wailing noise.

One of those subway entrances had curling tendrils of white smoke coming out of it. Eight Antidote, bruised and terrified and carried away out the doors of the terminal and into the bright, easy sunlight of a City afternoon, thought, *Was there a bomb in the tunnels?* and didn't know at all how to deal with that possibility. That wasn't supposed to happen. The subway was a perfect algorithm. The algorithm would notice a bomb if there was a bomb, wouldn't it?

The flow of evacuating people took him beyond the perimeter that the Sunlit were beginning to set up around the spaceport, and then stopped being a river and started being a confusion again: some Teixcalaanlitzlim standing around, some wandering off, hailing groundcars-for-hire or walking briskly away. Eight Antidote sat down on a low curb that bordered a garden plot full of tulips. *Tulip Terminal,* he thought. *Of course tulips.* His stomach hurt, and his shoulder, and the side of his face. He touched his cheek and winced at the sting, and wasn't surprised when his fingers came away bloody.

He wanted to go home.

He didn't know how to get home if he didn't have the subway.

He was *miles* from Palace-Central, and he didn't know what kind
of neighborhoods were between here and there anyway, if he
decided to walk. His cloudhook would show him a path, but it
was such a very long way, and he really never should have tried
to be a grown person out in the City. And if he couldn't do this,
how could he ever think he could be Emperor? Or even be a
soldier in the Fleet? He was sure Fleet soldiers didn't panic when
they couldn't use the subway. Or want to go home to someplace
that they understood the rules of.

He promised himself he wasn't going to cry right before he
started crying. Which meant he was crying and *embarrassed*
about crying at the same time.

When he managed to unscrew his eyes and wipe his nose
with the back of his sleeve (he was being such a *baby*), and look
up at all, there was a person in white crouched in front of him.

"Hi, Your Excellency," said Five Agate, the Emperor's *ezuazuacat*. "How are you doing?"

If he'd been two years younger—if he'd been two *weeks*
younger, maybe—Eight Antidote would have dived into her arms
and hung on tight. But he was too embarrassed. Too *ashamed*.

"Fine," he said, snot-choked.

"Okay," said Five Agate, and sat down on the garden curb next
to him. "How about we rest here for a minute so that the Sunlit
can finish securing the area, and then I take you back to Palace-
East?"

That sounded incredibly nice. That sounded *easy*. Eight
Antidote didn't trust it. Right now he suspected he didn't trust
anything. That was awful. He *wanted* to trust the Emperor's
sworn right hand. He always had before.

"What happened?" he asked.

"A lot of things," said Five Agate. "Which do you want to hear
about?"

He swallowed. Found himself asking, pathetically, ". . . Is it
my fault?"

Five Agate patted his back, just once. "No," she said. "Well.

Nothing's your fault aside from how Nineteen Adze asked me to go fetch you *myself,* and I was fairly busy at the time. But you did a fine job being findable—stayed on camera, stayed still. I only lost you for a few minutes."

He'd never really been alone at all, had he. Later, he might mind that. Not right now. The City had seen him and sent him Five Agate. Or Nineteen Adze had. Same thing, maybe. It was hard to tell, sometimes, where the City started and the Emperor stopped. "Sorry," Eight Antidote said. "For making you come out here."

"I accept your apology."

"Um. What—else happened? I saw smoke in the subway. Was there—" He didn't want to ask, *Was there a bomb?* Asking felt like it would make it real.

"A train derailed," Five Agate said. "Which is—a very complicated problem. A surprising problem. We haven't had a train derailment since before you were born."

"Not since the new algorithms, right?"

"Right." She didn't seem surprised that he knew about those. That he'd draw those conclusions. Eight Antidote remembered she had a kid, too. A little kid, but maybe he was a smart little kid and Five Agate was good at trusting kids when they were right. That would make sense. (He really wanted things to make sense right now.)

"Did people die?" he asked.

"Not yet," Five Agate said, after blinking through some data on her cloudhook. "Some people are being taken to the hospital, but no one has died."

"Good." He took a deep breath. "Did I— Did the train I was supposed to be on derail?"

Five Agate made a considering noise. "Maybe," she said. "It'd help if we knew exactly how the derailment happened. And also—what were you planning on doing, coming out here?"

Being a spy, Eight Antidote thought. *Finding things out on my own.* But that *maybe* was rattling around in his throat, awful enough to choke on. So he told the truth. Maybe if he told the truth he'd get to go home and stop being a spy for a little while. He said, "I wanted to ask someone who didn't work for Information or War about Envoy Three Seagrass."

". . . And you thought you'd find someone like that at the spaceport?"

"Um. She left on the *Flower Weave,* and—"

"Oh, *clever,*" said Five Agate. Eight Antidote expected the praise to make him feel good, feel proud, like when Eleven Laurel or Three Azimuth had told him he'd done something right. Instead he just felt tired. There was a long pause, a quiet contemplative space. He sniffled. He had a headache from crying, which was *also* embarrassing.

Finally, Five Agate stood up. Her white trousers had planter-dirt on them, and she didn't seem to care. "Let's go home, Your Excellency," she said. "The Judiciary and the Sunlit have the scene locked down. There's no point in hanging around waiting to see if it was a signal problem or an incendiary device."

An incendiary device. Like the one the *ixplanatlim* had been talking about in the throne room, days and days ago. A *bomb.* In the subway. That would be awful. That would be worse than a derailment. Especially if it was Eight Antidote's fault.

"Do you think," he tried, willing his voice to be even, "it *was* an incendiary device?"

"I think," said Five Agate, "that you and I both will be better off waiting for the Judiciary report on the incident before we start worrying about that. Wait for the real problem, Your Excellency. Don't borrow trouble that doesn't come to you on its own." She paused, and smiled, a quick there-and-gone expression. "Besides, I think I can do better than bringing you the captain of the *Flower Weave.* How would you like to talk to the envoy herself?"

———

The shuttle went down to the Peloa System with Swarm on it. Nine Hibiscus watched that shuttle's engines burn bright fuel and vanish into the atmosphere of Peloa-2 from the bridge, with Sixteen Moonrise right beside her where her adjutant should have been—the worst possible replacement for Swarm that she could imagine. There went Swarm, the envoy, the Ambassador, and her same four escort soldiers as the last time—all of them smelling harshly of chlorine and disinfectants even through fresh uniforms. Down to meet the enemy face-to-face, and the medical deck was still sealed off to all but emergency personnel. Sixteen Moonrise claimed that she'd been appeased sufficiently: there wasn't going to be an immediate outbreak of fungal-driven anaphylaxis, not just yet, but naturally a Fleet Captain (let alone a *yaotlek*) shouldn't take any chances. And of course, of *course* Sixteen Moonrise refused to return to the *Parabolic Compression* while there was any chance that she herself could be a vector. How noble. How convenient for her. How easy it was going to be for her to find out about the enemy planetary system before Nine Hibiscus was ready for her to know.

Nine Hibiscus wanted to hurt something. To *shoot* something. To have a target to unleash all of *Weight for the Wheel*'s energy cannons on, a conflagration to create. Nothing was making sense any longer. She'd understood Kauraan. She'd understood how to make her enemies trust her, how to give her soldiers strength in their loyalty—she'd *always* understood that—and here she was, paralyzed, waiting, with a dead cadet next to a dead alien in the autopsy cold-room. All of the power of the Fleet, all of the power of Teixcalaan behind it, all of her own skill and hard-won patience—and yet Swarm had gone down on that star-cursed shuttle to drown in desert heat and ask aliens questions. This had all been her idea, originally, and she wished she could take it back—if taking it back meant she'd have something to *do*. Something to give her people to do, aside from wait, and die in flashfire bursts when they were caught unawares by the sudden *appearing* of the enemy ships, peeling out of the void-dark of space.

(She could give them the planetary system. She could give

that order at any time, and waste half of every legion on *getting* there, and then—destroy a whole live planet full of sentients, and have the war continue forever. But it would be a war with targets. It would be a war to break herself open on, and be a song and a story before she was done.)

She wondered if she could get away with shooting Sixteen Moonrise, just by accident. Probably not. Not until she had an excuse.

"How long are you going to give them?" asked Sixteen Moonrise, and Nine Hibiscus regretfully concluded that question wasn't a sufficient excuse for court-martial and execution. It was the same question everyone else on the bridge wanted to ask—Bubbles, wrapped in her cloudhook's holoprojections of the Fleet's comm network; and Eighteen Chisel with his hands fluttering, ghosting over the propulsion and navigation interface, face hungry for anything she could provide.

". . . Two hours," Nine Hibiscus said. "Longer if Swarm sends back an all-clear signal. Which he will."

"You are very devoted to him," said Sixteen Moonrise. Nine Hibiscus found herself not even caring that the other woman was still trying to find an *angle,* information, ways to destroy and undermine her authority. It really didn't matter now.

"We've served together for our entire careers," she said. "Of course I am. Wouldn't you be?"

The distortion of his voice through the medbay intercom would stay with her forever, she was entirely sure. The careful choice of words. How he'd called her *Mallow* and *my dear* because he was nearly sure he was going to die and some sorts of protocol didn't matter then, even if you had made your whole life about being a perfect Teixcalaanlitzlim, a perfect Fleet soldier, except in all the ways you weren't.

". . . I would be," said Sixteen Moonrise, surprisingly, and sighed. A ghost sound, a breath, like ice on the inside of a broken Shard canopy, where vacuum had gotten in. "He is exceptionally brave. *His veins would drip starlight—and glow like fireflies in the sacrifice bowl.*"

That was "Reclamation Song #1." The oldest one, the one that had come out of the dirt with Teixcalaan, or almost. The first generation in space, under the First Emperor. The Reclamation Song no one ever assigned an author to, because why *would* you? It was the song about being Teixcalaanli. Nine Hibiscus was being manipulated, utterly, and that was—all right. "He *is*," she said. "And that's why I let him go down there with the envoy. He deserves a chance to ask these things why they almost killed him, and what for. And if they meant it."

The sound Sixteen Moonrise made wasn't a word. "Him, and not the rest of our dead? The rest of my dead? All of our people on Peloa-2?"

"He's the one who *gets* the chance." Whether that was bad luck or good she really wasn't sure.

"I," said Sixteen Moonrise, "want to believe in you, my *yaotlek*. Truly, I do. But there are powers at work here beyond you and me."

"What powers would *those* be, Fleet Captain?" Nine Hibiscus asked. Paranoia she'd expected. That was what Third Palmers were like, even retired ones who had ended up in command. Paranoia, but not coupled with this sort of honesty. This sort of—asking, to be allowed to be helped—

This time the noise that came from Sixteen Moonrise's mouth was a sigh. A grudging noise, the sound of a person getting ready to tell the truth. Fuck, but she *was* Third Palm, wasn't she. Nine Hibiscus couldn't trust her. Even if she turned out to be right—even if she couched her analysis in the language Nine Hibiscus understood as the one that ought to exist between commander and soldier, the mutual protection of *I would die for you* and *I will never ask you to, unless it is a last resort.*

Sixteen Moonrise said, "The ones who convinced Information

to take along a representative of a foreign government to negotiate a first-contact cease-fire. The ones who pushed Her
Brilliance the Emperor to encourage Minister Nine Propulsion
to retire early. Any power that wants us entrapped in this war,
instead of winning it."

Nine Hibiscus turned to her. She'd made some kind of decision; she didn't know what it was yet, only that she'd made
it. "Do you want to have this conversation privately, Fleet
Captain?" She tried to keep her voice gentle, as she'd ask one of
her own soldiers (like she'd asked Eighteen Chisel, when he'd
brought her the news that they knew the location of the enemy
planetary system). It was an offer: *Do you want me to trust you?
To protect you?*

And Sixteen Moonrise refused it. "No, *yaotlek*," she said,
all resigned politesse. "I can say all this right here on your
bridge. There are factions in the Ministry—as I know you are
aware—who would rather see you exhaust yourself on a war
of attrition rather than begin a war we could win. And those
factions are joined by those who would like power to accrete
to the Ministry, the sort of prestige we enjoyed before the
unfortunate incident with One Lightning. You *do* know where
Minister Three Azimuth was stationed, before she received her
posting?"

"Nakhar," Nine Hibiscus said, and nothing more. Of course
she knew Nakhar. Of course she knew how Three Azimuth had
subdued it, the careful and destructive violence she had done to
all of its insurgent factions, how she had installed her own people inside those factions and let them betray themselves down
to uselessness. She herself had done something similar in the
Kauraan engagement—

Abruptly, it occurred to her that the new Minister of War
might dislike Sixteen Moonrise and the Third Palm as much as
Nine Hibiscus herself did. And at the same time, might dislike
Nine Hibiscus equally much, for who her patron had been. For

using the same set of ideas, but not needing to have an epithet like *she who kindles enmity in the most oath-sworn heart* accrete around her like a chain.

"Nakhar," Sixteen Moonrise agreed. "Her Brilliance the Emperor Nineteen Adze, may she reign a thousand thousand years—she made the butcher of the Nakharese mind Minister of War. And sent your patron Minister Nine Propulsion home to Zorai, and you—and I—out here. With *this*." She gestured at the distant, still-spinning three-ringed ship. At Peloa-2, a glitter of reflected light.

Nine Hibiscus had only heard Three Azimuth called *the butcher of the Nakharese mind* in the *nastier* parts of Fleet bars, where poetry tended toward doggerel and the epigram so quick-spoken it eviscerated before you'd notice it had been said.

"I appreciate your candor, Fleet Captain," she said. "What do you want me to tell you? That I suspect we are all going to die slowly out here, the first wave of this war? That I believe that our illuminate star-blessed Emperor would start a war she had no intention of winning, just to root out the last of the elements in the Fleet that might have supported One Lightning? Would you like me to say that, whether or not it is true, so that you can carry it home to your Undersecretary?"

It was gratifying to see Sixteen Moonrise flinch. She hadn't known that Nine Hibiscus had figured out she was still Third Palm, had she. That was something. Some small thing.

"No," Sixteen Moonrise said. "That's not what I want at all. I want—I want this war *engaged*. I want us to *win it*."

Perhaps she wasn't even lying. Nine Hibiscus didn't have time to find out: Two Foam had stood up from her console and was saying, "*Yaotlek*—I'm sorry to interrupt, but we have a priority message from the Emperor Herself. She wants to speak with the envoy. The envoy and Ambassador Mahit Dzmare. As quickly as we can send the message back—the courier is waiting now."

The envoy and Mahit Dzmare. Who were down on Peloa-2,

arguing with the enemy, or possibly dying of fungal infiltration. Or heatstroke.

". . . Well, get them back up here, then, will you?" Nine Hibiscus said. The Emperor—her Emperor, no matter what Sixteen Moonrise was trying to make her think, make her doubt—wanted the envoy, and so that was what she was going to get.

FIFTEEN

INCIDENT RECORD LOOKUP—NUCLEAR SHATTER-
BOMB STRIKES (TERRESTRIAL) (?NUMBER) (must-include
FLEET)

There are three recorded instances of a Fleet vessel engaging
in a shatterbomb strike on a planetary system since the invention
of the technology. None of these instances has occurred in the
past four hundred years, though there was a public debate about
the usefulness of a threatened deployment in Nakhar System
two indictions ago; that public debate resulted in a general social
distaste for the idea . . .

> —*//access//INFORMATION,* access-limited database
> query performed 96.1.1-19A by Fleet Captain Sixteen
> Moonrise, personal cloudhook from secured
> connection on the *Parabolic Compression*

* * *

. . . ALL SUBWAY SERVICE IN INMOST PROVINCE SUS-
PENDED UNTIL FURTHER NOTICE PENDING INVES-
TIGATION BY THE MINISTRY OF SCIENCE. MESSAGE
REPEATS. EXPECT DELAYS. CHOOSE ALTERNATIVE
FORMS OF TRANSIT. ALL SUBWAY SERVICE IN INMOST
PROVINCE SUSPENDED . . .

> —public service announcement, wide broadcast on the
> Jewel of the World, 96.1.1–19A

DOWN in the sand and the heat again, Peloa-2 closed around her like a strangling cloak. Eighteen hours hadn't dimmed the sun. This planet rotated slow. Eighteen hours *had* thickened the smell of charnel rot. Mahit had expected it, and choked on it anyway. The body forgot pain. That was one of the first things Lsel Station's imago-integration therapists had taught her when she was small enough to just begin to think about how it would feel to be part of a long chain of imago-memory. The body forgets pain, but it also writes patterns into itself: endocrine response and chemical triggers. Biofeedback that sets patterns. That's memory: continuity plus endocrine response.

The charnel smell again, and the sick heat: repeated experience. Mahit wanted to gag. She thought, *Yskandr, were you ever on a killing field?*

And got back, <No. Not until you.>

So this was something new she was adding to their imago-line. She wasn't sure how to feel about that.

Walking back to their plateau-platform was different than it had been the first time. She was still frightened—still *terrified*, to be perfectly clear about it in her own mind if nowhere else—of the aliens they were talking to. But she had sung to them once, and she could do it again. And the composition of their little expedition was different: the same four escorts with their shock-sticks, the same canopy made from the most Teixcalaanli piece of silk Mahit could imagine bringing—but with the addition of Twenty Cicada, vicious with his tiny box of deadly fungus and his questions to ask. It was going to be Mahit's job, somehow, to find a way to ask those questions. In a language that wasn't language, on a planet so hot she thought she would faint.

Three Seagrass kept brushing against her as they walked. At first Mahit had thought she was staking some sort of claim—*I've had my hands inside you and now you're mine,* and she'd recoiled from the idea with a violence that evoked a wincing sympathy from the echo of Yskandr's memories of Six Direction and his

bed—but then she realized that it was almost certainly uncon-
scious. She was just standing closer. Some wall, dissolved. An
easy intimacy. Like any other lover Mahit had ever had. Not different at all. And the continuity of endocrine response worked
for everyone, Stationer or Teixcalaanlitzlim or something else:
endocrine response said, in that brutal language of the flesh,
*This person has had their hands inside you, and you welcomed them
in. Let's do it again. Here are nice chemicals to help.*

On the crest of the plateau, the aliens were waiting for them.
They weren't the same aliens.

First and Second were replaced by what Mahit immediately called Third and Fourth: two more of the same species,
but obviously two different individuals. Both of these were of
a height—a good foot and a half above Mahit's own, not counting their ears—and one was heavily mottled, dark and light in
a roan pattern, while the other was a nearly unmarked grey,
with one large black pigmentation mark that spread over half
of its face. They had clearly been waiting some time. Mahit
wondered if the whole lot of their negotiation team was going
to be eaten for rudeness before they even got around to saying
hello.

She decided to head that off at the pass. Either they'd be eaten
or they wouldn't be. (And was that easy fatalism the chemical
cocktail of endorphins and oxytocin in her blood, or just her being more Yskandr than they'd been before? That bravado. The
simplicity of decisions—) She walked up to Third and Fourth.
Came just to the edge of the reach of their claws. The sun raked
her, felt like a weight on her skull. And she opened her mouth,
took a lungful of desert air, and sang *hello* as loud and well as
she could.

She was still hoarse from the last time she'd done this. It would
be harder, this time. But—but Three Seagrass came up to her
side and sang with her, and even Twenty Cicada attempted to
join them. A light tenor. Not very resonant. But singing. And
Third and Fourth, after an agonizing pause, sang back. *Hello.*

They were in business.

The escort team set up the canopy and the audioproj—and their new toy, a cloudhook rigged for office work, the kind that spread a corona of files and feeds around its wearer—but this one manipulable by any hands that came near it. Three Seagrass had called it a *strategic planning modality*. Twenty Cicada had just said that it was a strategy table. The kind the Fleet planned wars on.

No time for language learning, now. No time, even, to decide if what they were learning was a language.

Given: these aliens communicated and understood communication.

Given: they communicated in a way that was not visible to Mahit, nor any other human being, as well as by sounds.

Given: they seemed entirely willing to eat entire planets alive, for scraps, and leave the waste to rot in the sun. All of those bodies, dead. All of those *people,* dead—

Given all of that, it was time for crude rebus drawings in holo.

The most disturbing part wasn't that Third and Fourth picked up what she and Three Seagrass were doing very quickly, drawing lines of light in the shimmering desert air with their claws. The most disturbing part was that they both simultaneously seemed to know *everything* First and Second had done the day before—and that they moved in that awful, unsettling-uncanny joint motion that First and Second had also displayed. Third would finish a gesture that Fourth had started. Draw the other half of a figure that Fourth had begun. And they had precisely the same skill in drawing. The same skill, and the same *style.*

It was like they were two links in an imago-chain—but both embodied at once. The idea made Mahit squirm. (But wasn't she herself a thing that was *wrong,* by all the standards she had learned on Lsel Station about what was the right and the wrong way to be a link in a long line of live memory?)

Communicating by rebus and song-snatch was slow and agonizing in the heat. They were circling around the idea of—it wasn't anything so concrete as *cease-fire.* Maybe something more like *managed retreat.* If Mahit could only figure out *why* these creatures did what they did, she could get closer to asking them to do it somewhere else. Somewhere far away from Lsel Station (. . . and Teixcalaan, and oh, Darj Tarats was probably going to give her to Aknel Amnardbat on a *platter*). But she couldn't get to *why.* She didn't have any abstract concepts to work with, at all, except—

Carefully, when it was her turn to begin the next—sentence, phrase, *communication unit*—Mahit drew the outline of a human being. The outline of a human being, with its guts spilled out in spirals of light. And above it, the outline of an alien, the long neck, the carnivore's claws.

Three Seagrass said, hurriedly, "I *don't* think this is a good idea, Mahit!" but Mahit had her mouth open already, and the shape of the sung-spat noise on her tongue was the pidgin word for *stop.* For *no,* or *cease,* or *stay away.*

Don't kill us.

There was a heatstruck silence.

Third lifted a claw—its hands were so delicate under those claws, and Mahit thought they were retractable, that they'd fold back for precision work—and did not rip Mahit open. Nor did it sing anything back to her. Instead it drew another human outline next to the eviscerated one. And another. And another. And another. As if to say, *But you can make more of you.*

How wide, after all, could the concept of "you" stretch?

Could it be as wide as a species?

On her other side, Twenty Cicada—his bald head gold-gone-angry-pink in the sun, his cheeks a sallow grey, heat-drained—sighed softly. "All right," he said. "Enough of this."

"What?" Mahit began, confused. But he had already produced his box of fungi, his box of maybe-poison, and held it out for both Third and Fourth to see. Held it like a prize, or like a challenge.

He pointed to the box. The alien eyes fixed on it like it had the gravitational pull of a black hole. And then he pointed to what Mahit had drawn. The dead human, torn up, wrecked. He shook the cube. The whitish fungus inside, dried to nothing now, *rattled*. The sound was too loud. (Were there no insects on Peloa-2? Was there really nothing here but silica sand and sunlight?)

The soundless communication passed between Third and Fourth, that impenetrable language again. They opened their mouths and sang, together, a bone-rattling noise, a wave of nausea. Mahit recognized something of the sound pattern she and Three Seagrass had identified as *victory*. But shifted. Made otherwise. She was so *lost*. She couldn't talk to these things—these people, they were people, she had to keep thinking of them as people even as she tried not to vomit up everything in her stomach—without language. If she was a poet

(*you should have been Teixcalaanli, what a poet you would have made*)

a poet like Three Seagrass, then all of the vast weight of Teixcalaan had sent the wrong sort of storytellers here. What good was poetry now?

One of the escorts was talking to Three Seagrass, rapid and hushed. In Teixcalaanli, and for one terrifying moment, Mahit didn't know language at all—all syllables were useless sounds.

<Breathe,> said Yskandr, in her mind, like he had before. But this time he said it in Stationer, the language she'd drunk in with her first breaths of oxygen, and it snapped meaning back into place for her. Sounds had meaning. Words were symbols. She could think in language again.

Three Seagrass touched her, her fingers on the underside of Mahit's wrist. "We have to leave," she said, and Mahit had to work to parse it. To hear words in Teixcalaanli that weren't all narrative, all implication. *We have to become absent, we have to excise ourselves from here.*

"What?" she managed, again, useless interrogative particle.

"Her Brilliance. The Emperor. Nineteen Adze, She wants us to send her a message. Both of us. Now. On *Weight for the Wheel*. The courier's waiting."

"We can't," Mahit said. "We're—they're not—"

Behind her, Third and Fourth were approaching Twenty Cicada. *Circling* him. He stood perfectly still, holding his box of fungal death. Perfectly calm. Mahit wondered if that was what being a homeostat-cultist meant. Not minding being about to die via enormous predatory enemies.

A claw tapped the box, once. The click of keratin on plastic.

<Nineteen Adze wouldn't ask for us if she didn't need us,> Yskandr said inside Mahit's mind, and with that came all of his certainty that Nineteen Adze was worth the absurd, agonizing, death-inducing amount of trouble she'd gotten him into, back when he was alive. All of his certainty that he'd loved her, and that it didn't matter in the end, and he'd loved her *even so*.

"Go on," said Twenty Cicada, strange and distant. "Take the shuttle and our escorts. I'll be all right here, I think."

"What are you going to *do*?" Mahit said.

"I'm going to bring them back a little piece of their dead," said Twenty Cicada, still not moving at all. "And then see if they understand anything about why I did. Go."

Third was drawing in the light again. A fractal shape, like the fungus. A shape that it laid over the image Mahit had made of an eviscerated human body.

"I don't know what's right," said Three Seagrass. "But Nineteen Adze sent me here—or at least she didn't stop me, and—she's the *Emperor*."

And Yskandr echoed: <She's the Emperor. And this adjutant can take care of himself here. Even if he can't sing.>

"Don't—die?" Mahit said, uselessly. She didn't even *like* Twenty Cicada.

"Everyone dies eventually," Twenty Cicada said, Fourth's maw inches from his face.

Mahit thought, *Everyone dies, except memory*—and then turned

to follow Three Seagrass back to the shuttle, and the Fleet, and
Teixcalaan, waiting.

They'd left Twenty Cicada down in the desert with the enemy.
Nine Hibiscus hated it, hated it *viscerally,* and she couldn't exactly argue with the decision. Especially since the envoy and
Dzmare (*the spook and her pet,* and oh, sometimes she'd really
like to excise all of Sixteen Moonrise's turns of phrase from her
mind) had brought back with them the sworn promise that it
had been Swarm himself who demanded to stay.

It was so exactly like him she believed it. It was precisely the
same kind of deliberate use of the self in possible sacrifice as
he'd done behind the sealed doors of the medbay, waiting to see
if he'd die of breathing fungal spores.

She hated it anyway. She could wish her adjutant—her dearest friend, her *longest* friend—was less interested in keeping the
whole world—the whole empire, the *universe*—in balance and
more interested in selfishly saving his own skin. For her sake,
if nothing else.

While the envoy and Dzmare went to answer their urgent
imperial communiqué, supervised by Two Foam, Nine Hibiscus took an hour of leave from the bridge. (She was owed nine,
but who needed *nine* hours of sleep?) She didn't go back to her
quarters. She went to Twenty Cicada's, straightaway, and—he
still hadn't changed the password, of course. The door let her in.

There was an autoplay message rotating in holo above the
work terminal he usually kept tucked away in a corner. It
read, in the perfectly neat glyph-style that Twenty Cicada wrote
in: *Mallow, if I'm not here, water the plants and feed the star-cursed
Kauraanian kitten.*

She was *not* going to burst into tears. That was a *fail-safe* message, not a goodbye.

Nevertheless, she watered the plants. And when watering
the plants revealed said star-cursed Kauraanian kitten, who had

been sleeping in one of the plant pots like a strange void-black root vegetable—a root vegetable that yowled at her when she poured water on it by accident—she fed it, too. There were small bits of vat-meat for it, which it seemed to enjoy.

She was still feeding it—it had come to sit on her knee, and purr, and eat vat-meat from her fingers, which was unfairly cute—when her cloudhook alerted her to a priority message, sent on the command-only broadcast band. She played it, without thinking. All messages on that band needed to be heard.

This one resolved into Sixteen Moonrise, her image flooding one half of Nine Hibiscus's vision while the other half stayed clear. She wasn't on *Weight for the Wheel* any longer. She was on her own bridge, on the *Parabolic Compression*. Nine Hibiscus knew she should feel relieved, but she didn't. Not in the slightest. She petted the Kauraanian kitten so it would stop yowling for meat (which only partially worked), and listened.

Yaotlek, said Sixteen Moonrise, on her distant flagship. *I feel it is incumbent upon me—considering that you are my superior officer, however much we disagree with one another, and also considering that you are aware of the terrible capabilities of our enemies, both in their ships and in their bodies—to inform you that I have learned what I am sure you already know: one of your scouts has found one of the enemy's home systems. Don't blame your officers. They were entirely closed-mouthed. But the Twenty-Fourth Legion is just as clever as the Tenth, and when the* Gravity Rose *altered its trajectory and search pattern to fly home right through my legion—it became obvious that they had found what we are all looking for. I have confirmed, with my own scouts, what the* Gravity Rose *found.*

I am preparing a strike force. I am willing, if you are willing to offer me the command, to lead it: the Parabolic Compression *beside* Weight for the Wheel, *cutting through our enemy so that we might get close enough to burn them all out of the sky. Sanitize what might infect us; what will, undoubtedly, eat us.*

I understand that you may wish to wait for your negotiators to return from their negotiation. I too, will wait. For a time.

My yaotlek, I would rather die ending this war before it leaches Teixcalaan of vitality than live through a long siege of attrition. I think you would, too. And besides, you are the hero of Kauraan: perhaps we'll all make it through alive.

The message ended. The other half of Nine Hibiscus's vision resolved to Twenty Cicada's garden of a suite.

"Ah, *bleeding fucking stars*," she said. The Kauraanian kitten looked at her, offended, and leapt off of her lap.

———

When the Emperor's *ezuazuacat* sent a message on fast-courier, it went even more quickly than when the Fleet sent one. Five and a half hours, Five Agate had said. Five and a half to get the request and Eight Antidote's list of questions to the flagship *Weight for the Wheel*, and then however long it took to record an answer, and five and a half hours back. She'd sent him to bed while they waited. He'd resented that, but he'd also guessed he'd deserved it: he'd gone out into the City, and had to be *rescued*, and there was the ever-present wondering of *signal problem* or *incendiary device* running through his head. He'd asked Five Agate if she'd heard from the Judiciary, and she'd told him to go to bed *more firmly* instead of answering, which either meant she hadn't or she had and it was the bad answer. The *incendiary device* answer.

But Eight Antidote had gone, and slept, was glad he didn't dream at all. He was sure he'd have dreamed of train derailments, if he had.

The message to the envoy was *supposed* to come back to Palace-Earth by noon the next day, but it didn't. It didn't come back by dinner, either, and Eight Antidote picked desultorily at his spiced livers-and-cheese in their lily-blossom wraps, even though he *loved* fried flowers normally. He was too nervous to eat. Everything seemed to be spinning just fractionally faster than he could keep track of. No one would tell him about the subway, and he didn't know how to get his cloudhook to give him more useful information than what anybody could find out on the newsfeeds.

He had to stop watching the newsfeeds, after a while. Seeing the smoke come out of the subway tunnel was making him feel sick.

It wasn't until just after sunset that Five Agate sent him an infofiche stick in the internal palace mail, asking him to come and see the answers to the questions he had asked. To see, apparently, not only Special Envoy Three Seagrass, but also Mahit Dzmare. Eight Antidote wondered if the fact that the message had *both* of them was a sign that Fleet Captain Sixteen Moonrise's message of warning had been correct—Information *was* compromised by the Ambassador from Lsel Station. Or if Three Azimuth had been correct: Mahit Dzmare disrupted protocol and the right functioning of the world wherever she was, whether she meant to or not.

When he got to the Emperor's suite, Five Agate was waiting for him on one of those white velvet couches. She wasn't alone. She patted the seat beside her, which meant Eight Antidote was going to watch this holo with the Emperor Herself sitting on his left and Five Agate on his right. Five Agate's child, Two Cartograph, who had made it very clear to Eight Antidote that he was *seven* years old, a *whole indiction,* and wasn't going to go to bed until he wanted to, was reading a mathematics textbook, sprawled out on his belly on the Emperor's tile floor. Eight Antidote didn't think he'd ever done that, when his ancestor-the-Emperor had lived here. He didn't think he'd ever been that *comfortable* doing it.

Five Agate asked him—or asked Her Brilliance, it was hard to tell—"Shall we hear what Three Seagrass has to say for herself?" and played the holo before she got an answer from either of them.

It wasn't just Envoy Three Seagrass. It was her, and Mahit Dzmare right beside her.

On the holo, both of them looked very tired, and sweaty, and not happy at all. They were in a small room with metal walls and a window. The holo didn't pick up much of the starfield that should have been outside that window, but Eight Antidote could guess what it looked like. He couldn't see if there was anyone else there, listening to them make this recording, but from where they'd both put their eyes—Dzmare kept glancing to her left, and Three Seagrass was very deliberately *not* looking left at all—he thought there was probably someone. Someone who made at least Dzmare nervous.

What he'd asked, in his message to the Fleet, was simple: *Why do you believe, Envoy Three Seagrass, that negotiating with our enemies will succeed? And why did you choose to go, instead of anyone else from Information?* Only those two questions. He just wanted to hear *her* justification. To try to understand her, at all, and see if he believed what she was doing.

Envoy Three Seagrass had a clear alto voice run ragged. She sounded like someone who had gone to a very loud concert and sung along with the band, or a person who had been *really enthusiastic* at an *amalitzli* game the night before. She looked straight at the recording-cloudhook, so now Eight Antidote felt like she was looking straight into his eyes. Direct eye contact. He wanted to look away, and she wasn't even here to look away from.

"Your Excellency," she said, in exquisitely formal tense. "*Ezuazuacat.* Your Brilliance. My most esteemed greetings to you on the Jewel of the World, from the flagship of the Tenth Legion, *Weight for the Wheel.* I apologize for the brevity of this message, but we are, as you might imagine, somewhat busy."

There was a pause. An emotion rippled across Dzmare's holoimage face, and Eight Antidote thought it might be stifled laughter. The laughing that adults did when they were horrified and didn't want children to know.

"You ask very complicated questions in small and simple packages, Your Excellency," Three Seagrass went on. "Ambassador Dzmare and I will not be able to give you the sort of response you deserve, considering time and—other factors. But she—Mahit, here"—she gestured at the Ambassador—"is of the opinion that you deserve answers when you ask for them, especially at such a remove."

Beside him, Nineteen Adze murmured, ". . . She would think that, wouldn't she."

"And you don't?" Five Agate said, as if Eight Antidote wasn't *right here* and they weren't all talking about him.

"Oh, on this the Ambassador and I have tended to agree quite profoundly," said Nineteen Adze, and Eight Antidote remembered, harsh and abrupt, what she'd said to him when she'd given him the spearpoint: *You're not Six Direction, no matter what your face looks like. I made sure you didn't have to be.* He wondered again what exactly she had done. For him, or to him—but the envoy was speaking again, the holo going on without respect for a conversation happening five and a half hours in its future.

"You want to know why *I* took this job. Instead of anyone else from Information. That's the simple question, Your Excellency. I wanted to. The request came in, and I—wanted to, wanted to do something more than sit in my office and not sleep very much and fail at writing poetry."

Next to her, Dzmare murmured, "Reed—" Soft and sympathetic. That must be the envoy's use-name. It was strange that the Ambassador knew it. Stranger that she'd *use* it. Three Seagrass waved her off, a little falling gesture of one hand that seemed to mean *later.*

"Ask Her Brilliance about wanting to *do something,* if you don't understand it, Your Excellency. I'm sure she's watching this with you. And if you still think you don't know why me and not anyone else from Information, ask her why she didn't *stop* me, or send someone else with me."

Nineteen Adze *laughed,* when the envoy said that. Laughed, and nodded. Eight Antidote was very sure he was being manipulated, over more than six jumpgates and five and a half hours of time—but it was so strange and refreshing to be manipulated by being earnestly told the truth. He needed to learn that one.

In the holo, the envoy sighed. "Your other question is harder. That's why I'm sitting here with Ambassador Dzmare. She understands languages better than I do, even if I'm a *much* better diplomat than she is— It's not her fault, she's—" Three Seagrass looked as if she'd eaten the first word she'd meant to say, swallowed it back quickly, and replaced it with "—out of practice. Why do I believe that negotiating with our enemies might succeed? Because they talk, Your Excellency. Because when we figured out how to make communicative sounds that they knew were communicative, they talked back. Because—oh, because I grew up reading Eleven Lathe. Get Five Agate to get you a copy of *Dispatches from the Numinous Frontier,* you're a ninety-percent clone of His Brilliance Six Direction, you're old enough to understand it."

Dzmare interrupted her, carefully. Like a swimmer diving into water without a splash. "Because, Your Excellency, the envoy likes aliens. Likes human aliens, at least—she told me so when she met me the first time—because she, unlike some Teixcalaanlitzlim, thinks humans who aren't Teixcalaanli might be a kind of human. It's easy to get from there to thinking that aliens might be a kind of—person. Even if they aren't human persons."

"Mahit," said Three Seagrass, like she was shocked.

But the Ambassador went on. "I don't know how they talk. I know they have more languages than the ones we've learned how to say words to them in, and that at least one of those languages isn't one a human can hear. I know they don't care about death the way we do, but that they do understand death. I know that they came back to the negotiating table, after the first meeting. And that they haven't stopped attacking the Fleet, even during the negotiations. I know all that, and not much more. But I think they might be a kind of person. And if they are . . ."

"If they are, Your Excellency," said Three Seagrass firmly, "there is the possibility of a brokered peace before we lose *too* many more Fleet ships. That's all."

A murmur in the background. Whoever else was with them, saying something inaudible. Dzmare looked frightened, or nauseated, or just annoyed. Stationers had too many expressions, and it was hard to tell what they meant. The envoy looked serene. "That *is* all. End recording."

And then the holo vanished, and there was only the Emperor's living-room suite, and Two Cartograph looking up from his homework on the floor, saying "Mama, does Eight Antidote do matrix algebra, because *I* can, and I solved *all* the problems while you were watching holo."

Eight Antidote missed being seven years old, he decided. Being seven was so much simpler than being eleven.

He got up off the couch. He wanted to think about what he had just seen, and *not* talk about it, not with the Emperor Herself or Five Agate or anyone. "I can do some matrix algebra," he said, and sat down next to Two Cartograph. "You want to show me?"

————

They came out of the recording room with the evaluating, watching eyes of Two Foam, *Weight for the Wheel*'s comms officer, still fixed on them. Three Seagrass had ignored her very determinedly the entire time they'd been on holo. It was easier to ignore her than to deal with simultaneously being *observed* by suspicious Fleet personnel—at least they weren't wearing isolation gear any longer—and being called back to the flagship to answer, not a summons from the Emperor Herself, but some sort of evaluatory question sequence from the imperial heir. It was like getting an are-you-a-good-cultural-fit-for-my-team job placement interview, from an eleven-year-old. An eleven-year-old who looked exactly like every picture of His Brilliance Six Direction from when Six Direction was a child.

Three Seagrass had been just about willing to turn around and get back on the shuttle to Peloa-2 and let the kid *deal with wanting to know* for a few hours—her answers would have been more complete anyway if she could have kept working on the negotiation, kept trying to make the enemy understand that really, they didn't like casualties very much at all, not even slightly. But Mahit had shaken her head. Had said, *If anyone deserves answers about why Teixcalaan does what it does, it's that child.*

And then Three Seagrass had remembered, quite vividly and with some embarrassment, that Eight Antidote had been born to *be* Six Direction. To have one of Lsel Station's imago-machines in his head, so Six Direction could have been Emperor forever. She guessed that Mahit felt complicatedly guilty about that. (And if Mahit was really more Yskandr Aghavn than she'd been six months ago, she probably also felt—thwarted. Frustrated. *And* guilty.)

(Which one of them had she fucked, last night? Which one of them had brought along that strange, lovely graphic story, with lines like *it's precious but it's not a memory* and *I'm everything you need?*)

(Did she really want to know? Probably not.)

When it came right down to it—when she was in front of the holorecorder, with Mahit to her right where she belonged, and a disapproving Fleet officer tucked in the corner, Three Seagrass decided to tell the kid as much of the truth as there was and see what happened. It was worth—well. It was that if she was going to do *anything* she was going to do it right. She'd been like that her whole life. The thing, entire, or not at all.

Nine Hibiscus was waiting for them on the bridge.

Three Seagrass bowed to her over her fingers, deeply, and Mahit did the same. Out of the corner of her eye she saw the imperial fast-courier shuttle glitter on its way to the jumpgate, their message inside it, passing across the windows of the bridge. There, gone. And here they were again, alone with the war.

"Have you heard anything from *ikantlos*-prime Twenty Ci-

cada?" Three Seagrass asked. She kept thinking of him, alone
with Third and Fourth and his box of fungi. Alone in the heat,
like she and Mahit were alone with the war.

"Not yet," said the *yaotlek*. "Nothing since you arrived. He
has—oh, another half hour, before I send you both back down
to get him. If he can be gotten."

Three Seagrass suspected that if he didn't radio in, there
wouldn't be much left to *get*. She'd—be sorry about that. Very
sorry. It would be a *waste*. A waste in the way Twenty Cicada
had explained it to her on the hydroponics deck. A flaw in the
way the universe should function. A perversity. A use of resources that wasn't the best use, or even a good use.

Maybe she'd become a homeostat-cultist, if she ever got home
from the war. Or at least read some texts about it.

"We should go back anyhow," said Mahit. "We weren't *finished.*"

"The situation has shifted," said the *yaotlek*. Three Seagrass
winced, internally. That was *never* a good line for a negotiating
partner to deliver. Not in any poem or handbook or case study
she knew.

"How so?" she asked.

Nine Hibiscus's face was unreadable. Everything about her
looked closed off, protective, *angry*. She didn't want to tell
Three Seagrass what she was about to tell her, but she was going to do it anyway, probably because she didn't want the Information Ministry—or Lsel Station—to screw up whatever it
was she had decided to do. This was going to be extremely
unpleasant. Three Seagrass attempted to brace herself. Mostly,
she felt exhausted.

"The scout-ship *Gravity Rose* has found one of the inhabited
systems of the enemy," said Nine Hibiscus. "A planet and its satellite."

"And?" asked Mahit.

"And I'm waiting for Swarm to come back with something
more actionable than *they want to keep talking* or *they're full of*

fungal infiltrates and we cannot trust their dead. And if he doesn't—well." For a moment Nine Hibiscus looked like she had the first time Three Seagrass had seen her: the absolute perfect image of a *yaotlek*. Star-bestriding and unmovable. "Well, then the Fleet knows where their heart is. And I am prepared to sink my hands into it and tear it out. If I have to."

INTERLUDE

THESE bodies: dry-weather bodies, endurance-gened bodies; one a body which had displayed stubborn determination as a kit, even before it was brought in to personhood; one a body which had displayed a cunning intelligence, a sneaky body, the sort of kit the *we* near it laughed at, finding it underfoot, babbling in kit-language, yowling its demands at all hours. These bodies, singing in the *we*: singing *heat* and *sand* and *confusion-interest* in the closed-off but persistent minds of the enemy, just as their precedents had. Singing also now in surprise, stutter-burst fascination / horror, disjointed chords. One of the bodies of their silent enemy had brought strands of person-maker. Had not *consumed* the person-maker, but locked it in a plastic box, like it was poison.

Like the *we* were poison.

The bodies in the sand and the heat tried to make sense of this. To not think language, or equivalence of narrative (why would we?), but to attempt to link concepts that had never been possible previously: to think, *not a person* and also *knows how to be a person* and also *does not want personhood; does not want to sing, fractal, reflected, iterating across the void-home.* To cross-reference: *those bodies that only sang an iteration of piloting, and were silent otherwise.* To echo fear across the *we*, fear in the shape of the silent enemy: to imagine *only wanting a partial singing.*

The silent enemy body speaks in the language of mouths, senselessly. When the cunning/sneaksome body plucks the person-maker from its clawless hands, it yowls briefly and then silences itself. It is very still, and very watchful, and the stubborn/

determined body sings *person* and the cunning/sneaksome body sings *not a person, not singing,* and these threads of melody reverberate endlessly through the *we*—

———

And at the same time, aflame with icy determination, the Fleet Captain Sixteen Moonrise, sometimes called *Ascent* by the man who was her most-beloved teacher, whom she wishes she could trust entire (but why then did he send her out this far, to this war, where she is like to die?), sends out orders to her legion. The Twenty-Fourth responds to her as if they were extensions of her hands, of her breath: they gather themselves, they assume strike formation, they begin, cautiously still, to advance.

And Sixteen Moonrise keeps a steady hand on their leash. She will wait a little longer yet. A little longer yet, for wondering why Eleven Laurel sent *her* here, and for the *yaotlek* to come to the inevitable conclusion that to avoid an endless war they must begin with an unanswerable atrocity: Peloa-2 a thousand times over.

———

The *we* slip in and out of black void-home the way the *we* slip in and out of jumpgate space: all places are in some sense the same, where there is the iterative song resounding, dirt-home or blood-home or starflyer-home in the dark between the stars. To think: *There is a change.* To think, knowing the confusion of the bodies in the sand and the heat, *The silent ones have turned away from the person-maker and move together now toward the nearest blood-home of ours.* To think to sing to *shriek,* ah, ah, ah, there are a million bodies there, a thousand million, too many to lose at once: so much silence to rebuild—

And, as all things do on the original dirt-home of the *we*, when they decide to move, their three-ringed ships a glimmer of distortion against the stars, they move all together, one murmuration in many directions. And this time, they move to flank their enemy and drive them away before they can even think to arrive at their ultimate precious destination: one swarm of diving, singing ships suddenly alive in the heart of the Seventeenth Legion, who scrambles, too late, all of their Shards to push the *we* away—

—and another murmuration heads for the jumpgate from where the silent enemy came, in all their vast spearpoint ships, came through this one point only into the parts of the void-home that belong to the *we*, came some time ago with their little resource-extraction colonies, and came much more recently with firepower and threat and the eternal inquisitive *reach* that should belong only to sentient persons. That murmuration comes hidden and flowing to the jumpgate, and begins to pass through, one and the other and the other and the other . . .

———

Dekakel Onchu wakes to alarms, to a nightmare she's dreamed often enough that she has to convince herself that it is real: the aliens are coming *through* the Anhamemat Gate. She moves on instinct and training, on the voice of her imago-line giving her enough space to breathe, to not hyperventilate or panic. She is the Councilor for the Pilots. Her ancestors brought Lsel Station safely to rest. If she has to, she will bring every last one of the Station's citizens to a new home, even Aknel *fucking* Amnardbat, who she has still not decided what to do about, except figure out how to make a Councilor not a Councilor anymore, and how to get Darj Tarats to help her do it—

But she doesn't want to have to find a new Station, dream up all those fragile numbers like the first pilot in her imago-line did, start the world over again. So she scrambles all of the military craft Lsel Station and every other sub-Station in Bardzravand Sector have, and prepares to meet the threat face-to-face.

She is in the hangar bay, watching her pilots climb into their ships, when she spots a tall, cadaverous shape who can only be Darj Tarats. Him, she stops. Him, she asks to justify himself:

now, after all this, after what he has done and condemned the
Station to suffer—*now* he is taking a flitter-ship and running
away? Alone? How many Councilors are going to betray their
duty to Lsel Station today? First Amnardbat—and how she is
going to deal with Amnardbat is clearly something that will
have to be considered after this conflagration, if there is an
after to consider problems in—and now Tarats, abandoning the
Station?

And Darj Tarats says to her, "No. I'm not running away. I'm
going to get Mahit Dzmare, and we are going to redirect this
war."

Onchu doesn't know—will never quite know—why she lets
him leave. Perhaps she thinks he'll die trying to get through
the Far Gate and none of it will matter. Perhaps she thinks he
might manage what he says he's trying to do—and if he can,
she will have less blood to mop up.

———

The cartograph table in Eleven Laurel's office is small; it fits on
a side table half as long as his desk. He runs it all the time; a sort of
background music, a thousand solved military puzzles replaying
beside him as he does the work he is required to do. He likes
to think it lets him remember his history. His history, his Ministry's history, his Empire's history. He's an old soldier, Eleven
Laurel is, and decades gone from a battlefront he personally
had to solve. Old soldiers need to keep their teeth, and Eleven
Laurel sharpens his on the knotty flesh of centuries' worth of
Teixcalaanli campaigns, played out again in pinpoints of light.

He has it on now; it is playing some battle in a double-star
system from two centuries ago, and he isn't watching it at all
except for how the lights shift across his hands.

His Ministry's history, his Ministry's successes. How fragile
they can turn out to be, in the hands of a *yaotlek* who would
rather be an Emperor, and the reactions of an Emperor who came
to her throne in the aftermath of that *yaotlek*. Eleven Laurel is

an *old* soldier. He thinks of the Shards, tied together with new technology from the Science Ministry, shifted and strange, not quite trustable—more like the Sunlit than his fellow soldiers now, in their worst moments, which are also their undeniable tactical best ones. He thinks of slow poison, and of trust.

Of what he has asked his favorite student to die for, all unknowing, in hopes of preserving his Ministry's history, his Ministry's successes. Cutting away what might be susceptible to rot—or the suspicion of rot. Sixteen Moonrise is an acceptable sacrifice if she takes Nine Hibiscus with her and wins a victory for War that will keep War relevant in the new Emperor's estimation for as long as the conflict continues.

———

In the Seventeenth Legion: all the Shards together, linked by Shard-sight and biofeedback and the *other thing*—the Shard trick, they call it, when they're alone amongst themselves, no superior officers, no nonpilots. The Shard trick, where sometimes it isn't just proprioception and pain that are shared between each Shard, but instinct—reaction time—and in moments of extremity or beauty, *thought*.

Not words, exactly. But communication. The ones who like it—and only a small percentage of Shard pilots *like* the Shard trick—have pushed its limits: recited poetry to one another without ever opening their mouths.

Recited poetry to one another from either side of a jumpgate, and heard. A distorted echo, a vibration in the bones. Something from a sector of space utterly disconnected from this one save for the stitch of the jumpgate, and the vast breathing Shard-sense.

All the Shards together, in the Seventeenth Legion, whether they like the Shard trick or not: dying under the slick dissolving ship-spit of the three-ringed alien enemy, under the flashes of energy-cannon fire. Dying, and it hurts, and there are a very great many of them dying.

A long way away, in the sector of Teixcalaanli space which holds the Jewel of the World, and also the Third Legion cruiser *Verdigris Mesa*, four Shard pilots on a training exercise return to the hangar bay screaming, weeping; they help each other from their ships, stand braced and linked as if they cannot bear to be alone, and one of them says, thread of sense within their sobbing—truly, it does not matter which one—"We need to speak with the Minister of War. Code Hyacinth. *Now.*"

CHAPTER
SIXTEEN

Two Alternator slipped a thumb-sized shockstick up her left sleeve and a garrote wire up her right, and grinned like a barbarian: all her square white teeth displayed. "How do I look?" she asked. "Think I can pass for a Lsel native?"

"For approximately twenty seconds," said Nine Foxglove, zipping up her tactical catsuit, "which is all you need, thank starlight. You look absurd. But absurd will work for twenty seconds of fooling that Station's customs officers while Five Filament and I get into their ductwork."

Two Alternator wrinkled her nose. "You're the ex-Information officer, *you* should be doing the persuasion," she said. "Especially if you're going to tell me I'm doing it wrong!"

"I would," Nine Foxglove said, "but they know my face just a bit too well."

"You didn't mention you'd been burned here when I signed on to this job," said Two Alternator, suspiciously.

"She has a very distinctive face," said Five Filament. He shoved a knife into his boot. "I've never stolen anything from a space station before. This is going to be *fun*."

—excerpt from *Fulcrum,* first in the series of Teixcalaanli
    popular novels by the Western Arc–born writer
    Five Spear

*   *   *

Top panels, three across page. First panel: Captain Cameron's ship approaches the underside of the Teixcalaanli warship we saw on the previous splashpage; it is so big it doesn't look real.

Second panel: close-up of Cameron's hands on the navigation controls, with the glowing echo of Chadra Mav helping him steer; through the cockpit window the warship has turned into a metal backdrop, super decorative with way too many flourishes, and also energy cannons like black eyes. Third panel: Cameron and Chadra Mav have slipped past the ship and into the black. It recedes into the distance. They are unnoticed.

> CAMERON (thought bubble on third panel): There's better stars out here than the ones the Empire sees or the Station's ever thought to look for.

> —graphic-story script for *THE PERILOUS FRONTIER!*
> vol. 10, distributed from local small printer
> ADVENTURE/BLEAK on Tier Nine, Lsel Station

EIGHT Antidote didn't dream, and was glad of it. He didn't remember falling asleep; only remembered waking. It wasn't dawn yet. He'd slept in his clothes, at his desk, his face pillowed on his hands, and woken himself up an hour or so later. He'd been thinking, when he fell asleep, having said good night to Five Agate and the Emperor Herself and gone back to his rooms. He'd tried watching holoproj shows, but he couldn't concentrate on any of them. He felt full up with ideas, with concepts, with horror; like he was a supersaturated solution and at any moment he'd crystallize and suddenly *understand*. He almost did. He kept coming back to *I think they might be a kind of person,* in Mahit Dzmare's voice. To *they don't care about death the way we do, but they do understand death.*

To what Three Seagrass had said. *They talk.*

And that had been obvious. Of course they'd talk, they had spaceships and weapons and a *society*—of course they talked. Maybe the important part wasn't that they talked, but that they talked *back*.

Maybe they thought humans might be a kind of person, too.

He'd been thinking that when he fell asleep, probably. And now it was still full dark and he was wide awake and the only things that were illuminated in his room were the camera-eyes, how they glinted in moonlight. The City, watching him. Keeping track. Like the Sunlit kept track. How the whole of the City knew where he was, even if where he was was (in a horrible subway derailment that wasn't supposed to be able to happen) (that might have been his own fault, meant for him, meant to—hurt—him) in his own room in Palace-Earth.

The idea was already all through him, like he'd dreamed himself full of it, without knowing or remembering the dream. It was exactly how he'd woken up understanding how the Fleet Captain Nine Hibiscus had won the battle at Kauraan.

The idea was: *they might be a kind of person.* The idea was, Eight Antidote thought he might know *what* kind of person.

Start with the Sunlit and the way they could see through all the camera-eyes of the City. The Sunlit were a complicated kind of person, all together. They were Teixcalaanlitzlim, of course they were, as human as Eight Antidote, but they moved together, they reacted together, they all saw through the same eyes that weren't human eyes but machine eyes, and that was *why* they moved and reacted together. They used the same algorithm process as the subway did, except they were people instead of a scheduling AI. They had become as good at it as they were when the new algorithmic principles were rolled out across Teixcalaan under Science Minister Ten Pearl. Everyone knew that: that now the Sunlit could see through the camera eyes, all together, like one mind made of a thousand observing pieces.

And if there was a human kind of person who could do that, could have many eyes and move all together easily and simply, it was easy to imagine other kinds of persons, who'd be better at it than the Sunlit ever had been. (Almost, Eight Antidote lost the shape of the idea, distracted by the vivid and surprising realization that he didn't know how a person became one of the Sunlit, not at all—but he *made* himself not think about it. Not right now.) If there was a human kind of person who could share vision and intention, and there *could* be other kinds of persons who would be better at it, who weren't human at all, then . . . then, they could be so much better at it that they wouldn't care about just one of them dying. Like Envoy Three Seagrass had said: *they'd know about dying, but not care the same way.*

If he was right—if he was right even as much as he'd been right about Kauraan, *almost* right with one piece missing—if he was right, he had to tell someone. The enemy moved the way they did, destroyed supply lines the way they did, showed up in unexpected locations too fast the way they did in all of those strategy-room simulations *because they had only one mind.* If he was right. And he thought he was.

The person he had to tell was the Minister of War. Because if the enemy thought all together, like one giant extra-powerful group of Sunlit, then that was why Three Azimuth and all the generals of the Fleet couldn't figure out how to go around them. He had to tell her *right now.*

So what if it was hours before dawn? He knew what the Ministry of War was like at the moment. He'd shadowed Three Azimuth for two whole days. If she was asleep, he'd eat a whole reflecting-pool's worth of lotuses.

––––––

Mahit and Three Seagrass stood on the bridge in front of Nine Hibiscus, still trying—or at least Mahit was trying, who knew what Three Seagrass was thinking, hearing a *yaotlek* of the Teixcalaanli Fleet say such poetic words as *I am prepared to sink my hands into their heart and rip it out,* a statement out of an epic conquest poem, said so casually and easily, the absolute weight of Teixcalaan's narratives settling over Mahit like a shroud she'd never really taken off—to figure out what to *say.* There was no immediate word from Twenty Cicada, down on Peloa-2 with his precious, absurd box of fungus, trying to take what she and Three Seagrass had established with the aliens about *maybe kill-*

ing us isn't all right, at least not indiscriminately, and link it up to whatever he wanted to explain about the fungal infiltrate. There was no message at all, and Mahit could see how the lack of one made Nine Hibiscus brittle and sharp, willing to contemplate the total destruction of a planetary system.

Have we ever loved someone like that, she thought. Not quite a question. *Enough to want to kill a planet in revenge for them.*

<Not a whole planet,> Yskandr said, and she rather wished she hadn't asked. What counted as killing a planet, anyway? Was it the deathfire of Fleet bombs, or was it also the gentle, wide, killing-strong jaws of Teixcalaan, wrapped around her own heart where Lsel should be?

She said, "*Yaotlek,* I do think we were making some kind of progress. Another few hours, or days, and—maybe."

"Oh, I don't doubt you, Ambassador," Nine Hibiscus told her. "But you're not one of my soldiers, are you? I don't expect you to understand. Eventually there are points where we in command ask our soldiers to trust us, not only with their lives but with their decisions. The Tenth has been waiting a long time."

Mahit wanted to tell her, *You're the one who dragged us up here to talk to a kid over infofiche message, we were working*—was about to, even with Yskandr on the back of her tongue slowing her, warning her, when the comms officer Two Foam interrupted them both to say, "*Yaotlek.* Message."

"Twenty Cicada?" Nine Hibiscus asked. Mahit winced at the naked hope in her voice, saw Three Seagrass wince, too.

"No," Two Foam said. "It's Forty Oxide's flagship, the *Chatoyant Sirocco*—the Seventeenth Legion is under direct attack. I think the enemy knows we know where they are—the Seventeenth is losing Shards. Fast."

———

Eight Antidote didn't bother changing clothes. Or telling anyone where he was going. He just put on his shoes—grey spy-shoes to go with spy-trousers and tunic—brushed his hair and rebraided it into a long queue, and took the tunnels. Like he was going to visit Eleven Laurel, before any of this had really gotten started. The tunnels between Palace-Earth and the Ministry felt soothing and familiar, except for how every small noise, every shift of dust, made him shiver and walk a little faster. He'd never been here at this hour. Even trying to sing the walking-marching song of palace architecture to himself—*as many roots in the ground as blooms into the sky*—felt like a kid's defense against monsters that might be under his bed. Or in his secret underground tunnels. (That was funny. Except in all the ways it wasn't. What would happen if an *incendiary device* went off down here? He didn't want to think of it.)

He climbed the ladder and came up through the trapdoor in the basement. There was no one there to meet him, and he was suddenly glad. He didn't want anyone to know he was here except maybe Three Azimuth. He wanted to hand her this idea— her, and Eleven Laurel if he was with her, *that* would show how good a student Eight Antidote was—and no one else. Not let it escape, until the Six Outreaching Palms had decided what to do about it. But if he was going to get all the way into her office without having to explain himself—even at this hour, when there'd be *fewer* guards, but more suspicious ones—he needed to be a spy for real. The kind of spy who could *sneak,* as well as talk and remember and keep his own secrets.

The camera-eyes would see him. That was just how the City was. But people—except for Sunlit—weren't camera-eyes. And he was small. He could hide in corners. He could be a piece of dust, a snatch of light reflected on a floor. He could be nothing at all. Someone who was supposed to be here, supposed to be where he was. Someone unimportant. A hallway cleaner, or a late-shift cadet doing inspections. He was too young to be either of those, but if he thought of himself as one of them—the hallway cleaner was easier. A person who was meant to be in the Ministry of War, making it look sparkling and new for the morning sunrise to glance off of.

He headed toward Three Azimuth's office directly. The camera-eyes and the Ministry's building-security AI would have seen him take this trip multiple times, and not suspect anything unusual. He was following a pattern the algorithm would expect from him. And if he saw a person—a person who wasn't a Sunlit—who didn't think he should be here, he'd either explain or he'd slip by them, pretending very hard to be a hallway cleaner. Thinking he was a hallway cleaner. *Believing* it. That was what spies in stories did.

He practiced believing he was a hallway cleaner until he reached the outside of Three Azimuth's office. He hadn't needed to talk to anyone. The only times he'd seen Ministry employees, he'd waited in a shadow and let them go past him. But now, right outside her office, in the center of the Six Outreaching Palms—right down the hall from it, enough to see the light from under its door and know he'd been right about the Minister for War not sleeping tonight—he heard voices. Raised, strained voices, drifting into the hall from that sliver of light.

He could interrupt them. He *needed* to tell Three Azimuth what he expected. He really, really did.

But instead he held himself very still, and made his breathing almost not breathing at all, no interruptions of sound or betrayal that he was there—and he listened. It was very hard, it turned out, to stop being a spy once you'd gotten used to being one. And Eight Antidote had gotten *very* used to being one.

(He wasn't sure whose fault that was. His, or his ancestor-the-Emperor's, either genetically or how he'd been raised, or the Emperor Herself's when she'd given him that spearpoint.)

"—time to wait. I'm not going to stand idly by while Shard pilots come to me hardly able to stop screaming long enough to make their warning coherent. Whatever else is going on out there, they are killing the Fleet's soldiers, and unless we unhook the Shards from their proprioception link, the *whole universe* is going to be exquisitely aware of it."

That was Three Azimuth. That was Three Azimuth sounding

more viciously animated than Eight Antidote had ever heard her. Three Azimuth, Minister of War, explaining what he could only think must be *the Shard trick,* and if the Shard pilots were somehow all linked together so that they heard each other die—as if they were Sunlit, except *broken,* Sunlit didn't hear each other die, at least as far as Eight Antidote knew—how *hadn't* the Minister of War come to the same conclusions Eight Antidote had? That the aliens they were fighting were *also* linked together? He took a step forward, toward the door, ready to interrupt and explain his idea.

And heard Eleven Laurel say, "Sending our ships down to that planet will surely expose our people to whatever fungal disease it is teeming with. *Really,* Minister?"

He didn't move. Didn't open the door. (Wasn't sure about *fungal disease,* the envoy and Dzmare hadn't mentioned anything like that.)

"A sufficient number of nuclear shatterbombs will wipe out even very determined fungi," said Three Azimuth. "I'm not ordering an *attack,* Undersecretary. I'm ordering a heart-strike. Wipe that one colony off the skin of the universe and see what sort of negotiations we get to have after they know what we can do."

A quiet, awful pause. Eight Antidote thought about what happened to a planet when its atmosphere was full of radio-isotopes. He had to think back a long way. Teixcalaan didn't do that kind of thing, anymore. It was too . . . A planet didn't come *back* from that. He'd read a whole codex-book about it, two years ago, when one of his tutors had decided he was old enough to learn about the atrocities Teixcalaan had smartly given up committing.

Into that silence, Eleven Laurel said, "Minister, speaking as the Undersecretary of the Third Palm, and nominally your expert on military intelligence praxis . . . negotiation is not going to be what you'll get after you order the Fleet to bomb a populated planetary settlement into radioactive winter. You'll get—oh, surrender, perhaps, or retreat. Or retrenchment, a war that goes on for decades out there in that little, ugly spot of black."

"Are you telling me it is a terrible idea, Undersecretary?"

". . . No," Eleven Laurel said, and Eight Antidote could imagine his smile. It would be the same one he used when Eight Antidote had gotten *most* of a strategy puzzle right. Pleased, but smug, too. "I don't think it's necessarily a terrible idea at all. Merely that you're unlikely to have *negotiation* be one of your outcomes—but then, negotiation's never been what you've liked, has it? Not on Nakhar. You prefer efficacy, Minister."

"And if I do?"

"Then you do."

Eight Antidote felt like he should be sick to his stomach, and wasn't. He wasn't sure if his stomach was near enough to him to be sick with. Everything was very distant and very frightening. The Minister of War was talking about killing a whole planetary system, and Eleven Laurel was agreeing. And if this was what being in the Fleet was really like, he was sorry for wanting it. Sorry for wanting to dance ships into being in a simulation room. Sorry for wanting to solve all the puzzles of command. Sorry for not thinking about how Shard pilots might scream when their fellow pilots died.

If he cried, he'd be overheard.

So he didn't.

". . . it has to be aboveboard," Eleven Laurel was saying. "From the Emperor Herself, no Shard trick to get ahead of the process."

"The Emperor still doesn't know about the side effects of the proprioception link, then. That's what you mean, Undersecretary."

A dry snatch of laughter. "Yes. I assume that is what I mean. I'd prefer to keep as much proprietary knowledge inside War as possible, Minister. In our current diminished state—after what One Lightning attempted—let us *not* give Her Illuminate

Majesty any reasons to send Information or Science in here to take over our decision-making."

"Sometimes," said Three Azimuth, with a tiny sigh that made all the hairs on Eight Antidote's arms stand up, "I understand why Nine Hibiscus prefers Information to you Third Palmers. Even so. Aboveboard, as you recommend. It won't be a problem; the message is already prepared."

"I do admire you, Minister. Enormously. My best student is willing to die in executing this plan, if it means we get what we need—"

"Sixteen Moonrise?"

"Yes. Right alongside the *yaotlek*. Two flagships ought to be sufficient to carve open a space in the enemy lines for the requisite number of shatterbombers to get through, don't you think?"

Eight Antidote had heard enough. He imagined how many bombs it would take to kill a planetary system, and how many bodies would be on that planet, even if they were all one mind like he thought they were, and he *didn't want it to happen*. It wasn't—just losing some Shard pilots made other Shard pilots cry. What would it be like to lose a whole planet if you felt all the deaths?

They understand death, they just don't care about it the same way, Dzmare had said.

But that didn't mean they didn't care about it at all.

Eight Antidote turned away, back down the hall, and headed into the tunnels. He was going to tell someone his idea. He *was*. But he was going to tell the Emperor Nineteen Adze, so that she didn't send that order that Three Azimuth wanted her to send.

———

"What does Fleet Captain Forty Oxide want?" Nine Hibiscus said, her voice gone very even, very serene. The voice of a person calculating lines of attack. Mahit wasn't sure she understood the question (what could a Fleet Captain under attack possibly *want* but for the attack to end with him victorious?), but Two Foam seemed to.

"It's not an all-ships distress call, *yaotlek*. It's a request for information. Have we done anything that would provoke an intensification of the guerilla strikes to direct engagement, do you have more specific instructions—their comms officer Nine Sea-Ice is waiting for our reply on open channel."

Before Nine Hibiscus could answer, Three Seagrass, her voice low and urgent and just as calm as the *yaotlek*'s, said, "Before you answer, *yaotlek,* find out if any of the other legions in your six are under similar attack or have changed position. I suspect this is not an isolated incident."

Nine Hibiscus looked at her with a weight of evaluation that made Mahit want to sink down under it, crushed by heavy scrutiny, heavier evaluation.

But Three Seagrass didn't flinch, and Nine Hibiscus, as if satisfied by that lack, said, "Two Foam. Do so. Status, from all captains."

It didn't take long. The order must have been a commonplace one—Two Foam reached above her head, her hands dancing in the holograph display of the Fleet, and transmuted incoming messages into a pattern of light, a stylized representation of what each legion in this sector was doing, how they moved, how many of their ships were under attack.

Even Mahit could see that the Twenty-Fourth Legion—Sixteen Moonrise's legion—had begun a slow, inexorable approach toward the aliens' planetary system. And that at the same time, or shortly after, the aliens had redoubled their attack on the nearest legion to that system—the Seventeenth. Cause and effect, as plain as sunlight.

"They understand retaliation just fine," she found herself saying. "*Yaotlek.* With the greatest of respect. I know I'm not Teixcalaanli, or one of your soldiers, and I know your people are dying, but if this is how the aliens react to the *suggestion* of approach—think of what they will do if you actually signal an attack."

"Also," Three Seagrass added, viciously dry, "I doubt that you ordered Sixteen Moonrise to take her ship in that close. Did you?"

Mahit had never seen any Teixcalaanlitzlim smile like a Stationer who hadn't lived near or known Stationers, but Nine Hibiscus did it now: bared her teeth, her lips curling back.

<Not a smile,> Yskandr told her. <A threat. A *displeasure*. A very Teixcalaanli expression, even if it looks like how we'd smile if we wanted someone to know we were going to *enjoy* hurting them.>

Close enough, Mahit told him.

"How right you are, Envoy," Nine Hibiscus said, still show-ing her teeth. "But you have reason to make me mistrust my Fleet Captain, do you not? You two—*the spook and her pet*?"

"You're the one who asked for Information's services," Three Seagrass said. "*Yaotlek.* It's you who commands me, just as you command the Fleet Captain."

"And how do I know, Envoy, if the attack on the Seventeenth is due to Fleet Captain Sixteen Moonrise's maneuvers—or some-thing you and Ambassador Dzmare said, down on Peloa-2?"

"You don't," said Mahit. "And neither do we."

Three Seagrass looked at her, flashfire-quick, her mouth twisted into the same amazed-wry expression she'd worn when Mahit had curled her fingers up inside her just *so*. Which was also the same expression she'd worn when she had watched Mahit turn the performance of barbarism directly against the Minister of Science Ten Pearl, at the very first event they'd ever been to together. That same pleasure, a twisted amazement and joy, a kind of possessive *wanting*. Mahit couldn't think about how it made her feel. She didn't have time to feel anything that strong. That—disarraying of the pattern of the world.

"The Ambassador is right," Three Seagrass said. "I would not promise you anything I could not guarantee. It may be our fault.

It may be the Twenty-Fourth Legion. It may be something else we cannot even imagine—our enemy is *otherwise* than any alien species I know of."

Clipped and vicious, Nine Hibiscus said, "For what did I bring you here, then, Envoy? If you cannot make these aliens make sense."

"For the attempt," said Three Seagrass.

At which Two Foam, apparently done with philosophy, negotiations, and barbarians all, said, "The *Chatoyant Sirocco* is still waiting for an answer," loud enough that Mahit almost flinched.

Quickly, Mahit said, "Ask the Emperor. Let this be, if it is to be, a destruction that is from the heart of Teixcalaan."

Eight Antidote had accesses he hadn't known he had. He'd never thought to use them. Never thought, before this morning—it was morning now, sort of, a grey morning that was going to rain at any minute, the sunrise mostly disguised—to walk through Palace-Earth and ask *locked* doors to open for him. To open for him because he was the imperial heir Eight Antidote, and his cloudhook was the second-strongest key in all of Teixcalaan.

Unless his accesses had been limited because he was a child. Which he was sure they were, somewhere—but he wasn't finding the edge. He kept not finding the edge, where someone— even the City, or the imperial security AI, or a dumb-locked door that needed a physical key—would stop him. He wanted—it was awful and stupid and unfair, but he wanted someone to stop him. That would mean it wasn't his responsibility anymore. That would mean someone else, someone grown up entirely, would be the one in charge of doing this. Of stopping a—a *planetary genocide*. Except: the grown-ups *were* in charge, and so far they weren't stopping anything at all.

Palace-East opened up like a flower blooming. Eight Antidote walked as deep as the imperial apartments went, past the post of the Keeper of the Imperial Inkstand, past the corridor that

led to his own rooms, past door after door and into the Emper-
or's own suite. He was bracing himself to try the last door—
the one he'd never been through, the one that would lead into
Nineteen Adze's bedroom, her private space—when a hand fell
onto his shoulder and he cried out, surprised, and forgot everything about how to fight off a kidnapper, just stood still, waiting to see if he'd be punished for trespassing.

It wasn't a kidnapper, of course. It was Her Brilliance the Emperor, all in white, bare feet soundless on the floor.

"Little spy," she said. It was not an accusation. More like an
invitation to explain himself.

"Your Brilliance," he said, and turned around. Her hand
stayed on his shoulder. He tried not to cringe or pull away. "I'm
sorry for disturbing you this early."

"No you're not," said Nineteen Adze. "You cut a swath through
all of the palace's security systems. You want very much to dis-
turb me. Now, would you like to tell me why?"

Her attention felt like a gravitational field. Something that
pulled a person in. "I was at the Ministry of War," he said. He
wanted to get this right, the first time. To not hesitate or hint. "I
overheard the Minister and Third Undersecretary Eleven Laurel
discussing using nuclear shatterbombs on an entire inhabited
planetary system full of our enemies. They're going to do it.
They're going to ask you to approve it. They're going to ask
you to tell them to kill an entire planet and poison it so nothing
ever grows there again."

"And you came to—what, to warn me?" Her face was expressionless. Eight Antidote felt completely lost. Why wasn't she
reacting? Why wasn't she making it *stop*?

"Yes?" he tried. "And to tell you that—I think that the aliens,
that our enemies, that maybe they're all one mind like the Sunlit sometimes are and killing a planet of them would be—it's so
awful I can't think about it, Your Brilliance."

"It is awful," said Nineteen Adze. "Have you had breakfast

yet? Come, sit with me a minute. I've got cassava and new-cheese breads—your ancestor-the-Emperor liked them. Do you, too?"

Eight Antidote did—they were one of his favorite foods, the delicious round cassava shell around the slightly melted, gooey cheese center, warm from the oven—but he couldn't imagine eating. He was sick to his stomach. He didn't understand *anything* about how Nineteen Adze was handling this. But he sat down next to her at a table by one of her enormous windows, and took a cassava bread from the platter of them that was there. He picked it apart with his fingers.

"Why aren't you making them *stop*?" he asked, finally, and Nineteen Adze sighed—just a faint sound, her shoulders settling back. She bit into a cassava bread. Chewed and swallowed while Eight Antidote stared at her.

Then she said, "I'm not making them stop because I believe it's the right idea."

He tore another piece of dough off his bread and squished it in his fingers. "*Why?*" he said, plaintive, hating himself for sounding plaintive. "They're people. Not humans, but people, I really think so, and you *said* it was awful to kill a planet, I just heard you."

"I did say it was awful," the Emperor told him. "And I believe it is. It is a terrible thing to do, and a terrible decision to make. But that's what Emperors are for, Eight Antidote. Terrible decisions. I'd rather—oh, I'll tell you the truth, my little spy. You're going to have to do this yourself, eventually, so the truth is better. I'd rather have a pyrrhic victory—display just what Teixcalaan is capable of, smash a living beautiful planet full of people—and yes, they probably are people, but not the kind of people we can understand—smash it to dust and deathrain. I'd rather one act of horror than an endless war of attrition, losing our people and theirs, on and on and on. Like a suppurating wound at the edge of the Empire, *forever.*"

She wasn't eating her pastry. She swallowed like her throat

was as dry as Eight Antidote's was. "Sometimes it is better to cauterize," she said.

———

Nine Hibiscus hissed through her teeth. Mahit wanted to flinch, or step in front of Three Seagrass, in case the suggestion of asking the Emperor for permission to begin all-out war, all strategy over, was so deep a breach of propriety that a *yaotlek* would—she didn't know. Have Three Seagrass shot. Court-martialed. Assigned to one of those glittering Shard-fighters to lead the assault.

She wished she could stop *imagining* worse ways for the narrative to play out. But there were so few better ones that she could see, and Yskandr was a shiver-quiet hum of pain in her wrists, all barely contained waiting that wasn't patience as much as a preparation for some unknown last-ditch action—

But then Nine Hibiscus said "Tell Forty Oxide to return fire, but not pursue." Two Foam nodded, a quick acknowledgment. Mahit tried to breathe in the space between the *yaotlek*'s sentences. She couldn't inhale and exhale fast enough.

"Not pursue *yet*," Nine Hibiscus went on. "But prepare to, on my order. And send a fast-courier to the City. I want the Emperor's voice on this order right along with mine." Then she looked back at Three Seagrass and said, much softer, hardly loud enough for Mahit to pick up, "I've always said that Information was better than the Palmers if you had to do counterintelligence outside the Fleet because Information's *prefucked*—no chance of getting yourselves enamored with barbarians for the first time and forgetting what the Fleet's for. You're already corrupt. But I didn't ever expect one of you to bring me a barbarian who uses Teixcalaanli imperial protocol to prove her points."

"Ambassador Dzmare is—unique," said Three Seagrass, and Mahit tried to decide who had insulted her, and if she should mind. She'd won, hadn't she? Briefly. She'd—bought them time. Time for Twenty Cicada to keep talking. Time for—something other than all of Teixcalaan's military bent to inexorable and total destruction, unnuanced, beautiful—an elimination of confusion, of incomprehension. A *loss*.

<A loss for whom?> Yskandr murmured. Mahit wasn't sure, or couldn't tell him, or he already knew. (A loss for *her*. For the spaces of language that let a person like her imagine Teixcalaan and still be a Stationer. The idea that there might be something other than Teixcalaan, when one said the word for *world*.)

One of the other officers on the bridge said, "*Yaotlek*. A ship has come through the jumpgate—*behind* us—"

"An enemy ship?" asked Nine Hibiscus, and Mahit thought, ice-clear and sudden: *If it is one of the enemy, coming through the Anhamemat Gate from the Stationer side, then they have already taken Lsel, and I never even knew when all my people were killed. I was here, talking to their murderers, and I never knew—*

If she breathed, she'd hyperventilate. If she moved, that thought would be true, and real, and she'd have to keep breathing afterward.

"No," said the officer, and Mahit exhaled so hard that she almost missed what he said next, lost in a sudden, imago-doubled flood of relief—a relief which vanished almost as soon as it rocked through her, leaving her shaking.

Because the officer had put the incoming ship's wide-channel broadcast on full audio, and the voice which was filling the bridge of the *Weight for the Wheel* belonged to Darj Tarats, Lsel Councilor for the Miners, first amongst six—and he was demanding to be brought on board to speak with Mahit herself.

———

Cauterize.

Eight Antidote didn't know what to say. He didn't know how to say it. How did he tell the Emperor Herself that she was wrong? How *could* she be this wrong? ". . . I don't understand," he managed. "You told me—you told me all those things about how my ancestor-the-Emperor wanted a Teixcalaan that could have another eighty years of peace, and you want to do this anyway? It's—"

"Go on," said Nineteen Adze. "Say what you think."

"It's a planetary genocide," said Eight Antidote, and said it *angrily,* and didn't burst into tears at all. That icy clear place beyond fear was back with him. "I don't care if it cauterizes. If you think it would cauterize. If someone murdered my home, I would fight them *forever.*"

"I do think you would," Nineteen Adze said. She wasn't *reacting* to him. He didn't know what he could say to make her stop being so calm, so already-decided. "I would have, when I was eleven. Maybe when I was twice eleven, too. But that was before I met Six Direction. We have to think beyond ourselves, and what we'd want. That's what I learned from him. What I learned from watching him rule, and watching the end of his reign. This is an ugly decision to make, and it hurts, Eight Antidote, and I'm sorry you had to find out about it in secret. I would have preferred to have been with you, so you could ask questions and I could have explained."

"You said. Before, in my bedroom—" He tried to remember the words. The *exact* words. It would have been easier if Nineteen Adze had recited a poem, but she hadn't. She'd just told him—". . . You said that Six Direction's Teixcalaan was an empire strong enough to be at peace. How are we going to get there from—from *killing a planet*?"

Nineteen Adze lifted one shoulder in a shrug, and put it down again. "You're really *not* like him," she said. "Or you're like he was when he was a child, and I never knew him as a child—he only told me stories. I'm glad you're not, you know. I meant what I said, in your bedroom. I'd rather have a clever, annoying successor than a dullard. Even if you are in my living room trying to make me feel ashamed of killing our enemies viciously enough that they will leave us alone. Your ancestor would have done what I am doing. We did it together once. On that campaign. The one in the holo that I gave you."

"You killed a planet?"

"A city. It—came to the same thing, little spy. There, and then, it came to the same thing."

He could imagine it. The two of them, on their horses. The bloody spears. He wondered how you killed a city without killing the planet along with it, and whether he'd know how when he was grown. He said, "You keep saying I'm not my ancestor. I know I'm not. I'm a *clone*. Most people are clones! It's not weird."

The Emperor put her hand on Eight Antidote's wrist. Her skin felt like skin. Warm and human, just like his. "You're exactly you," she said. "But—you could have been something else. And I didn't want that for you."

Eight Antidote was sure that he was being distracted, being led away from the horrible and certain knowledge that even *now* there was probably a message on an infofiche stick going toward the spaceport, on a fastest-of-fast-courier ships, jumpgate to jumpgate and only five and a half hours between here and genocide. But he couldn't help asking. He felt like he'd choke if he didn't ask.

He said, "What would I have been?" And waited.

Nineteen Adze closed her eyes. The lids were unpainted— she never really painted herself, Eight Antidote had always suspected that the white suits and the sun-spear throne were enough decoration for her—unpainted and thin. Every poem he knew said that Emperors never slept. Maybe it was true. Her eyes were still closed when she said, like the beginning of a story, the preamble to an epic, "Your ancestor the Emperor Six Direction loved many people in his time. Me—his crèche-sister Eight Loop, who you're named for, who is your legal guardian now—countless others. But once he loved the Ambassador from Lsel Station."

"Mahit Dzmare?" Eight Antidote asked, confused.

"No," said Nineteen Adze. "Stars, no, he met her—three times, I think. Three times I know about. He loved her predecessor, little spy. Yskandr Aghavn. And I—oh, Yskandr was easy to love. Like drinking too much and not minding being drunk. Like taking a strike force over a hill and not knowing if there's an ambush on the other side."

"He died, though," said Eight Antidote, and wondered if he should be offering condolences. Adults and the way adults loved had never made sense to him. What the Emperor was describing didn't sound like love at all.

Nineteen Adze nodded. Her eyes were still closed. "Yes. He died. I helped kill him, for what that's worth. Which was like killing a city, or a planet. There and then, it really did come to the same thing. Do you want to know why?"

". . . That's a stupid question, Your Brilliance."

She laughed. The sound was fragile and strange. "Of course it is. I set you up for it. But you do want to know, don't you?"

"Yes." He did. He also didn't, but he felt like being surprised with it later would be *worse*.

"Because on Lsel Station, where Yskandr and Mahit both come from—there is a technology that they use to put the mind of one's predecessor inside the mind of the successor. To—*share*, Mahit said. To have memory live forever. And Yskandr loved your ancestor-the-Emperor. I don't know, little spy, if a barbarian like Yskandr could believe in Six Direction's Teixcalaan, but he believed in Six Direction, and when your ancestor was old, and dying slowly, Yskandr offered him one of those machines. Imago-machines, they call them. A way to record himself, and put himself inside a new body, like a ghost. And have eighty times eighty years of peace."

There was a rock in his stomach, and he hadn't even eaten his cassava and cheese. "It'd need to be a close body, wouldn't it?" he said. His voice sounded thin. Babyish. He couldn't care. "A clone, if he could get one."

"Yes," said Nineteen Adze. "A clone would work very well. You're *quite* like him. Except in all the ways you're not."

He swallowed, dry-mouthed, and almost choked. "What would I have been like?"

The Emperor had stopped looking at whatever was on the inside of her eyelids, and was looking at him instead. He wanted to squirm away. She said, "I don't know. Not you. Not Six Direction, either. Something—*untenable*. Untenable to me. To Teixcalaan."

And yet it was tenable to her to kill a whole planet to *maybe* stop a war. Eight Antidote didn't understand. He didn't *want* to understand. He was glad he wasn't some ghost, some halfthing, his ancestor and himself wrapped up together, because he was *himself*, and he didn't want to understand how Nineteen Adze could kill her friend to save a kid and kill a planet to maybe do nothing but kill a planet.

"I'm not him," he said. "I'm *not* Six Direction."

"You aren't," Nineteen Adze said. "You are the imperial heir Eight Antidote. Nothing more and nothing less."

"You *let* me be myself," he said. Making sure.

"I—gave you the opportunity, when it would have been taken away, yes."

"Then I *am* myself, and I think you're *wrong*, Your Brilliance, you're *wrong* to go along with Three Azimuth's idea, this isn't *my* Teixcalaan. The one you're building."

And somehow he found that he could stand up, and turn his back on his Emperor, and walk straight-spined right out of her suite, leaving his uneaten breakfast behind him.

"Fire on that ship," said Nine Hibiscus, with the brittle determination that accompanied making an unwise choice that nevertheless felt better than making no choice at all. She knew this kind of thinking. She'd thought she'd grown out of it, long before she'd been a Fleet Captain, let alone a *yaotlek*. It was the sort of thinking that obliterated possibilities, unbalanced worlds. Twenty Cicada would be disappointed.

Twenty Cicada wasn't here.

"*Don't*," Mahit Dzmare said, her face twisted in some

incomprehensible expression. Grief or anger or another barbarian emotion that made no sense. *"Yaotlek,* please, don't. He is—that's Darj Tarats, he's one sixth of our government, *please."*

Such a simple request. She should deny it. Everything Sixteen Moonrise had warned her about—the compromising of Information by Lsel agents, the infiltration of Stationer concerns into what should have remained Fleet business—all of that was apparently true, by virtue of the presence of this barbarian in his little ship, demanding Ambassador Dzmare. And yet here was that selfsame Ambassador Dzmare, begging for his life, for the life of some member of her government.

"Hold," Nine Hibiscus said to Five Thistle, whose hands were already finished targeting the small skiff containing this Darj Tarats. "Why shouldn't I fire, Ambassador? That ship wouldn't be the first Stationer vessel caught in the crossfire of this war."

The Ambassador probably hadn't known that. She flinched. Everything was so visible on her face, so clear. And yet her expression wasn't anything that Nine Hibiscus was sure she recognized.

"He asked to speak to me," said Dzmare. "I am—duty-bound to defend him, to preserve the life of my fellow citizen—"

"Also it's rude," said the envoy Three Seagrass, perfectly bland. "To fire on someone who *announced himself* as friendly."

Nine Hibiscus wanted so badly for her to be wrong. For the both of them to be wrong. To be the sort of Fleet Captain who wouldn't *care* if they were wrong.

But she wasn't.

"Bring him on board," she said to Five Thistle, instead. "On board and to me. In restraints. I don't trust this timing, Envoy. Ambassador. I don't trust it at all."

CHAPTER
SEVENTEEN

It has always been Teixcalaanli policy to take in and provide for refugee populations fleeing natural disaster on their home systems, whether those systems are hostile or friendly toward the Empire. Those who flee disasters of their people's own making—war or persecutions—are naturally subject to more stringent integration requirements and evaluation (refer to Judiciary Code 1842.A.9 for procedural details). Given these policies, describe an appropriate course of action for a Teixcalaanli governor of a Western Arc planet confronted with a "worldship" claiming refugee status: 20,000 persons in a self-contained mobile space station, with unknown military capabilities and sanitation practices, parked in orbit around the largest planet in the governed system. Provide citations to defend your course of action.

> —set examination paper for selection into the political
> track of the Judiciary Ministry post-aptitudes training
> program, administered once yearly

* * *

For all the work that imago-memory does for us—the preservation of skill, the continuity of institutional knowledge that is so necessary to keep a closed and carefully balanced society-system like Lsel Station and its surrounding subsidiary Stations functional through the inevitably high loss-rate of individuals subject to cosmic radiation and the standard accidents of living in vacuum both—imago-memory has not managed to preserve for us the reasons that we Stationers came to Bardzravand Sector and stayed. Nor do we remember where we were coming from,

or where we were going. Fourteen generations down the chain
of live memory, and all our oldest lines have are dreams of numbers and a certainty that if we did this once, we could do it again.
Live memory does not retain the reasons for decisions; only the
ability to make them. And yet: we did this once. Could we do it
again, in reverse? Unpin Lsel from our gravitational wellpoint
and go traveling?

> —excerpt from the introduction to *A Pilot's History of
> the Future: Worldships and Lsel Station,* by the retired
> pilot Takan Mnal and published 291.3.11–6D
> (Teixcalaanli reckoning)

THE first thing that Councilor Darj Tarats of Lsel Station said
on the bridge of *Weight for the Wheel,* his hands cuffed behind
him in the sort of restraints Three Seagrass assumed were usually used for court-martials or other Fleet unpleasantnesses, was
"This is not what I sent you here to do, Dzmare." He said it
in Teixcalaanli, which meant that he wanted everyone else to
know that Mahit was his creature and no one else's. Three Seagrass thought that was, if nothing else—and there was *so much*
else—rude.

His face was cadaverously thin and highly mobile, and he
looked like he thought being restrained by Teixcalaanli soldiers
was a minor inconvenience of dignity, nothing more. He didn't
engage in the protocol of politesse: bowed to no one, acknowledged no one but Mahit. Mahit, who was standing next to her,
color draining from her cheeks like water disappearing into
desert sand. She didn't reply. It didn't help. Tarats kept talking,
and Three Seagrass could feel the attention of all of *Weight for
the Wheel's* bridge officers settle on Mahit, the stranger in their
midst—and on Three Seagrass herself, by proximity and asso-
ciation, if nothing else—like a pack of diving birds, waiting for
the silver belly-shine of vulnerable fish.

Behind them, Two Foam's strategy holomap of the Fleet's position showed Sixteen Moonrise's flagship creeping closer and closer to the marked-out location of the aliens' planet. Not stopping. Accelerating on a vector of her own choosing, and this whole bridge was looking at Mahit Dzmare instead.

You terrify me, Mahit, Three Seagrass thought, and found that the thought was galvanizing—terror and desire were wound so close inside her chest. Maybe she'd always been that way. Maybe it was Mahit's fault. Oh, but she wanted time to find out. How absolutely starfucked inconvenient, to discover that she wanted anything but to live through this, and live through it a credit to her Ministry and her empire—

When Mahit didn't respond to Tarats's first insinuatingly nasty comment, he went right on. "I sent you here to *keep this war safely over our heads*, Dzmare," he said, "and what have you managed? Nothing. Not a single communication. The first I hear from this front is the horror that you were supposed to keep entwined with Teixcalaan boiling through our Far Gate and toward the Station—even *now* Onchu is killing our pilots to keep them away from Lsel. And what are you doing?"

"Negotiating," said Mahit, thinly, right before the weapons officer, Five Thistle, put a pulse pistol under her chin.

Three Seagrass remembered what Mahit had told her, curled together in the dark: that she was meant to be a spy. Worse than a spy: a saboteur, intended to make this war go on forever, destroy Teixcalaan by attrition and waste. Meant to be a saboteur for this man, who repaid the kindness of sparing his life by putting hers in danger.

Three Seagrass always made decisions wholly and entire. All at once. Choosing Information at her aptitudes. Choosing the position of cultural liaison to the Lsel Ambassador. Choosing to trust her. Choosing to come here, to take this assignment—entirely, completely, and without pausing to look to see how deep the water was that she was leaping into.

"Oh, bloody fucking *starlight*," she said, stepping between Mahit and Tarats—between Mahit and Tarats and Nine Hibiscus, too, making herself the center point of a triangle. "If you all would stand down for a *brief* moment so we can sort out the actionable intelligence this Stationer has brought us from his other inopportune exclamations? There's quite enough shooting going on outside this ship, we don't need to start doing it in here."

Tarats said something in Stationer, which to Three Seagrass was still mostly a sequence of impossible-to-pronounce consonants, and Mahit—didn't answer him, which was very, very smart. It would be smarter still if Mahit didn't say a thing in any language but Teixcalaanli until Three Seagrass got that pulse pistol away from her throat. It was pressed so close. Like a mouth would be. Cool and patient, tucked up under her jawline.

No time to think about it. No time for anything! Anything save talking. And talking was what Three Seagrass was *for*.

"Precisely why, Envoy, *shouldn't* I have my officer shoot Ambassador Dzmare, as she is clearly, by her own superior's admission, a spy here?" Nine Hibiscus asked, soft and even. It was a bad tone. There was no hesitance in it. Three Seagrass needed to destabilize the situation further, before she could have any hope of putting it back together properly.

"Because that would be trusting the word of this man"—she made a little falling gesture with one hand, dismissive encapsulation of all of Darj Tarats—"without spending the time to investigate his agenda. Or Ambassador Dzmare's. Or mine. It shuts off options, *yaotlek*, and I believe we were just discussing how useful it would be to keep options *open*, given the current state of conflict with our enemy and the continued negotiations down on Peloa-2. Unless you've changed your mind because of one Stationer in a little flit-ship?"

Occasionally Three Seagrass wondered if she was going to die very young. Now might have been one of those moments.

That pulse pistol under Mahit's throat could be pointed at her own back by now, and she wasn't about to turn around and check. She was going to be fearless and assured, and it was going to work, it was, it was, it was.

"*Your* agenda," Nine Hibiscus said, still viciously calm. "Do you have one, Envoy? One of your own? Separate from that of the Fleet?"

Better. Not good—she probably *was* going to get shot! Just like Petal had, and wouldn't he laugh, if dead people could laugh—but better. Having the *yaotlek* focused on her was far more usable—safer—than having her play Mahit and Tarats off of one another. Three Seagrass shrugged, and said, "I'm a Teixcalaanlitzlim, *yaotlek*, and an *asekreta*, of course I have an agenda. But it is a simple one: the Fleet asked for a negotiator and I'm that negotiator. My agenda is to *keep talking*, and to be sure of any more final or drastic steps than that." She assembled a self-deprecating smile, wide eyes and a blink.

Nine Hibiscus stared her down. The *yaotlek* was like a pillar, a statue, a solid point with her own gravity. It was *very* impressive. She said, "Our enemy is not *talking*, Envoy. Our enemy is acting. In ways none of us predicted, if the Stationer is correct about their increased presence in Parzrawantlak Sector, as *well* as what they're doing to the Seventeenth Legion."

The scatterpoint lights of the Seventeenth Legion's Shards on Two Foam's holomap swarmed and fell to nothing, went up in fire, gathered themselves again, dove forward despite how many deaths they were doubtless experiencing. The whole sector-wide battlefield was evidence enough of *our enemy is acting*—and even if Three Seagrass thought it was mostly due to Sixteen Moonrise's forward momentum, it was still *true*. But it wasn't *all* that was true.

"Our enemy might be talking," she said. "Why don't you call your adjutant and find out, instead of waiting for him to report back? He was very much alive when we left him. And I doubt a person like Twenty Cicada dies easy."

The flicker of emotion, concern and upset and *anger*, that passed through Nine Hibiscus's face was gratifying. Three Seagrass had her now. She had the lever to move her, to destabilize and reform this negotiation, and—bleeding starshine, if she pulled this off she was going to write her very own epic poem about herself, no matter how gauche. Eleven Lathe had never done a negotiation like *this*.

"Keep that pistol where it is," Nine Hibiscus said, "and don't let the other Stationer out of his restraints." And then she walked over to Two Foam's comms console. Two Foam got out of her way. She didn't bother to sit down—this clearly wasn't going to be that kind of message—she just leaned in, reached through the holodisplay of death and valor to send a tight narrowcast beam down to Peloa-2, and said, "Swarm, if you can, report your status."

Three Seagrass kept being surprised by that use-name, even knowing that Twenty Cicada had the absurdity of an *insect* as his noun-sign. It had to be something related to his religion. She wished, absently, that she'd had enough time with him to really wrap her head around him. How he identified *waste* with *immorality*. Really, aside from how he was clever and surprising and confusing, he was the worst possible negotiator to have left on Peloa-2 with the aliens, who killed without understanding individual life and individual contribution—

A crackling, staticky noise. And then words.

———

Eight Antidote was not his ancestor-the-Emperor, and he was not Her Brilliance Nineteen Adze, and for a long moment, standing just inside the door of his own suite like a kid who'd been sent to his room to be punished, he was entirely sure that everything was over. He had tried, and he had failed. No one listened to him; he could be a little spy, and Eleven Laurel's student Cure, and even Minister Three Azimuth's favorite new political contact, and none of that mattered, because he was eleven and he'd *tried* and it hadn't worked. The war was already happening; by now the message ordering planet-killing destruction was in some jumpgate-flitter's hands, probably a Shard since they were the fastest and Fleet ships always had priority through the jumpgates, more than any other kind of mail—

Fleet ships had priority.

Shards had priority.

Shards could—if Three Azimuth and Eleven Laurel had meant what he was sure they'd meant—talk faster, one to another, than a message could pass through jumpgates.

And Her Brilliance the Emperor didn't know about that, at all. The only person—well, the only person who wasn't a Shard pilot and wasn't in the Ministry of War—who knew about that, was him. Eight Antidote, imperial heir.

He wasn't Emperor of all Teixcalaan. Not yet. Not for a long time, probably. But he was the closest thing. His word— his *orders*—they'd open doors all through Palace-Earth. They'd open doors all through the City.

They would, if there wasn't another order that superseded them, one from the *actual* Emperor, be as powerful as any order in all of the Empire.

He needed a sealed imperial infofiche stick. And he needed— he needed a Shard. Or a Shard pilot, but just the Shard would do.

He was still standing just inside the doorway of his room. There was a City-eye camera pointed right at him, he knew that. One on the door, one on the window, one on the window in the bathroom. The City always there, the algorithm watching him, keeping him safe. He tried not to let his expression change. Not show that he was shivering, exhausted-sick, and so full up with the possibility of *doing something* that he thought he might burst. He needed to be entirely—him. Normal. Disappointed and angry and definitely, definitely not picking up the open, empty infofiche stick made of animal bone that Nineteen Adze had sent him when she'd summoned him to talk to her, nights ago. The infofiche stick carved with the imprint of the sun-spear throne. Definitely not picking that up off his desk, along with one of the automatic wax-seals that didn't need to be heated up, and going into the bathroom, and taking off all his clothes to stand in the shower—without turning on the shower, he wasn't *stupid,* getting an infofiche stick wet while it was open would fry it—facing the tiled corner, away from the camera he knew about and any other cameras he didn't.

He didn't need to not be seen *forever.* He just needed to not be seen for *long enough.*

It took longer than he wanted, though, to compose the order. He'd never written one before, and his first try sounded like he was pretending to be a character in *Dawn with Encroaching Clouds,* all ancient verb forms that no one used anymore, even in imperial proclamations. His second try was simpler, and it sounded more like him—which meant it sounded like a kid, probably, but he'd rather sound like a kid than like a fake holo-drama emperor.

His Excellency Eight Antidote, Imperial Associate, Heir to the Sun-Spear Throne, he composed, drawing the glyphs in light, *on behalf of the government of the star-encompassing Teixcalaanli Empire, to the* yaotlek *Fleet Captain Nine Hibiscus of the Tenth Legion: Teixcalaan is civilization, and it is our job to safeguard it. This order forbids the use of civilization-destroying weapons or tactics on the alien threat beyond Parzrawantlak Sector, including nuclear strikes on civilian-occupied planetary systems, except in cases where such weapons or tactics are the only thing standing between us and certain civilization-wide death.*

That was probably strong enough. He wondered if he was in the process of setting policy for Emperors to come, and decided that he could do that, if he wanted. He was *himself,* and Nineteen Adze had let him be, and this was what he knew was true and right and Teixcalaanli.

He sealed the stick. His autoseals all had *his* name-glyph on them, but that was fine. He was *enough.* He had to keep believing that.

Now he just had to get the stick in the interstellar mail—and find a Shard pilot or a Shard itself to try to talk to—

Which meant he was going to have to go back to Inmost Province Spaceport. Immediately the hollowness of his stomach turned into a horrible churning. He didn't *want* to. Inmost Province Spaceport was where he'd been when the subway derailment happened. The alarms and the panicking people and everyone knowing what to do except him and *no way to get home* and *incendiary devices,* and he still hadn't heard anything from Five Agate about whether it *had* been an incendiary, like the one that had killed that woman out in Belltown—or anything about whether it had been his own fault it had happened, someone trying to kill *him.*

Even before the derailment he'd been terrified.

Terrified and stupid and alone with *too many people,* and he was so embarrassed about that he thought he might die. Even if no one was trying to kill him, he might die all on his own if he kept feeling this squirmingly *pathetic.*

But he *had* to go back. There wasn't anybody else to do it for him. And he didn't know where else but the Inmost Province Spaceport he'd find either a Shard pilot or an Information Ministry kiosk for sending imperial messages through the interjumpgate mail. His stomach felt like it was crawling up his throat.

Right out loud, he said, "Oh fuck," for the first time in his life, like a grown person would. And then he threw up, turning his head away from the infofiche stick, keeping it clean.

———

"Oh, I'm alive, Mallow," said Twenty Cicada, hardly audible through the hiss and pop of static. Three Seagrass leaned closer to the comms console, as if that would help her hear, even though she knew it wouldn't do anything at all. "For the moment. I'm trying to figure out if the heat or these claws will get me first—don't worry, I'm not being *chased,* I'm a—well, a hostage that talks, or draws at least. I can't talk long. They aren't very interested in our unmusical mouth noises, and you summoned all the singers back up to the ship."

"Don't talk," said Nine Hibiscus. "Don't talk to *me*. Talk to them. And don't die. This line is open, and I *will* send Shards for you—"

"If I needed Shards, I'd already be dead by the time they arrived. Hush. I think they're drawing fractals. Or—mycelium—"

More static. And silence.

Into that silence, Three Seagrass said, with all the vicious brightness she could summon, "See? Still talking. So I think we should wait for official word from the Emperor before you send in that strike force—because you know that the instant you attack that planetary system, he'll die down there on Peloa. And for what, *yaotlek*? What sacrifice are you making?"

Nine Hibiscus turned to her slowly—it was more threatening than a fast wheel would be. *Ah,* Three Seagrass thought, *weight,* weight *for the wheel, I see,* and tried not to let anyone know she wanted to have hysterics. Hysterics were for after the negotiation!

"I've already sent to the Emperor for confirmation, Envoy. No need to reiterate *that* argument."

"Of course," Three Seagrass told her, light, light, easy—and then whirled, within her triangle, to face Darj Tarats. "Tell us, Councilor," she said, dropping a level of formality and making herself sound vicious and bored, a poet having to speak to an illiterate at court (and wasn't this whole negotiation a sort of version of that hoary old trope? With Nine Hibiscus standing in for the Emperor and the bridge for the glittering fan-vaults of Palace-Earth—ah, but she *missed* the City, for the first time in a while, and intensely), "just *how* do you suppose that Ambassador Dzmare is responsible for your purported sudden invasion? As far as I am aware—and I have been with the Ambassador since you so kindly allowed me to borrow her from her deserved vacation at home—she has done nothing but contribute to the universal effort to minimize casualties and elucidate meaning out of meaningless conflict. What is it you said she'd failed to do? Communicate with you? Councilor, *when would she have had time?*"

It was a masterful little performance, if Three Seagrass was any judge of her own rhetorical abilities. She liked *elucidate meaning out of meaningless conflict*—it was a good paraphrase of Eleven Lathe, and someone (perhaps only her, but *someone*) would appreciate the allusion.

But Darj Tarats was depressingly unimpressed. He didn't respond to Three Seagrass at all—he looked at her, all disdain, and turned to say another brisk phrase in Stationer to Mahit, a blur of consonants. Three Seagrass caught the few words she was sure of: "Yskandr," and the Stationer word for "empire," which wasn't at all the same as the word for Teixcalaan. Mahit, the pistol still under her throat, shut her eyes— the lashes fluttered. When she opened them again, she looked different. Not quite herself. The curve of her mouth was wide. The gesture of her hand broad and lazy. Like she was possessed. Like she was—Yskandr Aghavn, probably.

(And which one of them had had her beautiful hands all over Three Seagrass? What a completely inopportune question for her to fixate on right now! Even if the answer was likely a horrifying *both*. She was never going to like the idea of imago-machines, was she. Not that it'd matter, if Mahit got herself killed now—)

Even her tone was different when she spoke. First in Stationer—there was that word for "empire" again, and another one Three Seagrass knew, "associate," because that verb was all over import/export documents. And then in Teixcalaanli, thank every single divinity anyone had ever sacrificed blood to: Mahit saying, "I have been tasked with making aliens understandable, Councilor, and with influencing their behavior toward our Station. As you have always tasked me, haven't you?"

Oh, but there was a history there. Three Seagrass wanted to

know it. Wanted to get her mouth around it, and her mind, and chew it up and spit it out again. If Darj Tarats had demanded that Mahit be a saboteur, what had he asked of Yskandr Aghavn, who had been the Emperor Six Direction's favorite barbarian? How much of what he had asked had Aghavn refused? How much had Aghavn *done*?

Five Thistle shoved the pistol up tighter against Mahit's throat, and she went still again. Silent. The movement of her jaw when she swallowed was a stifled gulp. He said, "Is that not a confession of spying, *yaotlek*? Stealing our secrets and trying to *influence our behavior.*" Which was tantamount to *should I shoot her now?* so Three Seagrass really needed to say exactly the right thing—

But Nine Hibiscus got there first. "One does not, Five Thistle, expect a barbarian to do anything but put her fellow barbarians first in her mind."

How correct! (Mahit was going to hate that it was correct! Three Seagrass could cope with that *later*.)

"And yet," Three Seagrass said, quick interruption, "Ambassador Dzmare was willing to come when I asked her to, to lend her skills to our first-contact effort. To serve not only her Station but all of Teixcalaan. Nothing is ever simple, *yaotlek*, not with barbarians. Not with Mahit Dzmare, who brought our Emperor to her throne, and warned us of our enemy, and knows us very well—and came with me anyway."

As she said it, she realized she was apologizing. For the stupid thing with Mahit's jacket. For not *talking* to her. For assuming she *would* come with her, of course she would—and not thinking that when the Empire asked, even in the person of a friend, a maybe-lover, there really was no way for a barbarian to say no and keep being the kind of barbarian the Empire thought of as a person.

That was a nasty realization that she was going to have to think a lot more about when people stopped pointing energy weapons at each other on the bridge. *Later.* (She wanted there to be a later. Rather badly, at this point.)

"And *you*, Councilor Tarats!" she went on, trying to talk her way toward that *later*. "Whatever it is that you wish Ambassador Dzmare had done already—if you continue to push us into believing that she is some sort of agent of yours, the officer *will* dispose of her, and what a waste that would be. Silencing a voice that speaks in *your* language, which we nevertheless understand." She forced herself to laugh, light, self-deprecating. "Well. Understand a little. You have *ever so many* consonants, Councilor."

There was a little, breathless, terrifying silence. And then Nine Hibiscus said, "Let the Ambassador go, Five Thistle. For the moment. And shall we have our visitor tell us properly what it is that is happening in Parzrawantlak Sector? In detail, Councilor Tarats. And in a civilized language, if you can manage it."

The pistol came away. Three Seagrass could hear Mahit's rapid, indrawn breath. She wanted to *hug* her. Hold her, maybe. Kiss her, definitely. But that would ruin all of the careful balance she'd just managed to spin, so all she did was look her in the eyes, directly, and smile with her teeth showing. It was possible she was getting better at it.

————

He was glad he'd thrown up in the shower, because that meant he didn't have anything else to throw up on the subway, or on the groundcar shuttle from the last working subway station to the spaceport. The City's investigation into the derailment wasn't over—or there *had* been a bomb and the repairs weren't done. Either way, there *wasn't* a subway to Inmost Province Spaceport proper: there was the biggest groundcar Eight Antidote had ever been in, with no seats, just poles to hang on to, stuffed with grown-ups and other children and luggage. He fit right in: probably everyone thought he was someone else's kid. A whole *lot* of people looked like they either had or wanted to vomit in the shuttle: it jerked when it started and stopped, and hanging on to the poles was *hard*, and the luggage kept rolling into the backs of everyone's legs and knocking them off balance.

The worst part was that he was doing this without a cloud-hook. Last time he'd left Palace-Central he'd had a *guide,* and he'd had the City watching over him—but he needed to move fast and quiet now. He wasn't sure whether Her Brilliance would let him keep being a spy, keep having the freedom to get in trouble and learn information he shouldn't know. Or that someone didn't want him to know. He'd disagreed with her to her face. And now he was in the process of countermanding her orders. If he let the City and all its camera-eyes cross-reference the location of his cloudhook with what images they could capture of him—well. If the Emperor wanted to stop him, he'd be making it easy.

So he left his cloudhook in the subway, right before he switched lines and got onto the horrible shuttle. Took it off to rub his eye—pretending he was a littler kid, an eight-year-old with their very first cloudhook, not used to wearing it—and set it on the seat next to him. When he got up and exited at the Plaza Central One stop (huge, and he was so glad he'd done this once *with* a cloudhook, because he'd never find his way through its seven levels of interlocking tracks alone) he left it there. Presumably it was *still* there, going around and around the subway, stop to stop, back and forth. And he was exposed, and free, and inside a crowd tall enough to *maybe* hide him from some of the City's eyes, and he hated it. He hated it a lot.

The infofiche stick with his replacement order was tucked inside his shirt, where he couldn't lose it or drop it or have it fall out. It was a sharp rectangular pressure, pushing into his belly every time some adult jostled him in the groundcar shuttle. When the shuttle's doors finally opened and everyone inside flowed out into Inmost Province Spaceport, Eight Antidote tried not to stay still, not to stop walking. If he stopped, he'd probably turn around. He didn't want to be here. The spaceport was so *loud,* and the subway entrances were still roped off, and he had to walk by a whole squadron of Sunlit and not look to see if their featureless gold helmet-faces had all turned to look at him, recognize him, tell the whole City and the Emperor what he was about to do.

(Maybe tell whoever it was who had derailed the subway to try again. That was a horrible idea, and he wanted to never have thought of it.)

Tulip Terminal to Nasturtium Terminal. At least he remembered the way. He felt like he was a tiny starship projected over a strategy cartograph table, moving on a designed trajectory set by someone else, someone who might have been him back in the palace but was a wholly different person than the scared kid he was right now.

The Information Ministry kiosk in Nasturtium Terminal was exactly where it had been, and there were *still* two Information Ministry officials inside it, looking bored. Eight Antidote fished his infofiche out of his shirt, rubbed it to polished gleaming on his trouser leg, and then—trying to look like an Imperial errand runner, out of breath because he'd come here *as fast as he could,* not because he was scared to pieces—came up to them.

"Excuse me, *asekretim,*" he said. "I have an Imperial order that needs to go into the jumpgate mail on fastest-courier override."

One of the two raised her eyebrows. "You do?" she asked.

Eight Antidote summoned all the righteous rage of a kid with a job who didn't get believed because he was a kid, and squared his shoulders. He put the stick on the kiosk with a *click.* "Yes, I do," he said. "From Palace-Earth. That's the Emperor's own infofiche stick, and it's sealed with an imperial seal. You can look it up. Don't you have a reference library of seals?"

". . . We do," said the *asekreta,* but she was still saying it like she didn't believe him. "And I'm happy to look up this one—but you *do* know that fraudulent use of an Imperial seal is a very big crime, right? I don't *have* to look this up, if you don't want me to."

Abruptly Eight Antidote wanted to laugh. She thought he

was doing this for a *prank*! It was amazing. She clearly had no idea who he was. Maybe she had never seen a close-up picture of him. Maybe he looked older now than the last pictures. Maybe kiosk workers were just really stupid. It was incredibly frustrating—but amazing. He repeated himself: "You can look it up, *asekreta*. This needs to be on the *next* courier, all overrides, as fast as possible."

"Scan this, would you, Thirty-One Twilight?" said the *asekreta* he'd been talking to, and handed his infofiche stick to her co-worker. "Let's find out about it. Make sure it goes to the right place."

Watching the stick disappear into the kiosk made another wave of nausea creep up through Eight Antidote's chest. He really hoped he didn't throw up again. It would ruin *everything* right now—

"The kid's right," said Thirty-One Twilight. "This is Her Brilliance's own private-use infofiche stick, and it's sealed correctly. Hey, kid—why did they send *you* with this?"

Eight Antidote had already come up with an answer to that. He'd figured he'd need it. "Because I run the fastest," he said, and smiled, wide-eyed and smug. "And I was on duty this morning, and everyone is *really* busy in Palace-Earth, what with the war. I said I could come deliver this, and no one with a grown-up job would have to waste half a day on the shuttle since the subway's still down and it takes forever to get here."

It was a good answer. The *asekretim* seemed to like it, at least—or Thirty-One Twilight did. The other one still seemed dubious. "Who's the addressee?" she asked.

But Eight Antidote knew this part, too. The addressee was *encoded in the message,* inside the infofiche stick itself. And he—if he was an errand runner, someone not important—wouldn't know what was under that seal. "I'm not sure, *asekreta*," he said. "It's above what I'm supposed to know about, I think. The imperial staff just said *fastest courier,* and it is going to the Fleet out on the front lines of the war. The rest is supposed to be inside."

That seemed to be enough. Maybe. The *asekreta* didn't give him back the stick, at least. Instead she said, "It's five and a half hours from point of origin to destination. You go tell that to your supervisor, all right? That's the *absolute fastest we can go.*"

"I'll tell him," said Eight Antidote, and tried not to giggle hysterically: his supervisor already knew, because he was his own supervisor. "Thank you! The Empire thanks you, also!"

He thought he'd managed it—he'd *done* it, his order would be on its way out to the Fleet—but he knew he couldn't stay to watch the Information Ministry workers send it. That'd be suspicious. *Fraudulent,* even. He wondered if he was committing mail fraud. He didn't think so. He had every right to give this order.

It was only what he was going to do next that was almost *certainly* illegal. No one was supposed to be inside a Shard except a Shard pilot, after all.

The Councilor from Lsel Station did not fit neatly into Nine Hibiscus's more-private just-off-the-bridge conference room: he sat at the table there like a twisted metal stake driven hard into rich ground. Tall and thin, with a high forehead marked with an old man's thinning curls. His hands were gnarled, arthritis-bulging where he rested them on the table, and still in restraints. His cheekbones looked as if they might be gnarled as well, with how the skin hung from them, dripping off their sharp and narrow points. He was the Lsel Station Councilor for the Miners, so presumably once he'd been hale enough to work ore out of an asteroid. Or perhaps he'd always been a shift boss. A man born to give orders to lesser men. Here on *Weight for the Wheel,* Nine Hibiscus found him to be an aberration and a discontinuity: but human. And thus something she could talk to, especially since he spoke language, as well as Stationer.

She sat down across from him, which was the sort of respect he deserved. He *was* a member of a foreign government. She could do him some courtesy while she interrogated him. And interrogating him would distract her from how strange Twenty Cicada's voice had sounded—from the hot-spark afterimages of Shard deaths, which seemed to live right behind her eyes now, even though she hadn't dipped into Shard-sight for more than a day—from the accelerating curve of Sixteen Moonrise's slow, barely plausibly deniable attack vector.

From how she wasn't sure if she wanted to stop Sixteen Moonrise at all, whatever Emperor Nineteen Adze's opinion of the matter turned out to be.

"Councilor Tarats," she said. "The Fleet extends its apologies for briefly identifying your vessel as an enemy ship, and is pleased that no harm came to you in the resolution of that misapprehension. Welcome to the *Weight for the Wheel*."

"How very like a Teixcalaanlitzlim, to say I am welcome and have me chained," said the Councilor.

"How very like a barbarian," Nine Hibiscus said, before she could think better of it—she missed Twenty Cicada, she missed him *terribly*, it was much harder to be both the voice of reason and the instrument of threat, with only one person talking— "to take a welcome as a chance to demonstrate ingratitude. I am the *yaotlek* of this Fleet, Councilor. I rule here as the outreached hand of our Illuminate Emperor, with all Her power deferred to me within my sphere. And *I*, who could be waiting for actionable communication from my soldiers on the bridge of this ship, am taking the time to ask *you* to tell me what you know of the advances of our enemy toward your Station. For your sake and that of your people, as well as for us here on this ship, I suggest you begin to give me what we both need to know."

"What should a *yaotlek* of the Fleet want with knowing that all her ships and weapons have done nothing but allow her enemy to slip behind her and pour through the jumpgate she guards?" asked the Councilor. His Teixcalaanli was stilted, assembled from parts, full of older forms of verbs—and quite correct, even so. Nine Hibiscus wondered how often this Councilor had talked to his Ambassadors, and how deeply. And in which language.

"To know *how many* and *how fast*, Councilor," she said, "and whether it is worth our effort to send a legion or two to defend your Station, or simply brace behind the *next* jumpgate and wait to see if your thirty thousand lives are enough to sate the enemy on. For *that*, a *yaotlek* of the Fleet would want with knowing." It pleased her to use his own strange constructions; she could see on his mobile, expressive, *confusing* barbarian face that he didn't like it when she did. Perhaps he thought she considered him a fool.

That she did not. She considered him a snake, and she was debating whether Mahit Dzmare was another of the same sort, or merely a person who had been *bitten* by a snake. Tarats looked at her unblinking, and then began with, "How many? Enough that we have scrambled all our pilots, which we have not done in seven generations; how fast? Perhaps you would like to tell us poor barbarian Stationers how to see the invisible, and then I could tell you."

She could imagine it: a black-void tide that swallowed ships and people faster than a person could count the losses. She could imagine it, because she had seen it. With her own eyes and with the eyes of her Shard pilots.

Why had she let the envoy convince her not to destroy these— *things*, these things that had eaten worlds and would eat more, these ship-destroying spitting things that had stolen her adjutant and killed her pilots and might kill her career, or just her body—why would she do *anything* but try to smash the source of that tide, if she could do it?

"I appreciate your candor, Councilor," she said, smooth, ice to hide the rage in her throat and chest, the burning engine of it. "In a moment I will send in my chief navigation officer, who will help you pinpoint on our maps the known incursion points. I have one more question for you: does your Station have *fast* ships? We may need all the help we can get."

"You would need to speak to Councilor Onchu of the Pilots to coordinate such a use of our resources, and she has reason to wish to keep them for herself," said the Councilor, beginning to lean forward, showing interest for the first time. "Councilor Onchu disapproves of even my small effort here with you, when you—in all your great power, O Teixcalaan—should have been enough to keep these monsters from our home. She is a little busy, at this moment."

Nine Hibiscus was about to snap at him, tell him that insulting all of Teixcalaan was not about to save his Station—but before she could, her cloudhook covered one of her eyes with green, green and white, Two Foam calling to her from the bridge: Swarm was talking to them again. Talking to them, and asking for her.

————

Over the static of narrowcast communication from Peloa-2, Twenty Cicada's voice had the particular edge that Nine Hibiscus remembered from some of their very first deployments together—a rapid, vivid, sudden prolixity that she'd most often heard when he was sleep-deprived, overworked, and absolutely sure of the shape of the universe because he'd seen the pattern of it. At least he wasn't calling her *Mallow*. Or *my dear*—if he ever did that again, she was going to kill him *first* before anything else had the privilege of breaking her heart.

He was talking, of course, with Dzmare and Three Seagrass, who had managed to take over the comms console in her absence. Two Foam stood next to them, sharply observant, as if she was waiting for the envoy or the Stationer to commit sufficient treason that she could cut the comm line entirely. Nine Hibiscus had come in on the tail end of a sentence: "—have a fair certainty that I understand not only how they communicate without speaking, Envoy, but also how they communicate faster than we can track—it's not *speech* at all, it's a networked collectivity."

"They share minds?" asked Dzmare, right as Three Seagrass

said, "They share *memory?*" at the same moment. She and Dzmare abruptly stared at each other, like they had some deep secret between them.

Dzmare said, "Minds *or* memory. If you can tell—"

"I can't," Twenty Cicada said. "Certainly not yet, at least—at the moment we're still *drawing* at each other, and they find me and my lack of networked connectivity profoundly disturbing, by the way—and what would memory even be like in a collective network of minds?"

"Mahit?" asked Three Seagrass, as if she expected Dzmare to know the answer to that entirely philosophical question.

Nine Hibiscus had more important questions to ask. "Swarm," she said, as warm as she could make it over the tinny-sounding void of space between them. "I'm sorry I wasn't available immediately—*how did you figure this out?*"

"*Yaotlek,*" Twenty Cicada said, and he managed to make her title sound like a name, sound like *her* name, he was that satisfied with himself and that glad to hear from her. "It's the fungus. That's how. They give it to their babies, and it—wakes them up, that's as close as I can tell. They drew me a picture—a small one of them being fed it, and then being connected to all the other ones with these fractal networks. It's some sort of telepathy drug—or a parasite that's gone symbiotic—what I wouldn't give for a team of *ixplanatlim* and a research institute, do we know anyone on *Weight for the Wheel* who has a hobby studying parasitic fungi—"

". . . I've never asked that question," Nine Hibiscus found herself saying, wondering if anyone would have a hobby like that *deliberately,* especially on a Fleet ship, which was determinedly free of fungi whenever possible. "I have no idea. The same fungus that killed that medical cadet, you think it makes them a—hive mind?"

"The very same. It wasn't Six Rainfall's fault that he died—I *still* think he had a massive anaphylactic reaction—and besides, our enemies don't inject the stuff, they *eat* it."

"An entirely organic way of preserving memory," said Dzmare, interrupting them in a low, fascinated tone. Nine Hibiscus ignored her. Hadn't Twenty Cicada just said that it wasn't *memory* the aliens shared, but minds?

"Not sabotage, then, to have that fungus ride along into our ship," she said. It wasn't quite a question.

"Not on purpose, no," said Twenty Cicada. "But nuance entirely escapes me, Mallow, I'm working in *rebuses,* and they're talking—or singing—to one another all inside their enormous fungal hive mind—I have an idea. You won't like it."

Nine Hibiscus wanted to laugh, to hug him, to *have him back on their ship.* "What is this idea that I won't like?"

"I think I am going to eat this fungus," said her adjutant, her dearest friend, her second-in-command for more than twenty years. "And then I'll be able to talk to them directly."

It was the worst idea Nine Hibiscus had ever heard.

[. . .] military applications seem a logical extension of algorithmic information-sharing processes already in use in law enforcement. While the interface for a pilot is necessarily more limited than what is available to one of the Sunlit (allowing for flexibility in time-of-use instead of relying on always-on algorithms), initial tests of shared proprioception are promising. Given the processing capabilities of Shard interface, Science strongly believes that Shards would be a first wide-deployment location for this new technology [. . .]

> —from "Report on Human-Algorithmic Interfaces:
> Military Applications," prepared by the *ixplanatl*
> team of Two Kyanite (Principal Investigator),
> Fifteen Ton, and Sixteen Felt, submitted to
> and approved by Science Minister Ten Pearl

* * *

The statistical chance of imago-integration failure leading to irreversible psychological and/or neurological damage is 0.03%, or three instances in every ten thousand. Heritage and Life Support both consider this level of risk acceptable.

> —from *Imago Surgery: What to Expect*, pamphlet
> distributed as part of routine medical evaluation
> before implantation of an imago-machine

EIGHT Antidote lost twenty minutes trying to find a Shard berthed somewhere in Nasturtium Terminal. There was nothing that looked like the sliver of tumbling sharp-edged glass that he thought a Shard should be, based on all of the specs he'd seen in the Ministry of War, the shape of glitter-point single-pilot fighters scattered over the black of a cartograph table. Twenty minutes before he remembered that almost all Shards would be inside a larger Fleet ship, hanging in berths.

He didn't need a Shard, exactly. He needed a Shard pilot, who would let him *into* a Shard.

That was worse, because how was he going to find a pilot—he couldn't go into a *bar,* he couldn't call up the Ministry and ask—and he was losing time every moment. Every minute he stood lost in the chaos of Nasturtium Terminal, Nineteen Adze's order to commit the Fleet to the total destruction of a whole planet got closer and closer to reaching the *yaotlek.* His own order was so far behind.

Eventually he found himself lurking behind the Information mail kiosk again, out of eyeshot of the *asekretim,* trying to imagine how he could get onto a Fleet ship. Maybe he could enlist? He wasn't old enough, but he could pretend to be . . . until someone looked up his genetic print and found out that he was the imperial heir and returned him to Palace-Earth like a lost kitten. That wouldn't work. He could maybe—climb into a crate being loaded onto a Fleet ship? Stow away?

All of his ideas were out of the *stupidest* episodes of holodramas, the ones he always turned off.

And then, as if he'd made them up, two Fleet soldiers walked right around the Information kiosk and straight toward him. They were both tall and had long dark hair in military-style tight queues, and the one on the left had, right below the patch on her sleeve with the emblem of the Second Legion—that binary star-system in mutual orbit was one of the easiest to recognize—a metallic triangle, all of its lines curved as if it was in motion. She was a Shard pilot. Right here. It seemed impossible. He needed one, and one appeared—except. Except it was the Shards which took the mail on fastest-courier override through the jumpgate mail-system, when the destination was the Fleet.

He had made this soldier up, in a way.

He'd made her *come to the kiosk to take his message to the Fleet,* and she'd just picked it up.

Eight Antidote swallowed. Straightened up to his full height, and wished he could be dressed like the imperial heir Eight Antidote, and not the errand runner Eight Antidote. But he didn't have anything but himself. He intercepted the soldiers on an angle, and stopped directly in front of them, making himself a nuisance that would either be tripped over or paused for.

"Honorable pilots," he said, not quite knowing whether *honorable* was the right respectful honorific, but he was about to demand a favor from them so he figured it would do. "I am the imperial associate His Excellency Eight Antidote, and I would be very grateful if you would allow me access to your ship for a short moment."

The two soldiers glanced at each other, and back at him. One of them—not the pilot, her friend—said, "You're *who,* kid?"

Eight Antidote gritted his teeth. "I am Eight Antidote. Heir to the sun-spear throne and the rule of all Teixcalaan. If you'd like, I'm sure your cloudhook will show you holos of me, for a visual comparison. I need access to your ship . . . Well. Her ship." He pointed with his chin at the Shard pilot. "I need a Shard."

"This is definitely the weirdest thing that's happened to me since we got drunk on Kumquat at that *really* horrible bar on Xelka Station," said the soldier. Eight Antidote really didn't want to know what Kumquat was, aside from a fruit. Or whether it could be an alcoholic fruit.

"What do you need a Shard *for?*" asked the Shard pilot, which was a lot better than anecdotes about getting drunk. Eight Antidote hoped that she'd told her friend about the Shard trick, because otherwise her friend was going to find out right now, in the middle of Inmost Province Spaceport.

"I know," he said, "that Shard pilots can feel each other when you're inside your ships. Feel, and talk maybe. Over impossible distances. Over jumpgates."

The pilot's face had gone statue-still, like a mask. "How did you come by this information?" she said.

Eight Antidote told the truth. It seemed the most effective method. "From the Minister of War Three Azimuth, in private conference." Not in private conference *with him,* but it was close enough.

". . . If you are really *that* Eight Antidote," the Shard pilot said, slowly, consideringly—and her friend interrupted her.

"Four Crocus, I am *sure* the kid who's the imperial heir is, like, one indiction old. If that. This guy's too old."

"Look it *up,*" Eight Antidote said, pleading. If they wouldn't believe him—if he was stopped *now,* he was never going to get a chance like this again, and half-done interstellar mail fraud was far worse than successful interstellar mail fraud. "Please. I need this. I'll order you as the heir to the Teixcalaanli Empire if I have to, honorable pilots, but I don't want to have to. Please."

The pilot Four Crocus did something with her cloudhook, her eyes moving very fast, shuddering in their sockets. Rapid-search.

". . . He looks right," she said. "And. And you don't know what it's been like, Thirteen Muon, in the Shard-sight these past few days. If he wants to see it—if the Minister sent him to see it—I have to get this message out, but I'll show him a Shard."

"It's on your head," said Thirteen Muon. "But you know I don't *stop* you, I never stop you, we'd never have any fun if I did."

"This way, Your Excellency," said Four Crocus, and Eight Antidote followed her and her fellow soldier back into the maze of Nasturtium Terminal's ships.

————

The Shard was smaller than he'd imagined it would be. It wasn't inside a Fleet ship after all—Four Crocus was on mail-courier duty, some complex sort of punishment or possibly reward that Eight Antidote couldn't understand from her conversations with Thirteen Muon while they walked, and thus she and her ship were right in the spaceport, not hanging in a Shard-berth inside her usual ship. That ship was the *Exultation*-class medium cruiser *Mad With Horizons* of the Second Legion, and it was waiting for her three jumpgate-trips away from the Jewel of the World, and from what it sounded like, she couldn't wait to get back and was worried about going back at the same time.

But for now her Shard nestled in Nasturtium Terminal like a splinter of glass stuck in a palm, ready to be caught up in one of the spaceport's skynets and launched orbitward. It was big enough for one grown person to fit in, if they didn't move too much. Eight Antidote touched its side. The metal was cool and smooth. He knew that the little ship could orient itself in any direction, on any axis, and the pilot would hang in the center, in her capsule, gravityless and free.

"Wait with him," said Four Crocus to Thirteen Muon. "Ten minutes, no more. I need to ask a favor from whoever else is on mail duty—this message is *really* urgent, and I don't know how long His Excellency is going to want to experience Shard-sight—so the next ship in line can take it through the jumpgate."

Eight Antidote was glad that Four Crocus took her job so seriously. He wished he could do something like—give her a commendation. Maybe he could, when he was Emperor, if she remembered him. That message—*his order*—needed to leave now. Even if it meant he had to spend an excruciating ten minutes under the supervision of Thirteen Muon, who clearly hadn't encountered a child since they'd been one themselves, and thought all children were interested mostly in star handball players (Eight Antidote didn't care) or star musicians that sold out enormous concert venues and made kids scream a lot (Eight Antidote *really* didn't care).

Eventually, out of agonized frustration at waiting, sure that at any moment someone would either set off an *incendiary device* or come to collect him and throw him back into his rooms in the palace like they were a jail, he asked what Thirteen Muon did in the Second Legion. This seemed to be a relief to both of them: Thirteen Muon was an engineering specialist who spent most of their time working on better ways to repair starship hulls, and Eight Antidote knew absolutely nothing about hand-held microthrusters for close navigation in zero gravity, which meant he could actually *concentrate* without vibrating out of his skin with impatience, because he had to pay attention if he wanted to understand anything Thirteen Muon was saying.

Even so, when Four Crocus finally came back, he cut Thirteen Muon off directly. "I need to go inside," he said to her. "I need to be inside Shard-sight, Pilot Four Crocus." And then, feeling himself blush with frustration at needing to ask for *everything*, "I need you to show me how."

Four Crocus glanced at Thirteen Muon, and then back to him. "Are you sure?" she asked. "It's a lot easier than you think. It's a lot *worse* than you think."

"He's a kid, Four Crocus, even if he actually is who he says he is—you came down to the Jewel of the World on leave and called me up to go get smashed because of what you said happened to you the last time you were in Shard-sight, and you're going to put a kid through that?" asked Thirteen Muon, and Eight Antidote really, really didn't have time for some kind of adult argument about whether this would be *good for him* or not, or whatever else their argument was about. He didn't understand it, and he didn't want to.

"Show me," he repeated. "Now. It's an order, Pilot."

"You'll need my cloudhook, Your Excellency," Four Crocus said. "And you'll need to be inside the Shard—Shard-sight works off of any cloudhook with the programming, but the *Shard trick*—I can't believe they're calling it that, it sounds like we're doing it on purpose—the Shard trick takes too much processing power for a little thing like a cloudhook. Or a mind. You need the ship." Her hand was on the hull of her Shard, stroking it like she would stroke a pet that needed to be quieted. "She's a good ship," she went on. "My Shard."

Very seriously, Eight Antidote said, "I believe you," because Four Crocus seemed to need to hear it.

She took a deep breath, like an orator about to begin a poem at court. "All right. Let's—get this over with. Fuck, but I really hope you're who you seem to be, because otherwise this is absolutely going to get me kicked out of the Shard corps—"

Inside, there was hardly space for one person, let alone two. Four Crocus showed him where to sit. Where to put his hands to call up the Shard's engine and onboard targeting AI without actually triggering a takeoff sequence. And then she settled her cloudhook over his left eye. It was too big, of course—he had to tilt his head to keep it exactly settled—but it worked just like his own. The interface was the same, except overlaid with a hundred commands and programs he'd never seen. Fleet hardware with Fleet programming. It was terrifying. All of this was. But he'd left being scared somewhere outside the Shard, somewhere in the boredom of waiting for Four Crocus to come back. All he had left was being cold. He thought he might be shivering.

"It's like a kaleidoscope," Four Crocus murmured. "You might throw up at first. People do. I did. But you'll see. You'll see what's *happening* to us. Ready?"

He nodded. He realized, for the first time in his life, that he had no idea what was about to happen to him.

"Wake up the ship, then," Four Crocus said, "and when the programming comes up, say yes to everything."

She got out of her Shard, and the shipglass hood of the pilot's chamber clicked shut behind her. Eight Antidote was alone. His hands on the controls—

He executed the sequence. Felt the ship come awake under him, a thrum, an impatience. Half his vision went black with starfields—the cloudhook coming online, some version of Shard-sight—there was a flicker of a prompt in the corner of that field, a *yes?* And he said *yes,* one blink—

And fell into the void, tumbling, thrown from himself as far as he had ever been. Into the void, and into how it was screaming.

————

"What *good* would that do?" asked Nine Hibiscus. "Even if you lived through it, which fuck knows if you would—"

"It's a system," said the static-distorted voice of Twenty Cicada. "It's a distributed system, and it's out of balance because they don't understand how we can be people and not be part of it. It'd do—a lot of good, Mallow. To have a—foreign graft."

Mahit watched the *yaotlek*'s face as she grappled with the basic Teixcalaanli horror of *artificial augmentation of the mind*. It was the one thing she never had quite understood—the *depth* of their cultural taboo, the central reason behind why Yskandr-the-man had died: he'd offered Emperor Six Direction the imago-technology, and neither the Ministry of Science nor Nineteen Adze could countenance what they seemed to understand as a fundamental corruption of the self.

<An imago is nothing like what that man is about to do to himself,> Yskandr murmured in the back of her mind. <If he lives, he won't even be human. He'll be part of something *else*.>

Isn't that what they say about us? she asked him. *That we aren't human, really, us barbarians with our mind-sharing technology—*

<Some of them,> Yskandr said, and he was all the old Yskandr, the one who had seduced an Emperor with the promise of continuity of memory. <But only some.>

Nine Hibiscus said, "Swarm. Your religion doesn't require you to balance the entire starfucked universe all by yourself."

"Who else would try?" said Twenty Cicada, and Mahit shivered, a violent little shudder of the muscles in her back.

"Do you think he's right?" Three Seagrass said to her, almost too low to hear. "They're a collective? Is it like—you?"

"Stationers are *chains*," Mahit said, "lines, not—he's describing a fractal web of minds, that's nothing like—yes, I think he *could* be right, it would make sense with how they always seem to know where their other ships are, with no lag over time. He could be."

Three Seagrass reached for Mahit's hand, caught it in hers. Mahit hadn't expected it—hadn't expected Three Seagrass to touch her at all, in public. But she didn't pull away. No one was paying attention to them right now. Not when they could be listening to the *yaotlek* and her adjutant argue about whether he should functionally join the enemy forces, biochemically, mentally, entirely, in hopes of being able to stop a war. And Three Seagrass's fingers were warm and tight on hers, like an anchor in a spinning world.

"If he does it," Three Seagrass said, "and he's right, and he lives—then he'll have achieved a kind of first-contact negotiation no Teixcalaanlitzlim has ever managed."

". . . Are you jealous?" Mahit found herself asking.

"I'm not brave enough to be jealous," said Three Seagrass, and looked away.

———

He died twice before he learned to talk. The worst experiences were the loudest, the strongest: they drew Shard-pilot minds like a black hole draws mass. A Shard dissolving from outside in, all of its shipglass coated with black squirming oil, liquid, thick, the ship-AI alarms all screaming at once and then silenced, and then the pilot himself screaming and screaming and silenced—and even before Eight Antidote could think, could stop tumbling end over end, made of a thousand minds and two thousand eyes, gyroscopic, ever-shifting

(how did anyone survive this, how did anyone learn to be this kind of pilot, to *feel everyone near them*—)

before he could find himself in the midst of the cacophony, he was spinning in a rictus of fear, engines cut, some other Shard-pilot's blanked-out panic in his throat as her Shard was struck by the edge of a three-ringed, slick-grey spinning wheel of a ship and she saw the flat pockmarked side of the asteroid coming up fast and faster and faster and *I love you I've always loved you remember me* and nothing. An afterimage of fire.

Two deaths, and almost a third—the spiral-caught tug of horror, a near miss of energy cannon, friendly fire in all its blue death right in front of his face—but that one wasn't a death, and Eight Antidote somehow found enough of himself to scream in words.

To weep and scream and say, *Stop, stop, whoever is carrying a courier message from Three Azimuth, stop, please, wait.*

And from a thousand minds and two thousand eyes: *What? Who are . . . ? Where?* Some attention, a scattering. Not all of them were falling apart. Not all of them were dying: some of them were just—flying, or fighting, or being together, and the nearer ones to him—in his own sector of space, he thought, snatch of coherency, *It's only the worst things that go all the way through accidentally*—heard him, and knew he wasn't Four Crocus, and wanted to know why.

Please, he said. He didn't know if he was speaking out loud or if he was thinking. *I'm Eight Antidote—the old Emperor's ninety-percent clone—I need to stop that message. It's wrong. It's false.*

And he tried, as hard as he could, not to think, *But you're dying, and it's horrible, and what if Three Azimuth and Nineteen Adze were right, and that genocide order is the only way to stop it?*

Because if he thought *that,* they'd never believe him.

———

Nine Hibiscus was pacing the bridge, back and forth, as if some internal mechanism inside the massive curves of her could not be still and talk to her adjutant at the same time. Mahit couldn't quite believe the degree to which the conversation they were having was public, where she and Three Seagrass and half the officers on the bridge could all hear how it flitted back and forth through the long shape of friendship, trust, arguments they'd clearly had a hundred times before, but were no longer theoretical, no longer abstract. But how could it be private, when

Twenty Cicada was down in a killing-desert and Nine Hibiscus was where she belonged, on the bridge of the ship he had kept running for her? Mahit imagined him with the tendrils of white fungus in their plastic cube, balanced on his palm. The sun would be finally beginning to set on Peloa-2 by now. She wondered if the aliens had claws to his throat or if they'd gone back to their own ship to wait, or retreat, or be smug (if they were capable of smugness) at having convinced a Teixcalaanlitzlim to ingest a poison deliberately.

She imagined how he would open the box, and put the fungus on his tongue, and be prepared to die, or to solve the problem, exactly as he had in the medbay of *Weight for the Wheel*. Imagined that, and found that Yskandr was thinking of Six Direction—or she was thinking of Six Direction—fever-flushed, worn to bones and eyes by age and illness. Prepared to die, or solve the problem, even if it meant he was not himself any longer by making use of a Lsel imago-machine.

Is it good to know that he wasn't the only Teixcalaanlitzlim who would make an attempt like this? she asked, forming the question deliberately in the empty mirrored room of their mind.

<I miss him,> Yskandr told her, which was a sideways answer. The rush of grief and longing and pride was clearer—*Yes*, he was saying, *but he never would have been in a situation like this one, so who knows.*

Nine Hibiscus was a shadow passing in front of the shipglass forward viewports, her silhouette hiding and revealing the still-present shape of that alien ship that had brought the negotiators down to Peloa-2. It hovered and spun, and she paced. Argued.

When Darj Tarats emerged from the little room he'd been taken off to, accompanied by one of the other bridge officers—Mahit *thought* that was the navigation officer, but she couldn't remember his name or what exactly he did—she was almost as surprised as she'd been by his presence at all. It was so much easier to not think of him. To not feel Yskandr recoil—to recoil herself, ashamed and angry and afraid.

"Councilor," she said, trying to let *everyone* know he was present. All of the Teixcalaanlitzlim on the bridge turned to look at him, and at her—all except Nine Hibiscus. She had better things to think about, clearly.

"Dzmare," he said to her, and approached. She found that she was standing up, as if she was going to back away—found that her hand was still in Three Seagrass's hand and saw Tarats's eyes go to that link, a diving glance that seemed to fundamentally satisfy him; his mouth curved into a brittle and vicious smile. In their own language, he said, "I see, now, what you have been doing. Why you were so *willing* to go with this woman—she offered you more than just a respite from Aknel Amnardbat and her covetousness of your imago-machine, didn't she? Something *nicer.*"

<Let me,> Yskandr said—and Mahit did. She was too angry to do anything but acquiesce. It felt like falling away into herself; her center of gravity shifted, the angle of her head changed. But fractionally. Less than before. They were closer together now. The trick of slipping in and out of Yskandr Aghavn or Mahit Dzmare wouldn't work, eventually. They'd be past it.

"And how many times," she said—Yskandr said, the faint drawl to his voice, the flattened Stationer consonants that came from utter confidence and too long speaking Teixcalaanli—"did you tell my predecessor that the seduction of empire could go both ways?"

Oh, she hoped no one else on this ship spoke enough Stationer to notice her playing games with Tarats—throwing all that long epistolary history between him and Yskandr back at him, to see if he'd flinch—and making herself seem like a spy with no loyalties to anyone at all, not Lsel and not Teixcalaan, while she did it. (She hoped Three Seagrass knew as little Stationer as she claimed to. That was the core of it. She didn't want to break whatever it was that they had managed to salvage between them. Not for Darj Tarats.)

"Look where it got him," spat Tarats, and gestured at Mahit

as if *she* was the affront to all his sensibilities. "Look where it's getting you."

"And where is that?" Yskandr said, with her mouth. "Where exactly are we, that you are not? Dependent on the actions of Teixcalaan to save or destroy us—how has anything changed?"

She'd never had the continuation of an argument that she'd not been present for, before. Her hands ached, prickled. Burned. *Careful,* she thought, but she didn't exactly want him to be careful. Didn't want, herself, to be careful. Only to win. She wished she knew what winning would look like—

"All of your line," said Tarats, vicious, "have no core of loyalty to rely on—if one of you ever did, the rest of the line would expose it to vacuum and wither it. Perhaps Amnardbat had the right idea after all."

Mahit—her, not Yskandr, Yskandr was a glimmer of horror and fascination—lifted her burning, insensible hand to slap him across the face.

———

Shard-sight was a cacophony; it was the chaos and movement and noise of Inmost Province Spaceport magnified by orders of magnitude, and Eight Antidote barely felt like he existed in the huge flow of it. The single point of *him*—where he was, his body, his life and what he knew—he kept losing *track*. He died again, caught in someone's firefight with a spinning ship, a burst of savage triumph as that pilot threw themselves *into* the enemy, becoming a spear, a piece of shrapnel caught in the heart of those whirling rings, an explosion. It hurt. It hurt every time.

And he kept saying, *Please. Listen to me. I need you to stop that message. One of you has it—one of you is carrying it through a jump-gate, one of you is about to carry it—and it's worse. It's worse than this. It's false and wrong and I am the heir to Teixcalaan and I am telling you if you let that message reach the battlefront all of this death will be a prelude—*

It wasn't words, exactly. It was feeling. Thinking *at,* or through, the whirl of eyes.

And at last, coming back to him: a singular voice, a person, his Shard on direct vector toward a jumpgate discontinuity, far (Still far! Still perhaps far enough!) from the dying of his fellow pilots. A voice unused to hesitance, and hesitant now, asking him, *If you're Eight Antidote, if you're that kid from the holovids and the newsfeeds, if you're the kid who was covered in our Emperor's blood when he died for us, then promise me you mean it. Promise me that if I lose this message, the way we are dying will stop.*

A silence, in the kaleidoscope. Another scream, stifled; Eight Antidote couldn't think of where his eyes were, or what eyes really were, if they did not feel everything at once. A *waiting* silence.

I promise, he said, meaning it, and not knowing if his promise was a lie.

Tarats's cheek was a stinging red where Mahit had slapped it. He lunged for her, a forward motion that seemed to be all teeth, his hands still restrained at the wrist. She darted backward, and Three Seagrass—amazed and horrified and utterly delighted, all at once, which was pretty much how Mahit doing anything made her feel, really—stepped in front of her. The Councilor from Lsel towered over her by a foot and a half. His chest was very narrow. Three Seagrass was narrow herself, but she was also a good forty years younger than Darj Tarats, and she figured if she had to, she could *probably* knock him over. It would be an enormous diplomatic faux pas, but what *wasn't,* currently? Everything about this bridge right now was a complete mess. All protocol dissolved! There wasn't an iota of Information Ministry training that covered tripartite negotiations from the bridge of a Fleet flagship, where one of the negotiating parties wasn't even human and one of the others wasn't Teixcalaanli, and *none* of the parties were Information agents except the negotiator. She should write a procedure manual.

If she lived long enough to be that bored.

Tarats backed off. Ah, so he was willing to attack Mahit, but not some Teixcalaanlitzlim. That was useful to know.

"*Yaotlek*," said Two Foam—the comms officer sounded agonized, having to interrupt her commander *again*, especially while she was still talking to Twenty Cicada down on Peloa-2. Three Seagrass turned to see what had caught Two Foam's attention *now*, and was entirely surprised by the person who had entered the bridge: a soldier with the bright pointed triangle of a Shard pilot on his sleeve, who was openly weeping.

She'd wept, of course. In public, even. And been embarrassed and horrified by it, or else felt entirely appropriate, because she'd been in *mourning*. But she'd never once wept like this man was weeping, endlessly and continuously, and come to report to her superior while she was doing it.

Nine Hibiscus turned to see the soldier, and Three Seagrass watched her face go grey under the space-kissed bronze of her cheeks. "Hold on," she said, still to Twenty Cicada. "Don't do *anything* while I'm not paying attention, Swarm, that's an order—Pilot. Pilot, what's your name? What's wrong?"

She came toward him, and he turned his face up to her like he was a flower planted too deep in the shade, reaching for sunlight. "Shard Pilot Fifteen Calcite, *yaotlek*," he said, without ceasing to cry. It seemed to be something that was *happening* to him, an autonomic process which did not deter him from attempting to report to his superior. The degree of loyalty Nine Hibiscus commanded was intense. Radiant.

He went on: "Shard-sight is—corrupted, or too intense, or—we don't know what's happening to us exactly, *yaotlek*, but it's not like Shard-sight was when you were a Shard pilot, it's the new programming, the collective proprioception—we keep feeling each other die, and there are so *many*, and I've turned off all my programming but I can't stop thinking about it. You need to know that there's a threshold—a threshold for trauma experience, I think—where the proprioception starts a feedback loop. I'm not the only one who can't stop crying, *yaotlek*. I'm so sorry. I don't mean to insult you like this."

Nine Hibiscus shook her head. "I am the farthest thing from insulted, Pilot Fifteen Calcite. Tell me a little more, if you can. I know about the—afterimages, in Shard-sight. I was one of you, not so long ago. But this—when did this start? Are the Shards still operational?"

"—When more than three or four of us died near each other, and all of the casualties were running the Shard trick—I mean, the proprioception upgrade."

Three Seagrass knew she shouldn't interrupt this—but she wasn't Fleet, bound by protocol, and she had *never heard about this technology*. "The Shard trick?" she asked, loud enough to cut through the heavy silence surrounding Nine Hibiscus and her soldier, the rest of the bridge quiet save for the static of the open channel down to Peloa-2, and Twenty Cicada listening.

Every head turned to look at her. She repeated herself. "The Shard trick?"

Two Foam, behind and to her left, murmuring in what Three Seagrass suspected was the hope of getting her to *shut up*, "New technology from the Ministry of Science—it lets Shard pilots feel where each of the others are in space, and eliminates a lot of navigational lag—it's based off the algorithm for the Sunlit—"

Three Seagrass was absolutely sure she—and all of the Information Ministry—were *not* supposed to know about this particular technology. War and Science again, working together and not letting Information in on the game—let alone the Emperor and her staff—just like it had been during the near-insurrection two months ago. The same pattern of influence. She said, much louder than Two Foam had, "The Fleet is using a *mind-sharing* technology for navigational purposes?"

And heard Mahit laugh, a brittle fast noise. ". . . See, Three Seagrass?" she said, "it's not so far a step from what Teixcalaan does already to what we Stationers have done with imago-lines for generations. Except we don't let anyone go in unprepared, like this pilot has—"

And cut herself off, realizing what she'd said.

Realizing, almost certainly, that she'd admitted the existence of imago-machines without any of Yskandr Aghavn's careful dance of secrecy.

But it was too late. Councilor Tarats, all his teeth bared—she was never going to understand how Stationers smiled, and what the expression *beyond* smiling was, and where the edges could be—leaned right *over* Three Seagrass to snap something nasty and fast in Stationer. Three Seagrass caught *imago-machine* and could guess the rest: *traitor, betrayer, exposer of our proprietary secret incredibly immoral technology, fuck you and everything you stand for.* Obvious, really. Obvious, from how Mahit reacted, too—how she blanched and then shoved Three Seagrass gently out of the way to meet Tarats head-on. (Everyone on the bridge was looking at *them* now. Even the weeping Shard pilot, who had mostly devolved to sniffling.)

Mahit started whatever she was saying in Stationer—one long sentence, a snarl of consonants—and then switched, fluid and easy, to Teixcalaanli. "And, Councilor—do you *really* think I am the first to trade our technology for our continued existence? Twenty years you wrote to Yskandr, and he fooled you the entire time." Her voice was silk, slick, sliding in and out of the tonality Three Seagrass was familiar with, and she knew that she was listening in part to Yskandr Aghavn (who was—so *very* like Mahit, but not at all her, and—oh, there'd either be time for Three Seagrass to panic about which one of them she'd slept with and trusted or there wouldn't be time for anything, so that didn't matter now).

Tarats said—in perfectly understandable language, he was capable, *obviously*—"If you are saying that Aghavn created some kind of—collective mind, that's not imago-technology, Dzmare. That's an aberration. A Teixcalaanli corruption, if it exists at all."

Mahit threw her head back and laughed. "Tarats. Oh, my friend, my predecessor's friend, my patron and foil—*no*, why would we do that? When all we had to do was what you asked, and let Teixcalaan fall in love with us, and promise the Empire memory eternal in exchange for our freedom?"

"What you're doing is *sick*," Darj Tarats said, "a perversion of imago-integration—you're not Yskandr. The pretense is vulgar."

"No," Mahit said. "I'm *not* Yskandr. I would never have offered the Emperor Six Direction an imago-machine, and I would never have died for it. I would have done something else you'd despise. Teixcalaan doesn't let us stay clean. Not you, not me, not Yskandr. I'm him *enough* to be sure of that. I remember what I am. What you helped make him, and what he has made me."

The low static of the open channel that Twenty Cicada was listening through crackled. Hissed. Resolved into his voice, serene and strange. "Ah, Mallow," he said, and Nine Hibiscus spun like she'd been stung, stared at the starfields outside the bridge like they would resolve into her adjutant's face. "I won't even be the first, it seems. Lsel is far ahead of us, aren't they? But we're catching up."

"Don't," said Nine Hibiscus. But she didn't say *I order you not to*. Nor did she say *please*. Three Seagrass thought the two might have been equivalent.

"It has been the deepest honor of my life to serve with you, my dear," said Twenty Cicada. "Wish me luck."

And then that open-channel static cut off to silence. Circuit closed.

Somewhere down on Peloa-2 a man who believed that *waste* was the worst thing that could happen to a society was letting himself be devoured.

———

Even after he'd promised, even after he knew he'd—succeeded, if success meant feeling some Shard pilot far distant from anywhere he'd ever been take a War Ministry–sealed infofiche stick and crush it, stamp it under his heel against the side of his cockpit—smash the battle-flag sigil, the sun all gone to spears, nothing left of illumination except the gold sealing wax—the splintered pieces floating up from around his boot, gravityless, sparkling—even after all of that, Eight Antidote couldn't quite *stop* being in Shard-sight. He was spread out so far. There were so many Shards, and he didn't know which way was up, or if *up* had meaning, or if *he* had meaning, really: he was only himself, and there wasn't a lot of himself compared to dying and desperation and the endless shifting overwhelming beauty of stars and void and moving all together, like a murmuration of birds.

He was scared, and proud. Those things were his, he was sure. But they were the Shard pilots', too, and it wasn't enough to be scared and proud. He felt like he was dissolving. Salt dropped in water.

Death and pain drew Shard-sight, but so did a sufficient number of Shards together: and there was one of those now, a center-point of a swarm, a group that knew one another even without the collective *feeling* that made the Shard trick work over impossible boundaries, impossible distances. That group hung suspended like a scatter of stars themselves, all around a flagship, all moving together, a shifting shield that kept the behemoth of their flagship-home hidden from easy view, easy comprehension. He caught the very edge of a name: that ship was the *Parabolic Compression*. That ship was the pride of the Twenty-Fourth Legion.

And it, and its Shards, were already—already, without ever being ordered, heedless of *anything* Eight Antidote had done or learned or promised—approaching the inhabited planetary system of the alien enemy, and they were aflame with triumph and vicious anticipation: they were going to end this all, now, together, at last—

No, Eight Antidote thought, but the word was gone, gone inside the wide stretch of linked-up minds. Too soft to hear. He wasn't enough of anything, anymore, to reach so far.

Please, no! One voice in a cacophony, in a choir of other negations, worse ones: *no, don't let me die—no, I can't do this, I am afraid—no, no, no, this cannot be happening—*

And the Shards of the Twenty-Fourth pressed forward, unafraid; unconvinced, if they'd even heard him at all.

CHAPTER NINETEEN

There is no instruction in the practice of balance that firmly forbids or firmly commands an observance: if a person chooses to bleed for the sun and stars of Teixcalaan, there is no harm in it, as long as they are willing to bleed also for the earth and water of each planet, or for the tears and saliva of a stranger, or for something so small and unimportant as a barren patch of garden.

> —from *Catena Commentary on the Practice of Balance,* vol. 3
> of 57, Anonymous Commentator G (blue text, left-hand
> side, dated to approximately one hundred Neltoc years
> post-conquest); Anonymous Commentator G writes in
> Teixcalaanli, which may be used to disambiguate them
> from Anonymous Commentator F (blue text, left-hand
> side), who writes in Neltoca. For arguments on the
> validity of F and G as separate persons, see *Catena
> Commentary on the Practice of Balance,* vol. 39 of 57.

THE war dissolved around Nine Hibiscus like spun sugar in water, too fast for her to grieve. She was *yaotlek* of this six of legions, and she was on the bridge of her flagship, and every report of the sudden hesitance of the enemy, the vanishing of attack forces, the hovering pause of three-ringed death-spitting ships, orbiting Teixcalaanli vessels now, observing and slow, instead of smashing them to pieces—every report came to her. She held them all. She spun up the cartograph strategy table and marked the position of her Fleet, the position of her Fleet's enemies, kept it updated in as close to real time as possible, while all of the crisis-flashpoint of conflict seemed to simply—stop. Hold itself in patient abeyance. The only moving piece was the Twenty-Fourth, Sixteen Moonrise's *Parabolic Compression,* and even she seemed to have slowed, surprised by the sudden lack of forceful opposition. Still moving, but—that was all right. She'd rather have the Twenty-Fourth in position if this strange détente ended, if what Swarm had done wasn't sufficient.

Whatever Swarm had done, he'd at least bought them time. She'd shouted—no, she'd *screamed* down the narrowcast band, even after he'd cut it off—screamed nonsense negation she was ashamed of, but it *hurt,* it hurt like a hole in the center of her, as if the alien acid spit was wearing her away like she was the metal of a ship. That he was either dead, or *gone,* or—not himself. Her friend. Her *dearest* friend. What was she going to do about all of his plants? About keeping the hydroponics deck in order? About that fucking Kauraanian kitten he'd been feeding? What was she supposed to *do,* other than watch the thing that she was for—prosecuting a war, in any way necessary, in all ways possible—become unnecessary, marked out in points of light?

She wanted to ask him: *Swarm. Swarm, what are you doing?* But he wouldn't respond to any message she sent. It was possible that he had simply eaten the fungus and *died* and the enemy had understood this as some sort of sufficient sacrifice.

———

No one heard him or cared to listen; all Shard-sight was grief or was single-minded determination that shut out grief and dying in a scintillation of light. Eight Antidote lost the shape of the Shards guarding the *Parabolic Compression;* died again, a simple ugly death, someone thinking so clearly *aw, fuck,* as a fast-moving piece of debris struck the side of their Shard, deformed it, cracked its bubble of shipglass from its seals—cold, shock-cold, and anger, and then quiet.

He wanted to stop. He wanted to get out. There was no out. There was no *stop.*

Except that:

—the eyes of Shard after Shard saw a sudden hesitance in the barrage of ship-dissolving acids and energy-cannon fire, a pause as if the enemy was thinking, all together, as a whole—a three-ringed ship, hardly larger than a Shard itself, hung motionless and then made a slow and lazy circle around two Shards without attacking them at all, as if trying to map their edges—alien targets vanished, leaving squirming visual discontinuity in their wakes, and Teixcalaanli hands trembled on Shard controls, hands that had been clenched so tightly they hurt as they were released—there was a stretched-out held breath, a thousand Shards and two thousand eyes trying to *feel*, to understand, to realize they were not dying any longer.

All except the Shards surrounding the *Parabolic Compression*, who did not hear, or listen, or care. Who had a purpose and a design. For whom discontinuity—even favorable discontinuity—was something to be undone, as if it had never been. Who had paused, for a moment of disbelief, the dissolve of opposition shocking to stillness—and then had heard some voice, some order, or just some heart-vicious *want* of their own, and accelerated again. Faster. Faster.

There was a convulsion. A shaking. Eight Antidote wondered if he was dying again, or if the Twenty-Fourth Legion had started the deathrain bombing and this was what it would be like—sudden light—hands—

And he looked up, dazzled, shocked back to his small singular body, as the golden featureless faceplate of a Sunlit removed Four Crocus's cloudhook from his face and scooped him out of her Shard like the stone from a peach.

When the order on the Imperial fast-courier ship arrived, sealed in one of Her Brilliance Nineteen Adze's own white-on-white seals (or a facsimile thereof, Nine Hibiscus had always heard that Nineteen Adze used animal bone for hers, but that wouldn't have gone through the transmission stations *between* jumpgates—this was a plastic copy), the order inside was almost unnecessary.

His Excellency Eight Antidote, Imperial Associate, Heir to the Sun-Spear Throne, it read, *on behalf of the government of the star-encompassing Teixcalaanli Empire, to the Yaotlek Fleet Captain Nine Hibiscus of the Tenth Legion: Teixcalaan is civilization, and it is our job to safeguard it.*

Interesting that it came in the voice of the imperial heir, not the Emperor Herself. A complex political maneuver—the Emperor commands war, her successor practices mercy. It was *very* designed, in Nine Hibiscus's opinion. Or maybe she was simply exhausted, and everything seemed to be a little beyond what mattered here on her ship, right now.

This order forbids the use of civilization-destroying weapons or tactics on the alien threat beyond Parzrawantlak Sector, including nuclear strikes on civilian-occupied planetary systems, except in cases where such weapons or tactics are the only thing standing between us and certain civilization-wide death.

There was no certain civilization-wide death. Not now. Not anymore. Not since Swarm had done what he'd done.

She looked up from the strategy table and said, "Two Foam. Send Fleet Captain Sixteen Moonrise an order to stand down—for the moment."

———

The Sunlit—there were more than one of them, of course, there were always more than one Sunlit—caught Eight Antidote by the upper arms when his legs wouldn't hold him up. The world kept spinning. Nasturtium Terminal seemed claustrophobic—but not because of how many people were in it, this time. Now it felt tiny compared to being stretched over sectors and sectors of space, so spread-thin that being all in himself again was a rush of hideously intense sensation. Eight Antidote squeezed his eyes shut. It didn't help. Even the reddish dark behind his eye-lids was so *present*.

One of the Sunlit said, "Your Excellency. We have orders to form an escort for you back to the palace."

Of course they did. The Emperor was going to *kill* him. Or maybe she'd let Three Azimuth do it. He was probably—definitely—a disruptive person now. ". . . You have my permission," he managed to say. His voice sounded like a drunk person's voice, not steady, sounds blurring into each other. Besides, they didn't need permission. They were going to take him anyway.

Distantly, he heard Four Crocus ask, "Did you get what you needed, Your Excellency?"

He didn't know what to tell her. *Maybe* wasn't good enough. Yes, he'd achieved what he'd set out to do, and no one would ever get that order from Three Azimuth to kill a planet. And no, he didn't think he'd made any difference at all.

"I hope so," he managed instead, and let the cool gold-gloved hands of the Sunlit lead him away.

———

None of them expected to hear from Twenty Cicada again, Three Seagrass especially. That goodbye had been so final. So absolutely exquisite. She wished she had recorded it—she could have written him such a poem. She might. She might write for him, since it looked like they all might live, at least for long enough to compose a single set of verses.

(Maybe not long enough for an epic, or anything with a complex caesura-dependent rhyme scheme—there was still the problem of Darj Tarats, and who knew how long the détente Twenty Cicada had bought them would last?)

So when that channel stuttered back into static, *open,* two-way communication instead of just the one-way frequency Nine Hibiscus had shouted down, Three Seagrass was not only surprised but shocked: she'd been almost sure Twenty Cicada was *dead*. Or so far transformed that it was a functional equivalency.

But there was his voice. It was static-distorted, still, but also—*off*. The rhythms of his phrasing were gone to syncopation, like he was trying to remember speech and assembling it from first principles. His voice flooding the bridge, because Nine Hibiscus hadn't adjusted the volume on that comms feed *at all*.

"Singing," he said, and then there was a pause. And again, "*Singing*, oh—we—"

Nine Hibiscus said, "Swarm?" with a kind of broken hope that made Three Seagrass cringe.

"Yes," he said. "Mostly yes—we are, it's appropriate, that name. Hello. Mallow. Hello, we. Our—*Weight for the Wheel*, Mallow, love her for us. For—me. And. We—us and the others, we—want to establish. Is there the envoy?"

"Yes," said Three Seagrass. "I'm here."

"And is there the other one? The—memory-person. The. *The spook and her pet.*" He sounded like he'd found the phrase somewhere in memory, a single phrase recalled all together. "The Stationer."

"I'm here too," Mahit said. Nine Hibiscus was staring at them, her eyes glitter-wet with tears she was clearly refusing to shed.

"We—we want to establish. Diplomatic protocol. For a period of cease-fire."

Three Seagrass looked to Nine Hibiscus, wordless, asking for permission. Nine Hibiscus nodded, a bare fraction of a movement.

"We accept a cease-fire," she said. "What sort of diplomatic protocol did you have in mind, Twenty Cicada?" Using his name, in case there was enough of him left that his name meant something.

"Send—send us people. People to prove we are people. The memory-sharers. To talk with."

Mahit said, "Stationers, you mean."

A long pause.

"Yes?" said Twenty Cicada. Or what had been Twenty Cicada. "Stationers. Pilots. Sunlit. All. *All.* And we are people. If. We are singing, *if.*"

All. Everyone. Everyone, Teixcalaanli or not, who had ever been part of some kind of shared mind. Three Seagrass looked at Mahit, helpless with how little she understood of what this *meant.* What kind of person could be useful here.

"Yes," said Mahit, and nodded to Three Seagrass. "The diplomats will be humans who understand—collectivity."

If it was even possible for anyone to understand the kind of collectivity Twenty Cicada had rendered himself up to. Three Seagrass wasn't so sure.

And then Two Foam said, "*Yaotlek*—Sixteen Moonrise won't answer our comms. She's still on approach target to the alien system. Approach and moving *fast.*"

Watching Nine Hibiscus try to reorient herself from talking to what was left of her adjutant to deal with whatever Fleet Captain Sixteen Moonrise was doing was like watching a warship attempt to reverse thrust; a wrench, a straining, not entirely effective. It made Three Seagrass wince.

"She's what?" asked the *yaotlek.*

"Still on attack vector," Two Foam repeated. "With shatter-bombs primed. She hasn't acknowledged any of the stand-down orders you sent—"

Nine Hibiscus's face was a mask. "They're not my orders. They're the *Emperor's.* Send it again. Tell her if she continues on this course, she is in direct insubordination to the Emperor of all Teixcalaan."

Two Foam turned back to the console. Her eyes flickered behind her cloudhook; her hands flew through the projected communication-space of the Fleet. There was a strangled, hideous silence; even the creature on the other end of the line, *Swarm*, it was easier for Three Seagrass to think of him as *Swarm* and not Twenty Cicada now, draw some separation—even he was quiet.

"No acknowledgment," said Two Foam, at last. "The Twenty-Fourth is speeding up. She doesn't—want to hear us, *yaotlek*."

Three Seagrass thought, *She doesn't want to hear us, or the aliens, or anything but her own course of action.* And then, bright and vivid and nauseating: *This is going to be the shortest cease-fire in the history of the Empire.*

She watched the mask of Nine Hibiscus's face crack, an internal decision made, one that flayed her as raw as a barbarian, all of her features twisted in certainty and grief at once, and couldn't figure out anything at all she could say—and she'd thought herself a negotiator!—that would change anyone's course now.

———

It was easier if Nine Hibiscus thought of the static-scattered voice on the other side of the commlink down to Peloa-2 as someone already a ghost. Or—equally heart-flaying, equally absurd—some other person she had never known, who happened to share a name with her dearest friend, the adjutant who had served with her for more than two indictions. A coincidence. No more, no less.

It was easier, and it made it possible for her to ask him—ask *it*, ask *them*, ask the thing down on Peloa, whatever it was—to ask without her voice catching, without weeping: "Swarm, I need you to do me a favor. You, and the rest of whatever you are now. It's a favor, and it's a sign of our good faith in whatever cease-fire you've brokered. Do you hear me?"

She shouldn't have called him *Swarm*. It was both too intimate and too appropriate now.

"We hear you," he said, and aside from the static and the use of a plural pronoun, he sounded exactly the same as he always had. Casual ease. A soldier in perfect command of all of his resources, and willing to bend them to her command.

Nine Hibiscus rolled her shoulders back. Braced herself, her hands flat on the cartograph table, grounded in her ship. "I am going to give you the coordinates and approach vector of Sixteen Moonrise and the *Parabolic Compression* to the inhabited planet she is targeting," she said. "The *exact* coordinates."

"We will see her coming, then," said whatever was left of Twenty Cicada. "We will be ready for her, when she comes. Reach for her. Stretch out ourselves. Net her and crack her open, give her to the void-home—" The sound that filled the bridge was a sigh, almost a melody—a falling tone.

The sound that filled the bridge was the grim silence of her own horrified officers. Nine Hibiscus had done this once before, not so long ago. But that soldier—*she* had begged to die under her Fleet Captain's hands, rather than dissolve in alien spit-acid. And this command was something altogether different. She had to be unwavering. Unwavering, and sure, and she was still going to lose these people—lose, at least, the effortless trust they'd had in her. She was going to let her adjutant and the aliens that had devoured him and killed a planet and destroyed so many of her ships already *kill another one*. Kill a Fleet Captain, and her flagship. All those lives on the *Parabolic Compression*—were they worth the lives on that alien planet? Were they worth the preservation of this uncertain cease-fire?

Could she dishonor Twenty Cicada's sacrifice by pretending one flagship was more important than ending a war?

No. She couldn't.

Somehow she had to stop those bombs from being dropped. And if the Emperor's command wasn't enough for Sixteen Moonrise—she'd have to let the aliens do her work for her— unless—

"Adjutant," she snapped, crisp command. Calling whatever was left of Twenty Cicada back to himself. To how they had always been together: logistics and command. "I will give you these coordinates and allow the aliens to strike the *Parabolic Compression* if and only if you believe that it is possible to take out the bridge and the bridge alone. There are three thousand Teixcalaanlitzlim on that ship. They are *our people.* Don't let them go to waste for Sixteen Moonrise."

A hissing sort of silence: the open channel. And then, soft as a haunting, Twenty Cicada saying to her, "I would never, Mallow. You know that. And so *we* know that."

She gave him the coordinates.

"Do you really think the Empire and what they've just yoked themselves to is going to want a *barbarian Stationer* as one of their negotiators, Dzmare?" asked Darj Tarats. He'd come to stand next to Mahit, too close for her liking—come to stand next to her and murmur to her in Stationer as they watched a *yaotlek* of the Teixcalaanli Fleet call down a precision strike on her own forces. Mahit hadn't ever imagined such a thing to be possible. The Teixcalaan she knew—the Teixcalaan Yskandr knew, that Tarats believed in, the ever-devouring elegant maw of an empire, teeth light across the throat of every non-Teixcalaanli system, light until they bit down and broke the spine, shook a culture to nothing—*that* Teixcalaan would never have cut away a part of itself to preserve a barely cohered peace.

She thought, too, of the Fleet Captain Sixteen Moonrise, an electrum-shaded flash in the dark of her assigned quarters, come to negotiate or warn. Mahit hadn't quite put her finger on which, and now she never would, and it didn't matter—the three-ringed ships would excise all negotiation and all warning that Sixteen Moonrise might have possessed, eliminate them as an option. Preserve themselves and their planet.

<Themselves, their planet, and the rest of the *Parabolic Compression,*> Yskandr murmured. <That's some little weight on the side of this alliance being a good idea at all—that they *can* understand now that humans die and are not replaced.>

Not very easily replaced, Mahit thought, and felt her imago laugh, electric shivering all through her. *Replaced with extreme difficulty and complexity.*

Darj Tarats clicked his tongue behind his teeth. "I see," he said, as if Mahit had said anything at all. "You either believe it or you don't care whether or not it is true."

She turned to him. She wanted—she *and* Yskandr wanted, a savage little flare—to talk to him only in the language that he hated and that she loved, speak the language of his enemy, drip poetry from her mouth—but it wasn't her language. It would *never be.* She knew that as clearly as she knew anything. In Stationer, she said, "They let me negotiate a first contact, Tarats. Right along with them. Why not have a Stationer as part of the diplomatic protocol, especially as they know quite well that we are *far* better at collective memory than they are?"

"They should never have known about imago-technology," Tarats said.

Mahit took a breath. Another. Slow. "No," she said. "Quite probably not." The bright stab of pain down her ulnar nerves, again, Yskandr's vicious displeasure at her disagreement with him. "But it's done now, Councilor. Done a long time ago. The Empire knows. And we might—if Lsel led this diplomatic delegation, we might have more bargaining power than we've had in generations—"

"And the price, Dzmare? The price of putting one of our imago-lines into that—*conglomeration*—that calls itself *we?* The price of Teixcalaan wanting even more of us than our self-possession and our language and our economic independence?"

Mahit said, louder, "The price was higher when it was the whole Station smashed under those three-ringed ships, and you *know* it." She hadn't meant to shout. Hadn't meant to attract the attention of half the faces on the bridge, the ones who weren't watching the convergence of the *Parabolic Compression* and a hundred spinning ring-ships on the cartograph table.

"I have," said Darj Tarats, "spent my entire life on a ruin," and gestured with his hand, as if to encompass not only the bridge and Peloa-2 beyond it, but all Teixcalaan and all Teixca-laan's enemies. All his long project of drawing Teixcalaan past its borders into an unwinnable war, undone. Teixcalaan would not beat itself to pieces against an unassailable shore. Not here. Not this way.

It was Yskandr who said, with Mahit's tongue, "Ruins can be rebuilt in peacetime."

And it was Yskandr who helped Mahit stay on her feet and keep her face still when Tarats said, "You were a mistake, and so was your entire imago-line, and I will make sure Councilor Amnardbat knows I agree with her. There is no place for you on Lsel. Don't ever come home, Dzmare."

CHAPTER
TWENTY

The motion of a swift is an impenetrable language; as incomprehensible to me as the thoughts of a flower when it opens its petals at dawn, without memory or mind. A coherent logic and a dance, but not one I can shape within myself. All my attempts are approximation. One cannot render meaning in a language one finds meaningless; nevertheless I know there is a design, a speaking, a world just on the other side of shadow, untouchable but nonetheless real. Three years since I came home from Ebrekt, and I still dream of the swifts, running: in dreams, sometimes I understand them.

—from *Asymptote/Fragmentation*, essay cycle by
Eleven Lathe

NINE Hibiscus knew the shape of the *Parabolic Compression* without ever having set foot on its decks: knew it as she knew her own ship. *Eternal*-class flagships were all built on the same bones, the same enormous and delicately balanced armatures of steel and shipglass. The same design. She could be standing on the *Parabolic Compression*'s bridge and have the arc of vision she had now, the consoles in the same places, only the uniforms changed, exchange the Tenth for the Twenty-Fourth, one Fleet Captain for another—

Almost, almost she wished that she could make that switch. Take Sixteen Moonrise's place, her hands on the navigational controls, flying her ship on a brutal-fast trajectory through alien space, her mouth shaped around the insubordinate words—*Don't listen. Even Emperors can be mistaken. There's nothing about these enemies worth talking to—all they do is poison us, and they will poison us forever if we don't burn them out.*

Nine Hibiscus could imagine it all too easily, and not only because she had cored out her own belly with guilt when she gave Swarm the order—the *permission*—to destroy Sixteen Moonrise if he—if *they*—could. Guilt wasn't a sufficient impetus to want to die in place of one of your soldiers.

Wondering if that soldier was right, after all—now, *that* was enough to wish yourself on the bridge of a distant flagship, even as it shattered under alien energy-cannon fire: a blaze of killing-blue, pinpoint-precise (Swarm was *always* precise—bloody *fucking* stars, this was never going to stop hurting, was it), and then a sparkling cloud, glitter of glass and metal, spreading slowly in the void.

What was left of the *Parabolic Compression* slowed its arc forward. Somewhere in that glitter was all that remained of Sixteen Moonrise.

.The alien ships withdrew, as quickly as they'd appeared; whatever cease-fire they had brokered was holding. For now.

Nine Hibiscus let herself wish it hadn't, wish it as savagely and miserably as she liked—she was a *soldier*, a leader of soldiers, she was not meant to have ended a war like *this*—and then locked her wishing away, as if she'd swallowed slow poison her own self.

———

Nineteen Adze brought him a bowl of tea. It was the second-most surprising thing Eight Antidote had ever seen her do. The first had been when she hugged him, without preamble, taking him from the guiding hands of the Sunlit in *public*, in the gardens right in front of Palace-Earth, and wrapping him in her arms. She was very thin, and taller than him, and her arms were ropes of muscle. He had thought she'd throw him in prison, or just lock him in his rooms forever, which would be the political version of the same thing, but—this. A fast, savage hug. He couldn't remember when someone had hugged him last. Hugs were for little kids. *He'd* hugged Two Cartograph, Five Agate's son, when they'd stopped playing, but that wasn't the same thing at all.

The Emperor hadn't locked him up, or locked him away. She took him to her suite. Kept a hand on his shoulder, firm and guiding, even when the world slipped sideways, a shadow in a corridor resolving into the shadow of some Shard's vision of three-ringed death—a memory, he told himself, *not real,* not anymore. Took him to her suite, and told him that she'd be back in a little while, when she had finished wrapping up the day. And left him there. Unguarded. Cloudhookless. (Probably his cloudhook was going around and around on the subway still.) He could have left, or gone out the window, or—anything—

Instead he sat on a window seat behind the long white tufted couch, and stared into the early-afternoon sun on the water gardens below, and tried to remember where he was. Where the edges of him were. He didn't know if he'd ever go all the way back to just being in one place, being absolutely sure of who and where and what he was. It was dizzying and awful, and he guessed he deserved it. The afternoon stretched into evening. He slept a little. Maybe. He might have dreamed he slept, or imagined it, or remembered someone else's sleeping. But when he was all the way awake again, the world outside the window was flooded blue and fuchsia with the end of sunset.

And then the Emperor Herself came back, and sat on the windowsill with him, and handed him a bowl of tea, clear green and sweetly astringent. He wondered if she'd *made* it. It seemed like the perfectly absurd sort of thing she'd do. He drank some. His hands still worked, and so did his throat, and he tasted the tea with only the tastebuds that were absolutely and definitely his, so that—helped. It did.

He said, "I'm not sorry," because he wasn't, and because if the Emperor was going to punish him, he wanted to deserve it.

Nineteen Adze looked at him for a very long time, long enough that he wanted to blush, and cringe, and get away, even though he did none of those things. Then she nodded, as if she'd come to some satisfying conclusion, and said, "Good."

Eight Antidote blinked in surprise. "Good?"

"Good. You're sure what you did was right. You had your reasons to do it, you made a plan, you executed that plan. You didn't harm anyone else in the process, aside from scaring that Shard pilot half to death, thinking she'd gotten the imperial heir killed or brain-damaged, and she'll be all right. So: good. What did I tell you about successors?"

"That you would rather an—um. An annoying one, than a dull one."

Nineteen Adze, when she smiled, looked *more* dangerous than when she didn't. "You are *absolutely* an annoying successor, little spy. And not dull at all."

"Did it—did what I did *work*?" he asked, suddenly helpless not to.

The Emperor held out her hand, tilted it one way and then the other. Maybe so, maybe no. "What did you want to have happen?" she asked.

Eight Antidote thought about being a spy: about keeping all his own desires as close as possible, unrevealed, even when asked directly. About choosing, always, if he was going to tell. He could keep doing that. He probably *should*. He'd be an Emperor, if there was an Empire left, and he couldn't just *tell people what he wanted to have happened*, they'd use it against him—

But Nineteen Adze had told him about his ancestor-the-Emperor, and the machines from Lsel Station. About what he might have been. She'd told him that, and he'd used it against her, and yet they were both still right here.

"I wanted the Teixcalaan you told me about," he said. "Eighty times eighty years of peace, and no one deciding a whole planet is worth killing just to prove a point. I wanted—I wanted to stop

Three Azimuth's order, and I wanted to send mine instead, and I want us to win the war anyway."

"The war is ending right now, and that planetary system remains intact," said Nineteen Adze. "I expect you were part of that. What you did inside that Shard . . ."

The war is ending, she'd said, but not how, or why, and Eight Antidote realized he was shaking hard enough that tea spilled over his knuckles. The Emperor took the bowl away from him. Held it for him. "It's called the Shard trick," he started. "They can all do it. Not just me."

"Pilot Four Crocus explained in detail," said Nineteen Adze. She didn't sound pleased. It wasn't really the sort of thing a person was pleased about, Eight Antidote guessed. Technology like that. Like the Sunlit, but *more.* (He *wasn't* going to tell her that it was still going on inside his mind. He wasn't. He didn't know what she'd do. To him or in general.)

"Eleven Laurel didn't want you to know," he said instead.

"—*Ah,*" Nineteen Adze said, like he'd given her something she needed. A last part of a pattern, slotting into place. "That's useful, Eight Antidote. Thank you for that. I wasn't sure which one of them—the Minister or the Undersecretary—was responsible."

"Are you going to . . ." He didn't even know how to ask the question.

The Emperor shook her head. "No," she said. "I can watch him much more closely inside the Ministry of War than I'd ever be able to if I let him out unsupervised into the Fleet."

"And me?"

"Am I going to do something to you?"

He nodded.

She sighed. "I wish, you know, that you could trust me. But you wouldn't be you, if you did. No, Eight Antidote. No, I'm not going to do anything to you, except wait for you to grow up and take this job out of my hands."

It was only in the quiet afterward, when he'd gone back to his own room, and crawled into his bed, that he remembered what Nineteen Adze had said about Fleet Captain Nine Hibiscus and why she'd made her *yaotlek* after what she'd done on Kauraan: *not because I thought she was too dangerous to keep alive, little spy. Because I thought she might just be dangerous enough to stay alive.*

Remembered that, and couldn't fall asleep at all.

———

Everything on the hydroponics deck of *Weight for the Wheel* was green. The air felt luxurious, almost too thick for Mahit to breathe. There were flowers—lotuses, lilies—all through the rice and the vegetable gardens, mixed in like they were as necessary as calories. Probably they had been, to Twenty Cicada. This had been his kingdom. Three Seagrass had told her so, told her all about the conversation they'd had, here, when she'd been convinced that the last thing Twenty Cicada would ever do would be to let Teixcalaan allow a species as wantonly and uncaringly destructive as the aliens had seemed, to exist.

The two of them were leaning on the decorative railing. Mahit wondered who was standing where: Was she where Twenty Cicada had been, or was Three Seagrass? Whose narrative was going around again?

<Ring composition,> Yskandr told her, and she said, *Overdetermined,* back at him. Call and response.

Without prompting or preamble, only taking enough time to set her shoulders and lift her chin, like Mahit was a problem that needed as much of her headlong determination as any of the negotiation she'd done on the bridge, Three Seagrass asked her, "Do you want to come back with me?"

At least she hadn't said, *Do you want to come home with me?*

"No," Mahit told her. She couldn't look at her while she did it. "No, but—where's *back*?"

"The Jewel of the World," said Three Seagrass, which—*of*

course. There was no other real place for a Teixcalaanlitzlim, was there. "I mean. I have a flat. I have to—do the dishes. Probably talk to the Emperor Herself, too. But—if it's the City you don't want, I could—I mean, there's got to be some system out there which needs an overqualified *asekreta* and has a halfway decent poetry salon—I could get transferred. Is what. I'm saying."

"Reed," Mahit said, soft, and Three Seagrass stopped talking, turned to her, tipped her head up. Her eyes were very dark and very wide. She was still so *small.* Mahit forgot, most of the time.

She bent down, and kissed her mouth. Not for long. Not long enough to be *yes.*

"Don't do that for me," she said. "Don't leave the City. Go *home.* Do your dishes. Talk to the Emperor, if there's time after doing the dishes."

Three Seagrass snickered. It was a wet sound; the sound a person made when they were laughing but had meant to cry. "Dishes, then Her Brilliance the Edgeshine of a Knife, in that order, yes. Fine. And where will *you* go?"

"I don't know," Mahit said. It was true. There were no places left: there was no such thing as home, not for her, not any-more. Darj Tarats had taken his flitter-ship back through the Anhamemat Gate. The ceasefire Twenty Cicada had brokered extended throughout the entirety of the alien fleet, whether its prey had been Teixcalaanli warships or Lsel itself. All humans were one thing, to them: one sacrifice had, for now, bought a collective peace. Lsel had not even been touched—Mahit had heard the transmissions from Teixcalaanli supply ships passing by that proved it. And yet she believed what Tarats had told her on the bridge: if she came back to Lsel Station while he and Aknel Amnardbat were in power, she would die under their hands. One, or the other. Heritage or Miners. All safety torn up, tossed away. And for what?

Now we are exiles truly, she thought, and couldn't even muster up an internal tone of recrimination: she'd been right, all along, and Yskandr hadn't. But Yskandr would have followed Three

Seagrass back to her flat with its undone dishes, its promise of poetry salons—Yskandr would have taken that offer the *first* time she made it, three months and a war ago.

"It doesn't have to be with me," said Three Seagrass. "If that's your problem with going back to the City—that I'd—I still don't understand why you feel *half* the ways you do about how much I like you, but I promise I'm perfectly capable of pretending we don't know each other or never kissing you again, and you're still the Ambassador if the Emperor says you are, so there's work . . ."

Mahit cut her off, a hand on her shoulder, gentle as she could. "No. It's *not* you. I— Reed, I don't understand why I feel half the ways I do about how much I like you, either. But I like you a great deal."

<You could keep explaining,> Yskandr murmured. <Sometimes even Teixcalaanlitzlim learn to see us.>

I want, Mahit thought, and with that phrase felt all the tumbling headlong desire to fall, and be subsumed, and be—oh, the Teixcalaanlitzlim she'd imagined herself in all those long-ago language instruction classes when she'd called herself Nine Orchid and thought poetry would be enough to make her the kind of person that a Teixcalaanlitzlim would automatically think of as a person.

"If it's not me," Three Seagrass asked, "then—what? If you tell me you're planning to join the fungal hive mind, I'm going to be *angry* and also not believe you. You're enough people already, and you like being *a* person, not a—that."

"I'm just Mahit Dzmare," Mahit said, wry. "Imago and all. Just one person."

I want, she thought again, and Yskandr finished for her. <To go home.>

No such place.

She tried again. "Three Seagrass, I want—work, and I want—things I can't have, that don't exist or never did, and I want—I want, if you ask me to come to the City with you a third time, I want to be able to say yes and mean it."

Three Seagrass was quiet. Listening. Turning over what Mahit had said; Mahit imagined the problem like a pebble in her mouth, an impediment to clear verse. After a moment she took a deep breath of the green-laced air and settled her shoulders. "I want someone to remember that I like being called *Reed*," she said. "And to—not be bored. You're never boring. I like your— that graphic story. I don't know stories like that one, and I'd like to. You make me have to *think*, Mahit, and that's not fair, no one else makes me work this hard and like it at the same time."

Mahit found herself laughing, soft, a hand covering her mouth. "Are you complimenting or insulting me?"

Three Seagrass considered this with more gravitas than Mahit thought it strictly deserved. "I don't know," she said, finally. "Both, probably. Mahit—"

"Yes?"

She could see Three Seagrass steeling herself, drawing her shoulders back, breathing from the diaphragm. Like Mahit was an oration contest she wanted to win. "What if—those other systems I mentioned, what if you went there?" she said. Mahit opened her mouth to reply, but Three Seagrass waved her quiet with a gesture of one hand. "You went there," she went on, "and I didn't. Her Brilliance would send you anywhere you wanted to go. It wouldn't be the Jewel of the World. It'd be somewhere—new. And you could write to me, if you wanted me to not be bored. I'd write to you. You could mail me more volumes of *The Perilous Frontier!* and I'd—send you new poems, and—anything else you'd want to hear, from me . . ."

"You would?" Mahit asked. After all this time, she had apparently retained the capacity to be shocked by sweetness.

"I would," Three Seagrass said. "And you could decrypt your own mail. Promise."

She was *bad* at smiling like a Stationer. She showed every tooth she had, the bright bone-white of them. A smile like starlight and threat. Mahit wanted, abruptly, to teach her how to do it right.

She smiled back. She felt brittle and fragile and on the verge of tears, and still she didn't want to not smile. It was—

<It's a good offer, Mahit,> Yskandr told her. <It's kinder than any I ever had.>

The Emperor Six Direction, promising peace in exchange for betrayal. Nineteen Adze, who didn't see light between loving someone and thinking they needed to die before they could do harm. Compared to those, letters and a temporary post on some distant provincial Teixcalaanli planet seemed like something she could countenance.

"I'd write back," she said. "All the time."

POSTLUDE

TO think as a person and to not think language. To think fractal scatter-song, the shape of an unfamiliar body, an inclusion like a garnet in the matrix of a stone—stone, still, but otherwise, crystalline and complete. Inside that crystal language—like the mouth-cries of unpersons, but made singable—lodges and reverberates, isolated until necessary. *We,* singing all through us, singing harmonic variance, vibration on an almost-interfering frequency. This body, that body: this body had a call-sign when it wasn't a person, and it is not the only one: this body was called LEAP! and that body greypattern, this body sweetling and that body Cleverer Than Littermates, and so, this new body, singing in the *we:* called Swarm, which is a laughing name now. Some call-signs are exactly like the person that is *we,* and that is glitter-sharp delight; the body LEAP! is a building-designing body, a structure-maker, whose structures are gossamer spaces for springing across. So too the body Swarm. To think that this body was a person before it was a person, and called itself appropriately even so!

We did not name this body, the unfamiliar body sings, *we were named. We were known.* The unfamiliar body sings the inside of a Teixcalaanli ship, a scatter of images and warmth: another body, a commander-body, a person-not-a-person in a thousand memory-points, reassembled. *We-when-we-are-Teixcalaan are known without singing,* Swarm tells the *we. We-when-we-are-Teixcalaan are known with language only, and still clearly.*

There is some disbelief, within the reaches of the *we.* To think language would be so transparent as to allow knowing!

Language is not so transparent, Twenty Cicada thinks—thinks *out,* a long reaching flicker through all of himself, which is all of the *we* together and still himself, *ourselves. Language is not so transparent, but we are sometimes known, even so. If we are lucky.*

Slide-shimmer query, the endless curiosity and *want* and reaching that is the *we,* thinking without language: *Show us, then!*

And on Peloa-2, in the desert night waiting for the shuttle that will take his body to a more hospitable environment, what remains of Twenty Cicada settles, cross-legged in the sand, and begins to try.

A GLOSSARY OF PERSONS, PLACES, AND OBJECTS

ahachotiya—An alcoholic drink, popular in the City, derived from fermented fruit.

Ajakts Kerakel—A life support analyst III on Lsel Station.

Aknel Amnardbat—Councilor for Heritage, one of six members of the governing Lsel Council; her purview is imago-machines, memory, and cultural promotion.

All Points Collapse—A Teixcalaanli band, playing in the shatter-harmonic musical style.

amalitzli—A Teixcalaanli sport, played on a clay court with a rubber ball that opposing teams attempt to throw, bounce, or richochet into a small goal. Versions of *amalitzli* specialized for low- or zero-gravity environments are also popular.

Anhamemat Gate—One of two jumpgates situated in Bardzravand Sector; leads from Stationer space into a resource-poor area not currently under the control of any one specific known political actor. Colloquially, "the Far Gate."

Aragh Chtel—A Stationer pilot assigned to sector reconnaissance.

Ascension's Red Harvest—A Teixcalaanli warship, *Engulfer*-class.

asekreta—A Teixcalaanli title, referring to an actively serving member of the Information Ministry.

Asphodel Drowning—A Teixcalaanli holodrama, currently in its fifth season.

Bardzravand Sector—The sector of known space within which Lsel Station and other Stations are located (Stationer pronunciation).

Belltown—A province of the City, divided into multiple districts; for example, Belltown One is a "bedroom community" for Teixcalaanlitzlim who cannot or do not wish to live in the Inmost Province districts, but Belltown Six is a notorious hotbed of criminal activity, urban congestion, and low-income residents.

Buildings, The (**epic poem**)—An ekphrastic poem describing famous architectural achievements of the City, commonly taught as a school text in Teixcalaan.

Captain Cameron—Fictional hero of the Lsel graphic novel *THE PERILOUS FRONTIER!*

Chatoyant Sirocco—The flagship of the Seventeenth Legion, *Eternal*-class.

City, the—The planetary capital of Teixcalaan.

cloudhook—Portable device, worn over the eye, which allows Teixcalaanlitzlim to access electronic media, news, communications, etc.; also functions as a security device, or key, which can open doors or give accesses; also functions as a geospatial positioning system, communicating location to a satellite network.

cuecuelihui—A Teixcalaanli military rank for non-officer specialist soldiers.

Darj Tarats—Councilor for the Miners, one of six members of the governing Lsel Council; his purview is resource extraction, trade, and labor.

Dava—A newly annexed planet in the Teixcalaanli Imperium, famous for its mathematical school.

Dawn With Encroaching Clouds—A Teixcalaanli serial holodrama depicting the history of the Emperor Two Sunspot and the attempted usurper, Eleven Cloud.

Dekakel Onchu—Councilor for the Pilots, one of six members of the governing Lsel Council; her purview is military defense, exploration, and navigation.

Dreaming Citadel—A warship of the Tenth Legion.

Dzoh Anjat—A pilot from Lsel Station.

Ebrekt/Ebrekti—The Ebrekti (singular "Ebrekt," adjectival form "Ebrekt") are a species of quadripedal obligate carnivores, whose social structure (called a "swift") resembles a pride of lions. The Teixcalaanli emperor Two Sunspot negotiated a permanent peace treaty with the Ebrekti, clearly defining zones of mutual non-competition, four hundred years ago (Teixcalaanli reckoning).

Eight Antidote—A ninety-percent clone of His Brilliance the

Emperor Six Direction. Heir to the Sun-Spear Throne of Teixca-laan. Eleven years old. Sometimes called *Cure*.

Eight Loop—The Minister of the Judiciary on Teixcalaan. Crèchesib to His Brilliance the Emperor Six Direction.

Eight Penknife—A member of the Information Ministry.

Eighteen Chisel—Chief navigation officer on the *Weight for the Wheel*.

Eighteen Coral—A Teixcalaanli artist who worked primarily in mosaic.

Eighteen Gravity—The captain of the *Flower Weave*.

Eighteen Turbine—An *ikantlos,* currently commanding Battle Group Nine of the Twenty-Sixth Legion, assigned to Odile System.

Eighty-Four Twilight—Captain of the scout-ship the *Gravity Rose*. A member of the Tenth Legion.

Eleven Cloud—A failed usurper who tried to overthrow the Emperor Two Sunspot four hundred years ago (Teixcalaanli reckoning).

Eleven Conifer—A patrician third-class, retired from honorable service in the Teixcalaanli fleet at third sub-*ikantlos* rank. Deceased.

Eleven Lathe—A Teixcalaanli poet and philosopher, best known for his work *Dispatches from the Numinous Frontier*.

Eleven Laurel—The Third Undersecretary of the Ministry of War. The Third Palm. Sometimes called *Wreath*.

Esharakir Lrut—Fictional character in the Lsel graphic novel *The Perilous Frontier!*

Esker-1—A planet in the Western Arc of Teixcalaan, known for choral singing.

Expansion History, The—A history of Teixcalaanli expansion, attributed to Thirteen River (attribution debunked; current literary scholars of Teixcalaan refer to the *Expansion History* as being composed by "Pseudo-Thirteen River," an unknown person).

ezuazuacat—The title for a member of the Emperor's personal advisory council; referred to as His, Her, or Their Excellency. Derives from the original name of the Emperor's sworn band of warriors, back when Teixcalaan had not yet broken space.

Fifteen Calcite—A Shard pilot. A member of the Tenth Legion.

Fifteen Engine—The former cultural liaison to Ambassador Yskandr Aghavn. Killed in an incident of domestic terrorism during the insurrection surrounding the ascension of Her Brilliance the Emperor Nineteen Adze.

Fifteen Ton—An *ixplanatl*, investigator on the research study "Report on Human-Algorithmic Interfaces: Military Applications."

Fifth Palm—One of the branches of the Ministry of War. Research and development.

Five Agate—*Ezuazuacat* to Her Brilliance the Emperor Nineteen Adze.

Five Diadem—Pen name of the famed Teixcalaanli historian and poet Five Hat.

Five Needle—Teixcalaanli historical figure, memorialized in the poem "Encomia for the Fallen of the Flagship *Twelve Expanding Lotus*." Died defending her ship after a series of field promotions left her the ranking officer.

Five Orchid—A fictional Teixcalaanli historical figure, the protagonist of a children's novel, in which she was the crèchesib of the future Emperor Twelve Solar-Flare.

Five Portico—A mechanic—of bodies and brains, amongst other things—living in Belltown Six.

Five Thistle—Chief weapons officer on the *Weight for the Wheel*.

Flower Weave—A Teixcalaanli medical supply skiff, operating out of Inmost Province Spaceport.

Forty Oxide—Fleet Captain of the Seventeenth Legion, on the flagship *Chatoyant Sirocco*. A member of the Teixcalaanli force sent beyond the Anhamemat Gate to prosecute war with unknown enemies.

Forty-Five Sunset—An aide to Her Brilliance the Emperor Nineteen Adze.

Foundation Song—Teixcalaanli song cycle memorializing the deeds of the First Emperor. Passed through oral tradition; more than one thousand versions are known.

Four Aloe—The current Minister of Information.

Four Crocus—A Shard pilot. A member of the Second Legion.

Four Lever—A *protospathat* in service to the Judiciary Ministry, in the role of Medical Examiner.

Four Sycamore—A newscaster, employed by Channel Eight!

Fourteen Scalpel—The writer of the poem "Encomia for the Fallen of the Flagship *Twelve Expanding Lotus*."

Fourteen Spike—Crewmember on the scout-gunner *Knifepoint's Ninth Blooming*. A translator and interrogation specialist in the Tenth Legion, of *cuecuelihui* rank.

Fourteen Spire—A minor Teixcalaanli contemporary poet.

Fulcrum—First in a series of Teixcalaanli popular novels about a band of thieves, grifters, and other criminals who take down corrupt officials for the good of the Empire and its people.

Gelak Lerants—A member of the Lsel Heritage Board, an accreditation body.

Gienah-9—A mostly desert planet, annexed with great force and considerable personnel loss by Teixcalaan, and then lost in a rebellion. Reannexed; subjugated. A popular setting for military dramas.

Glass Key—A Teixcalaanli serial holodrama depicting the history of the Emperor Two Sunspot and the attempted usurper Eleven Cloud. Approved for crèche-school use.

Gorlaeth—The Ambassador to Teixcalaan from Dava.

Gravity Rose—A scout-ship of the Tenth Legion, captained by Eighty-Four Twilight.

homeostat-cult, homeostat-cultist—A derogatory term for the Neltoc heritage religious practice of homeostatic meditation, or for a practitioner thereof.

huitzahuitlim—"Palace-hummers," a species of nectar-eating bird.

ikantlos—A military rank in the Teixcalaanli fleet, usually tasked with commanding a battle group within a legion.

imago—An ancestral live memory.

Imperial Censor Office—The office of the Teixcalaanli government tasked with determining what media is spread to which areas of the empire.

infofiche—A mutable, foldable, transparent plastic that can display images and text. Reusable.

infofiche stick—A thumb-sized container, often personalized, containing a holographic representation of a message that appears when the stick is broken open. It may also contain an actual piece of infofiche.

infosheet—A newsheet made of infofiche.

Inmost Province—The central province of the City, containing the government buildings and major cultural centers.

Inmost Province Spaceport—The major spaceport of the City, seeing 57 percent of inbound traffic.

Inscription's Glass Key—The flagship of the Teixcalaanli Emperor Two Sunspot.

Intertwined with Our Starlight: a Handbook of Syncretic Religious Forms Within Teixcalaan—An academic monograph by the Teixcalaanli historian Eighteen Smoke.

ixhui—A meat dumpling.

ixplanatl—Any accredited Teixcalaanli scientist (physical, social, biological, chemical).

Jasmine Throat—A Teixcalaanli supply vessel, *Succor*-class.

Jewel of the World—The colloquial (and the poetic) name for the City-planet.

Jirpardz—A pilot on Lsel Station.

Kamchat Gitem—A pilot on Lsel Station.

Kauraan—The habitable planet of the Kauraan System. A Teixcalaanli colony, recently the site of an abortive revolt.

Keeper of the Imperial Inkstand—The title for the Teixcalaanli Emperor's schedule-keeper and chamberlain.

Knifepoint's Ninth Blooming—A scout-gunner ship of the Tenth Legion.

Kumquat—A drink. Inadvisable. (Not to be confused with the fruit, which may be advisable.)

Lost Garden—A restaurant in Plaza North Four, famous for its winter-climate dishes.

Lsel Record of Origin—A collection of documents and accounts of the earliest activities of Lsel Station. Incomplete and contradictory. Highly valuable.

Lsel Station/Stationers—People living on any of the mining Stations in Bardzravand Sector. Planetless.

Mad With Horizons—A Teixcalaanli medium cruiser, *Exultation*-class. Assigned to the Second Legion.

Mahit Dzmare—The current Ambassador to Teixcalaan from Lsel Station.

Mist, the—The Judiciary Ministry's investigatory and enforcement body.

Nakhar—A Teixcalaanli-controlled planetary system, prone (until recently) to periodic revolt, insurrection, and unrest.

Neltoc System—A Teixcalaanli star-system with three inhabited celestial bodies: the planets Neltoc and Pozon, and the satellite Sepyri. Neltoclim practice a registered heritage religious tradition known as "homeostatic meditation."

Nguyen—A multisystem confederation near Stationer space, with whom the Stationers have a trade agreement.

Nine Arch—An ex-girlfriend of Three Seagrass's.

Nine Crimson—A Teixcalaanli historical figure, *yaotlek* of the Third, Ninth, and Eighteenth Legions of the fleet, approximately five hundred years ago.

Nine Flood—A Teixcalaanli historical figure, an Emperor from when Teixcalaan had not yet become a spacefaring power.

Nine Hibiscus—Fleet Captain of the Tenth Legion, on the flagship *Weight for the Wheel*. Sometimes known as the Hero of Kauraan. *Yaotlek* of the Teixcalaanli force sent beyond the Anhamemat Gate to prosecute war with unknown enemies. Sometimes called *Mallow*.

Nine Maize—A major court poet at the court of His Brilliance the Emperor Six Direction.

Nine Propulsion—The former Minister of War, now retired.

Nine Sea-Ice—The communications officer on the *Chatoyant Sirocco*. A member of the Seventeenth Legion.

Nine Shuttle—The planetary governor of Odile-1, recently reinstated after an uprising.

Nineteen Adze—Her Brilliance the Emperor, She Whose Gracious Presence Illuminates the Room Like the Edgeshine of a Knife.

Ninety Alloy—A Teixcalaanli holo production, episodic. Military romance.

North Tlachtli—A neighborhood in Inmost Province.

Odile—A Teixcalaanli planetary system which has recently been the site of insurrection and unrest.

One Conifer—A Teixcalaanli citizen, employed by the Central Travel Authority Northeast Division.

One Cyclamen—The Second Sub-Secretary of the Epistolary Department of the Information Ministry.

One Granite—The legendary first *ezuazuacat* to the First Emperor.

One Lapis—A historical Teixcalaanli emperor, succeeded by the Emperor Twelve Solar-Flare.

One Lightning—Formerly a *yaotlek* of the Teixcalaanli fleet, much acclaimed by his soldiers. A failed usurper.

One Skyhook—A renowned Teixcalaanli poet, often taught in schools.

One Telescope—An *ezuazuacat* from approximately two hundred years ago. A statue of her stands in the central transport hub for Inmost Province, commemorating her achievements.

Opening Frontier Poems—A multiauthor collection of Teixcalaanli poetry, popular in the Fleet.

osmium—A valuable metal, often found in asteroids. One of the exports of Lsel Station.

Parabolic Compression—The flagship of the Twenty-Fourth Legion, *Eternal*-class.

Parzrawantlak Sector—The Teixcalaanli pronunciation of Bardzravand Sector.

patrician (first-, second-, or third-class)—Ranks at the Teixcalaanli court, primarily representative of personal salaries received from the Imperial treasury.

Peloa-2—A Teixcalaanli resource-extraction colony that exports silicates.

Perilous Frontier!, The—A graphic novel in ten volumes, published by the Lsel Station small printer ADVENTURE/BLEAK.

Pilot's History of the Future: Worldships and Lsel Station, A—A work of popular history written by the retired Stationer pilot Takan Mnal.

Poplar Province—One of the more distant provinces from Inmost Province in the City; an ocean-crossing away.

Porcelain Fragment Scorched—A stealth cruiser of the Twenty-Fourth Legion, *Pyroclast*-class.

Pseudo-Thirteen River—The unknown author of *The Expansion History*, who used the name Thirteen River despite not being the Minister of the Judiciary of that name whose treatises on retributive justice are still taught in Teixcalaanli law schools.

Red Flowerbuds for Thirty Ribbon—A Teixcalaanli romance novel.

Reflective Prism—A Teixcalaanli warship of the Tenth Legion, captained by Twelve Caesura.

Ring Two—A designation for provinces in the City which are more than 300 but less than 600 miles from the Palace. Information Ministry slang.

Second Palm—One of the branches of the Ministry of War. Supply chains and logistics.

Secret History of the Emperors, The—A famous (and salacious) anonymous account of the lives of many Teixcalaanli emperors. Often updated. Never imitated.

Seven Aster—Second Undersecretary of the Ministry of War. The Second Palm.

Seven Chrysoprase—A newscaster, employed by Channel Eight!

Seven Monograph—The Fourth Undersecretary of the Ministry of Information.

Seven Scale—A junior aide to Her Brilliance the Emperor Nineteen Adze.

Shard—a single-pilot Teixcalaanli fightercraft, operated via biofeedback interface and cloudhook.

shocksticks—An electricity-based weapon, primarily used for crowd control on Teixcalaan.

Shrja Torel—A citizen of Lsel station. Mahit Dzmare's friend.

Six Capsaicin—Captain of the *Jasmine Throat*. Also, an *ixplanatl*.

Six Direction—His Brilliance the Emperor of All Teixcalaan. Deceased.

Six Helicopter—A former Teixcalaanli bureaucrat.

Six Outreaching Palms—The colloquial (or poetic) name for the Ministry of War; so named for the reaching out of hands in every direction (north, south, west, east, up, and down) which is the hallmark of Teixcalaanli conquest theory.

Six Rainfall—A medical cadet on the *Weight for the Wheel*. A member of the Tenth Legion.

Sixteen Felt—An *ixplanatl*, investigator on the research study "Report on Human-Algorithmic Interfaces: Military Applications."

Sixteen Moonrise—Fleet Captain of the Twenty-Fourth Legion, on the flagship *Parabolic Compression*. A member of the Teixcalaanli force sent beyond the Anhamemat Gate to prosecute war with unknown enemies. Sometimes called *Apogee*.

Sixth Palm—A branch of the Ministry of War. Engineering and shipbuilding.

starshine—"The Emperor's drink," a distilled wheat spirit used in Fleet traditional meals.

Sunlit, the—The police force of the City.

Teixcalaan—The empire, the world, coextensive with the known universe. (Adjectival form: Teixcalaanli; a person who is a citizen of Teixcalaan is a Teixcalaanlitzlim.)

Teixcalaanli—The language spoken in Teixcalaan.

Ten Pearl—The current Minister of Science.

Third Palm—One of the branches of the Ministry of War. Infosec, political officers, and internal affairs.

Thirteen Muon—An engineering specialist. A member of the Second Legion.

Thirty Larkspur—He Who Drowns the World in Blooms, formerly one of Six Direction's *ezuazuacatlim*, a scion of a major merchant family from the Western Arc. A failed usurper.

Thirty Wax-Seal—Captain of the scout-gunner *Knifepoint's Ninth Blooming*. A member of the Tenth Legion.

Thirty-One Twilight—An Information Ministry employee in the Epistolary Department.

Thirty-Six All-Terrain Tundra Vehicle—A Teixcalaanli citizen.

Three Azimuth—The Minister of War. Colloquially, *the butcher of the Nakharese mind*. She Who Kindles Emnity in the Most Oath-Sworn Heart.

Three Lamplight—A member of the Information Ministry.

Three Nasturtium—A Teixcalaanli citizen, Central Traffic Control Supervisor at Inmost Province Spaceport.

Three Perigee—A historical Teixcalaanli emperor.

Three Seagrass—Third Undersecretary of the Information Ministry. Formerly the cultural liaison to Mahit Dzmare, the Lsel Ambassador. Sometimes called *Reed*.

tlaxlauim—A certified accountant or financial professional in Teixcalaan.

Tsagkel Ambak—A negotiator and diplomat from Lsel Station, who formalized the Station's current treaty with the Teixcalaanli Imperium.

Twelve Azalea—A member of the Information Ministry. A friend to Three Seagrass. Sometimes called *Petal*. Deceased.

Twelve Caesura—Captain of the Teixcalaanli warship *Reflective Prism*. A member of the Tenth Legion.

Twelve Fusion—*Ikantlos*-prime of the flagship *Parabolic Compression*. A member of the Twenty-Fourth Legion, adjutant to Fleet Captain Sixteen Moonrise.

Twelve Solar-Flare—A historical Teixcalaanli emperor, who first discovered Parzrawantlak Sector, and thus Lsel Station.

Twenty Cicada—The *ikantlos*-prime of the Tenth Legion's flagship *Weight for the Wheel*. A homeostat-cultist. Sometimes called *Swarm*.

Twenty-Four Rose—A Teixcalaanli author of travel guidebooks.

Twenty-Nine Bridge—The current Keeper of the Imperial Inkstand, serving Her Brilliance the Emperor Nineteen Adze.

Twenty-Nine Infograph—A member of the Judiciary Ministry.

Twenty-Two Graphite—An aide to Her Brilliance the Emperor Nineteen Adze.

Twenty-Two Thread—The Fifth Undersecretary of the Ministry of War. The Fifth Palm.

Two Amaranth—A historical *ezuazuacat*, serving the Emperor Twelve Solar-Flare.

Two Calendar—A major court poet at the court of His Brilliance the Emperor Six Direction.

Two Canal—The Fleet Captain of the Sixth Legion. A member of the Teixcalaanli force sent beyond the Anhamemat Gate to prosecute war with unknown enemies.

Two Cartograph—The son of Five Agate. Seven years old. Sometimes called *Map*.

Two Catenary—The chief of medical ethics at the Twelve Solar-Flare Memorial Teaching Hospital. Author of a commentary on Eleven Lathe's *Dispatches from the Numinous Frontier*.

Two Cholla—The first Teixcalaanlitzlim to die while wearing the uniform of the Tenth Legion.

Two Foam—The communications officer on the *Weight for the Wheel*. A member of the Tenth Legion. Often called *Bubbles*, but not to her face.

Two Kyanite—An *ixplanatl*, primary investigator on the research study "Report on Human-Algorithmic Interfaces: Military Applications."

Two Lemon—A Teixcalaanli citizen.

Two Rosewood—The former Minister of Information.

Two Sunspot—A historical Teixcalaanli emperor, who negotiated peace with the Ebrekti.

Verashk-Talay—A political confederation of several systems and sectors, with a minor presence beyond the Anhamemat Gate. Comprised of two distinct populations, the Verashk and the Talay, each speaking a separate language, who seem to have resolved their resource conflicts via adopting a form of representative democracy.

Verdigris Mesa—A Teixcalaanli warship of the Third Legion.

Weight for the Wheel—The flagship of the Tenth Legion, *Eternal*-class.

Western Arc—An important and wealthy sector of Teixcalaan, home to major merchant concerns.

xauitl—A flower.

Xelka Station—A Teixcalaanli military outpost.

yaotlek—A military rank in the Teixcalaanli fleet; commander of at least one legion.

Yskandr Aghavn—The former Ambassador to Teixcalaan from Lsel Station.

Zorai—The home planet of the former Minister of War Nine Propulsion.

On the pronunciation and writing system of the Teixcalaanli language

The Teixcalaanli language is logosyllabic, written in "glyphs." These individual glyphs represent both free and bound morphemes. Teixcalaanli glyphs also can represent phonetic sounds, usually derived from an initial morpheme's pronunciation which has lost its meaning and become purely phonetic. Due to the logosyllabic nature of Teixcalaanli, double and triple meanings are easily created in both verbal and written texts. Individual glyphs can function as visual puns or have suggestions of meaning unrelated to their precise morphemic use. Such wordplay—both visual and aural—is central to the literary arts of the Empire.

Teixcalaanli is a vowel-heavy language with a limited set of consonants. A brief pronunciation guide is given below (with IPA symbology and examples from American English).

a—ɑː—father

e—ɛ—bed

o—oʊ—no, toe, soap

i—i—city, see, meat

u—u—loop

aa—ɑ—The Teixcalaanli "aa" is a *chroneme*—it extends the length of the sound a in time, but does not change its quality.

au—aʊ̯—loud

ei—eɪ̯—say

ua—ʷɑ—water, quantity

ui—ʷi—weed

y—j—yes, yell

c—k—cat, cloak (but never as in *certain*)

h—h—harm, hope

k—kʰ—almost always found before r, as in crater or crisp, but occasionally as a word-ending, where it is heavily aspirated.

l—ɣ—bell, ball

m—m—mother, mutable

n—n—nine, north
p—p—paper, proof
r—ɾ—red, father
s—s—sable, song
t—tʰ—*t*, aspirated, as in top
x—ks—sticks, six
z—z—zebra
ch—tʃ—chair

But in consonant clusters (which Teixcalaanli favors), t is more often found as "t," the unaspirated dental consonant in stop; l is often "l," the dental approximate in line or lucid. There are many loanwords in Teixcalaanli. When pronouncing words originating in more consonant-heavy languages, Teixcalaanli tends to devoice unfamiliar consonants, i.e. "b" is pronounced like "p" and "d" is pronounced like "t."

On the language spoken on Lsel Station and other Stations in Bardzravand Sector

By contrast, the language spoken on the stations in Bardzravand Sector is alphabetic and consonant heavy. It is easier for a native speaker of Stationer to accurately pronounce a Teixcalaanli word than the other way around. (If one wishes to pronouce Stationer words one's own self, and has only Earth languages to go by, a good guide would be the pronunciation of Modern Eastern Armenian).

ACKNOWLEDGMENTS

Second books are, proverbially, far more difficult than firsts. *A Desolation Called Peace,* despite my bravado and determined assurances to various persons—including, but certainly not limited to, my agent, my editor, a slew of fellow writers I'm honored to call friends, and my wife—was no exception. Bravado and determination will only get one so far in the face of *one hundred fifty thousand words,* a deadline, and the weight of knowing that, while you might have managed the trick once, each novel requires you to again learn how to write a novel.

I am still learning how to write a novel.

I will never, so long as I am privileged to write, be done with learning how to write a novel. I say this without resignation but instead with an acquired and giddy satisfaction: I hope I look back on this acknowledgments note in fifteen years and laugh at how little I knew, and how much more skillful a writer I have become. I hope all of you reading do the same. My first thanks is to you: everyone who picked up *A Memory Called Empire,* loved it, and made it a success. Without you I would not have any reason to pick up Mahit's story again and spin it a little farther on. I am profoundly grateful.

Eternal thanks go as well to that list of persons I inflicted bravado and assurances upon.

Thank you to my dear friends: Elizabeth Bear, who makes me want to be a better writer than I am, and a better student of ethics and character work as well, and whose friendship is a steady point I am honored by; Devin Singer, who told me I'd gotten it right when I needed to hear it; Marissa Lingen, who texted me "my DUDE Swarm" and thus entirely proved I'd written a book with the emotional valence I meant to convey; Max Gladstone, who once talked through Buddhist ethics with me long enough that for a brief moment I understood the *why* of it, and then wrote a book (*Empress of Forever,* which I entirely recommend, O readers who have followed me deep into the acknowledgments) that made me *believe* it for the space of a climactic space battle; and all the rest of the 'zoo and my agentsibs, too many to list here for fear of leaving out someone important. Thank you all; you are the community I have always wanted to find.

(A quick shout-out also goes to Scott and Anita at *The Read-Along* podcast, who accidentally saved me from an embarrassing continuity error; to David Bowles, for talk and teaching about Nahuatl; and to Rebecca Roanhorse, who has been an absolute cheerleader for this book, even before reading it.)

And thank you to DongWon Song, my fantastic agent, who trusted me to find my way through this book, and made sure I was all right through launching the first one at the same time; to Devi Pillai, editor par excellence, who insisted that I get the pacing right, and who is frustratingly, amazingly, *always correct* about what I need to do to a book (only 15k underwritten this time, Devi, I'm learning); to my brilliant cover artist, Jaime Jones, who apparently can see into my head; and to the entire marketing and publicity team at Tor Books, who have taken such good care of me.

Most importantly: I could not do this—write, this book, any book, any*thing*—without my glorious wife Vivian Shaw: spaceship consultant, world-translator, first and best reader. You are the center of every star chart; these things are ceaseless, my darling.

April 2020
Santa Fe, NM

ABOUT THE AUTHOR

Karen Osborne

ARKADY MARTINE is a speculative fiction writer and, as Dr. AnnaLinden Weller, a historian of the Byzantine Empire and a city planner. She is currently a policy advisor for the New Mexico Energy, Minerals, and Natural Resources Department, where she works on climate change mitigation, energy grid modernization, and resiliency planning. Under both names, she writes about border politics, rhetoric, propaganda, and the edges of the world. Martine grew up in New York City and, after some time in Turkey, Canada, Sweden, and Baltimore, now lives in Santa Fe with her wife, author Vivian Shaw.

arkadymartine.net
Twitter: @ArkadyMartine